Leaving Home

by

Casey Dawes

Mountain Vines Publishing

ISBN: 978-1-7340877-2-7 (print)

Book cover design by For the Muse Designs
Edited by CEO Editor (ceoeditor.com)
Interior design by Concierge Self-Publishing
(www.ConciergeSelfPublishing.com)

Knitting pattern used by permission of Brenda Castiel for purposes of this book only. All other rights reserved.

Published by Mountain Vines Publishing
Missoula, MT
Contact email: info@ConciergeSelfPublishing.com

*To all those who leave the known behind to search for
the unknown and the true purpose
of their lives.*

To my extended and loved family.

Chapter 1

The March wind hurtled down from Canada, blew south along the Rockies, and howled across the plains to the east. Not the best day to go to the airport and pick up his brother.

But then, the wind never really stopped. Living on the Rocky Mountain Front meant putting up with it. In return, the resident had an abundance of clear skies, majestic mountain views, and unexpected weather.

Dylan Beck checked the time on his phone for about the tenth time as he poured himself a cup of coffee from the ever-going pot in the ranch kitchen. He had to leave for the airport in about fifteen minutes, giving himself plenty of time to get to Great Falls, park, and find the right gate. Not that it would be a big problem in the small airport with only handful of planes landing at any one time.

Except so many things could go wrong—a flat tire, semi blown over by the wind, a bunch of cattle who'd escaped their enclosure, wandering over the road. He should leave now. No way was his wounded brother going to arrive at the airport with no one to great him.

"When is Cameron coming in?" Dylan's brother Jarod asked as he entered the kitchen.

"His text message said he left from Dulles at nine Eastern Standard Time, which put him into Denver at eleven their time. He had a two-hour layover and thinks he should be in Great Falls by three or four at the latest." He held up his phone. "I'm tracking the plane, and so far it's right on time. But I need to leave soon."

"You and your gadgets," Jarod grumbled as he poured his own cup of brew.

"I was right about the drone," Dylan said.

"I'll give you that."

"Someday you'll need to move beyond the twentieth century."

"I'm content the way I am."

"Now that you finally got the girl." Dylan glanced at his phone, then poured his coffee into a travel mug.

"CJ didn't want to go?" Jarod asked.

Dylan shook his head. "She thought it would be better if only one of us met Cameron so he didn't feel ganged up on. She also said a brother would be easier for Cameron to deal with than an older sister."

Jarod slumped into a chair, his legs splayed beneath the table. "I wish it had turned out differently. Cameron's such an outdoor guy. Losing a limb is going to hamper that big time." He looked up at Dylan. "What are we supposed to do? To say? What is *he* going to do?"

"They've got some amazing technology today. He's not the only one coming back from a war zone with a major injury. In some ways, we should be thankful it's only a limb. The military is having some success getting those soldiers functioning again. Brain injuries and mental problems are a whole 'nother animal."

"I'm not sure that's not going on with Cameron." Jarod sipped his coffee.

Unease tensed Dylan's muscles. Jarod was right. Since he'd been wounded in a bomb explosion several months ago, Cameron hadn't wanted to talk to anyone. After he was airlifted to a military hospital in Germany, CJ, the only one of them who had the cash, the time, and the passport, had offered to go over and stay with him until he returned stateside. He'd turned her down flat. Nor had he wanted anyone to visit him when he was going through physical therapy in D.C.

"Where's Birdie?" Jarod asked.

"Fixing up the master bedroom for Cameron."

"He's not going to like that."

"Birdie thinks it will be easier on him. He had a lot of internal injuries from the bomb detonation, too."

"He's going to like being treated like an invalid even less."

Dylan opened the mudroom door. "I'm sure we can figure out something to keep everyone's ego intact." He shrugged. "Maybe we've got it all wrong. Maybe he's fine with it all and ready to move on."

"Maybe pigs fly."

"I thought you were the religious one. Say a prayer and go feed the cattle. I'll be back in a few hours. We can't really figure out what's up until we get him home."

"Yeah, you're right. Safe trip."

Dylan nodded and went into the small room off the kitchen where a freezer hummed in a corner. The washer and dryer took up one wall; the other was covered with coats, hats, and other warm weather gear draped over pegs and looming over a pile of shoes and boots on the floor.

He zipped up his coat and tugged on his gloves, leaving his longish hair to warm his ears. Birdie'd been after him to get a haircut, but he kept putting her off. Summer would be soon enough.

Dylan put the ranch truck in gear and climbed the drive to the main highway. Turning left, he headed the short distance to Choteau, took the rotary partway around the courthouse, and headed out on the road to Great Falls. Next to the market, a new shop caught his eye: Waldron Creek Cheese and Pastry Shop.

Odd combination. It looked pretty upscale for a small town in the middle of nowhere, but the area was changing. The internet made living almost anywhere feasible. New people were moving in, attracted by small-town living and the awesome scenery. Plus, well-heeled tourists and retirees continued to pass through on the way to Glacier National Park. If the town could support a niche store like this, maybe someone would finally start a gallery where he could sell his paintings ... *if* he could sell his paintings.

He'd worn out his welcome at the Great Falls's venues when none of his art sold after a year. The sale of a painting last fall, which allowed him to get a commercial-sized drone for the ranch, had kept him in one gallery in Helena. But as each month passed without a subsequent sale, his spirits sank, in spite of the fact most high-end stores were slow in the winter season unless they happen to have a ski resort nearby, like toney Whitefish or the Big Sky Resort near Bozeman. Maybe those were places he should try to sell his paintings. He smiled. It might work. He had to try something different.

The road descended into the Freezeout Lake area. Migratory birds were starting to increase on the open water, harbingers of the great avian streams heading north every spring. Huge flocks of white geese stopped at Freezeout twice a year, providing a cacophony of harsh honks and a blur of fluttering wings as they took off in the morning to feed at nearby fields and returned at night to rest.

There was nothing better than the sights of nature to heal a person's soul. It had worked on CJ; there was a good chance the earth's rhythms could repair his younger brother, too.

Dylan followed the road's gentle curve as it passed the various ponds that made up the refuge. The overhead sky was gray, but not the deep hue that threatened snow, although the wind nudged the pickup with gentle bursts. The solid old truck didn't budge from its path.

Was his dream of being a painter unrealistic? His mother had dabbled with paint for a long time, but constant critiques—solid technique, but not unique—had finally forced her to stuff everything in a box and give it away. He should probably do the same thing.

But if he gave it up, who would he be? With his other four siblings firmly planted in careers, his lack of success stood out more and more. He was unsettled, drifting like an unmoored boat. At the ranch, he was second fiddle to Jarod. In the art world, he was nobody at all.

The road deposited him at the edge of Vaughn, and soon he was on the interstate going to the airport. Time to put away his own internal angst. His brother needed him, and family was the most important thing of all.

# # #

Dylan barely recognized the man walking toward him down the airport concourse as Cameron. His brother's face was drawn, with crevices where his smile creases used to be. Still dressed in the camouflage of combat, Cameron had an empty sleeve pinned to his chest, but the most striking characteristic was the lack of life in his brown eyes.

This was not the intrepid adventurer who had gone off to war.

Dylan slapped on a smile and walked toward his brother, his brain rapidly sorting through the best things to say first.

"Hey, kid," was all he could get out before he enveloped Cameron in a bear hug, a gesture to which there was no response. Around them, the sea of returning visitors parted, but most passersby's eyes were averted.

Dylan quickly let go.

"Do you have bags?" he asked.

"One."

"Okay. Let's head down to baggage claim."

"Thanks for picking me up, Dylan," Cameron said, words that sounded as if they'd been cut from a steel sheet.

"No problem. Did you have a good flight?"

"Yeah."

"Probably better than military transport."

"Yeah."

8

"Must be hot over there."

"Uh-huh."

At that, Dylan ran out of questions to ask, and they continued silently to the baggage carousels. He stared at the overhead television monitor while they waited. Same news, only with different names.

"There it is," Cameron said.

Dylan stepped forward to get it but was out-maneuvered. "I can do this," Cameron said.

"Sure." He was going to have to back off. "Need anything in Great Falls before we head back?"

"No, thanks," Cameron said.

They headed toward the exit to the parking lot. Once there, they had to fight to open the glass door.

"See the wind hasn't let up any," Cameron said.

"Not a bit," Dylan replied, the tightness in his chest dissipating a little. He beeped open the truck and let Cameron handle his own gear. He'd gotten that message loud and clear. If situations were reversed, he'd probably be the same way.

But the questions he wanted to ask his brother were thrumming in his brain. The most important was what the family could do to help Cameron get back on his feet. The one his brother was least likely to answer.

"Music?" is what he came up with after he paid the parking ticket and they were headed down the ramp to the interstate.

"Whatever suits you," Cameron replied.

The silence was going to fray his nerves so he flipped on the playlist he'd already set up. He'd chosen a combination of Mozart and Rachmaninoff.

Cameron didn't comment.

Dylan let his mind drift to the scenery around him and the notes filling the cab, a potent combination for him that would hopefully inspire a breakthrough painting. The Rockies were a smudge on the horizon, snow-covered hills cresting toward them. Freezeout Lake slashed a steel-blue streak in the near distance.

Maybe he should give up oils and take up watercolor. That seemed to be all the rage now.

Cameron stayed silent as they gradually climbed the five hundred feet of elevation between the city and Choteau. The dark clusters of cattle scattered on the surrounding plateau seemed to catch his interest now and again, but from what Dylan could tell, his brother mostly focused on the mountains.

"They don't have them like that in the Middle East," was his only comment.

"Probably don't have them like that anywhere but home," Dylan said. He'd never had the same longing to see the world that had taken most of his siblings to far-flung places. Even Jarod went to Las Vegas once a year, but Dylan had never left Montana and had no desire to do so. The Rockies were his anchor. They grounded him when the craziness of the world got to be too much.

"Will you be able to hike?" he blurted without thinking first. Crap. "Sorry, that was inconsiderate."

"No problem," Cameron said, but he didn't answer the question.

Dylan tried to refocus on the music and the landscape, but the tension made his shoulders ache. How was he supposed to relate to this stranger in the cab beside him, a man who'd seen more horror in a few years than anyone should have to bear in an entire lifetime?

"It will be some time before I can do anything strenuous for any length of time," Cameron said, finally providing some information. "The bomb did a lot more damage than what's visible."

"Just let us know what you need."

"Solitude."

There wasn't much of that around the ranch house these days. CJ came and went, Jarod's new girlfriend, Samantha, and her daughter, Audie, were a constant presence. With the cusp of spring, all types of activity would start as the town emerged from winter.

"I've got a small pickup you're free to borrow whenever you want," Dylan said.

"Thanks."

And that was the last thing Cameron said the rest of the way home.

The new bakery-cheese shop had closed by the time they made it to Choteau around six. Daylight was still strong, the lengthening sunlight lingering until the sun set at half-past seven. He completed the rotary circling the courthouse and headed south. Beside him, Cameron's stillness was like coiled metal, ready to spring into action.

Lingering effects of the war? Or something else? No one had ever been able to figure out why Cameron, who'd loved the ranch as much as Jarod, had suddenly enlisted one day and was gone a few weeks later, leaving one more hole in their dwindling family.

He glanced at his brother's face as he pulled down the driveway. It was unreadable. The service had trained him well.

Pulling up near the house, he positioned the truck so Cameron wouldn't have to deal with the remaining snow piles and would face a minimal amount of icy mud.

"We're here," he said.

Obviously. Stupid remark.

Cameron didn't comment. Instead he opened the door, hopped out, and gave it a satisfying thud when he closed it. Dylan knew better than to try to get the duffle, so he walked around to the steps leading up to the mudroom door.

"Birdie's edict," he said.

"I remember."

After divesting their boots and outer gear in the designated places, Dylan gestured for his brother to go into the kitchen first. There was a second when his brother's eyes widened, like a deer about to bolt, but then he swung open the inner door and entered.

"Cameron!" Birdie cried.

The duffle thunked to the floor as the small woman wrapped her arms around Cameron's waist. He gave her an awkward one-armed hug before pulling back.

Birdie took the hint and released him. "Supper will be in about a half hour. Do you need anything to tide you over? Jarod's still out in the barn working with his two training horses."

Cameron gave the housekeeper a half smile. "No, I'm good, thanks. I think I'll just head to my room for a lie-down."

"I fixed up the master bedroom for you," she said. "I figured it would be easier for you, considering." She pointedly looked away from Cameron's left side.

"I'd rather be in my old room," he replied. "My legs work just fine." He picked up the duffle and walked through the rest of the kitchen. The thump of his feet echoed his progress up the stairs.

Birdie looked at Dylan. "It's going to be a long road," she said.

"Uh-huh."

# # #

Megan Winkle stared at the poster board she'd propped up on her dining table. It was covered with pictures of alpacas, spinning wheels, and stacks of yarn she'd cut out of magazines. Additionally, she had found pictures of a loom and spools of thread for weaving. At the top, in elegant cursive, she'd written out "Megan's Homespun: From Fleece to Fabric."

All she needed was a fairy godmother. Wonder if Cinderella's was still available?

She leaned back in the chair and sighed. Choteau had seemed like the perfect place. She'd been able to find a small house on two acres of land, complete with a barn big enough for a pair of alpacas. God, she loved working with alpaca fleece. Properly prepared, it produced a soft, warm knit.

Granny had taught her everything she needed to know about alpacas when Megan had helped her out on her struggling alpaca farm near Ashland, the farm she'd expected to be hers. But her relatives had conned her out of it, convincing the mediator that they needed to be repaid for raising her and that Megan was too young to run a business.

Damn them. It had been her farm. All they'd done was turn around and sell it. But not before Megan had liberated Granny's old spinning wheel.

It would be a while before she'd be able to buy animals and have the money to take care of them, so the only thing to do was to start with the end process: creating unique yarns for the growing craft market. And for that, she needed a store front, a website, or both.

She cradled her forehead on her arms. Technology wasn't her strong suit. Why was life so difficult? Back in Ashland, she'd been known as the Winkles' daughter, descended from dirt-poor crop farmers who'd never finished high school and died from toxic chemicals in the land and water they'd used to grow their crops.

In the South, the history of a person's "people" too often defined how others viewed them.

Choteau was a fresh start. She had to keep her focus and make it work.

The alarm on her phone went off, and she put her dreams aside to attend to reality and her waitress job at the Waldron Creek Cheese and Pastry Shop.

After she parked her car, an aging Volvo station wagon she'd gotten with her babysitting savings when she turned eighteen, she entered through the back door, waving at the man and woman in the cheese room as she went to the tiny locker room to stow her gear.

The early morning rush for coffee, rolls, Danish, and bear claws was over, and a few tables were occupied by seniors lingering over sweet pastries. There was more energy in the air than she'd seen since she'd gotten here in January, sneaking across the snow-laden plains in the midst of the annual thaw.

It must be the slightly warmer temperatures. Spring was way overdue.

"Hi, Megan," Courtney Lewis, the shop's owner, called in a bright voice. "Could you refresh the coffee?"

"Sure." Megan walked behind the counter.

"The older folk can sure put it away," Courtney said with a smile. "You might check that the bathroom is well-stocked too."

Megan chuckled. Working with Courtney was fun. No matter what happened, her boss could find the humor in it, a trait she wished she owned. People had always told her she was too serious. She wasn't sure if that were true or she just preferred her own company.

As soon as the coffee was made, she restocked the bathroom and took over the seated customers. They were becoming regulars, and she was becoming easy with them. Although many were on fixed incomes, they never stiffed her on tips and always had a friendly word.

"What are you knitting these days?" an older woman with curly white hair asked. "That hat I bought from you last month sure does keep my ears warm."

"I'm actually doing some spinning right now. I got some roving up in Great Falls a few weeks ago."

"Roving?" piped up the woman's husband, a mostly bald man who buried his nose in the newspaper every morning.

"It's wool that's been processed—looks kind of like a long, fuzzy snake."

"And you make yarn from it?" the woman asked.

"Yes."

"I'd love to see some of your yarn one day. Maybe Courtney would let you display it like she did the hats."

"Worth asking," her husband added.

"Thank you," Megan said. "It's a good idea."

She forgot about the discussion until the afternoon lull when she found Courtney staring at a niche between the cheese room and the bakery. "What are you planning on doing with that area?" Megan asked.

"It looked so cheery when you had your hats there last month. I didn't realize they'd sell so fast. Got any ideas?"

"Well," Megan said, stalling for time. "I'm working on some

yarn that came from some sheep around Malta up on the Hi-Line. I'll think I'll have enough for a few skeins in a week or two."

"Yes, but that's not going to fill up the whole space."

"What about other crafters in town—there must be people who quilt or knit or maybe make candles. They'd probably love a place to display and sell their work. And you could charge a small commission."

"That's a great idea. You're a good businesswoman," Courtney said. "And I'll take whatever yarn or completed goods you have."

"Thank you."

It wasn't a storefront, but it was a start. Although she wasn't sure the part about being a good businesswoman was true. Whenever she thought about her business, fear and doubt raised their ugly hands. This job was her lifeline. How would she ever be able to take a leap of faith, give it up, and hope her business generated enough profit to live on?

Toward the end of the day, a good-looking man who didn't appear to be a born-and-raised Montanan walked into the bistro. He stared through the window at the cheese-making operation for a little bit, then wandered to the pastry display. At the end of the day, there wasn't much left. Fortunately, Trish had just brought in a tray of tarts.

"Can I get an espresso and one of those berry tarts?"

"For here or to go?" Megan asked.

"For here." He looked at her for a few seconds, his gaze assessing her as if trying to slot her into the local hierarchy. It was an echo of the scrutiny she used to experience back home before the onlooker's smile dimmed when they realized she was the Winkle girl.

"Have a seat anywhere you like, and I'll bring it over to you." She turned and started the espresso, the hiss of steam and the clunk of the porta-filter covering her discomfort.

Once the coffee was finished, she plated the fruit tart, grabbed a napkin-wrapped fork, knife, and spoon, and headed to the table he'd chosen.

"Thank you," he said. "You're new in town, aren't you?" He held out a hand. "Dave Brockman."

"Um ... yes. I moved here a few months ago." She kept it vague, like she did everything about her life except her love for fiber.

"I'm new here myself," he said. "Well, relatively. I've been here since last fall, although I went back to California for a month to remind myself there were places that weren't covered with snow right now."

"That must have been nice." She was getting better with the small talk required of a waitress.

"Very much so." Again there was that speculative look, as if he were measuring her for some task.

She smiled and returned to the counter. A half hour later, Courtney turned the sign to closed and dimmed the lights—her signal to the few remaining customers that it was time to head home.

As her boss closed out the register, Megan bussed the tables, pocketing the change most people left in tips as she did so. Everything was normal until she got to Brockman's table. He'd left his business card—no occupation, just his name, mobile phone number, and email—along with a five-dollar tip, more than he'd paid for the coffee and tart. On the back of the card it said, "Thanks, see you again."

What did the man want?

Chapter 2

By the time Megan returned to her rented house, twilight had faded, but the warm temperature beckoned. She dropped her bag on the couch, then returned to the back porch to as puffy clouds shifted from deep pinks and blues to fiery reds and yellows dancing atop the mountain peaks. So different from home. The Appalachians were shrouded with mystery and the ghosts of her relatives, but the hollows and valleys that ran through the ridges were heavy with the deeds of the past, and she was committed to the future.

At least she was most of the time.

Montana was beautiful, but it could be a hard place to live. According to the locals, weather alone discouraged many people. Newbies would arrive in the spring, cruise through the summer, and admire the battling of the fall elk.

Then winter would set in.

And the interloper would be left trying to deal with the locals.

Megan had arrived in January, huddled in her house, and dealt with winter's raw chill alone. She hadn't expected friends, and she didn't get any. Now, for no reason that made any sense at all, spring had brought a yearning for companions—just friends. There was no need for a relationship, something she would need to make very clear to Dave Brockman.

Making friends might be a challenge. People were nice enough, but most had lived in this small town all their lives. Their relationships were already cast in stone, and there wasn't much room for a newcomer in the chinks. The people she worked with were more acquaintances than friends. And none of them understood her obsession with fiber.

A gale blasted the side of the house, a simple frame structure in a ranch style, forcing her to retreat indoors.

After making a simple supper of fried pinto beans, a slice of the ham she'd purchased from the local Hutterites, and some overly sturdy broccoli, which seemed to be the sole vegetable to be found this time of year in the local store, she flicked on a podcast she was listening to and began to spin.

The pre-drafted batt of Leicester wool slipped easily through her fingers. She concentrated on developing a rhythm, watching the resulting thread to make sure the size was consistent. While a slub wasn't uncommon to a new spinner, people plunking down hard cash for yarn looked at the resulting bump as a flaw, unless they were buying "art" yarn where uneven dimensions and artistic knots were a feature.

Megan smiled to herself. The process took hold of her as she listened to a podcast on creating a craft business. If she was going to start a business, she was going learn to do it right.

# # #

Dylan stared out his cabin's windows at the peaks of the Rockies in the distance. What was he missing? The canvas in front of him seemed fine to him—well, technically fine. It even had life—the soaring of the eagle over the prairie, the lumbering brown frame of a grizzly in the distance, and the innocent cow chewing its cud in the foreground.

But it was flat ... boring ... just like every other journeyman's idea of what western art should look like. Although no one considered art of any stripe to be important anymore. There was gaming ... was that an art of a sort? But computer generation retained the same frenetic activity as most of the world, activity that served no functional or contemplative purpose. Instead, like the rest of the world's processes, it went at hyper speed and achieved questionable results.

He stared at the painting a few moments longer, put down his brush before he splashed it across the canvas, and went to the main house to get a cup of coffee.

Ridiculous, since he had a perfectly functioning kitchen in his own cabin. There was no one around, so he snapped the lid on the coffee cup and went back to work.

He'd created his home from one of the old bunkhouses left from the late 1800s when his great-whatever grandfather Jarod had built the house and ranch. Dylan had started imagining a place of his own at thirteen, right after his father had died. The main house had been both too noisy and too quiet for him. He was going to need a space that was his own, away from inherited heavy furniture and his mother's slow death.

At first he'd escaped by saddling a horse, strapping on paints and an easel, and riding into the hills. But winter trapped him at home. At fourteen, he'd started hanging around in the aging building. There had been holes in the walls, but the roof was solid and the fireplace still worked. Best of all, it was his, and he could get the solitude he needed. When he was fifteen, he started planning repairs, and a year later he'd gone to work after apprenticing himself to a carpenter for the summer.

By the time he was nineteen, Jarod had taken over the ranch, and CJ had left to pursue photojournalism. Every second Dylan didn't spend helping his brother tend cattle, repair structures, and ride fence, he worked on his art or improved the cabin. He'd moved in by then, and that's where he'd been for the last fourteen years.

It was perfect, until the walls closed in and life turned into the hamster wheel of painting work no one wanted to buy.

Resisting the temptation to slash the painting with a palette knife, he cleaned up and headed back to the main house. The mud and snow on the short path gripped the bottom of his boots, making him drag each step clear from the earth. Stomping up the steps got rid of some of the mud, but he wisely left them in the designated spot before walking in stocking feet to the kitchen.

Birdie was ensconced, as she normally was, at the table, coffee cup by her side and cooking show on the flat-screen television.

"Something new for supper?" he asked as he poured his own cup.

"Nope. Just fantasizing." She gestured at the screen. "Who has time for all that fussing? And you boys wouldn't eat it anyway. Chicken cordon bleu on a cattle ranch. Ha!"

Dylan chuckled. Birdie's meals were predictable, some might even say boring, but they were always good and always filling.

What more did a cowhand need?

"Cameron up?" he asked.

"He came down for coffee, but I haven't seen him since," Birdie said. "The shower ran a while ago."

Dylan slid into one of the other chairs. "What's he going to do? Can he stay in the army? Or have they already bounced him out? A desk job will kill him."

"You know the old saying, 'When one door closes, a window opens.' God will show him the way."

He smiled but didn't say anything. His parents had been churchgoers, but when they'd realized their father's prayers on Sundays had been preceded by infidelity on Saturdays, CJ and he had abandoned organized religion quickly. Somehow, it had stuck with Jarod, and it was totally ingrained in Birdie.

If he found God anywhere, it was in the drama and serenity of nature.

"Anything I can do to help him?" Dylan asked. "Do you think he'd enjoy going out to the barn and seeing the horses Jarod is working?"

"I think it's best to let him be," Birdie said, her gaze steady on Dylan. "He just got home and has a lot to deal with. There had to be a reason he didn't want any of us to be with him while he recovered. He's going to have to figure out how much family he wants around and when."

"I just want to do something."

"I know, but sometimes all we can do is live our lives the best we can and be true to ourselves."

He nodded. She was right, of course.

"What do you know about the new cheese place and bakery?" he asked.

"It opened a few months ago, but I think they were working out the kinks. Trish has her new tarts there, but says she won't give her pies to anyone but Mae's coffee shop and the Log Cabin Café."

Dylan grinned. Trish had been friends of a sort with CJ in high school, but where CJ had bolted town the day after graduation, Trish had married her high school boyfriend and immediately popped out two kids. The surprise had been when she started her own business. Soon her pies were in big demand in Choteau and beyond. She'd renewed her friendship with CJ after Dylan's sister returned to the States.

"I also hear," Birdie said, her voice softening, "they've got a redheaded waitress from somewhere in the South who is quite attractive."

Dylan leaned back in his chair. "I see where this is going. CJ and Jarod are now paired off, so you figure it's my turn."

"Well," Birdie's smile pretended innocence, "why not?"

He tilted forward and tapped his fingers as he enumerated. "One, I live in a small cabin on my family's land. I am not set up to have someone else in my life. Two, I don't have a real job. I'm a painter who can't sell his paintings. I work for my brother, who really runs the ranch."

"Wait—" Birdie started.

Dylan held up a finger. "Jarod runs the ranch. Everyone else in the family, including you, knows that." He ticked off the third finger. "Three, I will never date a woman who wasn't born and bred in Montana. Outsiders don't understand what it's like."

"That's a little biased," Birdie said.

He shrugged. "It's my life. I'm not running for office." He started to stand up. He was done with this conversation. Hard labor should set his angst to rights.

"But you should," Birdie said.

He sat back down. "What?"

"I heard Ross is resigning from the house legislature next year. Seems to me it might be a good fit."

"Why in ... heck ... do you think that?" Swearing out on the ranch set well with him, but doing it in Birdie's kitchen never felt right.

"Because you know how to find compromise. You've been doing it with your brothers for years. CJ was a little out of your reach, but she doesn't count."

"And just how do you propose I get all these people to vote for me? They won't even buy my art. Why would they trust me with their government?"

"You've got time to figure that out. The election isn't until next year."

He shook his head. "Not happening. I can't think of anything I'd rather do less." He stood again, ready to be done with Birdie's crazy ideas. "I've got work to do."

"Uh-huh. Supper will be at six. Tell Jarod we're having meatloaf. That should get him here on time."

"Will do."

He yanked on his coat. Run for office? He'd do that about the same time he fell in love with an out-of-state woman.

And yet, the preposterous idea ran through his head as he helped Jarod deal with the newborn calves. Using the ATVs, they ran a search pattern in the pasture nearest the ranch buildings, looking for the tiny animals. Much to the mother's dismay, they checked each calf to make sure it was thriving and tagged its ear.

"When do you think we're going to be able to get back up there?" he asked, gesturing toward the northwest corner of the ranch. So many weird events had happened in that part of the property. Last fall the fence had been cut, but they didn't find any cattle missing. There was also no evidence of a truck, the rustler's favorite way to extract cows, anywhere near the cut fence. A few weeks ago, an explosion occurred in the same area.

Dylan had sent his favorite toy, a commercial drone, to check out the landscape more than once, but it had never been able to give them any more information. Only boots on the ground were going to help them.

"Not long," Jarod said. "It's already melting far faster than it has in the past."

"Climate change?" Dylan suggested.

Jarod shrugged. "Who knows? Whatever is going on is making it a challenge to plan for feed. But I don't have time to figure out whether its change or the result of some convoluted idea like chaos theory. There's work to be done."

And that's how most people thought. They were just trying to get by, raise their kids the best they could, and leave a legacy, even if it was as small as a baby quilt, to be passed on to the next generation.

Except for Dylan. He didn't have anything to leave anyone. The ranch would go to any kids Jarod had with Samantha, and that would be that.

Dylan climbed on top of the ATV and gunned the motor. Something needed to change.

# # #

Dylan splashed paint all Sunday morning while Birdie and Jarod went to church. At least that's what it felt like he was doing. The painting was technically good; he could imagine it hanging over some rich man's fireplace, someone like their neighbor from California. But Dave Brockman could afford a Charlie Russell. Why in hell would he buy a Dylan Beck?

Why would anyone?

Still, people had bought Thomas Kinkade cottage kitsch for years before he died and the bottom fell out of that collectible market. There was no accounting for people's taste. Maybe, instead of trying to sell the paintings in Montana, where people could compare his scenery to the real thing, he should try someplace like Silicon Valley, Texas, or Omaha.

Putting aside the scenery, he pulled up a fresh canvas. He'd been toying with an idea ever since he'd driven by Freezeout Lake on his way to fetch Cameron. Turning the canvas horizontally, he picked up a pencil and began to sketch out lines that would become ribbons of color. At least that was the way he envisioned it, mostly horizontal lines, with a few vertical ones thrown in for contrast.

But what was the right media to use? Watercolor begged to him, although he hadn't done one in years. Once he'd settled on landscape painting, only oil made sense to him. The solid hues gave substance to the harsh land around him. The image he had in mind, however, needed the lighter touch and fluid edges watercolor gave.

The initial sketch was okay but still too mathematical to be real art. He closed his eyes and reimagined the lake from the few times he'd been there, the splash of a landing bird, a wading bird stalking something only it could see, the growing haze as the various ponds that made up the lake washed toward the horizon.

He erased, sketched, and erased some more. Finally satisfied, he picked up the brushes he'd used earlier and took them to a mudroom he'd built next to the kitchen. Using the industrial sink he'd installed for the purpose, he began the messy process of cleaning up.

He spent the rest of the early afternoon checking out his watercolor supplies and reviewing the art books he had on different techniques. Maybe changing his media could give him new inspiration, enough to garner some interest. There sure wasn't any in what he was doing now.

At the regular time, he walked to the main house. He was welcome to hibernate in his cabin during the week, but Sunday dinner was a command performance. Would Cameron come down? CJ and Nick, along with Nick's son, Trevor, were going to be there, and Samantha was joining Jarod along with her daughter, Audie. An almost full house. Kaiden said he would video conference with them all later.

The house was a noisy mess when he got there, Trevor and Audie were in a disagreement about which sibling was getting married first, CJ or Jarod. The two had definitely taken to the idea of being cousins with a vengeance.

Birdie was bossing Nick and CJ around the kitchen, while Jarod and Samantha had retreated to the living room, given the sounds of the basketball game. Good thing she'd learned to like sports, although she was lucky Jarod wasn't going to make her a rodeo widow.

"Anyone seen Cameron today?" Dylan tried to make it sound casual, but he wasn't fooling anyone.

"He was up early," Birdie said. "Had some coffee and left a note saying he was going for a walk. He hasn't come back yet."

Dylan checked the clock on the stove. "But that's eight or nine hours. Shouldn't someone go looking for him?"

"He's a grown man," Birdie chided him.

The mudroom door opened. Cameron stopped at the entrance, looked around him, and made an attempt at a smile that didn't quite make it.

"Sunday," he said. "I'd forgotten."

"Cameron!" CJ flung her arms around her brother, seemingly oblivious to the missing limb. "Damn, I've missed you."

Cameron's smile grew a little broader. "Good to see you, too. I'm glad you're back."

CJ released him. "Remember Nick? This is his son, Trevor."

"I remember." Cameron's voice had an edge as he looked at Nick. "I hope you've made up sufficiently for your past mistakes."

"Your sister and brothers think I've done the appropriate amount of groveling," Nick said, holding out his hand. "I've repented and see the error of my ways."

"He has," CJ said, putting a loud smacking kiss on Nick's cheek.

"Ewww," Trevor said.

"Precisely my thought," Cameron said, shaking first Nick's hand and then Trevor's. "Good to meet you."

Audie wedged herself into the middle of the group. "Who are you?" she asked.

God, Dylan loved that kid. She just cut to the chase and said what was on her mind. A great addition to a family more used to keeping secrets than anything else.

"I might ask the same of you," said Cameron, his features thawing a little more. "Considering you're in my house."

Audie shook her head with vehemence. "It's Jarod's house ... and Birdie's ... and Dylan's ... sort of." Then she cocked her head. "Are you another uncle?"

"Do you need another one?"

Audie counted on her fingers, her lips moving as she ticked off Dylan, Nick, and Kaiden. She held up her fingers. "I've got room for two more."

The resulting chuckle released even more tension.

"Then I'll be happy to be your uncle Cam. What shall I call my niece?"

"Audie. Audie Deveaux, but just for now. I expect to get a new last name soon." Audie smiled at Trevor with triumph.

Cameron crouched down and held out his hand.

"Why do you only have one arm?" she asked as she shook it.

He stood abruptly. "An accident." After looking around the room, he added, "If you'd excuse me, I'm feeling tired." Like the Red Sea, they parted to let him through.

Audie looked after him for a moment, shrugged, then walked to the living room.

"She'll be good for him," Birdie said, "but just not all at once." She glared at Dylan. "Don't stand there. Set the table."

"Yes, ma'am." Dylan tapped Trevor on the arm. "You're on dish duty with me."

Within twenty minutes the eight of them were seated around the old family table. Cameron failed to reappear. Grace was said, and they dug into the steaming chicken, potatoes, and boiled carrots.

"I am so looking forward to having time this summer to get to the farmer's market and maybe do a little canning," Samantha said.

"Salads," CJ added. "There is nothing like a fresh salad plucked from the ground."

"Then you better get started planting starters," Nick said. "The season is short enough as it is."

"Trevor and I have a project this week: plant some seeds and start watering. Over the summer we can build a cold frame."

"I've got homework," the teen said.

CJ gave him the stink eye she'd perfected on her younger brothers.

"But I'll be happy to help," Trevor said.

"Maybe you can help CJ build an arbor so they can finally get hitched," Dylan said.

The stink eye landed square on Dylan.

"Just to clarify," she said, pointing her knife at him, "whether and when Nick and I get married is none of your business. Right now, there are no plans for that particular action."

"Ever?" Birdie asked.

"Sorry to disappoint you." CJ put the knife down and softened her expression. "But neither of us is ready for marriage now or in the near future. We've both tried it once. Right now, we're happy the way we are."

Birdie pursed her lips, clearly not satisfied with that solution. Her quick glance to the ceiling let Dylan know she was counting on God to rectify that particular problem. He hid his smile.

"While we're on the subject of marriage," Jarod said. "I have an announcement to make. I have asked Samantha to marry me and she said yes."

Before the congratulations could erupt, Audie said, "And me too."

"I will never forget you," Jarod said, his eyes soft as he gazed at the little girl. He looked up at the rest of the group. "She said yes, too."

"We know it's quick," Samantha said, "but it feels right." Her smile was soft. "And if we want to get started on kids to pester Trevor and Audie, we need to start soon."

And then the commotion began. When it was all sorted, everyone knew that no, a ring, or in this case rings, hadn't been purchased and they hadn't set a date, but they were thinking sometime in the fall.

The family was moving on ... finally.

Conversation drifted back to more mundane topics: what Trevor and Audie were doing in school, Samantha's plans for the next semester, and Nick's upcoming fishing trips. Dylan let it flow over him, bringing contentment. As much as he needed solitude, he needed his family even more. They were a safe haven.

CJ dropped some news as the conversation began to wind down.

"I found birth records," she said with a big grin on her face. His sister's years of journalism were definitely paying off. "Thank goodness for the Mormons."

"Whose records?" Jarod asked.

"Alice's sons."

"Wow," Birdie said. "You're pretty amazing."

"That she is," Nick said and gave CJ a kiss.

Trevor groaned. "They do that *all* the time."

"Now, who was Alice exactly?" Samantha asked. "You told me something last fall, but it was a little convoluted for me and I don't exactly remember."

"Our great-whatever grandfather," Dylan said, "had two sons, Jacob and Seth. Jacob stayed here and ran the ranch, and Seth left, although no one really knows why. It was only a curiosity until the county decided to tax mineral rights."

"Then," CJ picked up, "we tried to find out if the mineral rights stayed with the ranch, went with Seth, or got sold along the way." She shrugged. "We couldn't find anything, and the deed isn't really clear, but the county made us pay them anyway."

"I remember that part," Samantha said.

"We hired a private investigator to trace Seth's family. We had some idea where to start, because the family Bible had a list of both boys' descendants. Seth's ended with Alice, born in the 1930s."

"After the PI told us he couldn't work on the case anymore—we have no idea why that happened either—CJ and I took over," Dylan said. "But she's better at it. She discovered that Alice married a man named Greg Stern in 1952, right after she graduated high school. And now ..."

"Alice had two sons, Greg Jr. and Tommy. Greg was born in late 1952, which explains the rushed wedding, and Tommy came along a year later."

"What happened to Alice and her husband?" Samantha asked.

"That's next on the list to uncover," CJ said.

"Maybe Cameron could help," Dylan suggested in a quiet voice.

"I don't think he's ready yet," CJ said.

"We've got to do something to help him."

"He's going to have to figure his own way back," CJ said, "just like I did."

"We didn't leave you to yourself," Jarod pointed out.

"No, you badgered me into helping out on the ranch. But I wasn't physically wounded."

Dylan chewed that in his mind, along with the chicken in his mouth. How would he like to be treated in Cameron's place?

"I wouldn't want to think I wasn't capable of keeping up my end," Nick said. "It's going to be especially difficult for a military man who's used to being at peak performance."

"So you're saying I should ask him for help," Jarod said.

Nick nodded. "Let him figure out what he's capable of."

"That's enough talk," Birdie says. "What if he hears you?"

The rebuke stung him, but she was right. "Speaking of not helping," Dylan said with a grin, "which day is best for me to disappear this week? I want to do some painting over by Freezeout."

"None," Jarod said flatly. "We're still running down calves, remember?"

"I can help." Cameron's deep voice made them all turn to the door to the other half of the house.

Dylan quickly stood and pulled another chair to the table.

Cameron hesitated for a second, then walked over and slid

his lanky form into the seat, his empty left sleeve toward CJ.

Dylan passed him the platter with the chicken.

Again, the small hesitation and then his brother selected a leg. The process was repeated with the rest of the dishes, while the others kept up a smattering of the small talk they'd already hashed through earlier. They were all too good at covering up painful situations.

Except Audie.

She was staring at Cameron, concern across her face. She leaned over and whispered something to Jarod, who tried to hide his glance at his brother.

"What is she asking?" Cameron didn't miss the look.

Jarod flushed.

"Audie, what do you want to know?" Cameron asked.

"Can you ride a horse with only one arm?" she asked.

"I don't know."

"Oh."

There was a moment of silence as Dylan, and he imagined everyone else, tried to figure out what to say next.

"Will you be painting birds or general landscape at Freezeout?" Samantha asked him.

"My intention is landscape, but I'm going to try some watercolor instead of oil," he said.

"Why's that?"

"Just to do something different." *And to make sure the dream I've had all my life isn't a dud.*

"I'll be interested in seeing one." Samantha looked around the dining room. "I don't think we have any hanging in the ranch house. We really should put one up, don't you think?"

Samantha was sweet for thinking of it, but the last thing he wanted was to see his paintings anywhere else on the ranch. Lately, he'd kept his artwork in the cabin facing the wall or covered.

The watercolors better work out.

"Do you think the Mormon database will have records about what happened to Alice and Greg?" Dylan asked CJ.

"What?" Cameron asked. "You found out more?"

"Yep," CJ said with a smile, and proceeded to fill him in. "Anyway," she ended, turning back to Dylan, "we have a few more resources when we're looking for adults. Back in the 1950s, parents didn't automatically apply for a Social Security number for their kids. That came later. But Social Security will have some kind of record of their adult years. I'm hoping we can track them down quickly, as well as what happened to the boys. Thankfully, they were both boys, so we don't have to worry about name changes."

"Are you going to handle that, or do you want me to look?" he asked.

"Why don't you start with the Social Security stuff—I'll send you a link and information to access our account. I'll continue combing the Mormon genealogy records."

"Sounds like a plan," he said.

"Time to clean up," Birdie said. "It's just about time for Kaiden to call."

Chapter 3

Megan hefted her castle spinning wheel up the steps of the Waldron Creek Cheese and Pastry Shop.

"Here, let me help you with that," a tall man with shaggy, black hair said, crouching as if to take the wheel but stopping short of actually touching it. "If it's okay with you, that is."

While she could do it, it would be nice to have help. "Sure. Thanks. Pick it up here, and I'll get the door." She pointed to the two best places to lift the wheel without damaging it.

"What is this thing?" he asked as he guided it carefully through the doorway.

"It's a spinning wheel."

"Doesn't look like any spinning wheel I've ever seen," he said with a grin that transformed his looks from dangerous stranger to friendly sprite. "Where do you want it?"

"Over here." She pointed to the corner Courtney had said she could use. "It's not the kind of wheel you see in movies, but it works just as well."

"This is a dumb question," he said as he lowered the wheel to the floor. "But do you spin?"

She chuckled. "Yes, I've done it for most of my life."

"Another dumb question, I'm afraid," he said. "But are you from somewhere in the South? Your accent ..." He gestured toward her mouth.

"North Carolina. Good guess. No matter how hard I try to soften it, people notice."

"I wouldn't change a thing," he said. "It sounds lovely."

"Thank you. Now, is there anything I can do for you?" No need to continue the conversation about her background. "My shift starts in a few minutes. Cup of coffee? Pastry to get you through the afternoon?"

"Coffee would be great." He held out his hand. "Dylan Beck."

"Megan Winkle." She shook his hand. Warm, callused, with a grip that was firm but didn't try to wrestle her for power. "Now let me get you that coffee." She walked to the counter and slipped on an apron.

"I wonder if he'll be next," Courtney said.

"What do you mean?" Megan grabbed a mug and filled it with fresh brew, the acrid smell vicariously providing a welcome afternoon jolt.

"The Becks own a cattle ranch south of here," Courtney said. "Dylan is the middle child. CJ and Jarod, the oldest, finally settled into serious relationships this past year."

"Some people take time to find the right one." Megan looked pointedly at Courtney, who was single, the best she could figure out.

"True, but in this case, the kids, all five of them, had their lives disrupted by a family tragedy."

"That's too bad." Growing up in the hills outside of Ashland had given Megan enough tragic stories to last a lifetime. "Well, right now he's a man who is looking for coffee, not a date."

"And a bear claw," Courtney said. "Rumor is, all the Beck men go mad for them."

Maybe Choteau was going to be too small a town to live in.

"Whatever you say, boss." She plated the bear claw and brought it with the coffee to the table Dylan had chosen. He sat there with the already-pored-over pages of the local weekly newspaper.

"Anything new?" she asked.

"Not in the paper," he said, glancing up with a smile that reached all the way to his gray eyes.

Why, the flirt! She'd need to be careful around him. Courtney may think he was ready for a long-term relationship, but she had no time or need to be involved with anyone right now.

"Courtney seemed to think you needed a bear claw," she said, placing the plate on the table.

"Courtney—is that Courtney Lewis?"

"Yes."

Dylan cranked his head around to look toward the counter. Courtney smiled and gave a little wave. He waved back.

"She work here?" he asked.

"She owns it," Megan replied as she slid the coffee on the table.

"Well, I'll be. She and I dated for a few months in high school."

"She said your family owns a ranch. Must be hard work," Megan said. It was good practice to chat with customers; it increased the tips.

"Some days," he said. "But, actually, I'm an artist."

"Oh, that's interesting. Where do you sell your art?"

"Helena mostly." There was an edge to his voice that hadn't been there before.

Bad subject. Disgruntled customers didn't leave nice tips.

"So what do you spin?" he asked.

"I make yarn from prepared fleece, then sell it on Etsy."

"Any money in that?"

"Some." The discussion was getting too personal. "Enjoy your paper and pastry," she said with a friendly smile. Had to work for her money.

"I will. By the way, there's not much money in art, either."

What was she supposed to say to that? Was he trying to bond over their shared lack of income?

"Oh. Okay. Do you need anything else?"

He paused. "Not right now, thanks."

Amid the low murmur and tapping of computer keys of the bistro's few patrons, she made her way back to the counter area.

"Looks like you and Dylan hit it off," Courtney commented.

"He's a bit of a flirt," she replied.

"Not normally. Of course, he doesn't get off the ranch much, and when he does, he's toting his easel to one part of the county or another."

"I take it he doesn't sell many paintings."

"What makes you say that?"

"Something he said."

"Well," Courtney said, "that may be true. I have no idea. I decorate my apartment with prints from the big box stores in Great Falls. Fine art, pretty as it is, just isn't in my budget."

"So, I was thinking." Megan picked up a cleaning rag to attend to the tables. "Would it be okay if I sat and spun a few times a day? During the slow times only. It would give me a chance to let people know about my business."

Courtney pursed her lips. "I'm not sure about that. It might distract people from watching the cheesemaking, which leads to purchase, or spending time in front of the pastry counter, which makes them order more than they'd intended. Spinning isn't part of *my* core business."

"Yes, I can see that," Megan said and grabbed the spray bottle.

As she walked to the first dirty table, her lungs deflated. She slipped into the routine of wiping the table, resetting it, and making sure the coffee creamers and sugars were well-supplied. She'd been counting on the bistro as a place to get the word out about From Fleece to Fabric. She was beginning by producing handmade yarn, but the next step would be to teach classes. If she let her dream really expand, she could see creating a small store and maybe even an annual fiber festival.

She sighed. It was probably never going to happen. She could barely afford to buy the supplies she needed to spin. And Choteau was too small a town to attract customers. She'd stopped here because she was simply so tired of running from her past.

The jingle of the bell over the door made her look up. It was that man again ... Dave something. He was smiling as he entered, but the expression became more guarded when he spotted Dylan.

Dylan had also looked up, but she couldn't see his expression. His body stilled though, like an animal that anticipates conflict. Dave walked toward him, his smile intact but not genuine.

Curiosity overcame her normal reserve, and she moved to another table that was closer to the pair.

"Dylan," Dave said.

"Hello, Dave."

"Good to see you." Dave's voice was hearty, like a used car salesman ready to sell you the biggest lemon on the lot. "Had any more trouble with fences near my land?"

"The snow's been a little too deep to get up there and look personally. Jarod and I should be able to get out there soon. There was a small explosion up there about a month ago. You wouldn't happen to know anything about that, would you?"

"An explosion? Was that when your brother was hurt? Cassandra mentioned she'd heard he'd been thrown from his horse or something."

"Yeah. Like I said, we haven't been able to spend any time exploring up there yet. We will, soon."

Was there a little threat in his voice?

"Well, I wish you luck with all that," Dave said. "Now I'm going to see about some of those great pastries they have here. You enjoy that bear claw."

Megan finished with a table. The heavy aroma of sandalwood caused her to turn around.

Dave stood in front of her. "You're looking very pretty today, Miss Megan," he said. "Can you help me choose the most delicious pastry you have?"

God, he was laying it on thick. She hadn't been smothered in this much sweetness since she left the South. But, mindful of her tips, she glanced over at the counter. No one was behind it.

"Sure," she said and walked quickly to the serving area where she dumped the rag and spray bottle before giving her hands a quick rinse. "Coffee?" she asked.

"Of course." He stared at the pastries.

As she poured, she surreptitiously studied the man—on the tall side; broad-shouldered; fussy, brown hair; and the slightly red face and curved-out belly of a man who enjoyed ingesting fine wine and food. What was a man like this doing in Choteau, Montana?

"How about one of the tarts?" she suggested to him. "They are a crowd favorite."

"Ah, yes, that gal Trish makes them. So talented. And her pies ... Why don't you carry those here?"

"She made a deal to sell them to Mae at the Bridges and the Log Cabin Café," Megan replied. "She doesn't want them to show up just anywhere in town."

"Smart businesswoman. Sure, I'll take a tart." He picked up another one of the used papers and went to a table away from where Dylan Beck sat.

She plated the tart and took it and the coffee to her new customer, glancing toward the rancher-artist as she walked. He was kind of cute looking in a raffish, artist way.

"So how are you enjoying the nightlife in our small town?" Dave asked with a grin.

"Is there one?" she quipped, adding a touch of syrup to her words. "You catch more flies with honey than vinegar" was ingrained in her DNA.

He laughed. "Not really, but if you'd like to go out to dinner some night, I'd love to take you out. By some miracle, we've recently acquired a fine-dining restaurant here."

The scrape of iron chair legs against hardwood flooring made her glance at Dylan's table.

He tossed the paper on the table, along with a few bills, and stalked out the door without looking back.

"Strange dude, Dylan," Dave said. "But then all the Becks have a bit of weirdness. They all but accused me of rustling their cattle last year." He snorted. "I've got no use for cattle; they're a relic, dying industry. The trend is toward vegan living and manufactured protein. Ranchers just haven't caught onto it yet."

"Enjoy your tart," she said, using a brief moment to escape

before he could launch into any other strange theories or invitations.

Courtney was behind the counter again by the time Megan finished the tables. "Is our latest Californian harassing you?" she asked.

"Nothing I can't handle," Megan said. Since she'd been in high school, too many guys had commented on her red hair and looks, some nicely, some aggressively. An aunt who'd been a waitress all her life had taught Megan how to avoid it without pissing off the man involved. It was one of the most useful skills she'd picked up.

"Well, just let me know. There's something about him that makes the hair on my arm stand up, and I'd be happy to find a reason to bounce him out of here. But he's always pleasant and courteous, so I've got no cause." Courtney polished the top of the already-gleaming pastry display. "So now that you have your spinning wheel here, what else are you going to display to make the exhibit complete?" She smiled. "I may not want you spinning, but your idea of having local crafts displayed is brilliant."

"I'm going to put up a few samples of what goes into spinning—roving, batts, that sort of thing. Then a few samples of yarn, some for knitting and some for weaving. Finally, a display of products, some knit, some woven, that you can resell."

"Oh, good, more money for me," Courtney said with a grin. Then she became serious. "Just make sure that you price them high enough so you make some money for yourself. It's the hardest thing to get artists and artisans to do around here. The people who trek to Glacier are usually pretty well-heeled and can afford the price. Even people who live here," she nodded toward Dave, who was finishing up his tart, "can afford a lot more than they'd like you to believe. They say the Scots are tight with a dime, but I don't think they can compare with the penny-pinching ways of a Montanan."

Megan refrained from pointing out that a great many of the early whites in Montana, particularly those in the mining trades, had been of Scotch and Irish descent. She'd done a lot of reading about her new state as she'd waited out the snow drifts of winter.

"I'll bring those samples over tomorrow and arrange them after I finish my shift," Megan said.

Courtney picked up the coffeepot. "And I'll go offer our remaining customer a top off, if you'll get started closing up. Only fifteen minutes to go, and the way the wind is picking up out there,

I doubt we're going to get anyone new."

Megan glanced outside where she could see the few young trees on the street straining against the supports that tried to keep them from blowing on down the road. She'd never lived in a place where the wind had such a dominant personality. Some nights when the gales from the north beat against her wood frame house, she could understand how early settlers sometimes went mad from the sound.

The ones who survived were hardy stock indeed.

Where did the Becks fit into that picture?

She shook herself. Dylan Beck was trouble. She could feel it in her bones.

When she wiped Dave's table again, she once again found a five-dollar tip and a note. This time the note read, "I really do want to take you to dinner. Text me."

She stuffed them both in her pocket.

# # #

Dylan carefully pulled the watercolor he'd done at Freezeout Lake from the back of the pickup and took it inside to the cabin. Once inside, he propped it on the fireplace mantel, sat in his recliner—the one he'd rescued from the ranch house after Jarod had decided he needed a new one—and contemplated the blues and greens that dominated the landscape.

It was different from anything he'd ever done, and he wasn't sure if he liked it.

Maybe he had to live with it before deciding.

It lacked texture. With oils, the paint had depth, highs, lows, and ridges. Some were intentional, some came along with the brush strokes.

Watercolor was pretty but flat. Maybe flat wasn't the problem. Maybe it was the pretty.

He'd been twelve when first his father and then his mother had died. All he remembered of his father were his frequent trips and his loud voice. His sweetest memories were like a black-and-white photo: his mother teaching him how to paint. That had ended when she'd experienced the first round of cancer with its attendant surgeries and poisons.

He'd poured himself into his painting from that point on, saving every penny for art supplies. It had saved him—kept him from going out of his mind. No ghosts haunted him when he was painting, and he never planned for the future.

That was the problem.

What if all art had ever been was therapy and he'd let other opportunities go by? He knew ranching and had a natural ability with technology, but what use was that combination?

The girl in the pastry shop had been cute, unusual, too, with her honey-draped vowels and gentle manners. But she wasn't a born-and-raised Montana girl. After the disaster of dating the woman from Massachusetts in college, he'd sworn to never look twice at a woman from out of state; they may make it through one winter, then they invariably wanted to leave and take him with them. They'd never understood that he wouldn't be able to breathe out of sight of the mountains.

But he wouldn't mind taking the new waitress out once or twice. Maybe he could convince her to sit for a painting, preferably in the nude.

He shifted uncomfortably in his chair and shoved the thought out of his mind. He was in too foul a mood to head to the ranch house for supper. After texting Birdie his decision to eat alone, he pulled a beer from his small fridge and flipped on a small flat-screen he'd installed, hoping he could find an old, depressing movie to suit his frame of mind.

The first thing that popped on the screen was a group of strange animals running around a field next to a road. They looked like miniature llamas, at least until the advertiser got done coloring their topknots in vibrant turquoise and violet.

They were cute in an odd sort of way. He searched his memory for a name for the feisty things.

Alpacas. Raised for wool. Did the spinning waitress use alpaca fleece? Where did she get it? While there were plenty of cows and sheep and attendant tension between shepherds and cowboys, he didn't remember seeing any of the long-necked beasts around. What would they be like to raise?

What fun it would be to acquire a beast like that, shear its fleece or wool or whatever, and present it to her like a magician producing a bouquet of flowers from nowhere. That would certainly turn her attention away from Dave Brockman.

Did she see anything in that man, other than his obvious wealth? Hearing him flirt with her had made his skin crawl so much he'd had to leave.

Why did he care?

Not something he wanted to dwell on. He flicked through the

channels until he found an appropriately gloomy movie and settled in to watch.

Chapter 4

The morning light woke Dylan at his usual time. For the first time in a while, the sky across the mountains was a deep cerulean blue that matched one of the blues he'd painted in the skies over the lake. In the dawn's light, the watercolor appealed to him much more than it had in the gloom of the night before.

He took a quick shower, then walked to the main house, the path not any drier than it had been a few days before.

"Morning," he said to Birdie as he walked into the kitchen. Coffee was brewing, eggs were out of the fridge, along with a package of breakfast sausages from the local pig butcher. Pans and plates lined the counter for an easy prep.

"Morning to you, too," she said and started heating the frying pan.

He finished filling his mug as Jarod walked into the kitchen. "Ready to get the hay out this morning?" his brother asked.

"My turn already?"

"Afraid so, but it shouldn't be too much longer. Already the cows are grazing across whatever they can find. Old hay just doesn't compare to green grass."

"Are some of the upper pastures clearing?" They didn't want to overgraze the wintering area. Jarod had been working with some environmental outfit to ranch as sustainably as possible. He was also talking about switching out some of the cattle for bison.

"I'm not sure. It's a nice day, and I'd really like to do some more prep for the arena, but I also want to check out those pastures and the fencing."

"I can send the drone."

"I know. And it's a great tool. But you know me. I like to be able to touch things to believe they're real."

"Sit down," Birdie commanded. "You two are eating breakfast before you go anywhere else." She plunked plates of steaming eggs and sausage in front of them.

"Thanks," Dylan said and dug in while Jarod silently added a prayer before picking up his fork.

"Tell you what," Dylan said. "How about I help you with the

arena after I get the hay out and then we can take a ride up the fence and take care of any problems we see. Building always goes better with two people." He wanted to see his brother's dream of building a rodeo training business come true. If he couldn't figure out his own future, he could at least help with someone else's.

"Thanks. I appreciate that." Jarod glanced upstairs. "Any news from Cameron?"

Birdie shook her head. "You're going to need to wait until he's ready. Take care of your own business. Remember, things need to get done before you can start thinking about that wedding you are planning."

"Samantha's got that covered."

Birdie's shake was even more adamant. "Start your life by planning it together and you'll have a better marriage. Now get out of here ... I got things to do." She picked up her cup of coffee and the latest book she was reading, a *New York Times* best seller on Roosevelt—the first one.

Dylan and Jarod poured their coffee into their respective to-go cups and headed out the door.

While his brother fed and turned out the horses, Dylan rolled a hay wheel onto the back of the modified pickup they used to distribute the hay, only sneezing once or twice from the dust. The rear had been removed, and the tires were the best available for heading across rough terrain in all kinds of weather.

And rough it was. Just like the area around the main house, the pastures were thick with mud, gripping the tires until the engine sucked the treads out of the muck. By the time he got to the primary pasture where they wintered their cattle, the truck body was covered with a thick, brown layer. He opened the gate, drove through, and hopped back into the truck after he'd latched it.

Heat from the sun seeped through the window, hinting of the summer to come. The big sky earned its name today, so close he could reach out and touch it. Being out here where he could see forever put his little dot of humanity in perspective.

Mother Nature provided the rhythm—they just all danced to it.

He stopped the pickup and clambered into the back as the cattle ambled toward him, making their dissatisfaction with the lack of feed loudly known. But Jarod was right; significant patches of grass were being chewed down before they had a chance to take, turning them into patches of dark brown mud.

Once the cattle were fed, he headed back to the barn.

"So what's your plan?" he asked Jarod after he'd put the pickup back in its usual place.

"Well, like I told you and CJ, the only place to build the arena and an adjacent corral is a little northwest of the main house and barn. There's enough room to level it out for the structures and designate a small area for cars to park."

Dylan nodded. "Makes sense."

"The whole thing has to be level. I can get Bobby and his bulldozer in here to do the final leveling, but the brush has to be cleaned out before I can lay out the exact location for him to clear for the arena."

"You're getting one of the pre-constructed jobs, right?"

"Yep."

"You've got final the measurements for the structure and corral?"

"Right here."

"Then let's get to work," Dylan said and started into the barn for the tools they'd need.

"Hey," Jarod said.

Dylan turned.

"Thanks."

"No problem."

The area was mostly clear of snow, and they started clearing at one end of the space Jarod indicated using a small tractor to pull out most of the larger bushes. Although the unfrozen ground made it easier to uproot the plants, the mud tried to hang on to what it owned. Still, it only took a few hours to get it clear enough to stake out.

Leaving behind stakes fluttering with pink tape, they headed back to the ranch house, pulled together some sandwiches and coffee, loaded up the supplies they needed to fix fences, and headed out.

After they'd chewed through the weather, the state of the beef market, and the current government nonsense, Jarod asked, "Would you mind if Samantha and I took over Mom and Dad's room when she moves in?"

Dylan hesitated for a moment. In spite of the fact that CJ had cleared out all their mother's things and saged the room, he could still sense his mother's ghost. But new life would help them all continue to move on.

"Not at all. You'll need room for Audie and whoever else

40

comes along. Cam has his space on the top floor for now, but he'll probably move on as well."

"I hope so. He's always at the top of my prayer list in church."

"Figured he would be. Any closer to figuring when to tie the knot?"

"We're leaning toward September," Jarod said as he slid off his mount to unhitch the gate at the end of the pasture. "Samantha says her teacher friends will be back but not so stressed that they can't have fun. The roads will still be clear, so people can travel."

Dylan guided both horses through, then waited while Jarod latched the gate and climbed back into the saddle.

"East side or west?" Dylan asked.

"Let's head to the west side first, then circle back down."

The first few miles were fine, which was pretty much what they'd expected based on the regular drone surveillance Dylan had instituted. They dismounted at the top of the ridge where the fence climbed out of a drainage.

"Think the cows'll be smart enough to stay out of the drifts?" Dylan asked, looking toward the heap of snow piled close to the fence. The structure had made it through the winter fine, but an unwitting calf might tangle himself up in the barbed wire.

"They are one of the dumbest animals on this earth," his brother replied. "Next to sheep, of course. But I think by the time they wander up here, these last patches will be gone."

They leaned against the rock where they'd laid out their sandwiches, cups of coffee, and the cookies they'd swiped from the jar. "Good thing CJ moved out," Dylan said. "More cookies for us."

"She sure could go through them," Jarod agreed.

Dylan took a bite from the ham and cheese sandwich he'd made and stared north toward the Bob Marshall Wilderness. It had been a while since he'd hiked in that area, or anywhere for that matter. When he was younger, he'd tote his sketchpad and paints, along with his tent, enough food for a few days, and a good-sized can of bear spray and be gone for days.

They were surrounded by such beautiful country, he needed to get back out in it, if only he could drum up enthusiasm for painting anything.

"What are you so blue about these days?" Jarod asked.

"Nothing," he automatically responded.

"Right."

Casey Dawes

"It'll sure be good to get up to that spot where the fence was breached last fall," he replied, as much to change the conversation as anything. "I'm curious to find out what the hell is going on up there that everyone is so interested."

"Well, it sure isn't cattle rustling."

"Do you think Brockman's in on it, whatever it is?"

"I try to think the best of everyone, but there's something off about him," Jarod said. "I can't decide whether it's that he's a Californian through and through or if he's involved with something not legitimate. The other thing that's troubling me is his involvement with Cassandra."

"You don't still have feelings for her, do you?"

"Not in the least," Jarod said. "But there's always been something she hasn't been truthful about. There's the picture that was in her office for one thing. The one CJ proved had been shot in that same area."

"You never did ask her about it, did you?"

"No ... well, Samantha came along and that was that." His brother's cheeks pinked.

Lucky.

Would he ever feel that way about a woman?

"Well, I think Brockman's a creep," he said. "Not only is he hanging around the attorney, but he's making moves on the new girl in town, too."

"Oh?" asked Jarod. "What new girl?"

"Just one of the waitresses at the new pastry shop."

"Is she pretty?"

"I didn't notice."

A nearby crow cawed.

Shut up.

"Uh-huh." Jarod rose and stuffed his reusable wrapping back in the backpack. "Let's get this show on the road so we can get home by dark. Audie had a school activity—Brownies or some such thing—so we pushed her lesson until tomorrow."

"Watching you be a dad is going to be quite a kick," Dylan said as he swung into the saddle.

"Your turn'll come."

As likely as eternal spring in Montana. Still, Megan had been cute. Not that he'd ever admit it to anyone, especially his family.

# # #

42

Reinvigorated by the accomplishments of the day, Dylan spent hours working on the watercolor, adding shading and using an ink pen to add in details and provide contrast. When he was done, he was as satisfied as he was going to get.

The painting reflected the mood Freezeout Lake and many of the other wildlife refuges developed from wetlands and potholes provided. There was an expanse, a timelessness at a place where birds dominated, and man was in service to nature. A peaceful place, ideal for reflecting on life and the world around a person.

Jarod had drawn cattle feeding duties the next morning, so Dylan took the opportunity to go through the work he'd done over the last few months and select a few more pieces for the gallery in Helena. Taking a deep breath, he dialed the number.

"Hey, Katie," he said to the owner. "Got a moment?"

"Sure," she said, but there was a tone in her voice that made him uneasy.

He cleared his throat and started in anyway. "I tried a new medium the last week—watercolor—and I'd like to bring it to show it to you, see what you think. I also have some new oils for you to look at."

The silence on the line edged his nervousness with black marker.

"I'm sorry, Dylan. We had a new artist come in to us last week. She's got a solid sales reputation in Billings and online. We have to have paintings that sell in order to stay in business. We need the wall space. I'm sorry. You're going to have to get here in the next thirty days to pick up your paintings."

"I see." And the truth was, he did. They were in business. He should be too. "I'll get there. Thanks for letting me know."

He stared at his watercolor for a long while, fighting the impulse to smash it across a chair and totally destroy it. With deliberation, he picked up the painting and placed it in the storage room with his watercolors, closed the door, locked it, and stuck the key in a kitchen drawer.

There endeth that chapter.

He yanked on a coat and walked out the front door of his cabin, not bothering to lock that. Pulling open the driver's door of the small pickup, he slid in and firmly shut the door. Resisting the urge to gun it—Birdie would have his hide—he climbed the drive to the main highway and roared north.

Maybe he should get a motorcycle.

By the time he got to town, he was no less keyed up than he

was when he'd left the ranch. Navigating the rotary around the courthouse, he continued north intending to push to the three Indians guarding the Blackfeet Nation before turning around. But a new thought overtook him, and he turned down a side street.

There was an open parking space in front of Bridges Coffee Shop. God, he hadn't been here in years. Even when it was a favorite high school hangout, he'd avoided it for places less populated. It was only after he'd graduated and bombed out at Montana State that he'd started taking long trips into the Bob or up to Glacier to paint. Stopping in to chat with the owner, Mae, before going home had become part of the ritual. But even that had fallen off over the last few years.

His downhill slide had been going on for a while.

The bell jangled as he walked in, causing Mae to glance over from the table where she was topping off the cups of two highway workers.

Must mean spring was firmly in the road repairers' sights. Locals quipped there were really only two seasons in Montana: winter and construction season.

He slid onto a stool and picked up the local paper that someone had sloppily refolded and left on the counter.

"It's been a while," Mae said as she stepped behind the counter and grabbed a mug. "Still taking it black?"

"Yep."

She set the mug on the counter. "Anything else? I've got a few slices of Trish's peach pie in the back."

"I'll pass," he said. "Thanks, though. Is that new pastry place affecting your business?"

"Not really," she said. "We get different kinds of customers. These guys"—she waved her almost empty coffeepot at the group of highway workers—"don't want fussy. They want food, and they want it fast. Same with ranchers." She put the pot back on the warming tray. "Now, some of those wheeler-dealer types are going to use the new place, and that's just fine with me. I'll take the working folk any day—you know, the kind that actually pay their tab when the time comes."

"That's good," he said and took a sip of the strong brew. Mae kept her coffee going all the time, but she constantly refreshed the pot so it was heavy on the caffeine but not so bitter a man couldn't force it past his lips.

A little bit of the tension went out of his shoulders. He snapped the paper to read the latest news from across the state, important stuff like the weather, market for crops and critters, and the all-important basketball scores.

Mae drifted back out to the tables, making sure folks had what they needed and bussing the few tables where people had left. The coffee shop had a familiar rhythm, like an old song he'd once known but forgotten.

The bell jangled and Sheriff Van Sutton walked in. Looking Dylan over with detailed scrutiny, he nodded and headed to one of the tables at the back. Mae grabbed a cup, set it in front of the sheriff, and poured.

The man nodded, took out his phone, and scanned the screen.

"A man of few words," Dylan said to Mae when she returned to the counter.

"His wife just left him," Mae said. "Give the man a break."

"Sorry. Didn't know that."

"She told him there wasn't enough to do in Choteau. Good riddance to bad rubbish is what I say."

"Could be." Rumor had it that the sheriff's wife had been seen with other men up in Great Falls where she'd go for a weekend visit. She always seemed to have more money to spend than a sheriff's salary should give her.

"Lots of excitement up at the ranch," Mae said topping off his cup. "First it was CJ and Nick, then Samantha and Jarod, and now Cameron's shown up. How's he doing?"

"About as well as you'd expect," Dylan said. "He keeps to himself, helps around for a bit, but mainly goes off by himself for long walks."

"Must be tough to figure out what to do given the circumstances. He was always going to be a man's man, if you know what I mean. Someone capable, strong, and active. The injury must put quite a crimp in his plans."

The injury. Losing an arm went way beyond that term.

"He going to get one of those artificial limb things?" Mae asked.

"Doesn't look like it. Not sure why, but he seems dead set against it."

"Huh." She hustled off to take care of the highway workers, who were shuffling out of their chairs. Once they'd left, he and the sheriff were the only ones left.

The bell tinkled and a man, somewhat on the short side with a shaved head, walked in. He didn't look at Dylan, simply walked around the counter and into the kitchen.

"My son," Mae said quietly. "He's going through some tough times. He's a good short-order cook, though, and it gives him something to do."

What was he supposed to say to that?

"Uh-huh."

"I guess we all hit rough spots in life," Mae said, busying herself straightening menus and filling the salt and pepper shakers she'd gathered. "What are you doing with yourself these days?"

Subtle. Like a brick.

"Still working on the ranch. It's a never-ending job, especially with Jarod finally launching his own training business."

"What about your art? I heard you were in a gallery in Butte or something."

"Helena. And 'were' is right. They told me this morning that I need to go get my pictures."

"Ah."

What did that mean?

He looked at the amount of coffee in his cup, slugged the rest, and set it on the counter. As he started to slip off the stool, Mae said, "Sorry. Didn't mean to overstep. Let me pour you another cup of coffee."

He hesitated, halfway between reality and possibility. He slid back on the stool and pushed his cup across the counter to her. Then he started to talk.

"I can't sell anything." He told her about the phone conversation with the gallery owner.

"Maybe you're trying to sell the wrong thing," Mae said, moving on to ketchup bottles.

"I tried a watercolor, but after that, I didn't bring it up."

"I can understand that."

He looked out the dim panes of the mullioned window surrounded by classic images of waitresses, coffee, and Coca-Cola.

"You know," Mae said. "When life hands you lemons ..."

"You need to make lemonade." He shook his head. "I was never very good at that. Just ask Birdie."

Mae chuckled. Then she shook her head. "Do you know anything about this coffee shop?"

"It's been here since the earth began?"

"You goofball." She waved her hand at him. "Although I

46

suppose you're right. It's been here for decades. Opened in 1951, I think."

"Isn't that when the earth began?"

"Ha. Anyway, it chugged along just fine. Kinda like me. I did what all you kids did. Got born, played for a while, went to school, went to more school, hit puberty, went to the school to end all schools, and got married. Some of you go on to college, but that wasn't my path." She rubbed the back of her hand across her forehead. "I loved Jimmy Senior, I really did. He was a man who did what it took to take care of his family. When the going got tough, he stuck. Jimmy Junior ..." She glanced over her shoulder. "Well, he's a good kid, but he's not all that bright. Well, when Jimmy was born, it took us a while to realize what the problem was. My husband took on extra trips ... he was long-haul trucker. Then the weather ... winter came early that year. He was headed west." She swiped at her face again, but this time her aim was lower. "He lost control on Homestake Pass outside of Butte."

"I'm sorry, Mae." Dylan put his hand on top of her dry and cracked one. They stayed quiet for a moment, in tribute to a man who'd died many years before.

"Thanks," she said, sliding her hand out from under Dylan's. She busied herself by cleaning off the coffee-making equipment on the far counter, her back to Dylan. "Anyway," she continued without turning around, "I never planned on operating a restaurant. But the owner was ready to sell at the right price, the insurance money had come in, and by owning my own business, I could have the flexible hours I needed for Jimmy Junior."

Maybe he should have had a piece of that pie. Looked like he was going to be here for a while.

"Well, we're all glad you're here. Putting up with us high school kids couldn't have been easy."

"Nah, it was fun watching you grow." She turned around and leaned on the counter, the strong light from the front window etching the age lines around her eyes and the deep grooves by her lips. The silver streaks in her light brown hair glittered.

Life was going by too fast.

"Anyway, the point is, sometimes you've got to look at the opportunity, whether it was planned or not."

"But I don't have any opportunities sitting on the horizon," he said.

"Sure you do. You just gotta look for 'em."

He studied his coffee and searched his brain for images of

opportunities. Pictures flowed—Freezeout Lake, the ranch, feeding cattle, the locked door in his cabin, a pretty redhead, and a spinning wheel. If the new café was doing exhibits of knitting, maybe they'd put up one of his paintings.

But first he should ask Mae. Loyalty was important.

"Would you mind if I put up a painting or two on your walls for sale? I'd give you a percentage if they sold."

She shook her head. "I wouldn't mind except it's the wrong place. You know the kind of folks who come in here. Hard workers but not people who'd hang original art on their walls. A print from Walmart but nothing fancy. You should check with the new bistro. Because of its location, it should get lots of traffic from people headed to the park."

He thought of the redhead again.

"Who is she?" Mae asked, folding her arms in front of her as she leaned in closer.

"Who?" he said, casually sipping his coffee.

"Whoever made your cheeks flush."

"I just got a chill, that's all. You know how spring is around here—hot one minute and cold the next." He rubbed a finger inside the back of his collar to keep it from sticking to his neck.

She just laughed and shook her head. "Someone's snared you good, Dylan Beck, and you don't even know it."

He slugged down the rest of his coffee and dug out his wallet.

She waved him away. "On the house. Come back more often. And have some pie next time."

"Will do. Thanks." He walked back to his truck, trying to figure out if Mae was right. If she were, he was going to have to work hard to prevent anything from ever happening. The redheaded girl with the Southern drawl seemed like she'd be pure heartache.

Chapter 5

Dylan spent the next two days working at the ranch. If there weren't chores to be done—and Jarod had a long list—he took a horse and rode fences, repairing the wire that needed it and keeping track of fence posts to replace once the snow dissipated enough that they could bring a utility vehicle where repairs were needed. Anything to exhaust him so that he tumbled into bed at the end of the night and didn't wake up until the morning.

But Saturday, life descended on the ranch.

"Uncle Dylan!" Audie called and flung herself into his arms.

He spun her around.

"You're going to make her dizzy," Samantha said.

"That's what uncles are for!" He grinned at his soon-to-be niece. "Isn't that right?"

She giggled, and he put her down. She was still charming and a little awkward, but already he could see the small changes of growing up. Her face seemed a little longer, her moods more mercurial.

"Jarod should be out in a minute. He was finishing up something with Birdie," Dylan told Samantha. "But," he said to Audie, "the barn cat recently had kittens, and he said you might check them out. They're tucked into the hay bales."

"I know exactly where they are." Audie flounced off with ladylike attitude that lasted only two steps before she broke into a run for the barn.

He laughed as he and Samantha followed.

"How is she doing with the whole wedding thing?" he asked Samantha as they watched Audie delight in the kittens and give the mother special orders on how to care for them.

"She has some definite opinions."

"I bet. Lord help us if the country finally decides it's ready for a woman president and she gets in."

"Well, at least there will be no question about what anyone is supposed to do," Samantha said with a smile.

There was that. When she wasn't asking questions of her future stepfather, she was telling Jarod what to do. He took it all in stride.

"You are planning on having more children, aren't you?"

"A few," she said, a blush coming to her cheeks.

"How will she cope with that?" Because she was on the Asperger's scale, Audie's reactions were always a little different than what could be expected.

"It will be an adventure, that's for sure."

Samantha smiled at her daughter, and an unexpected pang of jealousy startled Dylan. Ever since Samantha had come into his brother's life, Jarod had seemed more grounded, more purposeful, almost like an adult.

After watching Jarod put the little girl through her paces for a little while, Dylan saddled up Paint and took off for a ride. He didn't take his paints, and he had no destination in mind. He simply wanted to get away from family.

He took off toward the southwest, a place he hadn't been in a while. May as well double-check the fences and pasture while he was out there. Maybe they could start shifting cattle around. Jarod was anxious to do it because the livestock was putting a lot of pressure on the winter pasture. Seemed like the conservation group he was working with to develop better ranching practices was big on moving the cattle around, making it a bit more like it had been when bison roamed the west.

Unfortunately, the deep valleys between many of the foothills were still heavy with snow. There would be no moving cattle yet.

From the top of the most southerly rise, he stared out at the highway as it meandered down to the tiny town of Augusta. The sun polished the golden hills and glinted off of patches of snow and emerging grass. Over it all, the big blue sky arched.

A dirt road headed west from the highway close to him, leading to a small piece of land carved from the ranch. The neat two-story house and red barn were the same as they had been while he was growing up. Dylan couldn't quite remember the reason the property line took a jog like that, but he'd always admired the property. If he ever had a spread of his own, he'd want it to look like that.

# # #

Following Sunday's day of rest, was spent watching the second set of the Elite Eight in the main house. It started with him and Jarod, but soon Cameron joined them as they whooped, hollered, and argued their way through several games. On Monday, he was back to Jarod's damn lists, but by Wednesday he needed a break. Once he fed the cattle, he returned to his cabin.

The door to his art was still closed, but the impulse to destroy everything he'd ever created had passed.

With a click, the door opened, and he flicked on the switch. The evidence of his life, canvases stacked neatly together, mocked him.

He plucked the watercolor out from a pile. Was it any better than the oils? Heck if he knew.

But he liked it, and he needed to give his career one more try, no matter how small. Wrapping the painting carefully, he put it against the passenger seat of his small pickup. He hopped in the driver's seat and put the truck in gear.

Jarod waved at him to stop before he could start up the driveway.

"Where are you going?" Jarod asked.

"Town."

"We've still got chores to do."

"I fed the cattle. I need a break."

"It's a busy time of year," Jarod stated.

"It's always busy, except for the dead of winter, and even then everything centers around calving season. I told you. I'm taking a break for a little while. Everything will still be here when I get back."

Without waiting for Jarod to say anything else, Dylan moved forward, slowly gathering steam as he drew away from his brother. In the rearview mirror, he could see Jarod yank the cap from his head and slap it against his thigh before returning it to his head, signs his brother wasn't pleased with Dylan's decision.

Jarod could damn well get over it.

Dylan pulled out of the driveway and headed north on Highway 287. As he passed Dave Brockman's ranchette, he noted the lack of livestock anywhere on the roadside pastures. In the far distance, he could see a few horses, but that was it. What was the man doing here? It wasn't for the nightlife; Choteau didn't have any to speak of. It was a typical Montana small town. People got up, worked, most of them went to church on Sundays, and those churches were the center of most social activity. The teens got bored and caused a ruckus now and then, but a lot of them were too busy helping out on the family spread to cause continual trouble.

It had the usual small-town troubles: poor tax structure, inability to attract or keep good teachers, nurses, and doctors, and an exodus of young people after every graduation. Many businesses didn't stick, and glass storefront windows were covered with plywood only to be removed months later when the business changed hands.

It was drowning him, but he couldn't imagine living anywhere else than where he'd grown up. But maybe it was time to live somewhere on his own.

He drove right on through Choteau and made a left about five miles out of town to head toward the Bob. He needed to take a page from Cameron's book and walk.

About forty-five minutes later, he reached the trailhead and stepped out of the truck. Strapping on the bear spray that was a matter of course in areas where grizzlies and black bears could be emerging from dens, he headed up the trail. He didn't have the right shoes or any other hiking gear, but his ranch clothes and worn cowboy boots would have to do.

He pushed through the edges of his angst and let the soft quiet of the wilderness soothe him. As he walked, the conviction that he needed a place—and a life—of his own grew stronger and stronger, but what exactly he was supposed to do eluded him.

He wasn't a churchgoing man, but like many he knew who lived close to nature, he had no doubt there was a power greater than himself. Putting one foot in front of the other, he climbed the ridge, a fine sheen of sweat building under his flannel shirt. Reaching the top of the ridge, he sat on a nearby boulder that had been in the sun long enough to be bare of snow, and faced the fear that had been creeping through him since his gallery had rejected his paintings.

He'd watched his mother deal with the same rejections until it ate her alive. When they were all young, a time he could barely remember, she laughed and played with them, teaching them to finger paint as she laid out her own sketches to turn into homey paintings. Gradually, her enthusiasm waned, and it seemed like she withdrew from life. His father's infidelities had pushed her further into herself, and the cancer had thinned her to skin and bones.

The self-doubt that had started her down that fatal slope was circling him. He refused to let it win. Somehow, he'd figure this out.

He had to.

With a sigh, he pushed off the rock and headed back down the trail. Time to stop thinking and start acting.

Another hour had him back in Choteau and parking in front of the bistro. Carefully removing the watercolor from the truck, he carried it into the building. The lingering aromas of noonday dishes surrounded him, overlaid with the pleasantly bitter smell of coffee. A cup sounded really good about now.

The room was empty of customers, which worked well for him. Tough to talk to a restaurant owner when the traffic was heavy. Even Mae turned off her chatter.

Except there was no owner, no waitress, no anybody.

He walked over to view the completed exhibit of fiber arts. He chuckled at the expressions of alpacas, stroked the different examples of fleece and roving, and admired the spun yarn. Nearby, a set of shelves was stacked with woolens and woven goods. He pulled out a scarf made from different strands of brown yarn knit in an intricate pattern.

"She does beautiful work, doesn't she?" Courtney's voice came from over his right shoulder.

"Yes. How much is this?"

"I think she wants fifty for it."

"Wow. Not exactly giving it away."

Courtney chuckled. "My fault. I made her double the price she wanted to charge. Handmade goods should cost more than the mass-produced stuff you can get in the big box stores. I think it's worth it because you're supporting local artisans. Because it's pricey, you'll do more to take care of it, cutting down on the rampant consumerism in this country."

"For a woman who's a shopkeeper, that's a pretty radical statement," he replied.

"I'm used to being contrary."

"I seem to remember that."

"Cup of coffee?" she asked.

"That'd be great." He trailed her to the counter. "So what inspired you to come up with the harebrained scheme to put a cheese shop, pastry shop, and bistro combination in Choteau, of all places?" he asked as she poured him a cup.

"Got tired of hitting dead ends," she said, pouring a second cup. "Mind if I join you? I could stand a few minutes off my feet." She pointed to the package he had. "Besides, it looks like you might have something to discuss."

"Sure, that'd be great."

They settled at a table by the window. As she sat, he admired her lithe figure; she must still be the athlete he remembered.

"So," he began, "no serious romantic relationships since high school?"

She took a sip of her coffee and looked out the window. "I was focused on my schooling—I have a degree in business and accounting." She turned her cool gaze back toward him. "Yes, there were relationships, but not the kind you imagine. There was a reason we didn't work out."

"Oh?"

"I'm gay."

That left him speechless.

She smiled. "I kept it quiet until I moved away. Choteau wasn't exactly open-minded then. It's only slightly better now."

"So why come back at all?"

"It's my home. I tried it out there, but I missed the mountains. They're grounding, you know."

He nodded.

"Anyway, the last relationship went on for a couple of years, and I really had hope it was going to make it. But she wanted to have kids, and I couldn't see bringing any more people into this world, loved or not. So I let her go."

Saddened by the revelation, he placed his hand over hers. "I'm sorry."

"It's just the way it rolls sometimes." She shrugged. "Anyway, to answer your question, I spotted a place just like this in Deary, Idaho, population about five hundred, when my girlfriend and I were traveling through the state for some reason. I thought it was a really neat idea, so I worked the numbers, found a cheesemaker, a baker, and a chef, and here we are."

"Well, I hope you are successful."

"You and me both."

Her laugh was as light as he remembered it, reminding him of the times they'd dated, more like pals than anything else.

"So, Dylan, what do you have in that package?" she asked.

He hesitated.

"Show me," she said.

He took off the wrapping and propped the watercolor up on the table. "It's the first thing I've done in this medium in a long time," he said.

As she studied it, his pulse rapidly increased. He wanted her to like it. Even in high school she'd been astute about how things actually went. She didn't follow fads just to be trendy. Instead, she'd done the things that mattered.

"It's good," she said. "I can put it on one of the walls and try to sell it for you. I take a small commission."

"That's fine. As long as someone is trying to sell one of my paintings." He tried to keep the bitterness out of his voice.

"That bad?" she asked. After taking a sip of her coffee, she stared at the painting again.

"It's not easy." And because she was easy to talk to, he opened up a little more. "It's all I ever wanted to do, and if I can't sell it, then what's the point?"

She pursed her lips. "I have a hard time not saying what I think," she said. "Can you handle it?"

"Sure." Even though he wasn't ready at all to hear her opinion.

"This reminds me of your mother's work. It's nice. Pleasant. It would be good in a series of prints that could be sold as decoration for those of us who can't afford galleries. They do a really good job these days of making prints that look just like the originals."

Damning with faint praise. His chest caved inward.

"What *are* people buying these days?" he asked.

"From what I've seen, Remington and Russell still sell, as well as a lot of Native artists—both traditional and modern. Then there's photography, Tom Mangelsen and the like, although Mangelsen does a lot of print work, too."

He looked at the watercolor with new eyes. She was right. It was technically good but not original.

"While this is simply ... what did you say? Pleasant."

"And accurate. That was thing about your art in high school. It always represented the thing we were looking at almost exactly. Sometimes we need to accept who we are from a realistic perspective and find our skill and strength from that." She smiled. "I still want it, though," she said, her voice gentle. "Someone will come through who will want it; you'll see."

"Thanks, Courtney." He swallowed and looked her straight in the eyes. "For everything."

The bell jangled.

Megan walked in carrying a fabric bag. Her cheeks were a healthy red, and her eyes sparkled, matching the smile on her face that faded when she saw them together.

"Am I interrupting something?" she asked.

# # #

Megan tried to act casually as she continued. "I brought in a few more things for sale—skeins of freshly spun and dyed Leicester wool."

What were Courtney and Dylan doing together? Had they rekindled an old flame? They didn't look like anything was going on between them.

It was really none of her business.

They'd grown up here together. She was the outsider.

"You're going to have to get a shop of your own, soon," Courtney said, her smile broadening.

"Can I see them?" Dylan asked. "I don't think I've ever seen hand spun yarn like this before." His voice was kind, and he rose and walked toward her, taking her cloth bag and moving to another empty table. His nearness made her very aware of him as a strong man.

She better not be attracted to him; it would be like getting the measles the day before the prom—horribly bad timing.

"We're going to sell some of these soon," Courtney said, also getting to her feet. "I'm running out of space. If you'll excuse me, I have to finalize some things before we close for the day." She walked off to the back office.

Megan stood where she'd been, unsure of what to do.

Dylan took the bag from her and walked to a nearby table. "May I?" he asked, gesturing toward the bag.

"Sure."

After lifting the skeins from the bag and laying them out on the table, he ran his fingers over the fiber, as if testing the strength and texture of it. "That's a nice blue." He pointed to one of her favorite results. "But if your spinning wheel is here, how did you do this?"

"For this one"—she pointed to one of the thinner yarns, actually three yarns of complementary colors plied together—"I used a drop spindle. For the rest I used my grandmother's old wheel. It looks more like the one you're used to seeing in the Disney films."

"Interesting. There must be a lot more to this process than I've ever imagined."

"Yes," she said. "It's why I love it. There's so much to learn, simple in concept, and practiced in slightly different ways all across the world. There are even yarns made from used saris in India." She tried to tamp down her enthusiasm, but his eyes were bright with interest, so she kept going. "I want to handle everything from the animals used to produce the fleece to control over the processing of the wool, dying, spinning, and even weaving for those who want to learn."

"Sounds pretty ambitious."

"It's a dream I've had all my life," she said. "I'm not sure which baffles me most: raising alpacas or weaving. I'm okay at weaving, but I've never been completely thrilled with the results. They look so ordinary—not artistic at all."

"I know the feeling," he said, glancing at a watercolor that lay on the other table.

"That yours?" she asked, walking over to get a closer look.

"Yeah."

"It's ... pretty."

"That seems to be the general consensus," he said, a flatness to his voice.

"I'm sorry." She turned back to him.

He had a half smile on his face. "It's okay. I'm getting used to it." He looked at the yarn on the table. "Can I help you with that?"

She could do it herself. She should do it herself.

"That would be great," she replied.

He slid the skeins over his arms and walked to the display wall, looking like a mannequin destined to hold his arms stiff forever.

She chuckled at the look. "You're going to get tired."

"Nah. We Becks are made of stern stuff." His full-on grin made him look ten years younger, with a boyish attitude his unruly hair only enhanced. He had the look of all the Scotch-Irish bad boys she'd known in the hollers of home—the kind who always wanted to kiss her at the very least, the men with overactive hormones and one thing on their minds.

"I'll take your word for it," she said, sliding the nearest skein from one of his arms and hanging it on an old wooden rack she'd found at a garage sale and repurposed. She'd sanded it and painted it a jaunty yellow to attract the diners' eyes.

Taking her time, she arranged the skeins so their colors complemented each other. Each was labeled with the type of wool it was made from and where the animal lived. Whenever possible, she'd created several skeins the same so people would be enticed to create objects larger than a scarf or a hat.

"Looks good," Dylan said when she'd finished.

"Thank you."

"Megan, Dylan?" Courtney said. "Are you about finished? I'm ready to close up."

"Yes," they answered in unison.

"Oops," Dylan said, walking back to his table. "I left the coffee cup." He picked it up, took a swig, then took it and the watercolor to Courtney. "Thanks for taking this," he told her. "I appreciate it."

"Good luck," Courtney said, her smile warmer than it had been before. "I hope you find what you're looking for."

"Me too," he said, and his gaze finding Megan's.

Heat flashed through her body.

Courtney gave her a knowing look and headed back to her office.

"This may sound like I'm asking too soon," Dylan said, "since we don't really know each other, but do you want to go to John Henry's and grab a beer? I want to learn more about your ideas. I had a chance to see alpacas on a television commercial the other night. They're cute. Goofy looking, but cute."

Megan hesitated. She got so lonely sometimes, and she spent far too much time talking to herself. The routine of bantering with locals all day and going home to her solitary home at night was getting old. Being able to talk to someone—someone who seemed interested—about her business would relieve the pressure building in her brain.

On the other hand, Dylan Beck was trouble, the kind of man who was going to want a relationship even if he wasn't aware of it right this moment.

Loneliness won out.

"Sure," she said.

Chapter 6

John Henry's was the local pizza, hamburger, and beer joint. Megan had only been in it once or twice, when she'd first arrived and was trying to decide if Choteau was the right home for her.

The paneling that lined the walls was worn and marked with triangles of tape and paper that showed where posters had once been. The ceiling tiles were tinted yellow from age and smoke from before most Montanans finally accepted smoking was on its way out. A bar lined one wall, with high-back chairs along one side. The top of the bar gleamed with heavy layers of varnish that protected against the frequent spills as the night wore on and the families who'd come in to share a pizza faded away.

Dylan gestured at a table against the wall farthest from the bar.

"Trust me to get the beer?" he asked with a grin.

"Okay." She didn't know anything about beer. When she was growing up, if it was cheap, cold, and came in an aluminum can, the adults announced it a "fine brew." The whole world of microbreweries baffled her as much as discussions of fine wine.

He returned in a few minutes with two large glasses of amber beer. "Flavored with huckleberry," he announced.

It was cool and soothing down her throat, with a hint of sweetness that toned down its natural bitterness. "Thanks," she said. "It's good."

"So tell me about these alpacas," he said.

"I think the list of what I don't know is longer than what I do," she said. "I know they are relatively easy to take care of, playful, and can cost anywhere from $350 on up. The cost depends on the quality of their fleece."

"And what determines that?"

"Part of it is whether they are huacaya or suri alpacas. Huacayas are fluffy and suri are more silky. Then there's the density of the fleece. Then there are the things common to having any livestock. Are they being raised for breeding, geldings, or whatever?"

"Sounds as complex as figuring out the right breed of cattle

59

to buy."

"I don't know anything about cattle, but that makes sense."

"Except we don't have to shear them," he said with a grin.

"We only have to do it once a year," she replied. "Then the fleece has to be processed before I can actually spin it." And that's where her plan broke down. She had no idea how to make that happen on any kind of large scale.

"What's the problem?" he asked, sipping his beer.

She told him.

"'Fraid I can't help you there," he said. "This whole thing is a mystery to me."

"Me, too, I'm afraid," she said. "But I can figure that out later. The first problem is finding a classroom space and people to fill the classes. I'm not sure there are enough people in the area to do that."

"Could be a tough sell," he agreed. "People are busy with their own lives already."

"So I'm discovering."

"How'd you get this far from home?" he asked.

The question she'd been dreading.

"Things happened. My grandmother died and left me her spinning wheel and a little money. It seemed as good time as ever to move on."

"Sounded like you had roots in that area, like I do here. I can't imagine leaving Montana."

"Like with plants, sometimes you have to dig up the roots and transplant it." Especially when the rest of the family regards her as a thief.

He cocked his head and studied her before pronouncing, "profound," with a grin.

She had to grin back.

"Sometimes words come out before I think too hard about them," she said. Her grandmother had always teased her about having an old soul.

"Yeah, I get that." The smile faded from his face. "But it still seems like a radical step. I imagine the Rockies are quite different from the Appalachians and western culture a drastic change from the South. Do you think you're going to permanently live here, or keep moving on?"

Was he asking a straightforward question, or was there some deeper meaning?

"It's going to depend on whether or not I can get my business up and running," she said. "Here seems as good a place as any. So you never thought about leaving the state?"

"Nope."

"Never went to college?"

"Yeah, a year in Bozeman, but I was never much good at sitting in a classroom," he said. "So what do you like best about Choteau so far?"

She had started to feel like she was interrogating him, and he must have sensed that, too. She drank some more beer and answered his question. They spent the rest of the night talking about the good and bad of Choteau.

# # #

A flyer on the bulletin board at Rex's Market caught Megan's interest a few days later. "Lifelong Learning is looking for a few more adult-education teachers for the summer session." The flyer went on to say that the high school would provide the space and even announce the class on their local website, but instructors were also requested to help bring in students to meet the minimum required to hold the class.

Okay. It was something to shoot for.

Another flyer on the board announced a potluck at a local community church. If you wanted to know what was going on, religion was the answer. It didn't matter which one; they all shared the same holy telegraph.

But it was the know-it-all church ladies who'd helped force her from her home. They'd let Macon's father, Macon Joseph Bartlett II, know just what kind of girl his son was going out with. He'd blamed her for Macon's bad actions, whisked him off to college, and made sure the community shunned her.

A bitter pill after all the hard work she'd done to overcome her poverty-stricken beginnings.

"Thinking of going?" a familiar voice asked behind her.

Megan turned to see Trish, the tart lady.

"Probably not," she said.

"Oh, you should," Trish said. "I know you're new to the community, and I keep meaning to chat with you, but I'm usually in a rush from one thing to another between my business and my teenagers." Her smile broadened. "And we never use a hard sell ... although there *will* be lots of pies."

Megan chuckled. "I'll think about it."

"That's all I can ask," Trish said. Hefting her bag, she headed out the automatic door.

Using her phone, Megan took a quick snap of both flyers, than headed inside to do her shopping. As she browsed the few, and repetitive, vegetables that were displayed, she debated the wisdom of going to the potluck. Maybe she'd learn something new to do with broccoli, kale, and cauliflower. Maybe someone knew how to make potato salad like her grandmother had. With all the Hutterite chicken, someone had to know how to fry it just right.

By the time she got to the checkout stand, her mouth was watering and her basket was full of more things than she'd planned to purchase, including ingredients to pull together her grandmother's potluck mainstay: macaroni and cheese.

She hummed to herself as she drove the road north to her rental. The snow had receded on the rolling prairie, and bits of green grass broken up by sparks of yellow and lilac lined the road. The wildflowers didn't carpet the soil like they did in the lush valleys of North Carolina, but Montana had a stark beauty of its own she was coming to love, especially when she let her gaze roll west to the juncture of the prairie and the mountains.

After prepping and eating her meal of baked pork chop, couscous out of a box (her grandmother was rolling in her grave), and a token amount of green beans that had their taste frozen out of existence, she sat down with her laptop and crafted a class description that would be suitable for adults.

She checked Etsy for the drop spinners she needed to run the class and sent the crafter in St. Regis a note to see how fast she could get delivery from the western side of the divide. Somehow she was going to make this happen.

# # #

The following Monday, Megan took her plan to the high school. She handed in her application, and the secretary looked it over to make sure it was complete. "Looks good," she said.

At that moment, a woman who walked with the air of authority strode from a back office. Behind her was a man in a sheriff's uniform. "Good to hear that Jim is doing better in math. I knew he could do it," he said.

"He did it with Ms. Deveaux's support and help," the woman said in a kind but firm voice.

The sheriff nodded and held out his hand. The woman shook

it, and he left.

She then turned toward Megan, who stepped back. The woman's internal authority was an unexpected force, but it was splintered into shards by the woman's kind eyes and smile.

"Hello," she said. "I'm Rebecca Johnson, the principal. Welcome to Choteau High School."

"Hi."

"Ms. ... um"—the secretary glanced at the paper in front of her—"Winkle is submitting a suggestion for a class ... spinning."

"Drop spinning," Megan clarified. "It's easy, relaxing, and has been done for centuries all over the world."

"Interesting," Rebecca said and reached her hand out for the paper. She quickly scanned it and looked up at Megan. "You're not local."

"No, ma'am." And all of a sudden Megan was back in high school with her secondhand clothes and second-rate grades. "North Carolina." What was it about principals that made it impossible not to spill the beans?

"Welcome." Rebecca's smile scattered the image. "This looks fascinating. I might even sign up. I could definitely use something relaxing."

The secretary briefly nodded her head.

"I saw that," Rebecca said. "Well, I wish you luck. Nice meeting you," Rebecca said. "Please see me before you leave." She touched the secretary's shoulder.

"Will do," the secretary answered. Once the principal left, the secretary smiled at Megan. "I'm a knitter. It might be interesting to find out how yarn is made. If you're short one, I'll make up the difference." She smiled up at Megan.

"Thank you." Megan's smile came from her heart. People in Choteau were turning out to be surprisingly nice. She should try the potluck, if only to see who else she might meet.

As she walked out of the high school, the sun warmed her face. Spring was coming. It certainly took a lot longer in the northwest than it did in the Carolinas, but it might be worth the wait.

She walked down the sidewalk to her car, a smile on her face. As she opened the car door, she let her feet do a few steps of the jig her grandmother had taught her when she was young, back before her home life had exploded. Once there had been five of them: Mom, Dad, Peter, and her together, with Granny's house in easy walking distance.

Now she was the only one left.

Asheville had become too filled with pain and memories for her to stay. Leaving home hadn't been easy, and she'd drifted from town to town, continually moving west, searching for a new place to live that felt right. So far, she hadn't been content to stay in any one place for long.

Maybe this time would be different and she could finally root the plant of her life.

# # #

"You came!" Trish zeroed in on Megan the moment she'd walked through the door into the main church hall. "I'm so glad. You can put your dish down right over here. That looks amazing!"

Megan had made her go-to comfort food: macaroni, ham, and tomatoes smothered with tons of cheese. They didn't have her family's standby of Velveeta in the local market, but after discussing it with the cheesemakers at the bistro, they'd recommended something that had worked perfectly.

"Thanks," she said, and followed Trish to a table already stacked with casserole dishes.

"Beverages are over here," Trish said, guiding her to another table. "Nothing alcoholic, but lots of tea, coffee, and sodas. Why don't you grab something and I'll introduce you to a few people."

After selecting a mug, filling it with hot water, and dunking in a bag of Earl Grey, she followed Trish like a puppy dog, quickly overwhelmed by names, occupations, and relationships. Now she knew what outsiders who'd visited friends in the South complained about.

She smiled politely at each, her cheeks quickly reaching the point of pain with the prolonged gesture. The sharp aroma from her teacup kept her going.

Trish ended her tour with a diminutive woman who went by the appropriate name of Birdie.

"Can you take over?" Trish asked her. "I've got to get to the dessert table and figure out what those two are arguing about now."

Megan glanced over to see two women about Trish's age having a very polite but strong-willed disagreement involving finger-pointing and shaking heads.

Birdie chuckled. "Those two have been arguing since grade school. Trish has her work cut out for herself." She gestured to the food table. "Looks like people are digging in. I'll introduce you to Jarod, Samantha, and Audie, and we can get ourselves a plate."

The trio stood toward the end of the line: an attractive woman with light brown hair, a little girl who must be her daughter, and a man who bore an eerie resemblance to Dylan Beck. When Birdie and she got to them, the little girl looked up and asked, "Who are you? I've never seen you before."

"Sorry," the woman said. "Audie has a way of speaking her mind. I'm Samantha Deveaux." She held out her hand.

Megan shook it.

"And this is my fiancé, Jarod Beck."

"That explains the resemblance," she said, holding out her hand once again.

"You must have met one of my brothers," Jarod said.

"You have more than one?"

"He has three brothers and one sister," Audie pronounced. "There's Aunt CJ, Uncle Dylan, Uncle Cameron—he's sad—and Uncle Kaiden. I don't know him very good. Jarod says he's digging stuff from the ground."

"Wow," Megan said. "Big family."

"I take it yours isn't?" asked Samantha.

"Not anymore."

She gave me a quick nod and let the subject drop.

"So which brother do you know?" Jarod asked.

"Dylan."

"Oh," Birdie said with a smile. "You're the one."

Megan gave her a quick glance.

"Ignore her. She spends too much time tending everybody's business," Jarod said, then turned to the food table. "Looks like everyone brought out their A game," he said.

"First potluck of the spring," Birdie said. "Everyone's busting out with cabin fever."

That was something Megan could relate to. Winter was winter in the mountains, keeping people close to home for too long.

The relentless but gentle push of the churchgoers behind her made her concentrate on placing food on her plate. She had to admit the aromas drifting up from the casserole dishes started her stomach rumbling. It had been a long time since she'd eaten something that wasn't tossed together from the remnants of other things in her fridge.

"Come sit with us," Trish said, guiding her to a small table where a good-looking and tall man sat, a loaded plate in front of him. He stood as they approached.

"This is Brad, my husband," Trish said. "And this is Megan. You remember I told you about her."

"Yes," Brad said, extending his hand. "You work at the new pastry-cheese shop. How's that going?"

"Just fine," she said. A chill of cool air made her turn toward the door.

Dave Brockman walked in, a polished-looking blonde at his side. In her hands she had a glass cake stand with a perfectly iced white cake on it covered by a glass dome. Success oozed from every inch of her body.

Now *that* was the right woman for *him*.

All smiles, the couple walked to the dessert table where they deposited the cake before going to the coatroom. Moments later, they were in line at the food table.

"Who is she?" Megan asked.

"Cassandra Sanders, the best family lawyer in town," Brad replied, a bit of a gobsmacked look on his face. "I work with her now and again."

Trish cleared her throat, and he mentally came back to the table, only to meet his wife's glare.

Uncomfortable, Megan looked away from them.

Cassandra and Dave had gotten their food and looked around for a table. They drifted over to the table occupied by the Becks and chatted for a few moments, Cassandra letting her hand rest on Jarod's shoulder for a brief moment. He shifted and cast a quick glance at his fiancée. She smiled at him and shrugged her shoulders.

The woman may have been a fine attorney, but she was probably as adept at breaking up families as handling their affairs. Megan had known a woman like her back home, a successful shop owner who provided way too much personal service. How a person conducted their sex life didn't matter to her, as long as it didn't impinge on anyone else's choices.

She drew her attention back to the barbequed pork and beans she'd picked up—homemade and not from a can. As the attendees ate, a trio consisting of a bass, small drum set, and guitar set up in a corner that had been left clear of tables. As the food line disappeared, the music started.

Familiar tunes made her smile. The group didn't have the twang of the Southern country music she'd grown up with, but the melodies soothed the ache inside her, the one that had been there in some form or another since her father's agonizing death from the "accidental" poisoning of the well on the far side of the land he worked—the well he'd had a drink from every day of his adult life.

"Care to dance?" Dave Brockman stood before her.

Megan glanced over to see a few couples who were doing a two-step to the music.

"I don't know how to do that," she said, trying to avoid saying she didn't want to dance with him.

"C'mon, I'll teach you. That's what a potluck is for, isn't it, Trish?" He smiled at the pie baker. "To get to know people better."

"I thought you were with Cassandra," Trish said, a bit of an edge to her voice.

"We're just friends," he replied. "She doesn't mind."

Megan glanced over to the attorney who gave her a little wave.

"Don't blame me if I step on your toes," she said and stood.

But Dave turned out to be a good dancer and patient teacher. By the end of the first two songs, she'd begun to have fun, but then the music slowed. Fortunately, Cassandra showed up at that point to cut in.

Just friends? Or something else?

Megan smiled and graciously turned Dave over, actually relieved at the turn of events. She wandered to the dessert table, hoping to snag something filled with chocolate.

"How do you know Dave Brockman?" Samantha asked as she held a plate steady for Audie to load up. So far the plate was empty as the girl studied each dessert carefully.

"He's a customer—a big tipping customer, I might add."

"And when you're working for tips, that means you put up with more than you might actually want," Samantha said with a smile.

"You must have been a waitress at some point."

"I've been pretty much everything at some point," Samantha said.

"And now?"

"Now I'm a high school math teacher."

"I was there the other day. I'm doing a spinning class for the lifelong learning center, that is if I can get enough people to sign up."

"Wow, that sounds interesting," Samantha said. "I'm not

crafty, but I know a lot of the ladies in church are. If you make up a few fliers, I'll be happy to spread them around. I'm sure Trish would, too. She goes everywhere with her pies."

"That's a great idea," Megan said, her flame of happiness brightening.

"Glad to help." She looked at the still empty plate. "Audie, you need to pick something."

"But they all look so good and you said I could only pick two."

"Yes, one for you and one for Jarod."

Audie looked up at her mother and sighed. "This is soooo hard."

Megan had a hard time keeping a straight face.

"Well, I'm going for a brownie," she said, scooping one up and putting it on her plate. "Thank you again." She stood, undecided for a few moments. Trish and Brad seemed to be having a disagreement about something.

"Trish said you're the gal who makes all those lovely hats and scarfs at the new restaurant," a woman who looked to be about grandmother age said. Hooking a hand around Megan's elbow, she began to steer her to a table in the middle of the room. "You need to come tell us all about yourself. I'm Sally, by the way, and this is my friend, June."

Megan sat down to be polite but soon found herself laughing as the two friends told her stories about growing up in the prehistoric time before computers and the hijinks they'd gotten into.

An hour later, after helping people clean up, she headed home, satisfied and content. It was good to be part of a community. Maybe this time she'd stay.

Chapter 7

"Met Megan Winkle at the potluck," Jarod said as he filled his morning coffee cup.

Dylan was already at the table, chowing down the eggs, bacon, and biscuits Birdie had whipped up for the two of them for breakfast.

"She mentioned she knew you," his brother continued as he scraped his own helping onto a plate.

"I've seen her a few times at the new bistro," Dylan said, purposely leaving out the beer he'd shared with Megan. It was none of his brother's business.

"She was dancing with Dave Brockman."

Was Jarod deliberately trying to get under his skin?

Dylan shrugged. "It's a free country."

Jarod gave him a sharp glance.

"I'm thinking of going over to Helena in the next week or so." Dylan jabbed the biscuit at the eggs with one hand and scooped up a mouthful of eggs with his fork in the other.

"Picking up your paintings?"

"Yeah. Do we need anything else over there?"

"Nope."

The clomp of feet on the stairs announced Cameron's arrival at breakfast.

"Morning," he said.

"Morning," Jarod and Dylan echoed.

Jarod sat down, getting out of Cameron's way. They'd quickly learned not to offer to help, and Cameron had just as quickly figured out a way to get breakfast as fast as anyone else.

"What's up?" Cameron said as he sat down.

"Dylan's likes a girl who was dancing with Dave Brockman," Jarod teased.

"Oh?" Cameron said.

"Not true," Dylan said. "Jarod's only trying to get back for the teasing I gave him when he was first seeing Samantha."

"Sounds fair," Cameron said. "So who's this Dave Brockman when he's home?"

Dylan gave his brother a second look. It was the most conversation they'd heard from him since he'd been home.

"I don't know if you remember," Jarod said, "but last fall, Dylan and I found the fence cut on the northwest corner of the property. Some cattle had drifted across, but it didn't seem like rustling. Bad terrain for it anyway. No place to back in a truck."

"So what'd they want?"

"Beats me," Jarod said.

"We've tried to get the drone up there, but with the snow it just looks white," Dylan added.

"You've got a drone that can go that far?"

"Yeah. Commercial."

"Lazy kid was just trying to get out of riding fences," Jarod said.

"I can see that," Cameron said, a half smile on his face. The tines of his fork clunked against the plate as he stabbed his eggs.

"I'm getting some more coffee," Dylan said. "Jarod? A refill? Cam, want a cup?"

"That'd be nice," Cameron said as Jarod shook his head.

"Samantha thinks I should cut down on my caffeine habit," Jarod added.

"Henpecked already," Dylan said.

"You boys hush," Birdie said as she emerged from her set of rooms behind the kitchen. "It'll be good to have another woman in the house."

"You sure you can stay in the same kitchen?" Dylan asked.

"We'll work it out. She's easy. It's your sister who always gives me problems. Too bossy by far."

"Uh, yep," three voices chorused.

"It's a nice day," Birdie observed. "I'm going into town to do my shopping. Maybe I'll even stop at the bistro for a cup of coffee and a pastry and check out that nice young lady who was at the potluck." She winked at Dylan.

No one was giving him a break.

Once the housekeeper left, Cameron laser-focused on Jarod. "The cutting of the fence—you think this Brockman did it?"

"Or he knows about it."

"Then there was the explosion a few months ago," Dylan said. "It knocked Jarod right off his horse ... again."

"Making that a habit are you?" Cameron said.

Jarod shook his head.

"We've been waiting for the snow to go down before we try to

70

get up there and see what's what."

"That and Kaiden to come home for a visit," Jarod added.

"You think it's rock related?" Cameron asked.

"Not sure what else it could be. Has to be something mineral related, especially since we can't find the mineral rights. And I don't see how anyone could drill for gas or oil shale up there," Jarod said.

"Where are we with finding out who has the rights?" Cameron asked.

"CJ is on the trail since the PI we hired bailed. Right now she's accessing the Mormon records," Dylan said. "She's gotten up to Alice's children—remember Alice was the name in the Bible."

"Any particular reason the PI bailed?" Cameron asked.

"None that made any sense."

"Hmm."

The three of them were silent for a few moments. Then Cameron got up, rinsed his plate, and put it in the sink. "I'm going to take a walk," he said, turning back to Jarod. "Then I'll join you in the barn, see what, if anything, I can do." He headed to the mudroom.

"He does a powerful lot of walking," Jarod commented after they heard the screen door slam.

"Yup." Dylan rose as well. "I'll be out in a bit. Something I want to look up first."

"Okay. It's your turn to drop the feed. Don't take too long."

"Yes, sir, boss." He stuck his tongue out at Jarod. Sometimes regressing to twelve felt too good to give up.

Jarod shook his head, rinsed off his plate, and went to the mudroom.

Dylan sat in front of the ranch's computer in the office and opened a browser. Yes, he wanted to go to Helena to retrieve his paintings, but he had an itch not to do it alone. Soon he found a very enticing carrot.

But he'd wait until Birdie returned before tackling the Southern redhead.

# # #

It wasn't until the following Tuesday afternoon, the second week of April, that Dylan was able to escape the ranch and his prying family. Cameron had tried to help with the chores again that morning, but everything seemed to require two hands. He'd sorted hardware for an hour or two and then gone off again on one of his long, solitary walks.

Dylan hoped his brother would think about getting a prosthetic or something, but his mental healing was probably going to take a lot longer. And there was no way to help him without getting Cameron's damn prideful back up. It wasn't like there were huge numbers of veterans in the area, and if there were, they tended to isolate themselves, just like Cameron was doing.

It wasn't like the older wars where someone declared a victory and the army was welcomed home. Even Vietnam had ended, although in ignoble defeat. No, these wars just seemed to go on and on with no resolution and no way out that didn't involve sending thousands of civilians to their deaths.

God, how he hated it all.

Some days he thought he should take up politicking, just to see if he could make some sense of the world. But like war, government didn't seem to be what it used to be either. Instead of serving others, too many seemed to be intent on serving themselves.

He shook his feelings off, like a dog ridding himself of too much water.

Pulling into the parking lot, he took his time getting out, trying to determine the best plan of attack: casual or full-frontal? What if she wasn't even here? He should have gotten her phone number.

A knock on his window startled him.

Megan.

He punched the button to roll it down.

"Are you expecting delivery?" she said with a grin. "We don't do that here. You'll need to get out of the truck and come on in."

"Will do, ma'am," he said, rolling the window back up.

She waved and went into the café.

Following, he grabbed the local paper from the used basket and looked for the best place to sit. The lunch crowd was in the process of leaving, but most of the tables remained to be bussed. Courtney was busy ringing people out, the chattering line in front of the cash register stacked several people deep.

Megan must have assessed the situation and dropped her things off quickly because she was already hard at work. Dishes clanked into the bin she carried, and she moved purposefully, making rapid work of the mess left behind.

He finally settled on a table, content to wait until the rush had passed before trying to get a cup of coffee, but he'd barely started catching up on the local school sports when a mug, filled just the way he liked it, slid onto the table.

"Thanks," he said, smiling up at Megan.

"No problem." And she was gone before he got a chance to say anything else.

They were too busy. He'd chosen the wrong time to show up.

But as he slowly sipped his brew, the place calmed down and soon it was almost empty. Now all he had to do was get the redhead's attention.

"Do you want anything to go with the coffee?" Megan asked as she topped off his cup.

"No, thanks. I'm good."

"Seems like a long trip to go for a cup of coffee," she remarked.

"Sometimes I need to get out of the house," he replied.

"Funny, that's what Birdie said when she was here last week."

What else did she say? The housekeeper hadn't indicated anything when she got home from Choteau.

"Megan?" Courtney called. "Can you come here for a sec?"

"Sure." She whisked off.

Dylan went back to his paper.

Fifteen minutes later she came back to top off his coffee again. This time when she asked him if he wanted anything else, he said, "Yes. I need you to sit with me for a few minutes."

"I'm on the job. I can't really sit down with a customer."

"Then I'll stand," he said with a grin, and did it.

She promptly sat. "I guess it's okay for a few moments."

Okay, then.

"I have to go to Helena sometime in the next few weeks to get some paintings a gallery doesn't want to show anymore. This is a pretty time for a drive down that way."

She nodded.

"Well, there's a llama ranch kind of on the way, and I thought you might be interested."

"But I'm not looking for llamas. I'm looking for alpacas."

He was going about this all wrong, and he could see a car pull into the parking lot. His chance was slipping away.

"They have alpacas. They just call it a llama farm. I don't know why. They also ... um ... do something to fiber. Like you

73

bring it in after it comes off the animal and they hand you back stuff." He waved in the direction of her display. Not only were the words relating to wool unfamiliar, but he was stumbling over the ones he'd used every day of his life.

No wonder sheepherders and cowboys had such a troubled relationship.

But now she perked up.

"Fiber processing? It would be wonderful to talk with them about what they do and the ins and outs of doing it in Montana. Thank you! That would be great!"

The front door bell jingled, and she leapt from the chair.

"Let me know when you want to go and I'll get the day off." She took a step toward the ladies who'd just walked in.

"Wait! I need your number."

She spat it out at him and he quickly wrote it down on the edge of the newspaper, hoping he got the digits in the right order.

# # #

What had she just done?

Megan slapped a smile on her face and went to greet the familiar women. They were a Choteau beautification committee or something like that and came every Tuesday afternoon. Supposedly, they were working on plans for Main Street flower baskets, but she'd picked up a lot of gossip as she refilled coffee cups and delivered pastries. At some point Dylan slipped out, leaving the local paper open on his table. When she went to pick it up to stow it back in the reuse bin, she noticed a corner torn off one of the pages. It sat apart, boldly stating, "I'll call you!" followed by a smiley face.

Stuffing the corner in her pocket, she refolded the paper and put it where it belonged, then bussed the cup back to the stack by the sink, her mind rapidly trying to find ways to both see the alpaca-llama farm and learn more about processing and do it without Dylan. She should never have agreed to go. It only encouraged him, and a relationship of any kind with a man was totally out of the question.

The problem was, she enjoyed his company.

She finished up her shift without figuring out a solution.

As she drove home, the sun seemed to be a little higher on the horizon than normal, and a little farther north in the sky. It was one of the things she disliked about this far north community. The winters were incredibly long, dark, and cold. But they were giving a sharp contrast to the emerging colors of spring.

In people's gardens, purple crocuses pushed up through the snow, while bush and tree branches painted themselves maroon and canary yellow, presaging the emergence of new leaves and buds. Even though many mornings still left a dewy frost, the temperature was inching up.

It almost made up for the loss of a soft spring breeze through an open window and the insistent chirp of newborn chicks playing counterpoint to the low murmur of women as they spun, wove, or quilted in the Southern spring.

As petty as some of the women in her hometown could be, she missed the ones a person could depend on for sound advice, like when a guy asked you to do something more significant than go for pizza and beer.

She pulled into her drive and parked near a fence that bordered on a small pasture, plenty of room for a couple of alpacas. The land owner had told her the acre of pasture produced good grass, which would mean enough for four animals if everything worked out. It was a gorgeous setting, rolling grassland with white-capped mountains jagged across the distance.

She'd raise the animals, bringing the memories of home to her western abode. But did she really want to get involved in the shearing and processing of the fleece? It took a whole lot more time and skills, time she was already scarce on, at least until she gave up the security of her part time job.

The thought made her sweat.

It was sweet of Dylan to do the legwork to find the alpaca-llama farm, and she'd already agreed to go. There wasn't going to be a way to get out of it gracefully, and this was too small a town to go around offending people. Still, it was the wrong message to send him. He seemed to be a good man with enough pain in his past already.

The Becks were respected in this town. She'd caught a few snatches of conversation about some tragedy that had happened when the family was younger, but she couldn't quite piece it together. CJ had come into the bistro a few times, once with her boyfriend. She'd introduced him as Nick. Jarod seemed nice, if a bit uptight. Then there was the brother that was a soldier and had returned with some major injury. There was one more brother, but she hadn't heard anything about him.

How had CJ endured four brothers?

She pulled her hands off the rail and unloaded her car. After a quick meal of soup and bread, she put on some Carter family songs she'd made into a playlist and sat down to spin. The fine roving made from a combination of baby alpaca and about 20 percent dyed wool. The result was a soft brown that would be perfect for a beautifully draped spring or fall sweater. As she spun, she hummed along to the old melodies, songs she'd heard all her life.

"May the circle be unbroken ..."

The circle of her family had broken early.

"By and by, lord, by and by ..."

Faith-loving people, and she knew many, believed the circle would come together again in heaven. She'd lost her faith when her father was taken. *Someone* had been responsible for the water in the well becoming toxic. And that meant someone had made her father's death happen. Even if there were a heaven, which she wasn't sure about, breaking the circle of her family while she was just a little girl had been a cruel and thoughtless thing to do.

A movement outside her window caught her eye. A deer slowly grazed in a ripening meadow at the edge of her property, a spindly-legged fawn following behind. Megan stared outside while the fiber continued to twist in her fingers and build on the spool of the wheel. Beyond the deer, the sky colored deep pink at the cusp of the mountain peaks. It was a big sky, just like people talked about when they discussed Montana, a view a person could get lost in, its vastness suggesting there might be something bigger than human beings.

"In the sky, Lord, in the sky."

Maybe she'd find her faith in this wild land, and that faith would allow her to pursue her dreams with dogged determination. But she had to take a leap first, even if that meant trusting a man one more time.

After all, it was only a drive in the countryside. Nothing could happen.

Chapter 8

It was another two weeks before she could find a day that worked for both she and Dylan. Courtney had been off from work due to some family emergency, and Megan had been required to fill in. Then Jarod had taken off to some rodeo, and Dylan had to handle the ranch chores.

She got up early that day. Too early. She burned her toast and changed her clothes three times. Her minimal wardrobe should have made the choice easy, but it didn't. Jeans and boots were a given, but should she choose one of the three more feminine blouses or the more practical flannel for visiting a ranch? Problem was, they'd be stopping at Helena for a late lunch and to pick up the paintings. It was Montana, which meant no real dress code anywhere they went, but she wanted to look nice.

In the end she chose a sunny yellow cotton floral print blouse with buttons up the front. Her flannel-lined jeans jacket would have to protect her from the animals and their surroundings.

Still an hour to go.

She sat down to spin. Nothing but slubs and breaks.

Maybe knitting would soothe her.

Three dropped stitches later, she put it aside and began dusting her living room.

Finally, he arrived.

"Hi," Dylan said when she opened the door to him.

"Hi, yourself." She held up her knitting bag. "Any objection if I knit during the trip?" Maybe she'd be more successful when they actually *began* the trip. "I like to keep my hands busy."

"As long as you don't stab me with one of the needles," he said, "we should be okay." He grinned at her.

He really was a good-looking man, in her opinion better than his brother Jarod who looked like he was adept at hiding emotion. Dylan's smile took in his entire face, adding premature wrinkles to the corners of his eyes and deepening the lines that surrounded his mouth like a set of parentheses.

Once she was settled in the passenger seat, he closed her door and got in the other side. The engine rumbled as he turned it on but settled down to a purr as they left the drive and headed south.

"It shouldn't sound like that," he said. "I'll have to get Jarod to take a look. My brother's a mechanical whizz; he's kept machinery going on the ranch far after I would have junked it."

"My brother was like that."

"Oh."

The jaunty dinosaurs lining the streets, symbols of nearby discoveries, indicated they'd reached the northern limits of Choteau. She stayed silent while Dylan navigated the few stoplights and the rotary around the courthouse.

"How many siblings do you have?" Dylan asked as they passed the grain elevators at the southern end.

"None now. Peter died overseas—in the war."

"I'm sorry."

Megan shrugged. "It was a while ago." Reality was, it had only been a year. Peter had run away from their cousin's house, swearing he'd return for her so they could have a home together as soon as possible. But he'd gone into the army and found a home of his own there.

Miles rolled by.

"That's the entrance to our ranch," Dylan said, pointing at one of the traditional western gates over a dirt road.

"I didn't realize you lived this far south of town," she said. "I could have met you here."

He shook his head. "When I ask someone to come with me somewhere, I pick them up."

Okay. Was he controlling or just polite?

"I don't know how much you know about our family's history," he said. "But let's just say my dad didn't treat my mom right. When we got older, my brothers and I made a pact. We were going to be far better men than our father had ever been. We each do it differently, but we do it."

She relaxed a little. She knew what it was like to be determined not to grow up like someone else.

"It must have been hard, growing up like that."

"It was." He gave a big sigh. "But that's in the past, and I'd rather talk about other things. Like alpacas ... and what it was like growing up in North Carolina. Like I said, I've never been out of the state."

Totally incomprehensible to her.

"Where I grew up is way different yet a bit the same as Montana. Asheville, the city near where I lived, has a lot of sections with money—new and old—plus the crown jewel 'vacation home' of one of the late nineteenth-century robber barons, Vanderbilt's Biltmore." She added the air quotes.

"Don't think I've ever heard of that. I remember the time period—our so-called gilded age. Great for the men who had the monopolies, particularly on the railroad. Not so good for the working man or the small businessman."

"We agree on that one, but it's still an amazing estate."

"Have you seen it?"

"Only parts from the outside. Tickets were well beyond most of my neighbor's means."

"How much were they?" he asked.

"Ninety-nine dollars for a day pass last time I checked," she said.

He whistled. "Now I know why I never leave the state," he said. "That's way too rich for my blood."

She chuckled. "I know what you mean. My family—before my parents died—we lived pretty simply: barbeques with the neighbors, hikes in the nearby national parks like the Great Smoky Mountains. Things that were cheap and easy. Mom made a lot of my dresses, and we still lived by the motto of the Southern Depression: use it up, wear it out, make it do, or do without."

"I guess from that viewpoint we were pretty spoiled," he said. "The ranch was left to my dad free and clear, and he did well in real estate as well."

Different lives, but he seemed very down-to-earth.

She stared out at the fields of the high prairie. They were so high it felt like she could reach out and touch the sky. Out in the distance cattle grazed, eagerly snapping up the fresh green shoots coming up.

"Look!" she said and pointed, laughing as she did so.

He followed her gesture and cracked up. "Well, Martha," he said in an exaggerated tone, "what're we gonna do now to get out of this pasture?"

They zipped past the two cows standing on the far side of a cattle guard between two sections of fence. Each of the pair was looking down with one eye at the iron bars in their way, the other eye on their partner. There were no other cattle in sight. It would have been quite a photo, but they were halfway down the next hill before she had time to drag out her phone.

"That was too funny," she said.

"Yep," he said, slowing to take the sharp turns through the

tiny town of Augusta. A few blinks of her eye and they were out the other end. Small Montana towns were a bit like those in her home state, a post office and a bar as anchors, with maybe a church or an all-purpose hall that served as one when it wasn't doing duty as something else.

After a few more miles of vibrant prairie, they descended between two hills to an intersection. Dylan pulled to a stop, and even though there was no traffic, he looked west and paused for longer than necessary before checking for traffic and crossing Highway 200.

Tension emanated from his body, so she refrained from asking any questions. Whatever had happened on that highway had been bad. She'd wait for him to tell her.

The land around them became more rugged, with mountains rising to the east. Steep cliffs replaced gentle inclines and the road became more closed in. Her unused knitting bag lay at her feet.

"It's amazing countryside," she said, finally breaking the silence.

"Yes, and it's the perfect day to see it." The road began to climb again, putting them back on top of the world. "Once you get alpacas, what are you going to do with them?"

"You mean, besides feed and care for them?"

He chuckled. "Besides that."

"My idea is to help people understand the connection between the animals and the clothes they can make and wear. The whole process. I think we've lost touch with the basic origins of our lives. Everything is plastic, multicolored, and throw-away."

He nodded.

"But it's not only the connection to the animals and the land. It's a way of keeping the old traditions alive, of having connections to our past. Almost every culture spun something, including silk in Asia and human hair when nothing else was available."

"That feels a little creepy to me," he said as he took the on-ramp to Highway 15.

Soon they were speeding south along the higher parts of the mountainous region.

"Over there," Dylan said, waving toward the east, "are the Gates of the Mountains. The Missouri runs through there, tight between canyon walls. And, of course, where the Missouri went, Lewis and Clark went."

"They covered a lot of Montana," she said.

"That's for sure."

"I can't imagine what it would have been like, walking most of that way seeing animals, sights, and people like none they'd ever known before. But it must have been exciting, too."

"Some people like adventure," he replied.

"I guess I'm one of them." What would it be like to be so limited ... or content ... not wonder what was around the next bend in the road, to do something never tried before?

He became quiet, his hands shifting on the steering wheel as if they were tired of gripping so tightly. She stared out the window at the swarms of pines and firs, white clumps of lingering snow brightening the dark undergrowth. In the distance a ridge of peaks rose to the west, granite gray piercing the glistening snow.

No matter where she looked there was breathtaking beauty.

They descended from the mountains into a broad valley where civilization, in the form of ranchettes and farm equipment stores perched on the land like hotels on a Monopoly board.

"The llama farm is on the other side of Helena," Dylan said, giving her a quick glance. "You okay to wait for lunch until after we see them?"

"Absolutely. I had a good breakfast." She'd tossed the burnt toast and scrambled some eggs, which still sat undigested in her stomach. Why had this trip wound her up so much? Maybe because she had to navigate the narrow path between being nice to Dylan and not encouraging him?

"I thought we'd try a place on Last Chance Gulch for lunch. I know a few good ones."

Megan had read enough Montana history to Last Chance Gulch was where gold had been discovered in Helena in the mid-1800s. Since then, it had become a busy tourist area with restaurants and shops.

"Sounds good."

It was just business. Nothing more. Polite but noncommittal. She could definitely play that role. It was waitressing at its finest.

As they wove through the city, Dylan asked, "What do you think about how our state runs things—I mean the government?"

"I don't know. I haven't thought much about it. I mean, I grew up learning about North Carolina politics. And they are not for the faint-hearted, I might add. We take our debates, like the right way to make grits, very seriously."

He chuckled.

"I suppose we do, too, but we're more willing to let people make grits the way they want or skip them altogether for that matter."

"I'm certainly in favor of skipping them." She shuddered. While neither of her parents were big fans of the corn mush available on most Southerners breakfast tables, the relatives who had taken her in after her parents died were true fans.

And she hated them—the grits, not her relatives ... well, she wasn't fond of them either.

Then she thought back to his original question. "So what do *you* think about Montana politics?"

"On the surface, it works okay. We kinda split up the offices between the conservatives, who live mostly in the wide open spaces, and the liberals, who live mostly in places like this. And the legislature only meets once every couple of years for a few months. That means people have to have real jobs and come down among us common folk for a bit."

"Every other year? How do you get anything done?"

"The legislature has to pass a budget. And the government has to live within it."

"Well, that might work."

"For the most part," he said.

Gradually, they left the city behind and dipped back into ranchland. They turned onto a side road and within a short distance came to the ranch.

"I called ahead so Tom and Marsha Heismand are expecting us," he said.

"Oh." He was helping too much. Somehow she had to backpedal his enthusiasm.

The middle-aged couple, looking to be about in their forties, came out of the house as they pulled into the drive. Marsha had curly hair that looked like it would tolerate only one style of hairdo, and that was the one she had. Tom was losing his battle with his hair and kept it close cropped. He also had the erect posture of someone who'd spent a good amount of time in the military.

Once Dylan and Megan parked and got out of the car, they introduced themselves. "There's coffee in the kitchen," Marsha said. "And a bathroom nearby if you need one."

"Thank you so much," Megan said.

They trooped into the kitchen and Megan took advantage of the facilities. As she washed up, she stared at her reflection in the mirror. It looked the same as it always did: classic red hair and green eyes, without any sense of the person behind the face. Yet she must be attractive enough. Not one but two men in Choteau were interested in her.

Too bad she didn't want anything else.

She headed back to the kitchen.

"Where are you from?" Marsha asked Megan after she'd given her coffee.

Someday, she'd have to tone down the Southern accent.

"North Carolina."

"Oh, that's such a pretty state. My cousin on my mother's side lives in the north of the state, on a lake by Lexington. I've been to visit once or twice."

"I didn't get to travel much in the state," Megan said. "My family's from around Asheville."

"Well, I hope you're enjoying Montana."

"I am, thanks."

"What did you want to see first?" Tom asked, his voice all business. "The animals or the processing?"

"Let's start with the alpacas," Megan replied. "Dylan's never seen them in the flesh."

"Sure thing," Tom said and led them toward a fenced in area behind the barn.

"They're really enjoying this spring weather," Marsha said. "It's like they've all become crias again."

"Cria?" Dylan asked.

"Baby alpaca," Megan replied.

"We've got six alpacas now. We just added them," Tom said. "Shearing duties are going to be a little overwhelming, but whatever Marsha wants ..." He smiled fondly at his wife.

"Do you shear them yourself?" Dylan asked.

"Every one of them. And I try to hand shear as many as I can. The clippers are more efficient, but the noise can make them nervous and produce nicks. We like to keep them as calm as we can. With the enlarged herd, we may need to change that approach, but for now it's what we'd like to do."

Dylan nodded.

They got to the fence surrounding a small pasture. Four mature alpacas with white, brown, or red-brown coats roamed the area. Two crias bounced from one end of the enclosure to the other. One of the adults seemed determined to get a leaf from a tree. He, or she, was under it, standing on his hind legs, reaching with his neck as far as it would go. It still wasn't far enough. Finally, he gave a great leap and snagged the leaves he wanted before landing on the ground with a thud.

Dylan, Magen, and Marsha laughed. Even Tom broke a smile.

"They are funny animals," Dylan said.

Pulling out her camera, Magen snapped a bunch of pictures while they watched and Tom explained the type of alpacas they'd chosen and why.

So many factors went into choosing an animal, including type of fleece, ability to reproduce, disposition, and more. Her primary choice point was going to be price, followed by disposition. She did not need an animal that liked to spit a lot, which they were prone to do anyway.

"Ready to see the processing?" Tom asked.

"Sure am," Megan replied.

Flipping to her note taking app, Megan made notes about skirting, combing, and carding. Dylan asked a lot of technical questions that hadn't even entered her mind. In spite of her initial hesitation, she was glad he was there.

An hour and a half after they'd arrived, they climbed into the truck and headed back to Helena.

"They were really helpful," Megan said.

"Yes. Do you think you're going to send your fleece to them or some other processing outfit?"

"I think, initially, I'll try two or three places to see which one replicates what I want done. I don't really have time to add processing to my schedule. It's a lot of work."

"Smart idea." He sounded impressed by her thinking.

"I'm more worried about the shearing. My grandmother hired a professional shearer, but that can get pricy. I'd rather learn to do it myself. I figure," she said as they reached the edges of Helena, "if I understand what's going on, I get the results I want, and no one is going to cheat me along the way."

"Fairly cynical."

"Experience." She hoped he'd let the subject drop. Her past was ugly enough without reliving it with a near stranger.

Although Dylan wasn't that anymore. She was becoming more comfortable with him, letting down her guard. She had to be careful. While Choteau was looking more and more like the right place for her to set down roots, she wanted to learn to balance on her own two feet before attempting to dance with anyone else.

He parked on the street leading up to the pedestrian area of the old district and they strolled up the hill in the warm April sun.

"I figured Bert & Ernie's might be fun," he said.

"Really? There's a place called Bert & Ernie's?"

"Yep. Good food and a nice set of beers on tap. Wine, too, if you're into that kind of thing."

Her alcohol consumption was limited to a glass of white wine at holidays. Her father had been a heavy drinker. Not violent, he'd gently go to sleep after several glasses of whisky and a few beers, but she felt like she'd lost a chunk of what little time she'd been allowed with him as he snored every evening away in his recliner.

"Sounds good."

"Here we go," he announced as they stood in front of the sign announcing the restaurant.

She followed him through the door, too many thoughts and feelings swirling around to feel peaceful. There was so much to do to get her business really off the ground, and it was going to be hard to do it alone. But the alternative to doing it alone meant trusting someone, someone like Dylan.

And she was absolutely not ready for that.

Chapter 9

Dylan settled into his chair in the bright and spacious restaurant, his thoughts pinging from one thing to the next, all overlaid by his emotions regarding the woman across from him.

She was bright, interesting, and more driven in her ambition than he'd ever been in his whole life. But she was also North Carolina born and bred. She'd made it through one winter in Montana, but the novelty would wear off, particularly someone whose heritage involved the South.

"Alpacas sure are cute," he said after they'd ordered, both content with a burger, fries, and a Coke. She'd declined a beer, and since he was driving, he decided to abstain as well.

"They are. My first experience was helping my brother raise one for 4-H. She was one of my grandmother's crias, and he learned how to shear it—hand shear it. My granny sent the fleece out with her other fleeces to be processed, and then she started teaching me to spin. It was the softest roving I'd ever worked with."

"Roving?" he asked. This new world came with an entirely different vocabulary from raising cows.

"Fiber that has been processed in a way that makes it easier to spin." She looked off into the distance as if she wasn't seeing the wagon hanging from the ceiling as decoration but another scene entirely.

"Granny was such a good woman," Megan finally said. "Old-fashioned and strong. Her husband had died young, some kind of hunting accident, and when my dad died, it just about killed her. She was going to take me and my brother in when Mom died, but the foster system decided she was too old and our cousins were a better fit."

There was something in her voice at the end. Regret? Anger? Living with a prickly family and too many secrets had honed his instincts about when to push for more clarity and when to leave it alone.

Now was a time to leave it alone.

The waitress placed their food on the table and checked to see if they needed any other supplies before leaving them to their food.

"Isn't it risky to start building a place for animals on rented land?" he asked as he picked up his burger.

"No one in my family ever owned land," she replied. "It was all rented. I wouldn't know how to do it any other way. Where would I come up with the cash?" She shrugged. "It's not like there's people standing around waiting to give money to a girl with a business plan that begins on a dream board."

"Dream board?"

She looked away and her cheeks blushed pink. It only increased her prettiness. He wanted to help her, support her, but she seemed quite capable of doing everything on her own.

"It's, um, poster board. You paste pictures of things you want."

"Like alpacas."

"Uh-huh."

"What else do you have on this dream board?" He was genuinely curious.

"Buildings: places for the animals, a studio, a classroom, a store." She grinned. "A pickup truck that's not a clunker like my car."

"Any friends?" *Or lovers?*

She looked startled. "I hadn't thought about my personal life. I figured if I got the business off the ground, the rest would take care of itself. Besides, there's no space in my life for anyone else right now." She looked at him triumphantly, as if she'd just made a very important point.

No lovers. But no interest in having any either.

Could he respect her wishes and at the same time try to show her the error of her ways?

"I get that," he said, picking up a French fry and dipping it in the sauce that came with it. "I've dated now and then, but it was nothing serious." Not after college anyway. He'd believed Amelia was for life, but when she'd told him she'd slept with her high school boyfriend while home for spring break and protested that it was "only casual sex," he'd ended it right there.

He simply didn't have the kind of values where casual sex with an outside party during a committed relationship fit. Not after what his father had done.

"What are you going to do?" she asked. "I mean, now that you have to pick up your paintings from the gallery? Find a new one?"

He shook his head. "It's all I wanted to do in my life, and maybe if I'd stuck with it in college, I'd be a better painter, but I don't seem to have the raw talent people are looking for. It's a fine hobby, but not a way to make a living."

"You have the ranch, though—don't you get money through that?"

"The ranch's trust pays Jarod and me a salary, but he's always been the one in charge, the manager. He never went to college, but he's been learning about ranching from the time he was a kid, when he wasn't rodeoing, that is. He's got his own way of doing things, and the rest of us follow along." Dylan shook his head. "I need something just mine."

She nodded and took a bite of her burger. They were quiet for a bit while they ate. There was no strain to the silence, just two people content to be in the same space with each other.

Finally, she spoke.

"When I was living with my cousins, after my parents died, I thought I'd go crazy. We may have been related, but they weren't my people. My mom had been quiet, like me. She took care of the house, garden, and somehow got food on the table and clothes on us kids. We weren't rich—hand-me-downs and basic food—but we were cared for. Everything was clean and pressed. She made sure we did our homework and helped out at school. Every night, she made sure we spent an hour reading, all of us. No television or computers. Just country music and a book."

He nodded.

"Granny was still alive then. I think she hung on to see me graduated from high school. She thought I'd met a nice man and would have the best future a poor Southern girl could have." Megan swallowed so hard he could see the motion in her neck.

"I take it she was wrong about that."

"Yeah."

He let that be. Like an animal, human beings needed to develop friendships at their own pace, not on someone else's timetable. Instead, he took another bite from his burger as they resumed their companionable silence.

"Anyway," she said, "when the cousins became too unbearable, I'd escape to my grandmother's. She'd make tea, and we'd sit and spin. At times, it was if my troubles twisted away with the yarn."

The scene she described sounded peaceful to him, an antidote to the craziness it sounded like she grew up with. His life had been equally crazy, and with five of them, there never seemed to be a moment's peace. But he didn't have a grandmother he could remember. CJ said she could, and Jarod had a few hazy memories.

His peace had come from long horseback rides and hours in front of an easel. Maybe that was all painting had been, an escape, and because he'd never looked for anything else, he'd never found it.

Maybe that was his problem.

# # #

Once they'd finished their meal, he drove over to the gallery.

"Sorry about this," the gallery owner told him as he and Megan loaded the wrapped paintings into the back of the pickup. He laid them on an old blanket. Between that and the camper shell, they'd be safe.

"It's just, like I told you," the gallery owner continued, "other than that one, your paintings aren't selling. I need the room for other artists."

"It's okay," Dylan said shaking his hand. "I know it's a business decision. I can't say it doesn't sting, but I understand. Good luck." He opened the door for Megan so she could get in, then went to the other side of the truck and slid onto the driver's seat.

He was quiet as they drove through the city, and thankfully Megan let him be. A door closed, but he sure couldn't see any open windows.

"Is that the statehouse?" she asked, pointing to the huge gray building on top of a hill.

"Yes. Do you want to see it?" he asked, surprising himself.

"That'd be nice," she said.

He took a right turn. Walking would clear his head and it had been years since he'd last been in the statehouse—probably not since high school when some teacher had dragged them all in a yellow bus to see the government in action ... or inaction as the case may be.

After sliding the truck into a spot, they entered the state capital building through the heavy doors. A marble-walled hall led them to a set of counters built in a large circle. Signs on the counters indicated the function of the person behind it.

On the counter labeled tours, there was a map of the building.

Good thing, because there was no one behind the desk.

"This way," he said, his memory bolstered by the map.

He led the way into the rotunda.

"How pretty!" she said. "And how very western."

"Those are the kinds of people who settled, although at different times, the state of Montana."

"I'm not sure the Native Americans would agree with your assessment," she said, "but who are these people?"

She pointed to the four circular paintings that surrounded the dome.

"That's supposed to be Chief Charlo of the Bitterroot Salish," he replied, pointing to the man in Native dress. "That's Jim Bridger, a fur trapper, some guy who found gold—I can never remember his name—and a cowboy based on Charlie Russell."

"Who's that?"

"One of the best cowboy artists who ever lived. I can't believe you've never heard of him. I'll have to take you to the museum in Great Falls."

"I haven't spent much time studying art," she said, doing a slow spin as she examined the ceiling from different angles.

"Actually, there's one of Russell's paintings here. Let's go up to the second floor."

Without giving it much thought, he took her hand and led her to the stairs.

"Wow, that's beautiful," she said, staring at the brightly lit archway leading to the picture depicting the joining of the east and west branches of the railroad with a golden spike. "You guys sure take your history seriously."

"Doesn't everyone?"

"I suppose, but this is the stuff of movies and legends that the whole country understands. It feels like fantasy."

"But it was real ... mostly. Eastern history, the Revolution and all that, was well over two hundred years ago. Our history isn't so far back in the past. People in their sixties now remember grandmothers who were settlers. Besides, people born and raised here grow up feeling like they can touch the past in the rocks, the trees, and the water."

"I think you missed your calling," she said as they wandered toward the house of representatives chamber. "You should have been a poet."

"They make even less money than artists," he said with a shake of his head.

"True."

He explained the paintings in the house lobby before leading her to the gallery of the chamber. As they stood and stared at Russell's painting of Lewis and Clark meeting the Salish Indians, something stirred within him.

"The thing with this legislature," he said, "is that it isn't a full-time job. These are our friends and neighbors. The guy who represents Choteau lives on a farm. A lot of the bills he brings to the floor have to do with issues we all deal with—price of grain, beekeepers, milk, land surveys, that kind of stuff."

"You seem to know a lot about it. More than most."

He shrugged. "I get bored at night a lot." He looked over the seats of the representatives. What would it be like to serve? "Of course, there are problems with having people who do other things for a living."

"Really?"

"Conflict of interest. Does an owner of rental properties have the right to submit legislature that protects landlords?"

"Doesn't seem right," she said.

"Nope. But it's legal."

"Legal and moral aren't always the same thing," she said half to herself, still staring at the Russell. "That really is a beautiful painting. I'd love to see the museum."

"Then we'll go sometime. They've got some good restaurants in the city."

A frown crossed her face.

"I'm not really interested in dating, remember?" she asked.

"Is that what we're doing?"

She tilted her head. "I'm not really sure."

"Then I won't call it a date if you won't."

"Okay, I guess." But her voice was filled with doubt.

Megan kept up a lively conversation on the way back to Choteau. She brought up topics about everything under the sun, from her opinions on national politics, little stories about her grandmother, and most of all her plans for her business.

Dylan let himself get lost in her vision. It sounded so peaceful, raising the funny-looking camelids—a name Megan had supplied—without having to ride miles of fence or herd ornery animals from one place to another. All a person needed to do was take care of them and shear them once a year. And enjoy their antics. Kids must love them.

As she talked, he began to understand the whole process,

both from her clear explanations and her stories.

"I imagine you're a good teacher," he said.

"Well, I'm not sure. I taught a girl how to spin back home, but it took a long time. I guess my first test is this class I'm doing."

"When do you start?"

"In a week." Her voice sounded nervous.

"You'll do fine," he said. "So when do you think you're going to be ready to buy some animals?" he asked as he navigated the rotary around the courthouse for the third time that day.

"I've already started looking," she said. "There aren't many in the price range I have to work with, and I want to make sure they're sound. If possible, I'd like a female ready to be bred." She grinned. "And the matching male, of course."

"Three for the price of two."

"Yep. I just have to be patient and wait until the right pair comes along."

He pulled into her drive. "Mind showing me your set up? After seeing the Heismands' place, I'm eager to see what you have."

"Sure."

Megan took him out to the small pasture that would be more than enough to hold two alpacas. Dylan's practiced eye saw where the fence was weak and could be strengthened, but she prattled on about how perfect it was. The outbuilding was the same. It needed repairs and a bit more insulation.

But how could he bring that up to her? She barely had enough to get her dream off the ground now. Could he, or should he, offer to help? He could pay for the wood and other supplies from his salary; he really didn't have many expenses, especially now that he'd stopped painting. And the work was certainly within his ability.

But Megan was a prideful woman. She wouldn't take a gift outright. She'd need to feel she was giving something back in return.

He'd just have to figure out what that something could be.

Chapter 10

As Megan bussed dishes and wiped tables, all she could think of was the trip to Helena. Seeing the alpacas and their surroundings had only doubled her sense of urgency that the time had come to get started. Succeed or fail, she had to try.

Her first class started exactly a week from today. She'd already gotten the time off from Courtney, and the supplies she needed, small hand spindles and roving, had arrived. There were eight eager students, a nice group to start.

The doorbell jangled, and she looked up.

Dave Brockman.

He gave her a great big smile that she returned. A nice enough man, but what did he want with her? He wasn't bad looking, and while he didn't have as much money as the Vanderbilts, he had more than enough.

She was a waitress working for tips, at least as far as he knew.

Still, she walked behind the counter and started the brew he always ordered. Serving big tippers was always worth the extra trouble.

"How are you, Dave?" she asked him as he studied the sweets in the case.

"Good. Very good. Just sold a Santa Ana winner and made a bundle. I'm thinking of investing in some of those Appaloosas— you know, the horses with the spots. They'd look pretty as lawn ornaments and they're hardy enough to take this weather."

She nodded. What the heck was a Santa Ana winner? It had to have something to do with horses. "What can I get you besides the coffee?"

"I think one of those brownies with the swirls. Got a weakness for chocolate." He patted his stomach. "Got to watch it though. Once a week is all I can get away with."

"Well, you've picked the right dessert, that's for sure," she said. "Courtney shared this with us earlier. She got the cheese gals to make a cream cheese to her specifications and then swirled it in with her most decadent chocolate recipe. It's definitely yummy."

He took the cup of coffee she placed on top of the display case. "I'll be at my favorite table," he said, waving the newspaper he'd carried in at her.

The *LA Times*, no doubt. Either that or some financial paper.

Dylan would have tucked the paper under his arm and carried both the sweet and the coffee to save her the trip.

Stop it! She wasn't interested in either man, so she had no business comparing them.

She plated the brownie and brought it to him.

"So how's this place doing?" he asked.

"Fine," she said. "Do you need anything else?"

"No, really. You think there are enough customers to keep it going? It sure would be nice. About time we had some sophistication in this place. I mean, with Letterman and all, there's more money around here than people know. I even heard there's some rich dude ranch about a half hour west of here. Those kind of people need services, you know."

And the rest of us don't?

"Courtney doesn't tell me how the business is doing," she answered. "And I'm not here often enough to know if there are enough customers. Do you need anything else?" she asked again.

"No, thanks." He gave her that smile again, the one where she noticed his perfectly straight, gleaming teeth, the smile that made her close her lips when she returned it.

Although she couldn't blame him. If she had all the money she needed, she'd definitely get her teeth fixed. They weren't rotten or anything. They just made her look like what she was, a girl who'd grown up poor in the rural South.

She brushed away the voices clamoring for a pity party. The past couldn't be changed. Only the future was in her hands, and that started with the present moment.

She nodded and went back to the counter area to make sure everything was stocked. When it was ready, she pulled out the list she'd started making the day after she and Dylan had gone to Helena. Although he hadn't said anything, his sharp gaze told her he saw flaws with both the fence and the outbuilding. She'd planned on adding wire fencing to the inside of the rails that lined the pasture, and that should take care of any problems, but what had he seen in the building?

She'd gone back over it when she had a day off, and had seen a few needed repairs that she'd overlooked before. A trip to the local hardware store had given her the numbers she needed to add to her budget.

The rest of the list contained the things she'd need to properly welcome two new beings to her little—rented—spread. Next to each were the estimated costs. She'd divided the list into two sections, each totaled. Investments, like the animals themselves, were going to be covered by her grandmother's legacy. Everyday expenses had to be covered by her job, sales of yarn and woolen goods, and teaching fees.

Glancing at the display case, she realized nothing had sold in the last few weeks.

Of course. It was the tail end of April. Nobody was buying heavy gloves and scarves. She needed some light knitwear. She'd better get to it. And trade out some of the heavier yarns for light pastel colors.

Running a business took a lot of continual planning and juggling. She was only one person. How would she be able to make enough and not exhaust herself in the process? Plus, she had to keep working. She needed to know that she could pay her rent and put food on the table for both her and the alpacas. The safety net of a "real job" was going to be necessary for a long time.

A movement caught her eye. Dave looking her way.

She shoved the list back into her pocket and picked up the coffeepot, prepared to refill his cup.

"What has you so puzzled?" he asked as she poured.

"What do you mean?"

"The expression on your face while you were standing behind the counter. Whatever you were looking at had you deep in concentration, like you were trying to figure out something complicated."

She hesitated, not wanting to share her dream with anyone. But he was a successful businessman. He might have some advice, and there was no one else in the café.

"I'm starting a business," she said, placing the coffeepot on the table.

"Oh?"

"I'm calling it From Fleece to Fabric," she told him with a smile. She was very proud of that name.

"Nice name." He gestured at the display. "I take it you made the mittens, gloves, and whatnot."

"Yep."

"Have a seat," he gestured. "Tell me about it."

She sat and gave him an idea of what she was planning. His

dark eyes looked intelligent, and he nodded encouragingly.

"So what's your biggest challenge?" he asked.

"Money." She shrugged to show him she knew the ordinariness of the problem.

"Have you looked for investors?" he asked.

"No. I need to have full control over my business." The thought of any kind of partner disturbed her. She needed to prove she could accomplish this by herself first.

"If you retained 51 percent, you'd still have that," he said.

She shook her head adamantly.

"I see," he said. "Well, if you change your mind, I'd love to discuss numbers with you. It's always exciting for me to see new entrepreneurs get started and help them if I can."

"Thank you," she said and stood. As far as she was concerned, she didn't need his or anyone's help. She was smart, and she knew more about fiber than any investor. What knowledge she didn't have, she'd get from people who had already walked the path she wanted to take.

Dylan had been so sweet to take her to that ranch. That was exactly the kind of help she needed.

The doorbell jangled, letting in one of the groups of women who regularly stopped by each afternoon. This group was the younger set, mothers who were having a last relaxing moment before school let out. Megan set up the mugs and started pouring coffee. The group was eclectic in the pastries they ordered, but thankfully their coffee orders were always the same.

"Hi, Megan," one of them said when she delivered the brews. "How is the fiber business going? I'm so looking forward to the class next week. My husband is not thrilled I'm leaving him with the twins one night a week, but, boy, do I need the break!"

"Thank you. That's so kind. I hope you find it relaxing once you get used to doing it. You can do it anywhere. In fact," she said with a smile, "you might find yourself bringing it here to do while you talk with your friends. Unlike knitting, it doesn't take much concentration at all."

"That sounds fascinating," another woman said. "Is there still room in the class?"

She shook her head. "If it's successful though, I'm sure I'll do another one."

"Great! Can you add me to your mailing list?"

She didn't have one. Yet.

"Of course," she said. "Just write your name and email on a

piece of paper, and I'll pick it up when I bring your treats. Now what do you ladies want today?"

Pastries delivered, she checked on Dave to see if he needed something else.

"Yes," he said. "I would like to take you to dinner."

"Thank you. That is really kind, but I'm not interested in dating right now."

"Don't think of it as a date. I want to learn more about your business and give you some advice. I've run my own business for years."

Were there so few single women in this town that men were this desperate to "not date"?

"Um." She really didn't want to date, but his knowledge could be helpful.

"Tell you what," he said, folding his newspaper, standing, and sliding the paper under his arm. "You think about it, and I'll ask you again the next time I'm here." He handed her five more dollars than the bill required. "Keep the change."

He walked out the door.

After ringing up the transaction, she stuffed the tip in her pocket.

What exactly was he after?

# # #

The following Tuesday, Megan approached the school about a half hour before her class, which started at seven. The longer days made later night classes more accessible, the secretary had explained. Eight people had enrolled.

The room had been set up as she'd requested: two long tables that could seat six each and a third table where she could put the spinners and the fiber she'd already sorted into plastic bags. She pulled her own project from her bag and drafted some roving. Setting the spinner in motion, she drafted the fiber with one hand and managed the twist with the other. Soon the rhythm of the process took over and steadied her nerves.

She could do this.

"That's fascinating," a woman said.

After pinching off the twist, Megan looked up. The woman was familiar looking, but her oversized tote and pretty summer dress made her look like someone heading out for the day, not a class attendee.

"Samantha Deveaux," she said, coming into the room. "We met at the church potluck last month. I'm a teacher here at the high school. I stayed late to catch up on some paperwork."

"Oh, hello," Megan said, somewhat trapped by the project she had in her hands.

Samantha must have realized it because she moved farther into the room.

"I know you're new in town," the teacher said. "I only got here last fall myself." She shook her head. "A lot has sure happened since then. But anyway, I want to extend some of the courtesy the town gave to me. Would you like to have coffee or lunch sometime? I know you work at the bistro, but there are other places, particularly if you like hamburgers."

There was something soft and open about Samantha, very appealing. It would be nice to have a friend or at least a strong acquaintance.

"That would be nice," she said.

"Good. I'll text you to set it up."

"But you don't have my number."

"Does Dylan?" Samantha asked.

The last piece of the puzzle fell in place. This woman was Dylan's brother's fiancée. Was she getting tangled up in a web she couldn't get out of?

"Or you can tell me and I'll write it down," Samantha said, pulling out a small notebook. "I can understand not getting Dylan involved. I love Jarod, but the Becks ... well, let's just say they can be a family that takes a while to get used to."

Megan recited her cell phone number.

"Great. I'm really looking forward to hearing your reactions about our town and getting to know you better. I think you're going to be a real asset. Talk to you, soon." She started to leave, then turned back. "You should take some of your yarn and finished goods to the general store. Lots of tourists stop in there every day. Nick—he's CJ's partner—his parents own it. They were going to retire but settled for spending the winters in Arizona and the rest of the time back up here. They missed their grandchildren too much."

"Thanks, I will."

Samantha stepped aside from the doorway. "And here's your first student. See you later."

A slightly round, older woman hesitantly stepped into the room before Samantha went on her way.

"Hello," Megan said as she stood up to greet her. "I'm Megan Winkle. Welcome to spinning. And you are?"

"Roxanne," the older woman said. "I've never taken a class before. I'm here because my daughter thought it would be good for me. My husband died last year, and well, I didn't know what to do with myself."

It was amazing, the random stuff that people told her. It had happened all her life. Strangers in a grocery store would tell her what was bothering them. On her trip west, a girl on a city street had stopped to tell her all about the horrible experience she'd just had with a dentist.

"I'm so glad you've come," Megan said. "Let's get you settled, and I'll get you some supplies."

"What a lovely accent you have," Roxanne said.

"Thank you."

The woman with the twins who had been at the bistro a few days ago entered the room, the rubber from the bottom of her boots squeaking on the freshly polished floor. She pointed her finger at the older woman in the room. "Mom, I'm so glad you made it, but I told you I'd pick you up."

"I can still drive," Roxanne said.

"I know, but it's dark. You know you have trouble seeing in the dark."

"I did just fine."

"Here are your materials, Roxanne," Megan interrupted. She turned to the mother of twins. "And your name is?"

"Darcie. We met at the bistro."

"Yes, I remember. You have twins."

Darcie beamed. "Yes. How good of you to remember. Right now they are terrorizing my husband."

Roxanne cleared her throat.

Before the mother-daughter battle could begin again, Megan brought Darcie some supplies. At that point, others began to trickle in, including the high school secretary who introduced herself as Anne.

"If you need anything at all," Anne said, "just let me know. I've been here for ten years, and trust me, I know where every body is buried."

Megan chuckled.

Once they were all seated around the tables, she began her class. "Spinning is one of the oldest crafts in the world. What you will be learning in this class is hand spinning. Almost every culture has a type of hand spinner."

The words came easily, and after finishing up a brief overview, she showed the women how to pre-draft their material. Soon everyone was playing with fuzzy fiber and chatting away. Darcie and Roxanne had chosen different tables.

By the time she got to the end of class, Megan was satisfied but tired. One student had made great progress, but six of the others were producing what Megan encouraged them to call "art yarn," full of thin and thick stretches of yarn with periodic bumps. The last, a woman named Faith, had yet to spin more than a foot of yarn, and she'd complained every inch of the way. She was the first to leave; a waving hand and a general "goodbye" were the only things they got beside her backside.

The rest thanked her on the way out and said they'd see her the following week. Megan stopped Anne as she was leaving.

"Do you know Faith?" she asked. "Could she be a problem?"

Anne grimaced. "Every time she tries something new, which is often, she comes to the office to complain about the instructor, the classroom, and the materials. Nothing is ever her problem. So, you aren't alone. Don't let it bother you."

"Okay," Megan said, but she was dubious. She'd known people like Faith growing up, and they never made life easy for anyone else.

# # #

It took Megan a few minutes the following Saturday to find Bridges Coffee Shop, as it was tucked away in a spot of town she hadn't found before, odd because Choteau was so small. It looked like many of the local hangouts she'd seen all across America, no matter what state she was in.

The front was faded wood, with a brick bottom. A glass front window proudly proclaimed the name of the shop, although the gold lettering was chipped and faded, just like a lot of its coffee shop replicas kept alive by customers like retired men restless for something to do every morning, women who needed a deep breath between childcare/work and making supper, and those who needed the sympathetic ear of the waitress pouring the coffee.

It was a sentimental viewpoint, but one Megan preferred to keep. Otherwise, coffee shops were just one more fading business in Middle America.

Samantha was on a stool, listening to the woman behind the counter as she rattled on. It must have been a lull in business, because the small space was packed with a gamut of ages: parents with young children, young teens acting cool, older teens only interested in each other, middle-agers staring at their phones, and seniors alternating between chatter and staring out the window.

"So, you won't tell me who you're dating?" Samantha asked.

"Not on your life. It would be a scandal."

"Nothing you could ever do would be a scandal." Samantha swung around and smiled at Megan. "Besides, we don't want Megan getting the wrong idea."

"This being Megan," the woman behind the counter said.

"Yes." Samantha gestured Megan forward. "Megan is bringing the fiber arts to Choteau." Samantha pointed to the woman behind the counter. "And from my understanding, having only been here a short time, Mae knows most of the secrets of the high school sweethearts who have been eating hamburgers here for the past few decades."

"Hello, Mae," Megan gave a short wave. The woman intimidated her. She was like many of the older women of the hills, second sight bred in their DNA, even though science told Megan there was no such thing.

Then the woman smiled and lifted up a mug. "Caffeinated or low speed?" she asked.

"High test," Megan replied with her own smile. "Definitely high test."

"A girl after my own heart," Mae said. "This one"—she waved the pot at Samantha—"only believes in calmness."

"You can believe in it but never achieve it," Megan said without thinking. Then she put her hand over her mouth. She didn't know these women's histories.

And histories, Granny used to say, are everything.

"It's okay, honey," Mae said. "Welcome to Choteau. By the way, what is fiber art anyway?"

Megan smiled and launched into her standard answer to that question.

"Wow," Samantha said when she'd finished. "All that."

"Yep," Megan said, "all that. It's kind of why we aren't naked."

Mae shivered. "That'd be a little nippy on certain body parts in Montana."

The three of them laughed at the same time, and a warmth spread though Megan. Having friends ... well, acquaintances ...

meant there'd be people who smiled and asked how she was when they passed her on the street. And, in her short time in Montana, she'd learned when people asked how she was, they actually wanted to know the truth and were rarely satisfied with "fine."

Was this what home felt like?

The door protested but opened. A large family, about eight in all, ranging from an elderly man using a cane but still standing erect, to a little boy who looked to be about five. The kid was dressed in a T-shirt, jeans, and small cowboy hat. A sudden desire to crush him to her chest surprised Megan.

"Well, here come the first of the regulars," Mae said. "Your table's all set up in the back," she said in a loud voice to them.

"Thanks, Mae," a young man, most likely the boy's father, called back as they went trooping by to a long table at the back of the room.

"The Carsons," she said to Megan as she gathered up a stack of plastic-covered menus. "Now, you girls decide what you want so I can get it into Jimmy before this big order comes in. It takes fifteen minutes of jabbering before this lot decides they want the exact thing they had last week when they were all here." She hustled to the back.

"Well, what would you like?" Samantha asked.

"Which is the best burger?"

"The California Special," Samantha replied. "I hate to credit our out-of-staters with anything good, but they kept pressuring Mae for fresh veggies. She gave in but did it her way—with stuff she could keep in stock year-round."

"What's in it?"

"She won't tell anyone, and it changes all the time, but at one time or another she has added some special spices, sauerkraut, an avocado spread, and sautéed mushrooms—whatever's in season."

"Doesn't sound very California to me."

"And that's the joke." Samantha grinned.

"Sounds good to me." Megan raised her mug of coffee in a gesture of solidarity.

The door squealed open again.

"I'll have to ask Jarod to fix that next time he stops by for coffee," Samantha said. "Everyone tries to help Mae out now and then. Her son, Jimmy, is a great short-order cook but useless at much else." Her lips settled in a straight line as the person who'd opened the door came through it: the very official-looking sheriff, the same one Megan had seen when she'd first talked to the lifelong learning center about the spinning class.

"Hello, Ms. Deveaux," he said, running his hands over the brim of the cowboy hat he'd removed when he stepped into the coffee shop. "Glad I ran into you. The principal says my boy Jim's still doing okay in your class. That true?"

"Yes, Sheriff," she said. "In fact, he's doing better than okay."

He nodded. "Good. Good. Thanks for helping him out and giving him a second chance."

"No problem." Samantha's face relaxed a little bit. "Just part of the job."

"Hear you and that Beck fellow are getting married," he said. "Jarod's a solid man. Couldn't do better." His gaze flicked to Megan, and her respect for him increased. For all his "aw shucks" manner, his assessment was swift and hard.

It also made her somewhat nervous.

Although she shouldn't be. She'd never done anything wrong. Except take a spinning wheel that wasn't officially hers.

"Ladies," he said, nodding once again. "The usual, Mae," he said as he passed her heading to the back table by the window.

"On it, Jim," Mae replied. "What do you two want for lunch?" she asked when she got to the counter.

"Two California Specials," Samantha replied.

"Coming up," Mae said and whisked herself through the door to the kitchen.

A rectangular opening in the wall gave Megan a glimpse of the steaming kitchen beyond. A tall, somewhat round man focused on laying out burgers on a greasy grill. On the counter next to him lay piles of containers and a stack of buns.

He flipped a hamburger and broke into a smile as the thick patty of meat sailed into the air a few inches before landing with a sizzle back on the grill.

Her mouth watered.

"Let's go before all the tables are gone," Samantha said, slipping from her stool.

Megan followed, and soon they were sitting by the side wall midway down the long coffee shop. The wall was old planking that had been painted a bright yellow at some time but was now a faded lemon color. Over their heads was the famous picture of Rosie the Riveter.

Megan dragged her gaze from the picture and faced Samantha.

"So," her new acquaintance said, "I'm dying to ask about how you grew up and how you wound up in Choteau."

God, the dreaded questions. Megan's face must have betrayed her feelings.

"Oh," Samantha said. "Well, then, I'll tell you about me, boring though that is." She took a sip of her coffee. "I got in trouble as a teen, wound up pregnant, had my wonderful little girl. Audie is kind of special. She doesn't just march to her own drummer—she has a whole different band."

Megan smiled, as she knew she was meant to do.

"Anyway," Samantha continued, "I got my teaching degree, came to Choteau, intending to move on to a bigger place with more services for Audie. But then I realized how much more patient, good people could do for her. And, of course, there was Jarod." The edges of Samantha's mouth softened, her eyes moistened.

That was the problem when people told the bare bones of a story, especially a story of their lives. They left out the painful parts, the times they did incredibly stupid things and still managed to live, and the moments when they were hit over the head with the truth of what they'd been denying.

But it was a start. As their friendship deepened, if it deepened, she'd learn more.

Mae slid the plates on the table, just as the door squealed again.

"Need anything?" she asked as she stepped away from the table.

"I'm good," Samantha said.

"Me too."

Instead of heading toward the front to greet the new guests, Mae stepped toward the back where the sheriff was sitting. She was a super aware waitress, tending to each customer's needs while keeping everything running smoothly. No wonder the coffee shop had lasted so long.

Megan picked up her burger and took a bite.

The food didn't hurt either. The burger was juicy, not like the dried up patties she had often gotten in small-town burger joints. The sauerkraut wasn't something that had sat on a grocery shelf for a year but a robust flavor of tart acid and sweet caraway seeds. And Samantha had been right; there was a sharp tang of some spice that blended nicely with the rest.

"So," Megan began after savoring a few bites, "I was born into a farming family in a deep hollow near Asheville, North Carolina.

It's in the west of the state. Lots of national forests and lots of mountains. Not like here, those mountains are covered with trees of all kinds."

"Sounds pretty," Samantha said.

"It is." Megan hoped the pain of leaving her home wasn't evident in her voice.

"You must miss it."

"Sometimes." Megan forced a smile on her face. "But Montana has its own beauty I'm coming to love just as much." And it didn't have the pain of loss entwined with the land of her birth. "Anyway, my childhood was okay—not too much money, but it didn't matter. Until my parents died, that is. Then we—my brother and I—had to go live with our cousins. He was older, my brother, that is." She swallowed. "He didn't last long with our new family. Went into the army. He did really well."

She stuffed the burger into her mouth so she didn't have to talk any more. The unreleased tears helped the food go past the lump in her throat.

"So where is he now?" Samantha asked gently.

"He ... um ... died last year." Megan examined the detail on Rosie's blouse. It was bunched where the cartoon image had pulled back the sleeve with her fist to show her bicep.

Society's—well, men's—viewpoint of women took some strange turns at times.

"I'm sorry," Samantha said.

Megan shrugged. There wasn't much to say anymore.

They were quiet for a bit. Megan was content to eat her food. She should have rushed through her explanation, gotten it out of the way, like ripping off a Band-Aid or eating the required and detested lima beans before getting to the succulent roasted chicken and stuffing.

"It's not too different from Jarod's family," Samantha said. "Those five kids lost their dad and mom close together. And one of the brothers, Cameron, just returned from the war due to an injury."

"What happened?" Megan asked.

"I'm not sure of all the details," Samantha said. "But he lost most of his arm and so far is refusing to get a prosthetic. He walks a lot."

Poor guy. Of course, that was probably not what he'd want to hear.

"By the way," Samantha said, "Birdie insisted I invite you to

Sunday dinner tomorrow."

"I couldn't impose." The last thing she wanted to do was get any closer to Dylan. Getting to know his family was way too much intimacy.

"If I don't get you there, tomorrow, she'll have my hide. She's already taken a layer off of Dylan for not inviting you when he took you to Helena last week."

"She rules the roost."

"With an iron fist," Samantha agreed.

Another reason not to get involved in the family. Megan wanted to keep her independence, not lose it to a small woman capable of intimidating grown men.

"Please," Samantha said. "If you come, we'll finally outnumber the guys. And Birdie's making roast chicken with all the fixings for dinner." She leaned forward. "And her famous chocolate cake. Nothing made at the bistro could ever top it."

"Who else will be there?"

"Jarod, Cameron, Dylan, and CJ." Samantha ticked guests off on her fingers. "CJ's partner, Nick; his son, Trevor; Audie; and I. And Birdie."

Nostalgia stirred. Sunday suppers at her grandmother's had been crowded like that when she was a little girl. The swirl of talk, interrupted by phrases like "Please pass the black-eyed peas" had cocooned her. It had been a long time since she'd had the safety of family.

"What can I bring?" she asked.

Chapter 11

Mistake, mistake, mistake.

The words repeated themselves in Megan's mind as she drove south to the Becks' ranch. The day was filled with May sunshine, seed heads glistening on the miles of grassland heading east. She should be home working on product. Instead she was going to a family meal, but it was a family of strangers.

She'd eat and run. Her grandmother would turn over in her grave with Megan's lack of manners, but there was no other choice.

About ten miles out of town, she spotted the mile marker Samantha had mentioned and took the next driveway west, remembering it from when Dylan pointed it out. The pockmarked gravel and dirt drive wound down around a small hill, before emerging into a valley where the ranch house and outbuildings clustered.

Farther to the west, the hills flowed like rolling waves, but the ranch house looked like it was situated high enough to get a good view of the front from the porch.

Amazing setting.

She parked next to a beige Camry that looked like it had seen better days. Grabbing the bouquet of flowers she'd picked up from the market, she closed the door and walked up the wooden steps to the porch and what looked like the main door to the house.

Before knocking, she did a last-minute check of her sweater and jeans to make sure there were no obvious clumps of wool. She raised her hand and the door opened.

"Oh, I just heard you were coming," Dylan said.

"Well," she said holding out the flowers, "here I am!"

"For me?" he joked. "You shouldn't have."

She pulled them back. "They're for Birdie."

"I'm crushed," he said and grinned.

Her fears faded a bit and she smiled, unable to move.

He seemed to have the same problem, because he stood there.

"Dylan!" a female voice shouted. "Stop letting the damn flies in!"

"And that," Dylan said moving aside, "would be my older, and fortunately only, sister."

Megan stepped into what looked like a living room. "She sounds ferocious," she whispered. "When I saw her at the bistro, she looked perfectly normal."

"That was her disguise. She's man-eating," he agreed. "Fortunately, she's moved in with her boyfriend, so we don't see her that often."

"I know you're talking about me," the same voice yelled as CJ walked into the room. "Ah, she's here."

A little of her fear came back. Although CJ had a smile on her face, her gray eyes were sharp and took Megan's measure in a few seconds. Megan's status had changed from waitress to potential ...

Potential what, exactly? Why was she even here? Once again, she was sending mixed signals to Dylan.

"Don't let her get to you," Dylan said. "She's been practicing that look since she was sixteen and decided she was in charge of all her brothers. Megan, I think you've met my older, but not wiser, sister CJ." He looked at CJ. "Be nice to Megan."

"I'm always nice," CJ said, her smile finally reaching her eyes as she walked forward, arm extended. "Welcome to the chaos of the Beck household. We're glad to have a friend of Dylan's show up. I was beginning to wonder if he had any."

Megan shook the cool, slim hand.

"Samantha invited her," Dylan protested.

"Proving my point that you are essentially friendless." CJ waved her hand at the flowers. "I assume those are for Birdie. That'll make her happy. She loves things like that." CJ walked back the way she came. "Bring her along, Dylan."

"Bossy, isn't she?" Megan said a conspiratorial whisper.

"Definitely. This way." He took her hand and led her to a large, but furniture-crowded dining room already stuffed with people.

Megan slipped her hand away from Dylan's as eight pairs of eyes stared at her. Cameron was easily identifiable, the boy must belong to Nick, the solid-looking man next to him, and the little girl, her blue eyes widened by her glasses, was Audie, the one she'd met at the potluck.

"This is Megan," Dylan said. "And this"—he swept his arm to include everyone at the table—"is the family. I think you know some of them."

Megan waved her fingers. "Hi."

"Welcome, Megan," Birdie said. She looked around the table. "Stop gawking. I taught you better than that."

"You didn't teach me," the little girl said, drawing out the word *me*.

"Well, it's time you learned. You don't stare at people."

"But I have to look until I see everything," she explained patiently to the older woman.

"And welcome to the world as Audie sees it," Samantha said, rising from her position and coming around the table. She gave Megan a hug, deftly avoiding the flowers.

"I brought these for Birdie," Megan said to her new friend.

"Thank you," Birdie said. "Samantha, there's a vase in the sideboard behind you. Could you take care of them? Megan, have a seat. Food's getting cold."

As soon as she sat down, Dylan squeezed in next to her, so close the heat from his body was noticeable.

What had possessed her to come here?

"Take whatever you like," he said, holding a platter of chicken for her. "It's all wonderful."

She chose a few pieces of white meat, easy to cut up.

With a grin, he grabbed a leg and passed the platter along. "We're going to have to teach you to eat barbeque," he said. "The messy kind."

"I'll have you know," she retorted, "I not only know how to eat barbeque, *I* know how to make the best damn sauce in all of Buncombe County. My granny taught me." She immediately slammed her hand over her mouth. Her granny would also have tanned her hide for swearing ... especially at the dinner table ... more especially on Sunday.

Jarod and CJ laughed.

"You have met your match, little brother," Jarod said. "Well done, Megan."

"Sorry about the swearing," she said.

Birdie harrumphed.

"Mashed potatoes?" Dylan asked.

She gave him a mock glare at him and took the bowl. He was easy to have fun with. Too easy.

# # #

Somehow, Megan made it through the rest of the dinner without swearing again. Samantha and Jarod were perfectly matched, and Audie was a pistol. Nick seemed to take CJ in stride, and Trevor was the perfect foil for the little girl.

She tried to ignore the energy emanating from Dylan.

Cameron had been too quiet, had eaten little, and left to go on a walk. There was an elongated moment of silence after the front door closed, but then the conversation returned.

Birdie ran the show, smiling at everyone in turn, the love she felt for them visible on her lined face.

A family. God, how she'd missed having one.

"We're going for a ride," Jarod announced once the dinner was finished, the table cleared, and Birdie had banished everyone from the kitchen. "Anyone else want to come?"

"We've got to get back home," CJ said. "Nick has clients coming in tonight, and they'll be leaving first light to go on a fishing trip in the Bob."

Dylan glanced at Megan as if to ask if she wanted to go. Truthfully, she was ready to be alone. Having a big family could be fun, but it was wearing as well.

"I think we'll pass," Dylan said.

"Suit yourself," Jarod said.

She watched them all say their goodbyes and go on their separate ways before turning to Dylan. "I should go, too. My woolen goods won't make themselves, and I've got a fairly heavy work schedule next week."

"Sit for a while," Dylan said. "The porch is peaceful, and I'll let you be."

She checked his eyes for truth. "Okay," she said.

He led the way out the front door and to the rockers on the northern side of the porch. She settled down in one and leaned back, letting the sun wash over her body. The porch roof kept the rays from her face, but the westerly arc of the orb allowed light to sneak under and warm her.

She closed her eyes and started a gentle rock, reminding her of sitting on her granny's porch. The birds were different here, and there weren't as many of them as had been nesting and squabbling in the poplars, maples, and oaks surrounding the North Carolina house.

The familiar melody of the meadowlark pierced her consciousness.

For better or worse, this was her home now.

What if she didn't stay? What if she turned around in the fall and headed back to her native hill country? There were plenty of craftspeople there and outlets to support them. It sure would be easier.

But the thought deflated her. There would also be the same low expectations of the poor orphan girl from the hollow, the one who'd reached too high and gotten burned by the golden-haired son of the local banker.

"Where you going?" Dylan's voice interrupted her rumination. "All of a sudden you're rocking that thing so fast it's like you're going to take off for the moon or something."

He was right. She slowed down, opened her eyes, and looked over at him. His brow held a worried frown like he was genuinely concerned, the expression mirrored in his gray eyes.

She yanked in a breath. For a moment, it was if their souls were connecting, that communication went to a level where words weren't necessary.

He laid his hand on top of hers sitting on the armrest.

Oh, crap. He wasn't going to try to kiss her or anything, was he?

"Relax," he said, patting her hand before removing his own. "I just wanted you to remember where you are, safe and sound on a Montana porch." He put his elbows on his knees and his chin on top of his fists. "This state is a good place for people to heal. Because it's so big, we humans start understanding our place relative to the rest of things. While it sounds like something that should make people feel small, many of us find it comforting, like our problems can be managed because they aren't as big as the spaces around us."

He let his stiff posture go and leaned back in the rocker.

"I used to sit here all the time," he said. "I'd sketch or read. For some reason all my brothers and CJ hung out somewhere else. I think it was mutually decided alone time. This spot worked just fine until ..."

She let the silence linger for a few seconds.

"Until what?"

"Ah, it's a sordid story, not fit for a beautiful Sunday afternoon."

"You sound like an aging aunt from another century."

"Yeah, I get that from Jarod, too. Suddenly, I'm feeling very tired," he said. He leaned back and shut his eyes.

It was a phenomenally good idea, so she did this same.

# # #

Dylan dozed in and out, the world fading and resurfacing with his sleep pattern.

He could hear his father's voice getting louder. What was he saying? In the scenario Dylan's mind conjured, he was supposed to be studying for an English test. His sixth-grade teacher had warned them all it was going to be a big part of their grades.

He'd just come to sit on the porch for a minute, stop all the churning thoughts of the themes and characters for *Hatchet*, the book on which they were being tested. Why couldn't they just read the story? Why did everything have to be analyzed?

His father's words took shape.

"I know, I know," his father said to someone. Probably on the phone since the only other person in the house was Mom, and she was taking a nap in the bedroom. She seemed too tired lately.

"I do love you, sweetheart," the words continued. "But it's impossible right now. Jane's sick, and I've got to be here to take care of the children. I'll see you as soon as I can."

His father's voice sweetened. "You're everything to me, Marta. You know that. But it's impossible for us to be together all the time. I told you that from the beginning."

Dylan forced himself awake. The last thing he wanted to do was relive that moment, the second that innocence flew away and his father fell off his pedestal. The next few months he'd been in anguish, his heart heavy with the secret, until his father's death on a winter highway when he found out that both Jarod and CJ and known.

They'd only talked about their father's affair once, and then they'd stuck it away in a memory vault.

Would he ever feel safe enough to reveal the secret to anyone else?

He looked at the woman beside him, her chest rising and falling steadily as she napped. She had a sweet face in sleep, losing some of the harder edges that life had already etched. What had happened in North Carolina to drive her out? Even though she'd said little about it, he sensed there had been an event that had triggered her flight.

Would she stay? Her plans were ambitious, and he admired her for that, but maybe they were too much so. If she failed, would she move on?

What did it matter if she did? She was an out-of-stater, the type of woman he swore he'd never get involved with again. Besides, he wasn't in any position to be dating; he had no clue what to do with his own life, never mind in combination with someone else.

Because God or the universe or Mother Nature had a wicked sense of humor. He was attracted to the Southern redhead and wanted to know more about her, to support her in her dream.

Taking her to bed would be fun, too.

He grinned just as she opened her eyes and looked at him. A slow smile came over her lips. After a quick glance around, he leaned over and kissed her.

She stiffened for a second, then relaxed, softening her lips and returning the pressure.

It was as sweet as he'd thought it might be whenever he thought of her during the waking moments in the middle of the night. The time when his fantasies were most far-fetched. But he didn't linger too long. All he needed was to have one of his siblings spot them.

"Sorry," he said, "I couldn't resist."

She stared at him a moment, as if trying to decide her response.

"Don't be sorry," she replied with a wave of her hand. "It was nice. But let's stop it right here, okay?"

"Mind if I try to change your mind?" he asked.

Again, the consideration.

"I'm afraid so," she said. "My plans simply don't have time for this."

"Okay." He'd have to temper his feelings, probably stop seeing her altogether. If there was no future, it wasn't fair to either one of them. Maybe it was time for him to leave the state and start over again somewhere else. If she could do it, so could he.

# # #

Once again, Megan was set up by the time the class began to filter in. Roxanne was first, proud to show her the long piece of yarn she'd spun while watching television.

"You're right," she said. "It's much more relaxing in some ways than knitting. I'm always ripping out and having to do things over. I don't know how you make things good enough to sell."

"Oh, I rip out things, too. But I'll tell you a little secret. For complicated patterns, I thread a different colored yarn along with the needle every few inches. That way, you only have to rip out to the thread. It's called a lifeline."

"How clever!" Roxanne said.

"Once you get really good at spinning, you can create interesting yarns and use simpler knitting patterns," Megan said. "The yarn makes the garment."

"You really know a lot about this stuff," Roxanne said.

"Hi, ladies." Anne, the high school secretary came in, along with one of the other middle-aged women. Faith followed right behind.

Faith was one of those women who seemed to fade as they aged. Hair lost its vibrancy and skin took on a gray tone. Some fought it with hair dye and makeup; others let it be what it was. Faith was one of the latter.

"I don't know how you expect us to learn how to do this in four weeks," she said after dumping her stuff on one of the tables. "I spent *hours* trying to spin and all that happened was this." She held up a short piece of thread full of barely there thread and slubs, clumps of fiber on the yarn.

"Consider it art yarn," Megan said. "It's beautiful in its own way."

Faith shook her head. "It's far from perfect."

Megan was saved from further discussion by the Darcie's arrival.

"Sorry I'm late," she said. "The twins were squabbling, and my husband refused to let me out of the house until I settled them down."

"You let him get away with too much," Faith said.

Roxanne laughed. "The twins terrify their dad. It's amazing Darcie gets to leave at all."

"And I wouldn't have it any other way," Darcie said. "Poor man. He's never gotten past the fact that there are two of them when he expected one. He'll come around, though. My going out is good for him."

The rest of the women straggled in. Megan got them set up and then worked with each one to show them how to correct their errors and spin more easily. Everyone adapted except Faith. She fought every idea that Megan suggested until Megan was ready to offer her a return of her classroom fee in order to make her go away.

When the ladies were spinning, intent on their own work,

Megan got the other props that she'd brought, different types of fiber in various stages of processing from greasy wool that hadn't been washed to combed tops and roving that was natural and dyed.

"As you get more into fiber," she said, "you're going to find there are many ways to start, from obtaining an entire fleece to getting already dyed roving. It depends on how involved you want to get in the process."

"And what is the process?" Roxanne asked.

"A lot of it depends on what you ultimately want to knit from it," Megan said. "But it includes washing the fiber, dying it if you wish, carding and combing to get rid of fibers that are too short or too long, and removing anything else that doesn't belong there."

"Like poop," Darcie said, then covered her mouth and reddened. "Sorry," she mumbled through her fingers. "I've been hanging around the twins too much."

Everyone except Faith chuckled. Faith glared at Darcie like she was covered with excrement herself.

"But you're right, Darcie," Megan said, "although it's more likely to be grass or hay. Feel these different samples so you start getting an idea of texture. That's the wonderful thing about fiber arts, how they feel to the touch. You get to experience the craft through multiple senses."

"This is impossible!" Faith dropped the spindle on the table with a clatter.

"Let me take a look." Megan spent the next five minutes getting Faith unrattled and spinning again.

"You need to loosen your grip," she told her student. "Let your fingers do your thinking for you."

"What's that supposed to mean?" Faith asked, tightly gripping the fibers she was supposed to be drafting.

"Loosen your fingers. Feel for the twist coming up the thread and then draft a little more fiber."

"I should never have taken this stupid class," Faith muttered.

"Can it," Anne said to the woman. "The rest of us are enjoying it. Just keep trying and you'll get there."

Faith glared at her.

It seemed the woman didn't like anyone.

"Next week I'll bring in fiber from different animals and the yarn I've spun from it," she said after the students began to examine the different fibers with their fingers. "That way, you'll be able to see and feel the colors and textures."

"You've really thought this class out," Anne said. "Will you be doing more?"

"I was thinking about doing a knitting class next if you think people would like that."

"Are you thinking basic or intermediate?" Anne asked.

"I'm not sure. What do you think?"

"I'd love to have an intermediate class," Roxanne said. "Spinning is new to me, but I've been knitting for years. So has Darcie."

"And me," Anne said. "Something with colorwork would be nice. Or cables. Those two techniques have always baffled me."

"That'd be great," Darcie said.

"I'll think about that. I have a nice mitten and glove pattern that might be good."

Faith muttered something under her breath.

Megan ignored her, took out her own spinning, and began to work, her nerves calming with the steady flow of yarn onto her spindle.

Chapter 12

After spending the next two days at home spinning and knitting, Megan was ready to go back to the bistro to work. Her alone time was fine, and she knew she needed steady doses of it to stay sane, but too much isolation didn't work either.

"Wow! Smells good in here," she said to Courtney when she walked into the space right before lunchtime.

"I got the wood pizza oven up and running," her boss said, wiping an arm across her brow which was covered in sweat. "Once it got to the right temperature, I tried one of my new recipes." She pointed to a small, perfectly cooked pizza covered with tempting tomatoes, mozzarella, and basil.

"That looks great!"

"Let's have a slice and see how it tastes."

While Courtney plated a couple of slices for both of them, Megan poured glasses of water and retrieved two place settings. The first bite was like ambrosia, the flavors melding together like they'd been marinating for hours, yet each retaining their own distinct offering.

"I figure I can pair this with a small Italian salad," Courtney said. "I've even applied for a limited liquor license so I can sell bottled wine and beer."

"Catering to the ladies who lunch."

"Uh-huh. And they exist here, no matter how small and middle class the town looks." Courtney nodded to the display of crafts on a nearby wall. "Along with the tourists headed toward the park, they can and do pay well for handmade items, as long as they're well done. I hear Latigo and Lace in Augusta has whole busloads stop off to buy things at the store. All it takes is some strategic marketing."

She could learn a lot from Courtney.

"By the way," her boss said, "you need to bring in some more goodies. Those simple shells with the interesting neckline are selling like crazy. They are perfect for the warmer weather, classy but cool."

"Thanks. I'll get on it." In between working at the diner,

running her class, and searching for the exact right pair of alpacas, her time was getting squeezed. Of course, it meant less time to spend with Dylan, which was all to the good.

Although she hadn't heard from him since the dinner ... and the kiss. It had taken everything she had to appear casual when what she'd really wanted to do was get closer and explore the taste of him for another hour.

Yep. Staying away was the best way to avoid any complications.

"Uh-oh," Courtney said. "I know that look. Someone's gotten to you."

"Huh? Oh, no. Nothing like that."

The tinkle of the bell saved her from any further protest. Dave Brockman and a classy blond woman walked into the bistro.

"That is a great smell!" Dave said with a hearty smile. "I'll have whatever you're having."

"It's only an experiment," Courtney said, standing. "Not even on the menu."

"C'mon, you know I'm one of your best customers. Let me be your guinea pig."

Megan got up and bussed the table she and Courtney had used.

"Sit anywhere you like," her boss said. "Megan will be right with you." She stepped behind the counter where Megan was slipping on her apron. "I guess I should have expected that." Courtney checked the refrigerator. "I've got ingredients for about five individual pies. Tell anyone that asks that they're on special for $14.95."

Megan raised her eyebrows. "That much?"

"They'll go," Courtney said confidently.

Megan picked up her pad and a couple of menus and walked to where Dave and his guest had seated themselves. "Nice to see you again," she said. "I'll be right back with your water. Do you want anything else to drink?" She included the woman in her question.

"I'll have an iced tea," the woman said, her flatter Midwestern accent familiar from Megan's trip across the country. "I'm Cassandra Sanders. I'm an attorney, estate and family law mostly, but I can help you if you need anything else. I understand you're new in town. Dave has said nice things about you."

"Um ..." Megan glanced at Dave who was smiling broadly, the expression that seemed to come too easily to him. She snatched her manners back before they totally deserted her. "Glad to meet you. I'm sure Dave has been too kind," she said, her Southern accent broadening on the last two words.

Cassandra nodded. "He mentioned you were from North Carolina. It's lovely to hear you speak."

"Thank you. Dave, you need anything else to drink?"

"Just my usual," he said, still beaming.

"Be right back," she said, and turned toward the counter to get their drinks.

He shouldn't bother her; he was a successful businessman who might be able to help her get her business off the ground. He'd never been anything but polite and nice to her, as well as a good tipper. Yet there was that one spot between her shoulder blades that just itched so when he was around.

Granny had always told her to trust her instincts.

"Courtney said to tell you about the special pizza on the menu for lunch today. It's a new dish she's trying." Megan looked at the quick description her boss had written out. "Thin crust pizza, smothered in locally made tomato sauce, fresh basil from the New Rockport Hutterite colony, and mozzarella made right here in our store. They're made from scratch, so it will take about twenty minutes. The price for each individual pizza is $14.95."

"How about we split one?" Dave asked Cassandra, patting his belly. "I need to get this back in shape before I start working with the horses again. And it smells wonderful."

"That sounds perfect," Cassandra agreed. "Can I possibly have a salad on the side?"

"Me too." Dave said.

Megan jotted down the orders and she and Courtney got busy. Whenever she glanced at the table, Dave and Cassandra seemed to be in deep conversation, papers retrieved from the briefcase the attorney had brought in passed back and forth and returned to the case.

Shouldn't that type of work be done in the lawyer's office?

"I hear she's a cutthroat in the courtroom," Courtney said. "But demand for her services is high because she always gets what her client wants."

"Where's she from?"

"Rumor says Chicago, but she's closemouthed about her past. Whatever it is, though, she knows the law."

"Maybe you have to be ruthless to succeed in that business." Megan held herself stiff so as to not shudder at the memory of a sweet-talking but unsympathetic attorney told her she was being evicted from her granny's house. And another, this one a woman who'd been cut from the same cloth as Cassandra, delivering a check to buy her off from ever seeing Macon Joseph Bartlett III again.

Courtney shrugged. "Come with me and I'll show you how to get this in the wood oven."

While the pizza cooked, Megan settled a few others at various tables. Attracted by the spicy and savory aromas, two more people ordered pizzas. Her boss had a knack for making her business a success. Megan had so much to learn.

"I've left my payment with Cassandra." Dave's unexpected voice caused a hot coffee cup to slip in her hand. She set it down hard on the counter.

"Sorry," Dave said. "Didn't mean to startle you. I've got to be leaving. Cassandra's going to stay a while. I wanted to ask you something."

"Yes?" She clicked off the faucet and wiped the cup and counter with a rag.

"I'd like to take you to dinner. There's a great place a little north of town. Excellent food and atmosphere."

"I don't know ..."

"C'mon. It'll be fun. I promise I'll be the perfect gentleman. Think of it as a welcome to Choteau dinner." He leaned a little closer. "And I'd like to get to know you better."

Her cheeks heated. He was rich, and yet he wanted to go to dinner with her. In spite of her misgivings, a little part of her in her lost little girl soul was flattered.

"But aren't you and ...?" She waved the rag in the direction of the attorney.

"With Cassandra?" he asked and shook his head. "We're just friends. She's still recovering from her last relationship. Even though I tried to tell her, Jarod Beck's engagement to the schoolteacher surprised her."

All roads led back to the Becks.

"Okay," she said. "When do you want to go?"

"In a few weeks, I'm afraid. I've got to go back to California on business. I'll text you when I'm heading home, and we can figure it out then." He pulled out his phone and looked at her expectantly.

Oh, yeah. He wanted her number. She rattled it off, steadfastly ignoring the itch between her shoulder blades. It was only backwoods hooey, stuff Granny told her to keep her in line.

"Here's your tip. See you in a few weeks. I'm looking forward to it." He waved and walked out the front door. She stood there for a few moments before realize the man at table three was staring at her fiercely.

Oh, yeah. Coffee.

Once the next lull hit, she took the opportunity to stand in front of the display of her woolen goods. Courtney had replaced her spinning information with photographs from yet another Beck. CJ was definitely talented. Her favorite was of a newly born fawn peeking out from glossy leaves.

Was she still pricing too low? Courtney had just sold three small pizzas for about $15 each. The materials for each cost less than a skein of good yarn. It took under a half hour to produce a pizza. Megan worked on a pair of mittens for hours.

"Your work is beautiful."

What was it with these people? Didn't they know how to announce their presence *before* they opened their mouths?

"Thank you." Megan turned and smiled at Cassandra.

Like most people did, the attorney ran her fingers across a scarf of soft Merino wool. Megan had deliberately placed that one on top to entice people. Restaurants used smells; she used textures to entice.

"Oh!" she said as she looked at the price tag. The tone of Cassandra's exclamation was sophisticated, like everything else about her. "That's a bargain."

"Too low?" Megan suggested.

"Definitely. But I must have it. I'll give you a very large tip if you sell it to me this very moment."

The woman wasn't one for delayed gratification.

"I'd be delighted," Megan said.

Once she'd rung up the sale and wrapped the scarf, she handed it to Cassandra in one of Courtney's signature bags. The attorney proffered another large bill, along with her business card.

"A tip, as promised," she said. "My number's on the card. Call me and we'll have coffee sometime. I was new in this town not that long ago. It can be hard to break into old friendships."

"Thank you." Not too proud to accept charity, not anymore at least, Megan stuffed the bill in a pocket. "Um, I wanted to ask you something before you left."

"Yes?" The brown eyes gazed at her steadily.

"Um ... Dave asked me to go to dinner with him. He said there was nothing ... um ... between the two of you."

Cassandra's laugh had been developed for boardroom meetings.

"Nothing at all. We're old friends. We met in Chicago where he was a client with my firm."

"So you don't mind?"

"I couldn't care less. You have fun." Cassandra waved her hand goodbye. "And raise your prices."

Megan watched her leave, then picked up a dishpan to bus the table.

# # #

"Got time for a ride tomorrow?" Jarod asked Dylan late Friday afternoon after they'd made sure all the horses were fed and bedded for the night.

"Sure. Where to?"

"I thought it might be clear enough to get up where I had my accident during the winter," Jarod replied as the barn door squeaked closed behind them. "Got to oil that thing someday."

"Uh-huh. What about Samantha and Audie?"

"They've got some school thing going on. Apparently the last month of school is full of field trips, assemblies, and choral events that need planning and practice."

"Better you than me," Dylan said. Kids were not in his game plan.

"So you say," Jarod said with a grin. "I've never been so blessed."

"How many more you and Samantha planning?"

"Let me get the ring on her finger first. She's already had one without anyone beside her. She doesn't need a repeat."

"Not a chance of that." He may not want to follow his brother's footsteps, but there wasn't a soul more loyal than Jarod. If he had a fault, it was putting everyone's interests above his own.

"I'm looking forward to marrying her more than I ever thought possible," Jarod said.

"It's going to change everything."

"I want to think that it won't, but you're right." Jarod opened the screen door to the mudroom, turned to Dylan, and grinned. "Except for you. You're a confirmed old bachelor who never wants kids who'll be discovered some day stark raving mad with a paintbrush in his hand and crazy spatters on a canvas."

It was like a fist into his solar plexus.

"I've stopped painting," Dylan said.

Jarod stopped moving. "What? Why?"

"They aren't selling." Dylan shrugged. "What's the point?"

"Want to talk about it?" Jarod asked.

"Not really."

"And the girl?"

Dylan swung his gaze to his brother's face to check for any mockery, but Jarod's expression was neutral, a blank slate waiting for the written line.

"We're just friends. Remember, I have no desire for 'wedded bliss' or rug rats. Besides, she's from North Carolina, and I'm never dating a woman from out of state again."

"I never realized how bitter that gal in Bozeman made you feel. You need to get past that, man. Even if you don't go for the whole ritual, bitterness can poison you from the inside out."

"You missed your calling," Dylan said, his insides churning. "You should have been a preacher. Keep it at church. I don't need your philosophical bull crap." He turned and stomped away.

Was he overreacting? He continued his heavy stride to his cabin. No way was he dealing with the family tonight: Cameron's stoic silence, Birdie's effort to keep the conversation going, and Jarod's blissful happiness that he wanted to impose on everyone.

Nope. Baked beans out of a can would have to do.

# # #

The next morning they saddled up, neither of them resuming the conversation from the night before. This was exactly why Dylan would never have a long-term relationship again. Women had a distinct inability to let things drop.

"CJ been able to move the search along?" Jarod asked Dylan.

"I think she's closing in on Alice's oldest kid, Greg," Dylan replied. "She's trying to get Cameron to help her, but she says he looks at her, holds up his hand, and shrugs before leaving the room."

"We're going to need some serious intervention with that boy," Jarod said. "How long can we let him ramble around without doing anything? He's stuck."

"Leave him be," Dylan said, even though he thought it was long past time for Cameron to take action. "I don't think there's a timetable for recovering from losing a limb." He glanced at his horse and laughed.

"Look at Paint," he said. "He's all puffed up, just waiting for me to be dumb enough to get on this saddle and fall off." He smacked the horse's gut. "Suck it up, old man. You need to work today. Even though there's all that green grass out there."

Paint glared at him, then blew out his nostrils with a huff. Dylan yanked on the cinch and tightened it up to its usual notch. "Better," he told the horse.

"They do like to play in the spring," Jarod said. "That new horse I got to train is hard to settle down. Sometimes I have to run him for a mile before I can get anything through to him."

"How's that going?" Dylan asked, swinging a leg over Paint.

"He's showing promise. I should get good dollar for him when he's through."

"And riders?"

"I went to a few local rodeos in April, and I'll hit a few more in the next few months. Samantha got these business cards for me, and I'm handing them out." He shook his head then mounted the roan he was riding. "She says I need a brochure, that I need to look up how Prince is doing and get an endorsement from the kid."

"Strange world, running a business of any kind. When I was painting, I always felt this pressure to be selling."

"Uh-huh," Jarod said, heading up the trail to the northwest corner of the ranch.

Dylan eased himself into Paint's rhythm. He needed to change the subject before they went back to the argument of the night before. "Taxes are due again. We stuck for the mineral rights even though we aren't sure we have them?"

"Brad Small says it's best if we pay them. Puts more weight on our side if we have to go to court."

"Never argue with an accountant," Dylan said.

"Or a lawyer."

"Doing a lot of that lately?" Dylan teased.

Jarod glared at him. "You know I stopped seeing Cassandra a long time ago. She's moved on to that Dave fellow."

Then why had Dave Brockman been dancing with Megan at the church social? And why did it bother Dylan so much? He'd tried to put her from his mind after clear statement that she didn't want to be involved, but his desire simply wouldn't go away.

He took a swig of water from his canteen, then fell in line

behind Jarod as the trail narrowed through a set of rocky ridges. Most of the foothills leading up to the Rockies were covered with grassland, small copses of trees, and clean streams, but here and there were large outcroppings of jagged stone, looking like a bunch of Titans had had a war.

The grass was spring green and thickening, while the trees had leafed out with fresh vigor. Before the summer was out both would pale to ghosts of the vibrancy they held now. Mother Nature had an amazing palette.

Too bad his efforts to replicate it had failed.

How would alpacas do in country like this, if they weren't penned? They were related to llamas somehow, weren't they? Certainly more entertaining than cattle.

"I thought we'd take the fork off to the right and check the fence line," Jarod said. "I know the drone hasn't seen any damage, but there might be sections that need tightening."

"And I suppose you brought along tools for that," Dylan said.

"Of course. Along with a lunch Birdie packed."

"Okay. Let's get to work."

They took the fork and rode the fence, tightening wire in the few spots that it sagged. By the time they got to the spot where Jarod had been thrown earlier in the year, lunchtime was long past. They settled down on a boulder and split the sandwiches and coffee the housekeeper had packed.

"How are those two women going to share that kitchen?" Dylan asked.

"I don't know, but I'm sure of one thing. I'm *not* getting involved."

"Coward."

"Smart."

Dylan chuckled.

"We've finally set a date," Jarod said. "September 19. Samantha figures it's after school starts, so everyone should be back in town. Weather's still good, but not as hot as summer."

"You going to have it at the ranch?"

Jarod nodded. "Samantha's got her heart set on my building an archway for our vows—something she can decorate with flowers."

"I can give you a hand with that," Dylan said, a strange emotion that he couldn't identify making him antsy.

"You can do me one more favor," Jarod said. "Be my best man?"

"Nothing I'd like better," Dylan said, holding out his hand. "I admire you. You know that, big brother. You took over when no one else would, and now you've figured out how to go after the dream you gave up in a way that works now."

Jarod shook his hand, then pulled him close and smacked his back in what Dylan supposed was brotherly affection but made Dylan choke.

"Easy, brother," he gasped out after slugging a cup of coffee to calm his coughing jag.

"Sorry, but I had to thump all that sappiness out of you." Jarod stood and stretched. "Ready? Let's see if we can figure out what all the fuss is about."

They continued up the trail to the spot where they'd seen horse prints in the fall.

"Look," Jarod said, pointing to a muddy spot at the side of the trail. At its edge was the definitive rim of a horseshoe. "Someone's been up here recently." He slid off his horse, looked closer, then took a photo with his phone.

"But this time we haven't seen any breaks in the fence," Dylan said.

"Nope."

They climbed back on their horses and continued down the faint trail until it disappeared over the edge of a rocky ledge. Dylan looked around, then urged Paint down a grassy spot between some trees. On the other side, a meadow opened up and he could see where a horse had been tethered for long enough to take a healthy dump. Dylan turned Paint around and rode back to where Jarod waited.

"Looks like whoever was up here went someplace on foot," he said.

Jarod nodded and slid from the saddle. Dropping the reins to the ground, he walked to the edge of the ledge.

"Careful," Dylan said, getting off his own horse. "Don't know how crumbly that is."

Jarod nodded and dropped to his hands and knees near the edge. Lying prone, he slipped off his hat looked over the edge. Then he pushed himself up and stared at the lip of the ledge itself.

"It's pretty sturdy," he said over his shoulder to Dylan. "But look here."

Dylan walked close to the edge and stared at the section Jarod pointed out. Then he walked back several steps to an outcropping about ten feet from the rim. Bent and broken shrub branches indicated where something had gone from the edge to the boulder.

"I see what you mean," he said. "What do you think caused it?"

"I think someone started to lower themselves over the edge but thought better of it. See where the brush is broken in the first few feet on the side of the cliff?"

Dylan looked at where his brother was pointing. "Yep."

"But the rest of it is unbroken, and there's a lot of it, as if whoever went over the edge stopped and pulled himself back up."

"Luckily, we don't see a body at the bottom of that ravine," Dylan said. "It takes a lot of upper body strength to pull yourself up and down a rope, especially if you don't have the right gear."

"Uh-huh." Jarod pulled himself up and brushed the dust and bits of small gravel from his clothes. Then he walked south about ten feet and peered carefully over the edge again. "Well, looky here," he said.

A rusted steel bar about a foot long, its jagged end indicating it had been broken off, poked from the side of the cliff about five feet down from the top.

"What do you think that is?" Dylan asked.

"Maybe to support some kind of machinery that went down the cliff?"

"Machinery? Like to a mine?"

"Could be."

Dylan stared at the pipe. What the hell was it doing way out here? He examined the cliff face. There was no apparent opening. "Kaiden would know what kind of mineral could be found up here," he said.

Jarod nodded. "Can you get the drone to examine the cliff face?"

"Not really. The fence back there is about the limit of the range. We'll have to bring it up here and fly it into the ravine."

"Sounds good." Jarod straightened. "I'd love to know what was going on up here and how it's tied in with the mineral rights. And I wish we could find that deed or the record of it."

"I'll check with CJ to see where she's gotten on Alice's sons."

"And I'll contact Kaiden to find out when he's coming back up this way."

"Sounds like a plan." Dylan put his fists on his hips and turned around, staring at the land that comprised Choteau Ranch. This belonged to his family, and no one had better threaten it.

Casey Dawes

Casey Dawes

Chapter 13

The lumber Dylan had salvaged from Jarod's building projects thudded into the truck, causing the metal box of tools he'd put into the truck bed earlier to clang. He'd texted Megan earlier to make sure she was going to be home for the morning but hadn't told her what he was planning.

No use in giving her an advanced warning so she could decline his offer in that sweet Southern accent of hers.

Why was he continuing to pursue her?

Except he wasn't. He was just being neighborly.

Right.

"Anything else you need?" Jarod asked as he brought over another load of wood. "Nails, screws?"

"Already loaded," Dylan pointed to a cardboard box with sturdy paper bags inside it.

"You may not get the reception you are looking for," he said. "Samantha wasn't too pleased when I made a big gesture."

"Whatever she says, I'll enjoy listening to the sounds coming from her mouth," Dylan said with a grin.

"What happened to never dating a woman from outside Montana?"

"Things change," Dylan said, yanking open the driver's side door.

"Uh-huh." Jarod tapped the engine hood and headed to the barn.

Dylan put the truck in gear and headed out the long drive to the highway.

The late May weather was already heating up, and the prairie had lost some of its early spring green tone. Soon the grasses would develop their golden tone, a burnished sea of light brown stalks waving and glistening in the sun.

God, he loved this state.

He eased into the rotary around the courthouse, then north on the main street past the stores that had seen better days and the jaunty dinosaurs outside the ice cream shop with its gleaming white paint and red trim.

When he pulled into Megan's drive about ten minutes later, he jockeyed the truck around so the rear was close to the shed she planned to use to shelter the alpacas. By the time he'd finished parking, she'd opened her back door and was striding over to him, the expression on her face less than friendly.

"What are you doing?" she asked, legs astride and fists on her hips.

"Fixing your shed," he said, walking around to the back of the truck. What was it with women and accepting things?

"I don't need your charity," she said, her accent as strong as the Georgia clay was supposed to be.

"Don't think of it as charity. Think of me as part of the SPCA." He lowered the tailgate, pulled out the wood, and shouldered it. "Jarod's working on the inside of his arena. He had scraps left over and said I could have them. Using them here saves 'em from going into the landfill."

"You've got an answer for everything, don't you?" She was only slightly less calm.

"Comes from having an older sister," he said and walked to the shed.

"Anything I can carry?" she yelled.

"Nope." He was glad he was facing away from her so she couldn't see the grin on his face.

Once he had all his supplies in the shed, he gave the inside walls a closer inspecting, then went out the door to examine the outside. She was standing there, watching him.

"Come with me," he said. As they walked the perimeter, he pointed out where there were rotten boards and pieces that needed strengthening to make sure the roof didn't cave in. "And when we're done, we need to paint it to protect the wood so the rot doesn't continue."

"We?" She arched one of those pretty eyebrows, the shape of the W leaving her mouth in a puffy oval ... a very kissable oval.

He dragged his gaze away. This was not the right time.

"It needs to be done. I can help you get the paint—"

"No charity," she insisted.

"I know, but like lumber, there are people who don't use a whole can of paint."

Her smile started small but then slowly unfolded into a grin before it bloomed into a full-throated laugh.

"What's so funny?" he asked.

She waved at the shed but continued to laugh.

He turned but still didn't see anything.

Her breath rasped as she tried to slow down. "If we get lots of different cans of paint, it could be a coat of many colors."

All of a sudden he could see what she meant. He studied the shed. What if a problem became a feature?

"Yep, it could be," he said. "But it might draw attention to the place—good advertising."

She tilted her head, studied the building, and nodded. "That's a great idea. You're a creative man, Dylan Beck." This time the smile she gave him lit her face like the gleam on a sunflower lifting its head to the sky.

Something inside him opened up. Damn. He was hooked and there didn't seem to be much he could do about it, whether or not the woman was open to a relationship.

"Well then, I'd better get to the repairs," he said.

She took a few steps closer to him. "Sorry I'm such a grouch. It's just ... well ... it's not easy to accept things. My dad raised me with stubborn mountain pride, and when I've accepted charity, the cost was often more than I could handle."

"Yeah, some people can dish out a lot of judgment with a basket of food." He wanted to take her in his arms and rub all the hurt away.

And then he wanted to run his hands through those red ringlets, pull her close, and find out what those lips tasted like.

He shook his head to clear his thoughts.

"There are people here who are like that, too, but I'm not one of them. And there are a lot more like me, willing to give a helping hand because we all know we may need one someday. A moment's inattention on an icy road and you're in a ditch." Or worse.

"Anyway," she said, pink spots on her cheeks, "thanks for what you are doing. I'll be inside if you need anything." She almost ran back into her house.

He stared after her for a moment before getting his tools and starting on the outside of the shed. By the time he'd finished replacing the rotted boards on the far side of the building, Megan was back.

"I made you some lunch," she said, twisting her fingers in front of her. "You can eat it now or in a bit."

"Let me finish the one last board on the south side and then I'll be in. Thank you, for that." He hadn't needed it because the ever-efficient Birdie had packed a sandwich along with his coffee, but he enjoyed that Megan had made the effort for him.

After he finished the outside, he stored his tools in the shed and walked to her back porch. There was an old-fashioned rocker in one corner next to a wicker basket with a plastic bag of what looked like brown wool and several implements he couldn't identify.

"They're drop spindles," Megan said as she pushed open the screen door. Mercifully, it didn't shriek as it opened although the hinges were rusty. She must have noticed his glance.

"I do know how to use an oil can," she said.

"I'm sure you do," he said with a smile.

"Yes. Well ... come on in."

He followed her inside.

One main room dominated the house. At one end was a small table with a woven mat centered in the middle. On top sat a Mason jar with wild flowers. Mismatched plates sat on additional woven mats at either end of the table.

"Just some sandwiches," she said, stepping into a small room nearby and adding a plate with triangle sandwiches to the table. A small bowl of pickles accompanied them. "I put up the pickles back in North Carolina. It's the last jar." There was a sad note to her words.

"We've got cucumbers here," he said with a grin. "And plenty of jars, too. As you already know, winters are long here, and having a bunch of jars of canned summer helps us get through."

"Spinning helps me," she said, pointing to a beautiful walnut spinner in front of the main window. "I put on some classical music and just drift off to the feel of the fleece running through my fingers."

"Sounds peaceful," he said and stared at her a few moments longer than he should have.

She pointed to a chair. "Have a seat. I'll get the tea."

He sat, aware of the presence of Megan in every aspect of his surroundings. His shoulders let go of some of the tension that seemed to have taken up residence since he'd retrieved his paintings from the art gallery.

She poured his cup first, the deep sepia of the tea splashing into a thin, glass mug covered with blue flowers he couldn't identify. Hers was a complementary vessel with pink flowers. Sweet but bitter aromas wafted up with the steam.

"It's a special blend I order from the Lake Missoula Tea Shop in Missoula," she said. "I stopped in there when I was first exploring Montana to see if it fit me."

"Smells wonderful," he said. "But I think I'll wait til it cools before I taste."

"Good idea." She nudged the plate of sandwiches toward him, and he took a couple of the triangles, hearty-looking bread stacked with meat, cheese, and greens.

"No watercress?" he joked.

"That's only for ladies who lunch," she said. "Real men need real sandwiches." The smile turned saucy.

"Oh, and am I a real man in your eyes?" he asked, his heart beating a little faster.

"We'll see how well the shed holds up," she said, tilting her head.

"Oh, it'll hold up just fine."

"I imagine it will." Her voice was a little breathy.

He took a gulp of the tea, thankful it was cool enough to drink. What he really wanted was a cold shower.

"Who taught you to spin?" he asked, latching onto the first topic that came to mind. He suspected he already knew but couldn't come up with the answer. Not with her green eyes staring at him.

"Granny," she said, her gaze shifting to the wheel. "It was her wheel."

"So you said. You must have loved her very much."

"She was my anchor—the only sane person in my crazy world."

"Tough growing up."

"Yep."

"But you seem to have turned out well."

She looked at him incredulously and shook her head. "I've obviously gotten good at putting on an act."

"I don't think that's an act. I can read people pretty well, and you're a good person. Smart, too." He gestured to the spinning wheel. "And definitely talented."

"Are all the Beck men flatterers like you?" She put a pickle in her mouth and crunched it in half.

He took a pickle in his own hand and leaned back as if contemplating something deep and profound. Then he slowly shook his head. "Nope. I'd have to say it's only me." Then he popped the pickle in his mouth and chewed methodically, his gaze never leaving her face.

The red crept up from under her blouse, up her neck, to her cheeks. She picked up her cup and put it down. Lifting the pot, she added tea to the cup, concentrating on completing the task.

He should let her off the hook, but what he really wanted to do was increase the tension between them by getting physically closer to her. But that wouldn't be fair. She'd made herself clear.

"What's wrong?" she asked.

"Nothing really."

She arched a brow for a few seconds, then picked up her tea. "Somehow, I'm not buying that," she said.

He glanced at the sandwich plate. One lonely triangle was left.

"Go ahead," she said. "You've earned it."

He didn't hesitate. No matter how much he ate when he worked outdoors, he was always hungry. Plus a full mouth had the added benefit of not allowing a continuation of the conversation. As soon as he could politely do so, he stood from the table and reached for his plate.

"No need," she said, rising as well. "I'll clear."

"Thank you for the sandwiches. They were really good." He shifted awkwardly, trying to figure out what to say next, or more importantly, to refrain from taking a step closer to see if he could snag another kiss before she noticed. It seemed to him like heat shimmered between them like a mirage in the desert.

Was she really serious about not having a relationship? Or was that an act to protect herself?

"I'll get back to work." He headed out the back door.

# # #

Megan watched him go through the screen door, every molecule of her body aware of the strong shape of his back and the roundness of his ass. She'd made love with Macon before his father tried to buy her off, but that desire had been nothing compared to the flame that threatened to engulf her now.

This was pure desire. Best to keep to her resolve and stay away.

If she could.

Picking up the plates, she moved into the kitchen, switching on the music as she walked by her system. Soon the strains of Joshua Bell playing the theme from *Romeo and Juliet* filled her small cabin. The sweet sounds of the strings and the soothing ritual of washing dishes totally failed to distract her from the man working on her shed.

Once she finished straightening up, she sat down at her grandmother's wheel and picked up the fiber she'd been working, a mixture of baby alpaca fleece and merino wool dyed a rust color. The result would be perfect for a shell in a seed knit pattern.

Spinning worked its magic, and she drifted into an easy rhythm, sometimes looking out the front window at the nodding heads of the prairie grass. It never really stopped blowing in Choteau. The winter winds could be fierce. There'd been times her north wall had shuddered so hard she'd thought it was going to blow in, as if attacked by the wolf from the pig story.

But all the while there was a steady thrum under her concentration. Dylan.

When the spool filled, she used it as an excuse to stand up and stretch. The movement led to a step, and then another, and then she was on her way to the shed. She reached the shed and leaned against the door to watch him work.

His hands were steady, deliberate in their movements.

Did he make love the same way?

Shush. She didn't need to be thinking that way.

"So tell me," Dylan said without taking attention away from what he was doing. "Do you plan on having stalls for the animals in here or just penning them together?"

"Open," she said. "In fact, I'll probably leave the door open as long as the wind doesn't shift that way. They like the freedom of going outside if they want."

"Wind usually howls down from Canada," he said. "With a south-facing door, you should be okay." He stood. "I think I've got it pretty well tightened up. I'll just clean up my stuff and get out of your hair."

"How can I thank you for doing this?" she asked.

He looked over at her, then his gaze drifted pointedly to her mouth for a few seconds, then he shrugged and looked down at this clothes. "I'm pretty dirty. I should head home to a shower."

"I have water here," she said. "And an extra towel. I could make you a snack before you head home." The words seemed to be coming out of her mouth on their own accord. Once said, she couldn't very well take them back.

"That would be nice," he said after looking at her for a long moment. "I'll just clean this up and be in."

"Okay. I'll get things ready."

Damn. That sounded incredibly suggestive. She didn't mean it that way.

135

Not really.

Or did she?

Turning quickly, she almost ran back to the house. As the screen door closed behind her, she leaned against the doorjamb. Yes, she wanted him to kiss her again to see if it felt as good as the first time he'd done it. But that wasn't fair to him. She'd already told him she wasn't interested in any kind of relationship.

But was that really true?

And why had she agreed to go to dinner with Dave Brockman?

The shower was right next to her bedroom.

She should have let him go home.

Walking to the wicker shelves that served as her linen closet, she pulled out her best towel. Okay, she had only three, but this one she saved for guests, who had never shown up. Stacking it and a fresh bar of soap on the counter, she gave the surfaces a quick scan and ran a rag around the bottom of the shower.

There.

"Megan, I'm done," Dylan called out.

"Over here." She quick threw the rag in the laundry basket and headed toward the back door. "I've set out a towel and soap. Everything else should be fine. There aren't any tricks to the plumbing, fortunately."

"Sounds good." He smiled and walked past her to where she pointed. The door shut behind him.

Maybe she'd been worried about nothing. Maybe he wasn't really interested and she'd only imagined the tension in the shed.

What would happen when he was done? What should she be doing?

Spinning, of course. Nice, relaxing spinning.

Except it wasn't. Instead of being the consistent yarn she was accustomed to putting out, the thread thickened then thinned, and worst of all developed small clumps. As a result, she had to stop and straighten it out, cutting out the worst of it and rejoining a piece of drafting to the end of the spun yarn.

By the time she was done, the water had stopped running, so she gave it up and went into the kitchen. Would he like more tea? Water? Coffee? She didn't own anything stronger. Not that she didn't drink, but it was an expensive habit to maintain on a regular basis, and her budget had no room for pricy choices.

"A glass of water will do fine," Dylan said as he stood in the doorway to the kitchen. His dark hair was still damp from the shower and curled in places she hadn't been aware of before. The dark shadow of his afternoon beard framed his lips and as she lingered, the edges curled into a slow smile.

"You're staring," he pointed out, somewhat unnecessarily.

She looked away from his face, dropping her gaze straight down the rest of his body, feeling the heat flood her cheeks before she dragged her eyes away to look out the window.

He moved toward her. "Want do you really want, Megan? I'm not buying that there's nothing between us. Tell me." His fingers cupped her chin, urging her toward him.

She lifted her face to his and examined the depths of his eyes. Granny had always said the soul reflected in those orbs. She couldn't read anything. What was she supposed to do?

He dropped his fingers and shook his head. "I'm not going to rush you into making a decision you'll regret. If I could bother you for a glass of water, I'll be on my way."

The tension in the small space was making her crazy. "Sure, but you don't have to go. I'm trying to find the right words." She pulled a tumbler from the shelf, filled it with water, and handed it to him, her gaze focused on him again. "I just ... well, I've made bad decisions in the past, and I'm not sure how sound my judgment is."

"What do you need to know?" he said. "I can tell you I'm unattached. I've tested clean for any diseases since my last relationship. My only flaw is I've got nothing to offer anyone." His voice was sad. "And that's a big one." He took a long drink of water. "I figure I'm about ten years older than you, and that's a big gap."

"Well, that's certainly plain speaking," she said. Would he expect the same? Why not give it a shot? She took a deep breath and began. "I'm unattached as well, and I never thought of being tested. I've been with only one person a few times, but you're right—it's something everyone should think about. As for not having anything to offer, I think we're both alike that way, still trying to figure out what to do in life ... what's the expression? Find ourselves. And you being an old man doesn't matter to me at all." She gave him her best smile as an attempt to demonstrate her sense of humor.

"Funny," he said but didn't crack a smile. Instead he placed the tumbler back on the counter and walked toward her. Cupping her chin again, he cocked his head and gazed at her for a few seconds.

Her lips seemed to part of their own accord, and she leaned into him.

He pulled her close and slipped his mouth over hers.

She kissed him back like she'd been starved for affection for her entire life, which wasn't far from the truth. Her fumbling attempts with Macon hadn't prepared her for Dylan's hard body against hers, the connection of the kiss, or the need overwhelming her. She wrapped her hands around his chest and splayed her fingers, touching the hard muscles of his back. What would his bare skin feel like? Running her hands over those same hard edges all over him with no restriction would be sensory overload.

"Whoa," he said, pulling back a little. "I guess I got my answer." He grinned at her before letting the smile fade away. "And I'm happy with it, but I think we need to go a little slower. You said you weren't ready for a relationship."

She nodded but didn't let go of him. "Maybe a little fling would be okay," she said, her stomach trembling with fear as she said it. It was stupid. Foolish. But she didn't want to let him go.

He considered, then nodded before lowering his head again to kiss her.

With a sigh, she leaned into him and let herself be taken away by her own passion.

But only a little bit.

Chapter 14

After Dylan left an hour later, Megan stood on the back porch and stared at the mountains for a long time. Was a fling what she really wanted? She'd never been a one-night stand kind of woman. Even in high school, she hadn't participated in the drama of who liked who or which kid was two-timing another. It had all struck her as weird. Why couldn't people simply tell the truth?

But was she being truthful with Dylan? Or with herself? Or was she playing her own game of come here, come here, come here, go away, go away, go away without being really aware of what she was doing?

Dylan had made the shed snug and tight, telling her he'd be back next week with paint for the outside and some rails and chicken wire to secure the penned in area. He was a kind man and was already doing too much for a casual friend, even one with benefits. She'd never be able to repay him. And, damn it, she hated being obliged to anyone.

But if she didn't accept, how would she be able to move on to the next step in her plan? Well, she hadn't asked him to do any of it, so he couldn't expect anything in return. But the world, at least in her experience, didn't work like that. Everything came with a cost.

Her cousins had never let her forget she owed them. They'd raised her as their own little version of Cinderella, assigning the worst of the chores—like cleaning the boys' bathroom—to her. She'd escaped to Granny's whenever possible.

Her grandmother's home was civilized. There was always a soft tune playing in the background, hot tea in the pot, and soft wool to be spun. Nothing was demanded. She could spin or sit and listen to Granny's stories of the past: tales of hardship and fun or cultural stories of why things were the way they were. But Megan's favorite story had been about the courtship between her grandparents.

They'd been high school sweethearts, but he had felt a need to do his duty to the country and had done two years in the army, serving in the first Gulf War and returning home with the start of a college degree and a commitment to finding a better way for his country to deal with energy. So he'd run for Congress, but not before finding Granny, wooing her away from the boy she was seeing at the time, and bringing her to the altar.

The story always ended there. Granny never wanted to talk about her husband's death in a hunting accident or her son's death from unknowingly drinking poisoned well water over several years. Life in the mountains of North Carolina could be hard.

Megan never talked about her life with her cousins, either. They kept the conversation positive. She always went home feeling like she could deal with a few more days of her life.

And now she was living within the sight of new mountains, raw and jagged. Life here wasn't going to be easier than home, but it would be different.

Her phone buzzed with a new email message. She pulled it out of her pocket, glanced at it, and shrieked. The alpacas she'd asked about at a ranch near Valier were for sale. And, better yet, the asking price was in her budget!

She dropped into the porch rocker and sent an immediate response that she would like to come look at the animals one more time before making a commitment, but that she was very interested. Then she texted Dylan.

"There might be a pair of alpacas I can buy!!!!"

"Guess I better get busy, then. Do you need any help getting them to your place?"

"I need to give them a good look in person. Want to come?"

Want to come? She needed him to do less for her, not more.

"Sure. When do you need to go?"

They worked out the details for a few more moments and settled on some dates she could suggest to the rancher.

When he signed off, once again she stared at the mountains before turning back into her house to get ready for the next day when she had to waitress. Fatigue forced her to bed, but possibilities ran rampant through her dreams.

# # #

"I really would like to take you to dinner," Dave Brockman pressed the following afternoon. "Nothing serious—I just want to know more about you and your plans, as well as to welcome you to our little town."

"I can't. Really."

"But before you said you would go."

"I ... um ... changed my mind." Whatever was going on with Dylan was none of his business. She walked toward the counter to get his coffee and the pastry he'd already picked out.

"What does he want?" Courtney asked as she slid the items on top of the counter.

"Dinner," Megan replied. "Someplace fancy nearby."

"Oooh, probably LaGorille," she said.

"That was it."

"You'll eat really well," Courtney said.

"Um ..." Megan shook her head. "It doesn't feel right."

"Dylan?"

Megan shot her boss a look. "What do you mean?"

"Remember, I went out with the man. Even though we could never be romantically involved, we were good friends. I see how he looks at you." Courtney smirked. "Kind of like a cat sitting outside of a goldfish bowl trying to figure a way to get the fish without getting wet."

Megan laughed at the image.

A new customer came up to the pastry counter.

"You'll figure it out," Courtney said, pushing Dave's order across the top of the counter.

Megan picked up the coffee and dish and took it to him.

The number of customers picked up, and she busied herself with pouring refills of coffee and bussing tables. It was only when Dave prepared to leave that she went back to him. He tipped well, he was connected to the killer lawyer in town, and it paid to keep him on her good side.

"Thank you," she said. "I do appreciate the gesture, but the meal could be misinterpreted as something more than it is. You understand, don't you?"

"I'm disappointed," he said, but then he smiled. "But I'm not someone who gives up easily. How about lunch? People meet all the time for business conversations, and I'd like to hear more about your proposed business."

"I suppose that could be okay." What harm could a simple meal do? And like he said, people met over lunch all the time.

"Good. I'll text you a few times and places."

He was gone by the next time she returned to the table, but, as usual, he'd left a healthy tip.

# # #

The weather on Memorial Day morning matched the solemnity of the occasion. Megan had made it a practice to attend services, however they were offered, to honor her brother. So by 10:00 a.m. she was seated at the high school gym in a metal folding chair. She made it through the bugling, presenting of the flags, and the short address by a veteran.

But then a fresh-faced high school student arose and, accompanied by a pianist, began to sing "The Star-Spangled Banner" in a clear, melodic voice.

The tears filled Megan's eyes, and she let them fall as the notes soared throughout the gymnasium. She was in her own puddle of pain, oblivious to the men and women around her. After the last note died, she swiped her eyes and glanced at the people in the gym: some had stoic faces staring straight ahead, others' eyes were misted like her own.

She swallowed hard and listened to the address given by a local pastor, the prayer, and the reading of the names of the local veterans who had died in the wars America had fought. Mentally, she sent up a prayer for her brother.

As people rose to leave, she turned toward the exit. Immediately before her, rapidly walking toward the door, was a tall man she thought she recognized. Then she saw the awkward definition of the back of him, the asymmetry caused by the lack of one arm. It must be Dylan's brother, Cameron. Should she approach him, or would he prefer to slink off without having to deal with a relative stranger?

As if possessed by a sixth sense, he looked over his shoulder and spotted her. A moment of confusion crossed his face, then he smiled, an expression that barely managed to encompass his lips.

She grinned back, trying to add as much lightness as she could, given the solemnity of the day. To her surprise, he waited for her by the door.

"Megan, isn't it?" he asked.

"Yes, I was with your family for Sunday supper a while back."

"Dylan's girl."

"Well, I'm not sure I'd go that far."

"I see."

Not sure exactly what Cameron saw, she simply smiled.

"Do you need a lift somewhere?" she asked and then felt the heat flame in her cheeks. Would he think she's was making a big deal of his disability instead of offering a friendly ride?

"Birdie should be along shortly. She wanted to attend a service at her church, and it was easier for her to take her car there herself. Although I *am* capable of driving myself." Cameron's smile took the sting from his words.

"Sorry," she said. "I didn't mean to offend."

"No problem," he said, but he didn't offer anything more.

Should she stay to greet Birdie or go?

"Well, I'll see you around then," she said. Wishing him a happy Memorial Day didn't seem quite right, so she gave him a wave and continued out to the front hall that led outside.

The weather had changed. Where before there had been clouds and cool temperatures, the constant wind on the front had urged them south, leaving bright sun, blue sky, and the chatter of noisy songbirds.

As she walked to the sidewalk, a familiar-looking faded blue sedan pulled into an open parking space. Birdie got out of the driver's side and hustled to the sidewalk.

"Is it over?" she called to Megan. "I didn't want to be late picking up Cameron."

"It just ended," Megan said.

"Good to see you again." Birdie touched Megan's arm lightly. "Was it a good service?" She glanced around. "Did Cameron make it through okay? We were all a little worried that he wanted to come." Then she took a second look at Megan. "It looks like it might have been a little rough for you, too. Did you lose someone?"

"My brother. Some time ago." It was nothing she wanted to discuss.

"I'm sorry."

"Thank you. Have a good day." Megan started to walk toward her car.

"Um, Megan? Do you have anywhere else you have to be today?"

Megan paused and turned. "Not really. I was planning on spending the rest of the day spinning."

"Well, if you are up for it later, come on down to the ranch around three or four. The whole family's having a barbeque. Even Kaiden has made it home. I'm sure Dylan would like to see you."

"Thank you so much. I'll give it some thought, but I can't decide right now." Holiday gatherings with the family implied more than the fling she and Dylan had agreed to.

"It doesn't matter when you get there; I want you to know you're welcome."

Megan nodded, a lump in her throat. Maybe someday she'd get used to people being kind to her without expecting something in return.

Slowly she drove home, memories from growing up overlaying the scenery around her. Playing with Peter on their farm before everything had changed: his gentle tutelage as she struggled to raise her own rabbits for a 4-H project, his joshing, but understanding actions when her supposed best friend didn't invite Megan to her birthday party.

But the sensitive boy who'd been her brother had changed when they'd moved in with the cousins. Like her, he'd been treated as a lesser being, but unlike her he'd not been able to stand it long enough to finish high school.

He'd met her at the bus after school one time and walked toward home with her as their cousins walked ahead.

"I'm leaving," he'd said. "I just can't do this anymore. I wish I could take you with me, but you need to stay. They won't look for me too long. I have ways of disappearing and some friends who will help me."

"But what are you going to do? How will you survive?"

"I'm going to go work in a farm in Georgia. They'll help me get my GED. Then ..." His shoulders straightened a little bit and his eyes glinted with determination. "Then I'm going to be a soldier, fight for our country."

"No, you can't!" Her yell was loud enough that the cousins turned around.

Megan forced a smile and waved.

One of the cousins made a looping motion with her finger at her temple and with loud laughter, they continued down the road.

"You can't go!" she hissed at Peter again.

"I have to," he repeated. "Once I get back, I'll find you. I promise." He'd hugged her tightly, given her an awkward little wave, and headed down the road in the opposite direction.

She'd watched him for a while, tears falling down her cheeks.

But he'd never come back for her. Instead, two men with uniforms had climbed the steps to her granny's house one day.

Megan swallowed hard and forced herself back to the present. How could she go to a family barbeque and pretend that everything was fine? How could she start a new life when Peter was never going to be in it?

Because it was all part of life, her granny's voice seemed to say in her mind. The older woman hadn't been a churchgoer; she was more of a spiritual person, gleaning her beliefs from a number of different sources, much to the horror of the more traditionally minded people in her family. As a result, Megan's faith was more like her grandmother's in spite of her cousin's family's insistence that she attend church with them every Sunday.

As she pulled into her driveway, she saw a hawk circling low over the stubble in a nearby field. All of a sudden, it seemed to stop mid-air, then plunged to the ground. Instants later, it soared back up, a thick, black snake struggling in its grasp. The hawk fought to hang onto the reptile, its wings flapping with strong beats, flying up and then sinking down as the snake writhed harder, trying to escape.

Ultimately, the struggle proved too much. The hawk dropped the snake and headed toward another field where it probably hoped the pickings would be tamer.

It was the way things were.

She made herself a sandwich for lunch, turned on the classical music, then sat down to spin. With a new batch of roving, it took her a little while to produce the result she was looking to attain, an even twist that produced a thin strand that would be perfect for light summer-weight garments when spun into a three-ply yarn. The roving had been dyed a light peach that almost glistened in the sun streaming through her living room window.

A few hours later, she stretched and smiled at the pile of yarn wrapped around the spool. It had been a good afternoon's work, but it was toil that brought her peace and joy. The hours flew by.

Walking into the kitchen, she refilled her water glass and leaned against the counter to drink it. The dry weather west of the Mississippi took its toll on her skin and her body. She'd learned quickly that maintaining her water intake was key to feeling good.

Should she go to the barbeque? The alternative was grilling a lone hot dog on the small unit that had come with the rental.

Depressing.

She looked around the small kitchen for something she could take with her. Pulling together some greens, she made a salad in the largest bowl she had. It was probably only enough to feed four people, but at least it was something.

Her heart sped up as she searched through her closet and drawers for something to wear—casual but not too far gone. In the end she decided on a pair of shorts, a denim-blue blouse, and a pair of sneakers. A straw hat that she'd worn for gardening back home would do for coverage from the sun. At the last minute, she grabbed a light shawl she'd knit a few years prior.

Before she could change her mind, she put the salad in her car and headed out.

It would be okay. It was only a barbeque, not a commitment.

She made the right into the ranch drive and headed down the gravel road, slowing as she took in the view.

Beyond the rolling green of the foothills, the sharp peaks of granite, most still topped with snow, rose starkly in front of her. It was raw power, the kind people tried to imagine they had but could never dream of matching no matter how much they tried to fool themselves into believing they could.

The mountains humbled her, but they didn't make her afraid. The key, she'd learned during her long solitary walks on Appalachian trails, was to be respectful of what she couldn't do and constantly improve her ability to handle unimagined circumstances.

Like barbeques.

She took a deep breath.

After rounding the bend that led to the house and outbuildings, she realized she had no idea where on the property the event was taking place. It couldn't be too far from the main house, could it?

Then she spotted an awning up a slope from where she'd parked her car. A stone-lined wide path led the way there with a couple of easy switchbacks. Someone had planted wildflowers between the copper-colored slabs.

Carefully, she made her way up the path. She was about halfway up when Dylan appeared in front of her.

"Hello there!" he said, his greeting overly enthusiastic. "Birdie said she invited you. I'm glad you came." He smiled, the expression calmer, and added, "Very glad. Frankly, I'd like to kiss you right now, in front of God and everyone, but I suspect you aren't ready for that."

"No, not really," she said, her cheeks growing hot.

"You'll be okay. It's just a barbeque."

That's what she had told herself. Just a barbeque. Just a kiss. Just a little fling.

Chapter 15

Dylan forced his arms to stay at his side. All he wanted to do was taste the glistening lips in front of him. But from Megan's wide eyes, he knew he'd been right to avoid the gesture. Besides, he could feel the stares of every one of his siblings drilling laser like in his back.

"Let me take that," he said, reaching for the covered bowl she held. "Ladies first." He gestured up the path.

"I'm so glad you came," Birdie said as soon as Megan reached the top of the small knoll.

"What would you like to drink?" Jarod asked. "We've got beer, soda pop, or water."

Did his older brother always have to be so helpful?

"Or there's some iced tea over in this jug," Dylan said, proud that he'd thought to ask Birdie to make some.

"Oh, that would be just the thing," Megan said, her smile broadening.

He grinned smugly at Jarod, who refrained from rolling his eyes but just barely.

"Hello, Megan," Samantha said. "Don't let these ruffians bother you. You'll get used to it."

"I'm not sure about that," CJ added. "I grew up with them and they still get on my nerves."

"That's only because you're raising a teenager," Nick said. "Good to see you again, Megan."

Dylan watched his family gather around Megan, drawing her into their nest. Hopefully, they wouldn't overwhelm her. He loved them, but they could be a bit intense.

"Who's the new girl?" Kaiden asked.

"She came up here in January," Dylan replied, not bothering to correct his brother's use of "girl." Someday, someone was going to take a wrench to his head if Kaiden didn't change his Neanderthal ways. "She's from North Carolina."

"She's a looker. You interested?"

"Stay away from her."

"You *are* interested. Aren't you a little old for her though?"

"I can still take you down, little brother, and don't forget it." Of all his brothers, Kaiden had always been the one who got under his skin the most.

"I won't tromp on your territory," Kaiden said, palms up in surrender. "But can you introduce us?"

"Behave," Dylan hissed as he walked toward where Megan was surrounded by all the females, Kaiden following behind.

"This is the only Beck you haven't met," he said to Megan. "Our baby brother, Kaiden."

Was he the only one who saw the flash of temper cross Kaiden's face? His brother had always been a scrapper. Kidding him could be dangerous if he decided to take it the wrong way.

"And probably the best looking of all of us," he added, jabbing Kaiden's arm lightly with his fist, trying to defuse the situation.

"True," Kaiden said.

"I'd debate that," CJ said.

"Me too," added Samantha.

Megan grinned at Dylan, then gave Kaiden the full wattage of her smile, hitting Dylan straight in his gut.

They did look striking together. Six-foot-plus Kaiden with his trim, dark hair, perfect teeth against a deep tan, and blue-gray eyes and petite Megan, all five-foot something of her with her red hair and fair complexion. His brother was also closer in age and had a real job.

Dylan turned away from the sight and snagged a few tortilla chips from the bowl.

"Is she going to join our family, too?" Audie asked from her perch on a lawn chair. "If she does, Jarod is going to need to get her a horse."

Dylan laughed. That girl was always good for his soul. If she had a question, she asked. No pretense or hidden motive.

"I don't think so, but you never know."

"Oh. Okay. But she should. She's nice."

"Yes, she is." He perched on a nearby bench. "How are your riding lessons going?"

"Good! And Mommy is finally learning how to canter. She was scared of that. Said it was too fast. We're all going on a long ride and take a picnic."

"Giving my future daughter the third degree?" Jarod asked, coming up behind him.

"What's a third degree?" Audie asked. She wrinkled her forehead. "I don't even know what a first degree is." She shrugged and took a big bite out of the hot dog she was holding.

Both of them chuckled.

"She's something else," Dylan said.

"That she is."

"Seems like your training business is picking up," Dylan said. "You've got two riders you're training?"

"Yes. And I've got my eye on a new horse. Another one like Prince was—too much horse for the city kid that bought him."

"I'm glad." And he was. But Jarod's success made him look even more lost at sea.

"Don't do that to yourself," Jarod said. "You'll figure out what you're meant to do. Have a little faith." He nodded toward Megan. "And don't let our kid brother horn in on your territory."

Jarod was right. He shouldn't give up without even trying. After filling a cup with iced tea, he walked back to the small group of Megan, Samantha, and CJ.

"Here's your tea," he said, handing the cup to Megan.

"Thanks," she said with a smile. "I was getting parched."

"Do you want anything to eat?" he asked. "I could throw a hot dog or burger on the grill."

"There's also salads," CJ said, "if you're not a beef eater like my brothers."

"I'm not quite ready to eat yet," Megan said. "Samantha was entertaining us with stories about her students."

"High schoolers haven't changed since we were kids," CJ said. "I'm not sure how I'm going to handle it when Trevor gets his hormones all riled up."

"Or when he falls in love for the first time ... all that drama," Samantha said.

"We think that might have already happened," CJ said. "There's one girl he's been 'hanging with' since he got here. He even got suspended for defending her because, unfortunately, he decided to use his fists."

"Yep," Samantha said. "Hormones and love, bad combination."

"Well, if you ladies wouldn't tempt us with your wily ways ..." Dylan added with a grin.

And he was immediately booed and shooed away.

"This is important girl talk," CJ said. "We need to let Megan know what she's getting into."

Megan's cheeks tinted.

"She's not getting into anything," Dylan said. "She's simply

149

here because Birdie was neighborly and asked her. Give it a rest, CJ."

The pink deepened.

Wrong tactic. After all, he'd kissed the woman passionately a few days ago, and now he was saying there was nothing between them. Yep, definitely put his foot in it.

"Let me know when you're ready," he said to Megan, then escaped to have a chat with Nick and Trevor about his big sister's overbearing ways.

The arrival of a few more people from Birdie's church as well as some neighboring ranch families relieved the pressure. Dylan made himself indispensable at the grill until Jarod told him to go eat his own food. After grabbing a burger and dropping some salads on a plate, he headed over to a spot on one of the picnic tables he and Jarod had carted up here with the pickup a few days earlier.

He looked around but couldn't see Megan. Had she left? God, he was incompetent at everything.

"Hey, stranger," Megan's soft voice floated to his ears as she sat on the bench opposite him.

"My sister get to you?" he asked, indicating the can of beer in her hand.

"It's been a while since I've been around this many people."

"Especially since I bet they all want to know every detail about your life."

"Kind of." She looked at him steadily. "You've made yourself scarce. Um ... did I misinterpret what happened the other day?"

"No." He struggled to come up with the right words, ones that would express what he needed to say but not send things any farther south.

"Oh." She sipped her beer and her gaze drifted to the scene around them.

For once, his extended family was leaving them alone.

"Like I said," he continued. "I ..." He glanced around again, and lowered his voice. "I enjoyed what happened. I want to continue. But I want to make sure you're okay with everything."

"I won't break, you know. I may look like a sweet Southern girl, but I'm made of steel."

What looked like residual pain in her eyes belied her statement.

"But I might." He put on a sad expression and laid his hand on his heart. "Being a sensitive guy and all."

She swallowed rapidly.

"Uh-huh. Still willing to get the alpacas with me on Thursday?"

"Absolutely."

"Good."

"So there you are," Jarod slid next to him while Samantha took the seat next to Megan.

So much for a heart-to-heart, even if he could have steered Megan away from her business and back to what was going on between them.

He let his brother and future sister-in-law take over the conversation and used the opportunity to watch Megan's interaction. She was easy with them, but he could sense her guardedness in the way she deflected certain topics and, like she had with him, turned conversations back to her business and her experience with her first class.

As she talked, Jarod and Samantha's easy ways seemed to put her at ease. Her face became more animated, and her fingers relaxed their tension around the beer can. The lazy afternoon and full stomach began to get to him, and he shut his eyes briefly, letting the voices float around him as he lost track of what everyone was saying.

One thing was becoming more apparent to him, even if everyone else disagreed with his analysis. If he didn't find a way to get his feet under him, learn to make a living away from the ranch, any possibility he had with Megan, or anyone else like her, was going to fade away.

# # #

Tuesday afternoon, after he'd helped Jarod bring down the benches and the awning, Birdie sent Dylan into town to replenish items they'd used up during the barbeque. The day was heating up, a promise of scorching temperatures during the worst of the summer months. Instead of the air conditioner, he rolled down the windows, listening for the sounds of wildlife as the fresh air filtered into the cab.

He'd always lived his life by what suited him at the time. He'd needed to get away from the ranch, so he went to college in Bozeman. He'd needed to get away from memories of Amelia, so he came home. Painting provided him the solitude he craved from the rest of the family, so he painted.

And now the gallery's dismissal had made him stop painting.

Even Megan was as much happenstance as anything else.

He was a drifter, just like great-great whoever ancestor, Jarod Beck, had drifted until he'd landed a piece of land, a woman, and started a dynasty.

Almost by routine, Dylan pulled into the bistro parking lot, a few hundred yards before his destination of the grocery store.

May as well get a cup of coffee and drown his sorrows in the local paper. There'd no doubt be something in either national or local politics to rile him up and drag his self-pitying focus somewhere else. Once inside, he looked around but didn't see her.

"Megan here today?" he asked Courtney, who was behind the counter.

"Nope." She looked at him sharply, then folded her arms at the edge of the glass. "What is it you're doing with her, Dylan? Just because you're at loose ends doesn't mean you get to mess up her life. She's got goals."

"Are you saying I don't?"

She shrugged. "If the shoe fits ..." She turned to the coffee urn and grabbed a mug. "The usual?"

"Yeah." His insides churned with the slam. Intended or not, she'd hit the mark.

Picking up the cup of coffee Courtney put in front of him, he turned and stared at the tables. A portly man with gray hair and moustache, with a blue dress shirt and jeans, waved at him. The man looked slightly familiar, but Dylan couldn't place him.

The man waved him over. When Dylan got close to the table, the man stood. "Ross Fitzsimmons," he said holding out a hand. "I'm your representative in Helena."

"Hello." Dylan shook hands. What did the man want?

"Sit, sit, sit," Ross commanded. "I like to get to know my constituents, find out their concerns. What's your name?"

"Dylan Beck." He sat. What the hell. He didn't have anything better to do.

"Beck. I know of a Cameron Beck. Good soldier. Any relation?"

"My brother."

"It's sad what happened. You tell your brother if he needs anything at all, running interference with the VA, anything, just give me a call." Ross's face lost its ruddy bonhomie. "It's criminal what we're doing to our veterans."

Dylan nodded, unsure of the response the man wanted.

"Anyway, what's your top of mind?" Ross asked, his smile returning.

"Property taxes," Dylan answered. It was the easy answer. Without a state sales tax, everyone's property taxes were high to cover local expenses and education.

"That's a common one," Ross nodded. "Not much we can do about it, I'm afraid. People are dead set against a sales tax, and nobody really makes enough money in this state to fund the government off income tax."

Those were all true statements. But then there were the out-of-staters with money to burn, like Dave Brockman. Were they paying their fair share?

"But it's good to know we keep our budget balanced," Ross said. "Unlike the feds." He chuckled.

"Yes," Dylan said, sipping his coffee. "Can I ask you—what made you decide to run for office?"

"Truthfully?"

Dylan nodded.

"My wife wanted me out of the house." Ross chuckled again. "I'm a retired insurance guy. We've got a little spread, but it wasn't enough to keep me occupied during the winter months. Our rep retired, so here I am." The cheerfulness dimmed a bit. "Not sure if I'm going to stick, though. My wife passed last winter, and my daughter's after me to move to Texas to be with her and her family."

"Sorry to hear that," Dylan said.

"But I don't think I can leave if I can't find someone reliable who's interested in running. You know, someone who understands our way of life, not some outsider trying to impose their values on us." He raised a hand. "I know, I know, the times are changing. Global warming and all that." He gave Dylan a politician's grin. "Although it sure didn't seem like it this past winter."

"Nope." Where was the man going with all this? Dylan took a sip of his coffee.

"But back to your question about property taxes. Is there something in particular you're concerned about?" Ross dropped all his legislative demeanor and genuine concern showed through.

No wonder he kept getting reelected.

Dylan told him about the missing deed to the mineral rights and the impact on the family of the new taxes the county had levied. He wasn't telling family secrets; the information was in the county records if anyone decided to look.

Had anyone checked into the mineral rights status? It would be interesting to know.

"Unfortunately, I've got no say in the county, other than as a private citizen," Ross said. "But I do know they're trying to adjust the rates depending on development. So if a landowner doesn't develop the mineral rights, he pays a lesser amount than someone who is actively mining for something or another."

"That would be a step in the right direction."

"I'll pass that along," Ross said, finishing up the last bit of coffee. "Well, I've got to get home, tend to the animals." Loneliness wrapped around his words as he stood. "Think about running, Dylan. The legislature could use some young blood, people with roots to the land." He held out his hand again, and Dylan shook it. "See you, Courtney," he called out as he walked toward the front door.

Run for office? He'd never considered the possibility. But the legislature only met a few months every other year, so it wouldn't need to be a full-time job, just serving the state he loved with his whole heart.

The rest of the time, he could help Jarod run the ranch.

Or support Megan in her business. Surely, one person couldn't do everything by themselves. And with his background on the ranch and knowledge of animals, he could be a real asset with the alpacas. All he had to do was convince her.

With a lighter feeling than he'd had in months, he paid for his coffee and left.

Chapter 16

Megan paced the porch as she waited for Dylan. He'd made arrangements to borrow the ranch's two-horse trailer. Thank goodness. She hadn't given a thought to how she was going to get the one- to two-hundred-pound animals back to the ranch. They definitely wouldn't fit in the trunk of her car.

If she didn't start thinking more clearly, she wasn't going to get the business off the ground, much less keep it afloat. As soon as she got the animals settled, she needed to put in the application for the next class, this one on intermediate knitting.

She'd found a beautiful hat and mittens set for her class to make. It was full of complicated color patterns, challenging enough to keep the advanced knitters occupied. She hoped Faith wouldn't make an appearance. The woman didn't have enough patience to try anything complex.

The rattle of the truck on the drive made her look up.

Dylan pulled to a stop well off from the shed, then executed a well-practiced turn so he'd be able to pull right back out onto the highway.

"Ready?" he asked as he stepped from the truck.

"Yes. Just let me get my bag." The screen door slammed as she ran back into the house, grabbed her purse, and snagged the loaf of sweet bread she'd made the day before.

The screen door thumped on her way back out.

"Hey," he said as she got to the passenger door where he stood. "Slow down. It'll take us a while to get to Valier. They'll be there when we get there." Then he leaned forward and brushed her lips with his. "I hope that was okay."

"Sure."

Truthfully, she hadn't expected it. She'd managed to slip away from the barbeque without really being alone with Dylan, helping CJ and Samantha carry some things back to the kitchen before slipping out to her own car, not willing to have the family think there was anything more than casual friendship between her and Dylan.

But the instant of intimacy had added a burst of fuel to her physical passion.

Down, girl. She had animals to inspect and, hopefully, buy.

She climbed into the truck, as did Dylan, and they rumbled north on the highway.

"A person can sure spend a lot of time driving in this state," she commented as she looked at the expanse of road in front of her. To the left, the Rockies rose in a dark smudge against the horizon; everywhere else mostly treeless hills undulated toward the next geographical change.

"Yep," Dylan said, his hands easy on the steering wheel. "It's worse in some areas than others. The eastern half is fairly desolate. People have to drive a hundred miles or so to get to a decent supermarket or one of the big box stores. I pity the UPS drivers in those areas."

"I know. I drove through there."

While she'd come into the state on a two-lane from South Dakota, cutting through a small corner of Wyoming to get there from the Black Hills. She'd hoped to find lodging but had slept in her car more than once. Desolate didn't even begin to cover it. The unfamiliarity of the Indian reservations she'd driven through had set her nerves on edge. Not that she was afraid, but it was so profoundly different from the small enclaves of people she'd grown up with.

When she'd stopped to see the Battle of the Little Big Horn Monument, something in her heart broke. Hundreds of people had died from a clash of cultures, happenstance, and hubris. From that spot, she'd turned north, ready to leave this vast unknown place and find a more populated area.

Billings, with its smelly oil refineries, hadn't appealed, while Bozeman and Missoula seemed too crowded to be comfortable. She'd needed middle ground and had begun to suspect she might not find it in Montana.

"I've never really asked," Dylan said. "How did you pick Choteau?"

It was if he'd been reading her mind.

"The classic way," she said with a chuckle. "I broke down."

He joined her laugh.

"Once that happened, I had to find a mechanic. The guy was so friendly, even though he overwhelmed me a bit. He's a big bear of a man, red hair and beard."

"That must have been Perry," Dylan said. "You lucked out. He's the best."

"Well, between him and my enforced stay, I began to appreciate the town. I know it's somewhere between prosperity and blowing away in one of those cold blasts from the north, but it feels hopeful."

And that's what she'd needed most at the time: hope.

"Yes, it's a good place to be. Are you going to stay? I mean, winters are going to be tough for a Southern girl like you." He grinned at her for a second before turning his attention back to the road.

"There are Southern girls and there are Southern girls," she said, letting her voice drift lazily into a drawl. "I'm more of a steel magnolia than a limpid lily."

"Is that right?" he asked. "What exactly does that mean?"

"It means I'm determined to get what I want and don't mess with me." As she said it, she realized it was true, that it might even become a mantra—something she could look at to remind herself of who she really was.

"I have no intention of messing with you," he said. "And not only don't I want to get in the way of your business, I want to help you with it."

"You've already done too much," she said.

He went silent, his mouth in a flat line.

How was she going to help him understand? If she didn't do this all by herself, she wouldn't believe she could truly succeed on her own. No one had ever believed in her, and she had to prove them wrong.

"What if I became a silent partner?" he asked.

"A what?"

"It's something I've been thinking about. I have a couple of ideas on what to do next now that ..." He stared straight ahead for a moment, then seemed to shake off whatever shadow had clouded him. "Anyway, your ideas intrigue me. I'll probably never spin or knit—"

"Don't count on it," she said with a smirk in his direction.

"Oh, I don't doubt that you're determined to get everyone you know to become interested in your business. And no, I don't think knitting isn't manly enough for me. It just doesn't intrigue me that much."

"Maybe you're a weaver," she said.

"Huh?"

"It was Granny's belief, and I believe it too, that certain fiber arts call to different people. Some people knit, crochet, spin, weave, or do something entirely different with fiber. Maybe the beginning of the process is what speaks to them, like raising the animals, or preparing and dying the wool."

"I get it. But I've got some money—we all have trust funds. CJ is using hers to start her business. I don't have anything in particular to do with mine. I thought if I invested it in your business, you could get started quicker. I'd share some of the profits when you make some."

"I could *never* do that!"

"Why not? People do it all the time." He seemed surprised at her harsh reaction.

"Why not?" Indignation made her blood hammer through her veins. She'd trusted him to understand. "Because it would be *cheating*!"

He went silent again.

She stared out the window, the artery in her neck throbbing and her temples beginning to ache. What had she been thinking, accepting help from anyone for anything? She should have gotten a trailer on her own and towed the damn animals back herself. For god's sake, she'd driven a trailer from one end of the country to another. She could handle it!

"Which part would be cheating?" Dylan's voice interrupted her internal boil.

"What?"

"I asked which part would be cheating."

He was making no sense.

"Which part of what?"

"My being a silent partner. The fact that I'd be silent or that I'd be a partner?"

"Both."

"Ah. It's necessary to do things all by yourself in order to claim your success."

"Of course." Her aunt and uncle never stopped reminding her that she wouldn't be healthy and fed if it weren't for them, and as for her good grades, she wouldn't have achieved them either without help from her cousins and the teachers giving her a break.

"The truth is," he said as he pulled into the alpaca ranch, "none of us do anything entirely on our own. The myth of the self-made man is just that, a myth."

She opened her mouth to argue with him and then realized a man was walking toward her with a big grin on his face.

Later. *Then* Dylan was getting an earful.

"Hello there," the man said, extending his hand to Megan. "I'm Fred, and I own this place. You must be Megan."

"I am." She gestured toward Dylan. "And this is Dylan. He's helping me get the alpacas back to Choteau, if we can reach an agreement, that is." She wanted to make sure Fred knew who was in charge.

Dylan wasn't ever going to be a partner, silent or not.

"Like I said on the phone," Fred said, waving them to follow as he walked to a small shed. "These are huacaya alpacas, one female, one male. What I didn't realize until yesterday is that the female is pregnant. Not sure if that's going to make a difference or not."

That complicated her plan. She hadn't planned for raising a cria. And what would the quality of the baby alpaca's fleece be?

"So, I take it you aren't sure which other alpaca was involved," Dylan said, asking one of the questions on her mind.

"Unfortunately, no," Fred said. "I had a weak fence I didn't get repaired in a timely manner, and she got through to another pasture. Nature took its course, and I guess the timing was right."

"But you have only huacayas, right?" she asked.

"I have two suris. Just got them. Male and female."

"So it could be a cross."

"Could be, but not likely. The suri male's a little on the young side. Let's go inside and take a look at the animals and see if they're what you had in mind."

A cria. They were so cute. Something she could raise herself, but not so closely that the animal imprinted on her and became berserk. And three for the price of two!

The shed was cool and shaded with enough air flowing through to keep it from stifling her. Hooves thumped against the cement floor, and the aroma of hay filled her nose. Two curious brown heads lifted and balanced on the long necks. Both eyed her with brown eyes topped by lashes a movie starlet would covet.

Megan sucked in a breath.

Be calm. Be professional.

Fred opened the stall door for her, and she slipped inside, Dylan right behind her. Fred grabbed the alpaca's halter, and she began to examine the animal, starting with its head.

The ears were good, no damage she could see. And the facial bones were normal conformity.

"You want to look at the mouth?" Dylan asked.

She nodded, and Dylan pried open the animal's mouth, much

to its annoyance. A quick look while she held her breath showed her there were no abnormalities that would cause the alpaca to have problems eating. After Dylan released the head, she stepped back.

"Well, at least she didn't spit," Megan said as she ran her hand down the spine. A slight concave in the back caused her to pause. She glanced at Fred.

"I got her that way." He shrugged. "Hasn't been a problem. Previous owner said she'd been in a fight with a male that had gotten aggressive."

But it might be why he was willing to let her go as inexpensively as he was. If it was truly an injury, it wouldn't be passed to the cria, but if it were genetic, that was another story.

Crouching, she examined the legs. They were solid, shaped correctly, and not stiff.

The slight swayback was the only issue she could see. That, and the unexpected pregnancy.

"This one's okay," she said. Showing enthusiasm as a buyer never worked well.

They went through the same process with the male who was sound, except it was evident he was much older than the female.

"He's still a good breeder," Fred remarked when she asked about the alpaca's age.

She nodded but didn't comment.

When they were done, they left the shed.

"I told you what I'm asking," Fred said, "and that remains the same, even though there will be three eventually. The other condition, though, is you're taking them as is. If there are any problems down the road, they're yours to handle, although the possibility of that happening is slim to none with this pair," he finished confidently.

"Can you give us a moment to discuss this?" Dylan asked.

She pushed away her irritation at his interference. Truthfully, she did want to think about it before her final decision, and talking it out with him was as good away as any. Her pique was her own sheer orneriness.

"Sure," Fred said.

They walked toward the fence surrounding the open pasture where a few dozen alpacas grazed in the distance. The spring green grass waved lazily in a soft breeze and songbirds chirped in a nearby tree.

"Idyllic," she said, leaning against the fence and looking

across the expanse.

"Yes." Dylan positioned himself next to her but didn't say anything more.

If she bought these two animals, she was taking a bit of a risk. This was the female's first pregnancy—who knew what could go wrong? And though the older alpaca male might be breeding just fine now, there was a reason he was going so cheaply: he was nearing his expiration date.

On the other hand, they were a start. They would both provide fleece that would allow her to build the next steps of her plan. The fleece she'd examined had been average but solid to work with. She could learn without investing too much.

"What do you think?" she finally asked Dylan. He may not know alpacas, but he knew animals.

"I'm not much of an expert on alpacas," he said with a grin.

"But ..."

He changed his position so the front of his body was facing her. "It might be best to wait until something else comes along. That is, if you're planning on breeding them. If I were buying cattle, I'd want a track record. From what you told me, Fred doesn't seem to have one for either one of these animals. I have a feeling he buys cheap and takes his chances."

"I'm going to have to do the same. I don't have the money for any fancy alpacas. If this works out, then I've got a base to build on."

"And if it doesn't?" he asked.

"Then I guess I'm back to square one and I'll need to think of something else."

"Look, I know you were dead set against the idea when we got here, but I'm still willing to invest in your business. However you want to structure it is fine by me. It could even be a loan. Wouldn't that allow you to get a better pair to start with?"

"I'm not taking your money," she said, her voice steely.

He looked back out toward the herd.

Damn. He was only trying to help, and she was being bitchy.

"I don't mean it the way it sounds." She touched his arm to get his attention back to her. "It's just ... well ..." She fumbled for the right words as he swung his head back toward her, his wolf-gray eyes feeling like they were drilling right through her. "I need to feel like I built this business on my own, that no one—no government agent, no banker, no friend, and especially no relative—will ever be able to take it from me."

He nodded. "Okay, then. I guess I'm going to have to learn a lot about alpacas."

"Why? It isn't your job."

"Because," he said, leaning closer, "I want to get closer to you, and that seems like a damn good way to do it." He planted his lips on hers and kissed her. "Now let's get these guys home."

He took her hand and they walked back to where Fred waited.

# # #

The next few days were a blend of excitement and exhaustion. Finn and Flora, as she decided to call the alpacas, turned out to have pleasant dispositions, although Flora could be a little temperamental at times. Megan chalked it up to hormones.

"I understand, sweet girl," she told Flora. "Some strange thing has entered your body and you have no idea what's going on. It's got to be confusing."

Flora simply stared at her for a few moments, then went back to eating.

Dylan had helped her get them adjusted, but then told her he wasn't going to be around that weekend. Something about helping Nick out on a fishing trip.

She told herself it was no problem.

But every time she hit a situation where an extra pair of hands would be helpful, she hoped he'd have nothing but empty hooks for abandoning her.

Every night she fell into bed exhausted, and every morning she practically leapt out of bed with joy. She'd done it! She was on her way.

"They are so adorable," she told Courtney when she went back to work on Monday. "I can't wait until the cria arrives!"

"Cria?" Courtney stopped loading fresh bear claws into the pastry case.

"Baby alpaca."

"Why can't they just call it that?" She went back to loading the pastries.

"I don't know, but that's what it is."

"So when is this little critter going to arrive?"

"Well, the previous owner didn't know when exactly she got pregnant. But it takes them between eleven and twelve months from the time of conception to birth."

"Ugh. Poor things."

A sweet, bright aroma reached her nose. "Mmm, something smells yummy."

"Raspberry Danish," Courtney said. "The berries are coming into season. It's the perfect start for the first day of June."

The bell rang. Two of the women who'd become their regulars came into the shop.

"I told you!" one said to the other. "Cora up at the Hutterite place told me the new lady came in and bought a bunch of raspberries." She gave an exaggerated sniff. "And it smells like they're being used well."

"I wonder when I'll stop being the new lady," Courtney said.

Megan chuckled. And so the morning began.

Most of regulars stopped in, as if released by the change of the month. The lunch rush was busy for a Monday, and Megan found herself creating box after box of pastries for the last week of school. She was about to end her shift at three when a group of six giggling teenagers came in.

"Would you mind staying another half hour?" Courtney asked. "Or do your fur babies need you?"

"They'll be okay on their own. They actually don't need all that much close care," she replied. "I can stay."

"Thanks."

The kids were polite but indecisive, probably more used to the Cokes and burgers at Mae's place.

"How about iced coffee and some chocolate chip cookies?" she suggested. "They came out of the oven a short time ago, so they are nice and warm."

"Good for me," one guy said.

"Can I have iced tea instead?" a pale teen asked. She looked young to be with this crowd.

"Sure." There were a few more requests for tea, then Megan went back to the counter and started pulling the order together. She'd delivered it when the bell rang again, and Dave Brockman walked in. He gave her a big smile, grabbed a newspaper from the pile, and headed for the pastry counter where Courtney was waiting.

Megan took her time returning to the coffee area. She hadn't responded to the list of available times Dave had sent. Whether it was because he made her uncomfortable or she didn't want to be seen with him in public, she wasn't quite sure.

When Courtney waved at her to come get the man's coffee, she didn't have much choice.

"Here you go, Dave," she said. "Anything else?"

"You haven't answered my text," he said with a smile.

"I've been a bit busy. I purchased my first two alpacas on Thursday."

"How exciting for you," he said, his smile broadening. "That makes our meeting more important. When are you available for lunch next?"

"Tomorrow," she said reluctantly. He'd find out from Courtney if she didn't answer.

"Good. Let's do it then."

"Okay." May as well get it over with.

"I don't suppose you'd want to come here."

"Not really," she said. "It's my day off."

He nodded. "Our only other choice is a burger somewhere, then." He seemed to be disappointed at the idea. "Unless ..." He leaned forward. "Why don't you come over to my place? I'll have the housekeeper make up some fresh salads—she's really good at it—and I'll pick up one of Trish's pies from the market. I've built a nice patio so we can sit outside. What do you think?"

"I ... um ... I'm not sure that's a good idea." Her aunt's voice thundered in her brain. *You went to a boy's house. And you were alone! You'll deserve whatever you get.*

Her aunt hadn't been a particularly sympathetic woman.

Dave snapped his fingers. "I'll tell you what! I'll invite Cassandra as well. Then you can get an attorney's perspective on what to do to make sure you're never sued or something like that."

Who knew a fiber business could be so dangerous? But it would be good to know more people in town, and an attorney was a good person to get to know.

"Okay. I'll be there."

Chapter 17

Basket of fresh-baked scones in hand, Megan reached Dave's house at about eleven on Tuesday. As she pulled down the long driveway, she noted the contrast to the Becks' entrance a little farther south. The ranch's wooden gate was tall, all polished wood. The road itself was freshly graded.

When the house came into view, she stopped her car. It was huge!

A balcony crossed the entire second story of the peeled-log home providing an overhang to the first story where plate glass windows peeked out from between the uprights. The upstairs, with its three peaked dormer windows, also gleamed with glass. Everything was polished, trimmed, and orderly.

The place screamed money.

Oh, she was so out of her element.

She parked her aging Volvo next to a Toyota Tacoma, also shiny with care, although that seemed out of place on a working ranch.

Which obviously this wasn't.

She took a deep breath and walked up to what she assumed was the front door. The sight of a doorbell was reassuring. She pressed it, which created booming bell peels throughout the house, almost like she was standing right outside a church steeple during an important celebration.

Dave opened the door and smiled at her as the bells were fading away. The scent of sandalwood wafted over her.

"Come in, come in."

"Nice chimes."

He chuckled. "It's a bit of an overkill, I'll agree, but they remind me of a trip I took to England about ten years ago."

And that's why they fit into a ranch house. Right.

"I made some scones."

"Great. Great. Follow me. Cassandra's waiting on the patio."

He shut the front door behind her, then led the way through a living room decorated with leather furniture and scattered rugs over rust tile. A doorway in between a state of the art kitchen and a traditional dining room dominated by a massive wooden table led outside.

Inside the kitchen, a small, Hispanic woman sorted her way through a mound of vegetables as she created three good-sized salads.

"She came with me from California," Dave said as he pushed open a screen door. "Her husband is my horse trainer. He's here, too."

What exactly did Dave Brockman do for a living?

Cassandra looked like she belonged exactly where she was, sitting on a rich man's patio with a crystal glass of white wine in her manicured hand. Megan forced herself not to look down on her own clean but broken nails.

What was she doing here?

"Welcome, Megan," Cassandra said, bestowing a pleasant smile on her. "Would you like a glass of wine? We've got it on ice right here."

"Uh, sure."

"Let me take those into the kitchen," Dave said, reaching for the scones. "I'll have Angie plate them."

"Okay."

"It's all a bit overwhelming, isn't it?" Cassandra asked after Megan had taken a seat. "Dave never did know how to do things in half measures."

Swallowing the wine she'd gulped in the name of steadying her nerves, Megan grabbed the conversation lifeline. "So how long have you known him?" she asked.

"We met in Chicago, oh, let's see, about five years ago now. Not too long before I decided to come here."

"Why on heaven's earth *did* you come here?" Megan asked.

"Well, so did you. Why did you uproot yourself from the South and move to the wild, wild West?"

"I needed to get away from some things," Megan said, hoping the answer would satisfy.

"The same. And family lore says that a distant relation lived here a long time ago, so I figured I'd check it out. I needed a change of pace from the big city. This was perfect, the old-boy lawyers needed some female competition, so here I am."

"You do family law?"

"And estate planning, real estate, that kind of thing."

"Oh." Maybe Cassandra was different from the attorneys her relatives had hired, the ones who'd stripped Megan of any significant assets. They'd even claimed her cousins owned Granny's antique spinning wheel, even though she'd never seen any of them pick up a knitting needle, much less a piece of wool.

"Angie should have our lunches ready soon," Dave said coming over to them, a second bottle of wine in his hand. "I brought out another Riesling, too," he said, displaying the bottle to Cassandra and Megan. "This one's from the Mission Mountain Winery, which I think is on Flathead Lake somewhere."

"Should be interesting," Cassandra said, a faint note of sarcasm in her tone.

"You need to expand your thinking," Dave said with a grin. "You Midwest women are all alike. Once you find something you like, you stick to it."

"I try lots of different wines and you know it," Cassandra said with a small smile and shake of her head. "I just like to stick to recognized wine regions—you know, France, Italy, California, New Zealand."

"She's a total and complete snob," Dave said to Megan, but his tone was affectionate.

They really were good friends.

Dave's gaze lingered a little longer on Cassandra, like he wanted more than friendship, but she wasn't interested.

Then why was he chasing Megan so persistently?

She'd best step carefully.

"So, Megan," he said, abruptly turning to her, "why don't you lay out your business plan for us."

She took a sip of her wine to buy time. Other than Dylan, she'd never explained her ideas to anyone with business knowledge, afraid if she did that they wouldn't be good enough. But she'd already started laying out money, so advice would be better than doing things in a vacuum.

"I want to create a business that covers the entire process of making a garment, from raising the animals for fleece to creating garments. I also want to teach people about the process—you know, like the farm-to-table movement. This is the fleece-to-fabric movement. In fact, that's what I'm going to call the company: From Fleece to Fabric."

"Great name," Dave said with enthusiasm.

"You should get that trademarked," Cassandra said.

"I wouldn't know how to go about doing that," Megan said.

"I can help you."

"I ... uh ... can't really afford to pay you." She shrugged. "I'm a waitress, you know."

"You don't have to pay me. I do a certain amount of pro bono work as part of giving back to the community."

Megan hesitated, ready to get into her default mode of not taking any handouts, but if it was something Cassandra was willing to do, she shouldn't let her pride get in the way.

"You should also incorporate or get an LLC," she said. "Just to protect yourself and your assets in case anyone sues."

"What would they sue me for? I'm not doing anything that could injure anyone."

"A, you have animals. They could get out and hurt someone. B, you'll be working with machinery of a sort, your spinning wheels." Cassandra ticked her reasons off on her fingers. "C, people are very imaginative when it comes to trying to get money out of other people."

Dave chuckled. "You can say that again. Especially the animal part. I've been sued over injuries presumably caused by my horses more often than I can count. Even by one guy who was trying to steal the beast!"

People actually did things like that? She couldn't even imagine the mental twist it would require to sue a man while trying to rob him.

"Keeps attorneys busy," Cassandra said. "Anyway, I'll point you in the right direction. You'll need to do all the work and handle the fees yourself; I'd simply be an advisor."

"Thank you. That's very kind of you."

"I like helping new business owners get started, especially women."

Angie came through the door with a tray in her hands, the surface covered with three brimming salads.

"Where did you find those amazing vegetables?" Megan asked.

"In the Hutterite colony," Angie answered. "It's the best place to find greens in this state. Everything else is limp."

The plates were deposited on the table with grace.

"Angie is a stickler for feeding me well. When she first came up here last year, I thought she was going to drive me crazy about the food. Brown, brown, was all she said."

"I also don't understand why they consider Jell-O a salad up here. It is sugar water with a few slivers of cabbage and carrot." She gave a mock shudder as she added the plate of scones to the table.

"I don't know what I'd do without you," Dave said with a smile.

"Shrivel up and die, I think," Angie replied as she turned back to the kitchen.

Dave roared with laughter.

Very different from Megan's experience growing up. The South, no matter how modern it may seem, had rules, and one had best follow them, especially as a servant.

Or if you were someone perceived as trying to rise above her level by marrying the banker's son.

That was why people had come west in the beginning: to escape the strictures of civilization and start a new life, just like she was doing.

She smiled at Cassandra and Dave. They were good people. She had nothing to be suspicious about.

"Dig in," Dave said. "I promise it's as good as it looks."

And it was.

Thankfully, there was no escarole. The stiff stalks and short curly leaves were tasty, but impossible to eat with any kind of decorum. And this situation required she not create any greasy food stains.

The conversation meandered between places Dave and Cassandra had been, Megan's trip across the country, and the plusses and minuses of living in Choteau.

"You absolutely need to go to Freezeout Lake when the geese come through in the fall. It's too late now for the spring migration," Dave said. "It is an unbelievable sight. All the birds seem to land and take off at once. And the noise! It's damn loud there!" His laugh was hearty.

"I went once with Jarod when I was dating him," Cassandra said.

"Ah, yes, the Becks." Dave turned to Megan. "They live next ranch to the south," he said.

"Yes," she replied. "I've been there."

"Oh?" Dave said, his smile dimming.

"Dylan helped me with the alpacas," she replied. No need to mention she'd been there for the Memorial Day picnic.

The silence lingered for a few seconds, and Dave exchanged looks with Cassandra.

What did they know that she didn't?

"You must hear a lot as a waitress," Cassandra said. "We heard that a while back there was a fence cut between Dave's and the Beck land way back into the foothills. Do you know if they've had any other troubles?"

"We're curious because if they have any kind of trouble, it's bound to migrate next door," Dave said.

"I'd think they'd tell you themselves," Megan said.

"We don't see them much anymore," Cassandra said. "Ever since I broke up with Jarod, it's been … well … awkward." She fluttered her hands like a Southern belle.

That woman had never been helpless in her life. And why was it a "we"? Wasn't this simply Dave's ranch?

Questions she didn't have answers to, and questions wasn't going to ask.

"Sorry," she said. "I haven't heard anything."

Dave leaned back in his chair and picked up his wineglass.

Had he relaxed, or was he only attempting to look that way?

She preferred Dylan's straightforward manner.

After picking up her own wineglass, she stared at the mountains in the distance for a moment. Was there a graceful way for her to leave?

The screen door clanked shut and she looked up to see Angie returning with three plates on her tray and what looked like a slice of pie on each.

"Perfect timing as always," Dave said.

Angie nodded and began the process of putting down the plates and picking up the salad bowls. Her movements were as economical as Megan's were when she was serving. She could see why Dave thought of Angie as a valuable employee.

But there was no way she could make her excuses to leave before eating the slice of pie.

"Thank you," Dave said and Angie returned to the kitchen. "Dig in," he continued, "Trish does make some of the best pies I've ever tasted."

"We digressed before you could tell us more about exactly what you're planning with your business," Cassandra said. "Why don't you continue?"

So Megan told them in more detail. It actually helped to spell it out for the two of them, because she was forced to be clear about the steps she needed to take and the order in which they needed to happen. Both asked pointed but helpful questions.

As they talked, she grew more animated. She'd been dreaming about this business since she was in her teens. Now it was about to come true. She had alpacas. She'd taught her first class. She was on her way.

Nothing could stop her now.

# # #

On her drive back home, Megan cranked up the music, belting out the lyrics to "Drunk in Heels" as Jennifer Nettles sang the verses about the innate ability of women—well, some women—to manage their lives while teetering on a skinny nail. As the saying went, Ginger Rogers did everything Fred Astaire did, only she did it backward and in heels.

A talent Megan had never been able to manage.

But how well did Jennifer Nettles spin? These were the questions of life, Granny used to say. It was useless to aspire to have every talent out there, best to be satisfied with the ones God granted you.

Once in town, Megan circled back around the county building and headed down a side street to the post office. The clerk waved as she walked into the building, and she smiled and waved back. Her feelings of success bubbled inside her. She'd made an appointment with Cassandra to go over the particulars of setting up an LLC and registering a name. Dave had recommended checking with an insurance agent as well.

The box clicked open, and she pulled out the regular dose of newspaper circulars, credit card offers, and request for charitable contributions. As she sorted through the small pile by the recycle bin, she was startled to see an envelope with a return address in Asheville. No one knew where she was.

Dropping the reset of the mail in the bin, she ripped open the envelope. Inside was a thin piece of pink paper with a faint rose watermark. She glanced at the signature and saw it was from one of the girls who'd been friendly to her in high school.

After scanning the letter, she took in a deep breath and began more slowly from the top. When she'd read it again, she stuffed both it and the envelope in her purse. Then she returned to her car, the prick of fear bursting her bubble of euphoria.

# # #

Ten people showed up for Megan's knitting class. She was happy to see the return of Anne, the school secretary, and the mother and daughter team. But when Faith walked in, she wanted

171

to groan.

After making sure that everyone had the right sized circular needles to begin the hat, she distributed the yarn they'd need.

"I'm assuming everyone knows how to cast on," she began. "Is there anyone who thinks they may need help?"

No one said anything.

"Great. Then cast on 92 stitches if you're making this for a young person or 104 stitches if you're making it for yourself or another adult."

She cast on her own stitches while keeping an eye on her students. Once she was done, she walked around the table to make sure everyone was being successful. Darcie and her mother finished quickly and were chatting. As she'd predicted, though, Faith was struggling.

"I forget how to do this every time!" The needles clattered to the table in frustration.

"How do you cast on?" Megan asked. There were many methods, and she didn't want to confuse Faith any more than she was.

The woman showed her a complex strategy involving looping the yarn around one hand, slipping the needle through a loop, and snagging the yarn on the needle. It looked like Faith was attempting a style of long tail cast on but had invented her own variation.

No wonder it was so difficult.

"Have you tried simply knitting the stitches on?"

"What do you mean? How can you knit stitches that aren't there?"

"Like this." Megan made a slip knot, slid the needle through, and showed Faith how to knit and leave both stitches on the needle.

"I like my way better," Faith said after attempting to mimic the pattern.

"This might be easier, though."

"I dunno."

Megan moved on to the next student. From the corner of her eye, she saw Anne step over to Faith to help her.

Once all the stitches were cast on, Megan proceeded to the next step of the pattern. "The purpose of this first group of lessons is to learn to work with different colors and to read a chart. Knowing this will allow you to create all kinds of lovely pieces."

"Definitely," Roxanne said. "This set is beautiful. It's one of the reasons I decided to sign up for this class."

"Me too," Darcie said. "That, and I needed another break from the twins."

The group laughed in common understanding. All except Faith, who was steadily glaring at her needles.

Twins. Megan couldn't even imagine having a single child, never mind two at once.

For the next twenty rounds, using the main color, the group descended into the genial comradery that usually accompanied a group of knitters. Adding the next color was fairly simple, even Faith managed it. When they got to the chart, however, Faith's struggles began again.

Megan tried to help her, but there were plenty of other students to attend to, and soon Faith's yarn was a mess.

"I am so frustrated and you're not helping me!" she accused Megan.

"Oh, Faith, I'm sorry, but this lady needs help, too. I can't be with everyone at once. I assumed most people taking this class were experienced knitters."

"I can knit," Faith said. "You can't teach!"

"Now, now, Faith," Anne said, laying her own knitting on the table and coming over to the distraught woman. "We all know you can knit, but most of what you do is basic knit and purl. This is a bit more complicated than that. Perhaps you want to practice more on simpler projects and take this class later on."

"Are you saying I can't do this?" If the woman got any tenser, her gray curls would no doubt turn into corkscrews, as impossible as that was in reality.

"No," Anne replied patiently. "I'm thinking maybe you can't do this *yet*."

Faith's lips opened, closed, and practiced acrobatic movements for the next few seconds.

"I'll be teaching an easier class in the fall," Megan said, hoping to smooth things over. "I'm sure the lifelong learning team would be happy to transfer your class fees to that one." She glanced at Anne, who nodded.

Without speaking, Faith stuffed her materials in her bag and walked out of the room, letting the door thud closed behind her.

Everyone stared at the closed door for a few moments.

"Well," said Roxanne, "that was fun."

The hard knot of tension dissipated from the room, and soon the clack of needles and low hum of conversation replaced it.

Casey Dawes

"Don't worry," Anne said placing a hand on Megan's shoulder. "Faith gets like that. Always has. I'll handle it in the morning and get her fees refunded. I'm afraid you're out the yarn, though."

"Small price," Megan said.

Hopefully, that was all she'd have to pay.

Chapter 18

"Hey, Cameron," Dylan said to his brother. "I need to go into town for supplies. Want to come with?"

Cameron shook his head. "I'll be going out for a walk shortly."

Dylan blew a breath between tight lips. The only place Cameron ever went was to the VA administration in Great Falls and the veteran's hall in a small, rundown building on a side street in Choteau. His brother wasn't really living, just marking time.

"I'll go with you."

"Why?" Cameron looked at him, his brows narrow with suspicion.

"So we can talk, man."

"I don't need any help."

"Well, I do. I need to sort some things out, and you were always good for that."

Cameron's shoulders relaxed a bit. "A woman."

"Kind of, but there's more than that."

Cameron nodded slowly, as if trying to fit this unusual request into the order he'd made in his mind. "Give me an hour to clean up and handle some things and I'll be ready."

"Good."

He headed up the stairs, his slippered feet barely making a sound. Cameron was becoming a ghost, a shadow of his brother who'd shipped out years ago. Like the rest of them, Cameron had found it necessary to put distance between himself and the family tragedy. Like CJ, he'd chosen to put miles between himself and Montana. Jarod had buried himself in keeping the ranch going, and Kaiden had focused on his rocks and his education.

And he'd taken every chance he could to wander off to paint, immersing himself in color and style. All to no avail.

After helping Jarod with a few of the morning chores, he returned to the house to find Cameron sitting in one of the porch rockers staring at the distant mountains. When Dylan climbed the front steps, he rose as if knowing he was there without even looking.

No words were exchanged. Cameron simply got up, headed

over to the side steps, and descended.

Dylan followed.

The air was still cool enough at nine in the morning, although the sun was already soaring toward the center of the sky, the summer solstice only a few weeks away. They'd be blessed with almost sixteen hours of the sun, double that of the shortest day of winter. As they walked, he sensed the warmth filtering through the fabric of his clothes and the pores of his skin, seeking to heat the marrow of his bones.

After a too-long winter, it felt good.

At six feet, Cameron's stride was slightly longer than Dylan's, and his pace was quicker, the result of long daily walks since he'd gotten home a little over three months ago. Soon Dylan's pulse beat faster, his breath became quicker, and he was struggling a little to keep up. Cameron was oblivious.

So much for a nice brotherly conversation.

When they reached the top of an incline, Cameron stopped and, with his hand on his hip, stretched backward to lift his face to the sun.

"Every day," he said, "I thank God I'm alive, and then I curse Him for allowing wars to occur." He righted himself and looked at Dylan. "Then He reminds me about our free will."

Dylan chuckled. "Yeah, we're really good at messing up. Not so good at putting it together."

"So what's on your mind?" Cameron asked as he started down the hill, although at a more restrained pace.

"I'm thinking about running for office."

"You want to join that mob in Washington? Whatever for?"

"Nope. Local office. Representative in Helena. The old guy is retiring."

"How do you know that?"

"He told me. I was at the bistro one day, and we got to talking."

"Do you think you have a chance?" Cameron asked.

"I've got no idea. I've got some time to explore the possibilities. Filing doesn't open until January."

"Oh." The path swung to the left. Across from them, on another green-swathed hill, a doe and two fawns grazed. She looked up as they walked, then dismissed them as no threat and went back to nibbling. Above, a crow rode the air drafts, the faint caw reaching them from afar.

"I feel like I need to contribute something to the state, put in my share. And no offense, but the military seems a little drastic to me."

"It's not for everyone, that's for sure. The hardest part isn't the training or even being away from home. It's that everyone back here is going about their daily lives without thinking too much about what goes on over there. It doesn't really hit you until you come stateside after being away, but once you realize that's what's going on, you feel separate from the rest of the country. And no matter how many times someone says, 'Thank you for your service,' it doesn't quite make up for it."

"I didn't realize you were so bitter about it."

"I'm not, really. It's just a fact of life—one of the unintended consequences of an all-volunteer army."

Dylan let silence linger as they made their way down a steep slope that became rockier as they reached the bottom. A rivulet meandered through the narrow canyon with a lone Russian olive tree flourishing on its banks.

"Damn trees," Dylan muttered. "I wish we could get rid of them all and give the natives a chance to come back."

Cameron didn't comment. He settled on a boulder not too far from the stream and pulled out two sticks of jerky and handed one to Dylan.

"So, what are you going to tell people to convince them you're the best person for the job?" Cameron asked after he'd bitten of a piece and chewed for several minutes.

"I'm a lifelong Montanan."

"When are you going to stop beating that drum?" Cameron shook his head. "Yes, it's important to a lot of people—too many, probably. But it's not the be-all and end-all. Like it or not, Montana is changing. If we're ever going to lift this state out of the bottom 25 percent of the nation, we're going to need to do some different kind of thinking."

"Sounds like you should be the one to run for office," Dylan said.

"Not me. I did my time, remember? This is your harebrained idea. I'm just saying that being a born and raised Montanan isn't something you should lead with, especially if it comes out that you've never left the state. Thank God you got past the idiot idea that you wouldn't date anyone who hadn't lived here all her life."

"I'm just helping Megan out." Dylan stood up and walked away. Where did his brother get off being so critical?

"Right. I've met her. And if you don't think you're interested, you're in serious denial."

Dylan grit his teeth and let it ride.

"So, what other reasons do you have to give for being the best person for office?" Cameron stood and walked down to where Dylan was watching the water go by.

"Because I care," Dylan said, reaching down into himself for the truth of the matter. "It matters to me that we have clean water and enough of it to irrigate our land, use for our daily needs, and still be able to throw a line in a trout stream and catch something. Native women should get to stop worrying about being abducted. And you're right, the economy could do a better job. When a retail chain that's the largest employer in the state is paying only minimum wage, there's a problem."

He surprised himself with the amount of passion he had. Totally unexpected. Maybe he did want to run after all. Did he care enough to put up with the wrangling that sitting with a huge group of people with diverse backgrounds, beliefs, and goals meant?

"Well done," Cameron said. "Let's walk." He led the way farther down the creek where they had to go single file, then up the next rise on a narrow path.

How long a walk were they going on? It could be hours. No one ever knew where Cameron went or how long he'd be gone. It just happened every day, no matter what the weather.

They walked in silence for another half hour, although his mind was full of chatter for the first fifteen minutes. What would be the best way to go about campaigning if he did put his hat in the ring? Should he start before the filing happened? Coordinate with the outgoing rep and get his endorsement?

"You're thinking too hard," Cameron said. "It's disturbing the atmosphere. Try just being here."

As if he had any choice.

So he tried to concentrate on the colors, as if he were preparing to paint the variety of greens spread on the palette before him. Even the way the sun hit the grass changed its hue. Here and there patches were becoming golden as the days warmed.

The blue sky was so crisp that the edges of the hills seemed outlined by a knife, with little tuffs of blades that had managed to escape poking into the air. A dark shape caught his eye.

"Cameron," he whispered and pointed.

The bear and her cub came into focus, its flat dish face and recognizable hump proclaiming it a grizzly. Yet another important icon of disagreement. Ranchers wanted them penned back in the mountains where they'd been for decades. Environmentalists fought for their expansion. Finding a compromise would require more skill than negotiating a truce between his family members ever had.

And he'd definitely been the peacemaker in the family, settling feuds between all his siblings. Somehow, he'd found a way to make one person understand what the other was thinking. Surely he could leverage that ability in the courthouse.

A certainty arose from within. He could do it.

With a smile, he picked up his pace and matched Cameron's stride.

# # #

Jarod and Cameron were in the office when Dylan brought the mail in a few days later. Cameron glanced at the letter addressed to him, then slipped it in his pocket. Jarod used the letter opener on the desk to open the very official-looking envelope Dylan had handed him. He scanned it, then handed it to Dylan.

"Shit," Dylan said after reading it, and then passed it to Cameron.

"Who the hell is Choteau Mineral Development?" he asked.

"No idea," Jarod said.

Dylan sat at the desk and pulled up the internet. "Says here it's a privately held corporation, but there are no details on the owners. If we got that notice of mineral exploration from them, they must be the ones who own the rights."

"But there's no record of it in the courthouse," Jarod said.

Dylan clicked a few more keys. "There is now. It was filed by the corporation. Apparently they obtained the rights from some unnamed third party."

"How did that third party get the rights?"

"That's the key question," Cameron said. "How are you and CJ coming with the research?" he asked Dylan.

"CJ found some information in the Mormon database. Alice died in the 1980s of cancer. Her husband, Greg, lived until sometime in the 2000s when he died of heart problems."

"And the kids? What were their names?" Jarod asked.

"Greg Jr. and Tommy. We thought we had Greg's info, but

179

Casey Dawes

the trail disappeared somewhere near Cairo, Illinois."

"Where's that?" Jarod asked.

"Southern Illinois, near the Ohio River."

"Local records might have more information," Cameron mentioned.

"Maybe, but we don't have the PI anymore," Dylan pointed out.

"Then someone needs to go—feet on the ground," Cameron said.

Jarod and Dylan looked pointedly at their brother.

"Oh no. Not me." He touched his pocket. "I may have something else I need to take care of."

"Well, it can't be me," Jarod said. "I've got a new horse to train, and someone has to keep this ranch going."

"Not to mention a wedding in three months."

"That's Samantha's department."

"Somehow," Dylan said, "I don't think she'll let you get away with being a silent partner."

Jarod grinned. "Probably not."

His older brother looked so damn happy it made Dylan's heart ache.

"Well," he said, "let me talk to CJ, see if she has time."

"We should also get a lawyer on this," Cameron said. "There must be some way to establish who held the rights before this corporation. It could even be the same people or person who held the rights before."

"Should probably be an attorney from Great Falls," Jarod suggested. "Whoever is doing this looks like they know their way around the law. We want someone experienced."

"And someone who will work for the little guy," Dylan added.

"I can look into that," Cameron said. "It's too bad Kaiden isn't here."

"Yeah," Jarod agreed. "He'd know the right questions to ask."

"Time to loop him in," Dylan said.

"Yep." Jarod looked around at them. "The Becks are fighting back."

And, just like they had when they were kids, they stacked their fists and pumped them up and down together.

# # #

Dylan hummed as he got ready to head out the next morning.

180

For the first time in a long time, his family was pulling together. Placing his iPad on the passenger seat and his mug of coffee in the cupholder, he started to close the door and head out to CJ and Nick's place.

"Wait a sec," Cameron called out. He walked down the front steps with more energy than Dylan had seen since he'd come home. "I need to ask you something."

"Sure." Dylan stepped back out of the truck.

"The letter I got ... it was from a buddy of mine ... his wife's sister, actually. He was killed in combat."

"Oh, man, I'm sorry."

"Yeah. He was a good man, lived in Oklahoma. His wife and her sister came over to Europe one time and we both got leave to head to Italy. They were great women, and we had a lot of fun. Anyway, the letter is from the sister. It seems my buddy's wife has a six-month-old, and she's devastated. The sister thought it might help out if I took a trip down there."

Dylan suppressed all kinds of questions, the primary being about just how much fun Cameron had had with the sister. "So what do you need?"

"I'll need a ride to the airport. I wanted to talk to you before I made the reservations."

"Sure." Dylan shrugged. "It's not like I have pressing plans. Any time should be good."

"Thanks." Cameron turned and headed away from the house and truck, up toward another path he'd worn through the fields in his relentless walking.

There was obviously a lot more going on with his brother than was apparent on the surface. Dylan climbed back in his pickup and headed out to the cabin CJ shared with Nick and his son.

In about a half hour, his truck climbed the gravel drive to the small knoll where Nick had situated his house. It was a perfect location, enough room to hold the horses and storage areas Nick needed as an outfitter but also room for a nice size home with million-dollar views of the mountains.

Before CJ had fully moved in, Nick had built an addition to the house to house her photography studio and office, complete with separate entrance and necessary coffee machine.

"Hey, sis," Dylan said as he opened the door.

"Hey yourself." She shuffled some papers around and swiveled the monitor so he could see what she'd been working on. "Updated the website. What do you think?"

The images faded from one to another, seamlessly interpreting a world seldom seen by the average person. Here a lynx peeked from a ring of ferns, there two bear cubs wrestled each other; bison scenes merged with teepees from a Blackfeet summer camp that transitioned into an action shot from Indian horse races. The last few showed less happy aspects of the human condition—homeless in an alleyway, the dead eyes of a woman working the streets of Seattle—before returning to the sweet hand of a newborn nestled in an old man's hand and the final shot of bear grass framed against the rising sun in the mountains.

"Wow," he said, "you're doing amazing work."

"Thanks. I just keep plugging away. Unless I have a deadline, I don't rush the process. Sometimes, when a picture isn't working, I go curry a horse or something." She shrugged. "Seems to readjust my perspective."

He grunted. It was a little too close to home to delve into. Would he ever pick up a paintbrush again with the same confidence he'd once felt?

"You'll figure it out," she said, digging out a folder from the pile to the side of her desk. "Meanwhile, let's see if we can track down these relatives and find out what the hell's up with these rights. We can't let them drill on our land. We just can't."

"I've built a family tree from the records I could find at the ranch," he said. "I don't know about you, but a picture works better for me than words."

"Got it. So what do you have?"

"The Beck family, a bunch of them, according to the diary we have from that time, came to Montana around 1882. They came because they believed all that horseshit about beef being a great way to get rich."

"And then the winters of 1886 and 1887 hit, and frozen beef was strewn across the plains," she said.

"That's when Charlie Russell painted 'Waiting for a Chinook,'" Dylan said, the memory of the starving steer surrounded by wolves vivid in his mind. If only he could create art that lasted for more than a hundred years. But Russell hadn't been an instant success and was still only a household name in the West. Maybe he'd given up too quickly.

"Great-whatever grandfather Jarod Beck stayed," CJ continued. "While everyone else returned to the Midwest somewhere."

"Be interesting to know where that was," Dylan said. "Might

have some bearing on where the mineral rights wound up."

CJ grabbed a pad and wrote down the question.

"So Jarod got a law degree, married Elizabeth, and set up practice in Choteau. They had two sons, Jacob and Seth." Dylan pointed to the appropriate spot on the family tree.

"And he bought the ranchland."

"Probably for a song at that point," Dylan said. "Jacob, being the oldest, inherited the ranch which was the custom at that time. But we are assuming Seth got the mineral rights, so he would have an inheritance."

"Equitable father," CJ said. "But why couldn't he have noted that somewhere?"

"Seth moved back to the Midwest, married Rose, and they had Alice in their thirties, which was late at that time."

"There could have been a lot of miscarriages and infant deaths. That was also prevalent at the time."

"True," he said. "Or maybe it took Seth some time to settle down. Weren't there some notes in the diaries that indicated Seth had some issues with alcohol?"

"I remember reading something like that."

"Some believe alcoholism is hereditary," he said. "I wonder if either of Alice's two sons were affected."

"Well, Tommy seems to have gotten married based on the newspaper records I found from Fort Wayne, Indiana. But I lost track of him after that. His name isn't in any death record I can find."

"So he may still be alive. Could be, but he'd be close to seventy now, wouldn't he? And what about Greg Jr.?"

"Seventy isn't that old, not anymore," CJ said with a shake of her head. She tapped her pencil on the box Dylan had drawn for Greg. "He seems to have disappeared after high school. He graduated in ..." She consulted her notes. "In 1970 from Jasper High School, the same one Tommy did." She looked up at Dylan. "Feel like taking a trip to Indiana?"

"Other than Yellowstone, I've never left the state and you want my first trip to be to Indiana? Couldn't we go somewhere more glamorous, like the Grand Canyon or something?"

"Unfortunately, Greg didn't go to high school in the Grand Canyon."

"Well, then I guess Indiana it is."

"Sounds like a plan. We can go next week. Nick is heading out on an all-guy fishing trip and taking Trevor with him so he can help with the gear. That'll be the best time for me to get away. Does that work for you?" she asked.

"It's not like I have other things to do," he said.

"I'm sure Jarod would disagree."

"He always does." Dylan grinned at his sister. Getting away for a while might give him a new perspective on his life.

Chapter 19

Megan bussed the last remaining tables and checked the antique clock on the wall. Two o'clock on a Friday afternoon in June. Courtney had left to run errands, and there were only two hours left of work, but there was no need to rush because there was no Friday night date. Nor any plans over the weekend other than a few hours of work on Sunday afternoon.

Snap out of it. She had plenty to do. The alpacas would keep her company, and she could finish knitting the second spring shell she was making. There was sure to be something on one of the streaming services to keep her company.

And to keep her mind off the letter she'd received. According to her friend, the only person in North Carolina she'd sent a postcard with her post office box number, her relatives still hadn't given up the idea that Granny's spinning wheel, along with the rest of her belongings, belonged to them.

They had everything else that was important to her. Every. Single. Damn. Scrap.

Tears threatened to leave Megan's eyes, and she blinked rapidly.

Her friend had said they'd consulted with some distant cousin who was an attorney, and he'd advised that they file a complaint with law enforcement. She didn't think it would go anywhere—police had more important things on their minds—but it was still a threat.

And if anyone did a background search on her, they'd find it.

Good thing she'd gotten all that taken care of a few months ago when she'd applied to teach the adult ed class. And most people in Montana, she'd found, preferred to judge a person's character by talking with them rather than looking up a bunch of things on "the Google."

The bell jangled and she looked up.

Dylan.

He smiled, but a flash of concern crossed his face.

That man saw too damn much.

She gestured him to his usual spot and made for the coffee

machines behind the counter. Taking a few cleansing breaths, she pulled herself together. There was no time to worry about possibilities when there was coffee to serve.

"Here you go," she said. "Do you need anything else?"

"Is something wrong?" he asked, concern in his gray eyes.

"Nothing. I'm fine."

"I do have a sister, you know," he said with a smile.

"Huh?"

"I long ago figured 'I'm fine' generally means the opposite."

Megan shrugged. "It's going to have to do."

"Have I upset you somehow?" he asked.

"The alpacas are fine, thanks for asking." She hadn't realized she'd been irritated by his lack of contact until the words came out of her mouth.

"It wasn't that I wasn't interested, and I'm glad they're doing well." His tone became defensive. "But you want to keep this, whatever it is, casual, and I'm trying to respect your wishes."

"Sorry. You're right." Angst cramped her chest. Some days everything was hard. "I'm feeling my way. I like you, but I don't want to lead you on."

He shook his head. "How about you let me figure that out." He touched her hand. "As long as we keep talking, it will be okay."

Her eyes watered. He was a good, decent man. Why couldn't she relax and stop trying to control everything?

The bell couldn't have come at a more welcome time. Two couples, strangers to her, walked into the bistro. They were laughing over some funny story someone had apparently just told.

She snatched back her hand as a twinge of jealousy went through her. The group seemed so normal. So opposite of what her life had been growing up, or even now.

"What a darling little place!" one woman exclaimed. "Out here in the middle of nowhere."

The whole state was out in the middle of nowhere. Evidently, the woman hadn't noticed.

Megan put a smile on her face. "Welcome to Waldron Creek Cheese and Pastry Shop. Please take a seat anywhere. If you want to have a pastry, please feel free to look at what we have in the glass case. Cheese is over there." She pointed to the cold case by the window overlooking the cheese operation.

"Wow, that's interesting," the man said and walked toward the window. Everyone else followed, except for one woman who stopped by the shelves featuring Megan's knitted goods and spun yarn.

"These are beautiful," the young woman said. "Is this done locally?"

"Actually, they're mine," Megan said. "Do you knit?"

"More than that. I'm part owner of a yarn shop in Great Falls. We're always on the lookout for local yarn. We also feature patterns and samples of garments made with the wool. Is that something you do?"

"I hadn't thought about it before. Most of these are made from patterns my gran taught me. Sometimes I take her basic pattern and jazz them up, like these," Megan said, pointing to the one set of hat and mittens she had on display for the spring and summer months. Both had several strips of colorful patterns in a Fair Isle pattern, and the hat was topped off by a jaunty pompom.

"That's super." The woman fished a business card from her purse. "Tell you what, I'll take these two skeins of the yarn and let you know if we want to carry it. Do you have a business card?"

"Um, no." Something else to take care of. "I'll get you my name and phone. You can text me if you decide you want to stock them." Her chest clenched in anticipation.

"That'll do," the woman said. "Helen Samuels," she said, holding out her card. "It's great to meet you. And if you do have the patterns written down, I'd love to see them, too."

"Um, sure. Thanks. I'll ring these up for you."

I might have an outlet!

She tried to stay calm. What she really wanted to do is jump up and down and yell. Definitely not appropriate.

Instead, she quietly walked to the counter, hit the correct numbers and icons on the Square register, and flipped it for the customer to slide the credit card and sign, smiling and nodding the whole time. Quickly scribbling her phone number and name on a scrap of paper, she handed it to Helen.

"Good," Helen said. "I'll be in touch."

She spent the next half hour serving the group pastries and tea, without much time to do more with Dylan than refill his coffee cup. She needed to figure out what to do with him. Or not. It would be easier if she didn't like him so damn much.

Before leaving, the other woman in the party bought one of the two soft shells Megan had made. She was really going to need to get knitting and spinning.

By a miracle, Dylan was still there when they left. She grabbed a cup of coffee of her own and sat across from him.

"I'm sorry," she said. "I didn't mean to get all thorny on you. It's just that there really hasn't been anyone in my life that I've felt I can trust. Make that I knew I couldn't trust them."

"That's hard," he said. "Not even your grandmother? Sounds like you and she were close."

"Well, I thought I knew her." Granny's betrayal was a hole in her heart.

"What happened?"

"She always said she'd leave everything to me so I could have a place of my own. She knew my dream. With her house and property, I could have realized it easily. She promised."

Megan swallowed several times before she could continue. "I took care of her as she got older, did her shopping, errands, dealt with phone companies, that kind of thing. But after she died ..."

"She hadn't left it to you," Dylan supplied as Megan stared at the grain of wood on the table.

"No. At least that's what my cousin's lawyer said. And I couldn't afford a lawyer of my own to fight it." She glanced at him quickly. "I did take a few things from the house, things that were special to me, before I left."

"Like the spinning wheel."

"Yes. And now they want that back too. They've gone to the sheriff and filed a complaint. They said I stole it. It was mine! They have no use for it! Not one of them knows how to use it." She put her face in her hands and pulled in air. Anything to keep herself from bawling.

The bell jangled again.

Not now!

But she wiped her eyes, grabbed another sip of her coffee, and rose to see who had come in.

"Hello, Cassandra," Dylan said before she could react. "You're timing couldn't be better." He stood and gently pushed Megan back into her chair. "How about I get you a cup of coffee while Megan explains her problem to you."

"Giving away my legal advice?" Cassandra asked, her perfect eyebrows arching in a way that looked like she practiced for hours in front of her mirror.

"In this town, we help each other," Dylan replied and walked to the counter.

"I like my cappuccino with a decorative foam leaf," Cassandra retorted. "Megan does a great job."

"You're going to have coffee and love it," Dylan said. "But to show I have your best interests at heart, I'm even going to pay for your drink. Now talk to Megan, would you?"

Cassandra shook her head. "You Becks are a royal pain in my you-know-where. Now, what's going on?"

Megan hesitated for a moment.

"Give me a dollar," Cassandra said.

Megan fished one from her pocket of tips.

"Good. Now you're my client for the next half hour, and I can't repeat anything you tell me."

"What happens after the half hour?" Megan asked.

"You pay my regular rate. Better talk fast."

That took care of any other hesitation Megan had. Swiftly she told Cassandra what was going on.

"Do you have anything in writing that says your grandmother wanted you to have the spinning wheel?"

Megan had packed up a lot of things before she'd left, including her grandmother's diaries, lots of photos, and old recipes. Fortunately, her relatives hadn't thought any of that was worth pursuing. No, they wanted to strike at the thing she treasured most, and the item most likely to bring in serious cash.

"I don't think so, although I haven't gone through all of Granny's diaries. She might have put something in there."

The espresso machine hissed in the background.

"Then I suggest you go through them as quickly as you can. That's your best bet."

"Won't they say I stole those too?" Megan asked.

"They might, but that's easier to explain away than a big object like a spinning wheel. I suppose it's valuable."

"It's worth something, but they aren't as valuable as people think. Most aren't worth as much as a thousand dollars. And it depends if someone wants to spin with it or use it for decoration," Megan replied.

"You know your stuff," Cassandra said.

"Yes, she does," Dylan said, sliding the drink on the table.

"Thanks," Cassandra said.

"I aim to please. Now, can you help her?"

"We're working on it. Stop being so impatient. You're too much like your brother. How's he doing, by the way?"

"Good. The training business is progressing nicely and the wedding is in September."

Something flickered across Cassandra's face. Everything Megan had heard about her described the attorney as a hard woman, but the expression she'd just seen made Megan wonder. Maybe, like everyone else, there was a little bit of vulnerability hidden under the tough exterior.

"Do you remember any conversations you had with your grandmother about the spinning wheel?"

"Lots," Megan said. "Every time we spent time spinning together. At first, I use a hand spinner. She insisted I had to learn the rhythm and the feel of the twist with my hands before I started to rely on the mechanics of a wheel."

She could still hear the whir of the wheel as her grandmother spun in her memory. The low murmur of her granny's voice lilted over the steady rhythm—stories of the gradual immigration into the hollers and the excitement when the Vanderbilts came to town to stay at the Biltmore Estate. Megan had never been to the estate herself. The tickets were too dear.

"Good," Cassandra said. "Jot down the ones you can remember and the dates if possible. It's particularly important if she mentioned anything about leaving you the wheel."

"Okay. You really think that will help?" Megan asked. It seemed pretty thin to her.

"Well, it might not do much in a court of law, unless you can find written documentation. But it might help us to get them to cease and desist."

"We?" Megan asked. "You mean you'll help me?"

"For a small fee," Cassandra said.

"Oh."

"Don't worry. I'll make it something you can afford. Or perhaps we can find some pretty garment you can make me in trade."

"I'd love to do that," Megan said, thinking it would be a good idea to do that even if she did pay Cassandra.

"Good. Now that I've heard you out, can I get one of those great tarts Trish makes?" Cassandra pulled a file from the briefcase she had. "I've got some work to do and a need a sugar jolt to get it done."

"Of course." Megan plated the tart, rang it up, and took the payment from her own pocket before taking it to the table to which Cassandra had relocated.

"On me," she said.

"Thank you," Cassandra said with a gracious smile. "There's one more thing I need to discuss with you."

"Yes?"

"Can you sit?"

Megan looked around at the almost empty shop, the tourists having gone a half hour before, and sat.

"I wanted to let you know I heard a rumor you might want to take care of if you want your business to succeed in this town."

"What's that?"

"There's someone who's using every opportunity to talk about how bad your spinning class was."

Faith. It had to be. Damn that woman.

"That's wrong, but what do I do about it?" Megan asked.

"I assume there's just one bad apple," Cassandra said.

"As far as I know."

"Then talk to the others. You don't have to say what's going on, but get them to talk up the class and any others you're giving, in a good way." Cassandra drummed her impeccably manicured fingers on her papers. "This town can be hard on out-of-towners. If one person has a bad impression and they talk, they can give someone a reputation they don't deserve."

Was Cassandra talking about Megan ... or herself?

The attorney shook her head. "I just thought I'd let you know." She picked up her folder. "Thanks for the tart."

Megan rose and went back to the counter to make sure all the coffee urns were full. It was almost time for some of the locals to start wandering in for their afternoon shot of coffee.

Cassandra Sanders was turning out to be a better friend than she'd ever anticipated.

# # #

Helen Samuels's interest spurred Megan to work Friday night when she got home. She took out the notes that she used for the different patterns, including the Fair Isle mittens and hat that had enthralled the yarn shop owner. They were mainly scribbles, but if she organized them, she could make a good pattern. Her granny had been a patient teacher, logically breaking things down into steps that had helped her learn.

All Megan had to do was follow the same method.

She spent time on the internet, looking at patterns on the Ravelry site to see what made some easier to follow than others. Then taking out several pieces of paper, she began to chart out the patterns she used in the knitted goods. The computer would work fine for the finished products, but Granny had taught her with

191

old-fashioned methods.

"A pencil in your hand is like the touch of wool on your fingers. It gives you another sense to understand where the truth of something lies," she'd say when Megan wanted to use her phone to look up everything. "This way you develop patience and the ability to stick with something."

Megan had sighed, but Granny had been right.

After a few hours, she walked out to the shed. The alpacas, already into her rhythm, waited by the fence, impatient for their food.

"Hey, guys," she said. "Did you have a fun day?"

Flora gave a little hop as if to tell her things were okay, but they'd be better if she'd speed it up with the food already.

Finn, the more standoffish of the two, stayed by the shed, keeping a close watch on her. He'd already spit at her once, and she was just as happy he kept his distance.

After pouring the food in the bins, she let them into the shed. Flora needed to eat more than Finn so the cria growing inside her would get enough to grow properly. She leaned against the door and watched the female eat. It would be great to have a baby alpaca running around the place. Hopefully, Flora would be a good mama and Finn would be tolerant of the young animal.

She moved her attention to Finn. Had buying him been the right decision? The guy wouldn't have sold her Flora without Finn, but something wasn't right with him. Nothing she could put on paper, just a sixth sense that nagged at her.

Well, she had to get the vet out to check on Flora anyway, so she'd have her look at Finn, too. Sheila Nielsen was new in town, but Dylan had mentioned his brother Jarod had used her when the old vet wasn't available, and he was impressed with her skills.

If it was good enough for the Becks, it was good enough for her.

She went back inside to prep her own supper, a grilled cheese sandwich and tomato soup, her Friday night go-to meal, before settling in front of her spinning wheel and streaming a movie.

This was the perfect way to live. No permanent entanglements and no need for any.

Chapter 20

Cameron was quiet on the way to the airport that Saturday. Dylan was almost getting used to his brother's taciturn style; it was the way it was. None of them were the same as they'd been when they were teens.

"How long do you think you'll be gone?" Dylan asked after they pulled on to I-15 near Vaughn.

"Depends on how much help she needs," Cameron replied.

"Are you talking about the wife or the sister?"

"The widow," his brother replied in a tone that shut down that line of questioning.

Silence rode south with them.

"You and CJ going to Indiana, then?" Cameron asked a few miles down the road.

"Taking off Monday. CJ's covering the tickets." Dylan shook his head. "First time leaving Montana and I'm headed to the heartland. Row after row of corn and soybeans."

"It's not going to be that bad," Cameron said. "You don't exactly live in the most hopping place in the country. Who knows? Maybe it will get you painting again."

Dylan snorted. "Here's a nice picture of a cornstalk to hang on your wall."

"Warhol made soup cans an art. Anything's possible."

"You got me there." Dylan navigated the roads to the bluff where the airport huddled against the ever present wind. "We'll be back in a few days, I'm sure. Plenty of time to pick you up if you want. Or you could ask Jarod."

"I'll wait til you get back," Cameron said. "Jarod will talk my ear off about what needs doing at the ranch."

"True," Dylan said, although he couldn't blame his older brother. Cameron had been home for months with no apparent intention of doing anything else. Maybe time with the widow and her sister would push him out of his rut so he could get back to actually living his life.

He pulled up to the curb and started to get out to help Cameron with the luggage.

"I got it," his brother said. "I'll call when I get back." He flipped open the camper top and yanked out his bag. Then with a wave, he was gone.

"Hope you find what you're looking for, bro," Dylan said to the glass doors as they whooshed close. Then he put the truck in gear and headed out of the airport to grab some lunch before heading home.

Near Choteau he pulled into the Freezeout Lake entrance and drove to one of the best areas for watching waterfowl. He pulled over and grabbed his binoculars. He was rewarded with a bevy of birds: the clusters of coots, darting from one place to another, a few mallards and goldeneyes plunging halfway into the water, their white rumps a bright flag against the brown vegetation. A willet stalked his prey on one edge of the water; an avocet did the same nearby. Two herons stood like statues by the reeds across the pond.

His fingers itched to paint. Giving it up these past few months hadn't seemed like a big deal, but now it was an ache, as large a loss as his brother's missing arm.

With a jerk, he yanked open the passenger door and pulled a sketchpad from the glove box, along with the few drawing pencils he always kept there. Leaning against the truck, he sketched the willet, capturing its long legs mid stride, with its straight bill as counterpoint.

He didn't think; he drew. Shading came automatically, and the bird came alive under his hand. Yes. This was what he'd been missing. A sense of life in his veins coming alive on the paper in front of him.

After drawing a few more birds, he got back into the truck, carefully stowing the pad and pencils. Maybe there was hope for him after all.

He wove through the dirt roads to get back to the main highway, exited the wildlife area, and headed back to Choteau. When he reached the town, he checked for Megan's car at the bistro but didn't see it. Just as well.

If he were honest with himself, he didn't really want a fling. He wasn't built that way. But he didn't have anything to offer her that might make something more seem interesting. He should let it go.

But he couldn't.

Ten minutes later he pulled into her drive. The two alpacas trotted to the fence nearest the house to check him out. They stayed there as he went toward the house, their ears twitching in alertness for danger.

"Oh, hello," Megan said. Her hair looked like she hadn't bothered to run a brush through it but tossed it up in some kind of clip. She had on a sleeveless T-shirt and a loose skirt that fell gracefully to her mid-calf. Her bare feet sported bright pink toenails.

"I stopped by," he said. *Well, that had been obvious.*

She smiled and pushed the screen door wider. "Cup of coffee?"

"That would be great. I got up early today to get Cameron to the airport."

"Oh? Is he going back to duty?"

"I don't think that will ever happen," Dylan said, following her to the small kitchen. "Besides his refusal to get a prosthetic to replace his arm, I don't see my brother becoming any kind of paper pusher." He accepted the mug she handed him. "One of his buddies didn't make it, and his family apparently needed some help."

"So he went."

"Yep."

She refilled her own mug, then gestured to the small table where they'd had lunch. "You haven't spoken much about your parents," she said. "But it seems like you've all turned out to be honorable people. Pretty impressive."

"Uh, I think that might be in spite of them, not because of them."

"How so?" she asked.

He took a deep breath. He hated going into the family tragedy, but if they were going to be friends, she deserved to hear the truth from him, not some second-hand story.

"My dad was into real estate in addition to the ranch. He always had a desire to be rich. I think he was jealous of the wealthy out-of-staters and their pristine ranchettes. He worked hard, but later I learned he was known to drive a hard bargain, one where he inevitably came out on top." He took a long swallow of his coffee.

Megan waited, her gaze intent on him.

"Anyway, I don't think he and my mom loved each other after a while. They obviously had sex—there are five of us—but there wasn't a lot of warmth between them. Dad liked to be overt with kisses and touches, and I think he liked to feel he was the boss

195

over her. Old-fashioned that way."

Dylan swallowed hard. He only vaguely remembered his dad. CJ and Jarod told him he had been fun to be around when they were little kids, but he started to change dramatically when Cameron was born.

"Mom wasn't demonstrative." He leaned back in his chair. "Most ranch wives are pretty matter of fact about the birds and the bees, but whatever sex education we got was through observation and whatever we learned during school. Thankfully, CJ had girlfriends. Otherwise, I don't think she ever would have been prepared for a period."

"That's awful."

"Pretty much. They were a pair, our parents. Makes you wonder why some people get together."

"Or why they stay that way."

"Yeah." He'd run out of steam, and he hadn't even gotten to the ugly part yet.

"You don't have to tell me any more if you don't want to," she said. "This family stuff is hard."

He waved his hand. May as well get it over with now that he'd started. Kind of like ripping off the bandage.

"Need to finish now or I may never be able to," he said. "Anyway, Dad, no surprise, started hanging around with other women, those he could manipulate. Or those who went out of their way to demonstrate they listened to whatever he told them to do. Totally opposite of Mom.

"Then sometime ... I think I was ten or eleven ... he found this woman in Lincoln. She ran a bar and knew how to handle men like him. At first we all thought it was more of the same, but from the bits of arguments we could hear from behind closed doors, it sounded like Dad wanted to throw Mom out and marry the lady from Lincoln."

"How could he do that? She was the mother to his kids. Besides, they ran the ranch together, didn't they?"

Dylan shook his head. "He kept the ranch in his name. I told you. He was old-fashioned that way. He wanted to buy a nice house for us in town and have us come out to the ranch on the weekends. He figured money would make up for what he was taking away."

Even saying it out loud made the bile rise in his stomach. The ranch had been their home. CJ and Jarod had already started high school. How could their father think they'd ever be happy anywhere else?

"Is that when he died?" Megan asked.

He nodded.

She put her hand on his arm. "I'm sorry."

"He was coming back from Lincoln one night. The highway was slick, and he took it too fast. The car plowed into a bridge, and he didn't make it. They called my mom, but she sent Jarod."

"Oh my god," Megan said. "That's so unfair."

"Yeah. It took a while for Jarod to get past that one."

Megan shook her head. "I thought I had it tough, but at least I had Granny. Wasn't there anyone?"

"Shortly after that, my mom's cancer returned. She'd had a bout with it and recovered, but now she had to rest ... a lot. Somehow she found Birdie to come take care of the house and, by extension, us." He tried to smile. "Birdie pretty much raised us. If anyone's responsible for how we turned out, it's her."

Emotion choked him. The time between his father's death and Birdie's arrival had been the bleakest in his life. He and his siblings had fought all the time, and bloody noses occurred every day. Even CJ had sported a black eye for a while. His mother had retreated into the bedroom, not coming out even for meals. The two oldest had tried to keep food in the house, driving to the store on a learner's permit and robbing their mother's purse and their father's desk stash to pay for things.

Then Birdie had shown up and never left. It was the only thing that saved them.

"I'm sorry," she said again.

"It's in the past," he said. "I wanted you to hear it from me. So now you have. You don't have to wonder, and we never have to talk about it again."

"Okay." She cocked her head and looked at him. "I know, though, pain like that never really goes away until you find a way to make it fit into your life in a more healthy way."

"Is that what you're trying to do?"

"Yes."

"How's it working so far?" he asked.

She smiled. "Not there yet."

"What would help?"

"I'm not sure." She released his arm and stood. "More coffee?" she asked.

"I was thinking something sweeter." He stood and walked to her. "You know, the thing that I remember most from that time is the sheer loneliness of it. Our parents weren't there, and we were so angry we didn't have each other." He looked at her pretty face, the vulnerability in her eyes, and the soft lips he'd sampled.

"I felt that way when Peter left. But at least I still had Granny."

"And it still wasn't enough."

"No," she said, "not enough." She tilted her chin up. "Not nearly enough."

"Are we still talking about our families?"

"I don't think so."

"Me either." He lowered his head and kissed her.

Yep. As soft and sweet as he remembered. Her lips quivered against his, lighting his urge to protect her, keep her safe from the pain he'd felt growing up. Letting her go, he peered into her eyes and stroked his fingers against her cheek. "You're so damn beautiful," he said. "Soft and sweet."

"But not fragile," she replied. "Don't ever think I'm made of glass, Dylan Beck. Southern mountain women have steel cores."

"I don't doubt that for a minute."

She laced her hands around the back of his neck and pulled him down to her where she showed her determination by taking his lips and owning them. He took accepted her tongue and then wove his around it, heightening their battle for equality as they traded possession.

He pressed his body next to his, one hand snaking around her back and the other sliding over the soft mound of her breast, alert for any sign of her hesitation. He'd fight her for temporary dominance, but never take what wasn't freely offered.

Instead, he got a moan, emboldening him to pull her closer, knowing how hard he'd become, stiff enough so she'd notice. Hungrily, he slid his mouth from her lips, instead using it to caress the smooth flesh of her neck, fluttering kisses down to her upper chest. In response she arched her head back, leaving herself open to his ministrations.

He paused when he reached the upper edge of her top, then used his fingers to gently push aside the fabric and use his tongue and lips on the upper part of her breast.

"Bedroom," she whispered.

"Are you sure?"

"Absolutely." She straightened and held out her hand.

He waited a few more seconds, then let her lead him to the back of the house.

The bed was an old-fashioned white-painted iron bedstead, fluffy with embroidered pillows and handmade quilts. It suited her, but he felt too big for its stature. This room was her, and by letting him in, she was giving up a small part of who she was.

She must have sensed his hesitation, because she tugged his hand.

"Are you sure?" he repeated.

"Stop talking," she said, slipping off her shirt to reveal a pearly pink bra.

"Do the panties match?" he asked with a smile.

"Still talking. I must be losing my touch." She trailed a finger down from his chin to his top shirt button and undid it.

Letting her take the upper hand, he left his hands at his sides, merely experiencing the release of letting someone else run the show. It was a delicate dance between a man and a woman these days. Too far too fast and the man was too aggressive. Too slow and the woman lost interest. Of course, women had the same problem. She was either a slut or frigid.

The world would be better off if people would let people evolve into being whoever they truly were.

The touch of her fingertip on his nipple brought him back to the bedroom with a thud. No point in worrying about what the world thought. He had more than he could handle here and now. He slid off his shirt, then pulled her close and unhooked her bra. Soon her sweet breasts were against him, tickling the hair on his chest. He pushed her back on the bed and yanked off her pants, leaving her in her panties.

Her underwear totally matched.

"You too," she said.

He obliged, fumbling through his wallet for the foil wrapper that had been there since he'd given up his last mutually agreed-upon sexual encounter. He tossed it on the nightstand, then returned his attention to the almost nude woman on the bed.

# # #

It wasn't fair to compare, but Dylan had mad skills compared to Megan's two previous lovers, one who hadn't gotten very far. High school fumblings were just that. She had never allowed her teenage boyfriend to get too far to be anywhere near risky.

But she'd given it all to Macon Joseph Bartlett III. She'd thought it was for keeps. Thank god she hadn't picked up any nasty diseases or gotten pregnant. After six months of a hot and heavy relationship, his father's attorney had shown up with a check. It was Megan's as long as she stayed away from the banker's son.

To her shame, she'd taken it. Granny was gone, the cousins had taken everything, and no future was possible in her hometown. The money gave her enough to get out of town.

She gasped as the heat from Dylan's mouth touched the flesh between her legs. No one had ever been that intimate with her before, and she wasn't sure she liked it. It was like her entire inner self as a woman was exposed to his sight and ministrations. She made a fluttering motion with her hand, not wishing to push him away, but not sure she wanted more.

He sensed her hesitation and moved his kisses back up her body where his mouth settled on her breast, sucking the tight nipple in and sending currents of sparks to all the sensitive parts of her body. She groaned, unable to help herself.

"Please," she said, "Please ..." She couldn't say the words out loud. She couldn't beg him to join with her, satisfy her, even though she wanted it to her very core.

He raised his head from her breast. "Are you sure?" His eyes were filled with concern, making sure it was what she really wanted.

She nodded, unable to speak.

He lifted himself off, unwrapped the condom, and soon he was back, poised between her legs, probing her inner being.

"Yes," she was finally able to say.

He pushed into her, gently, stretching areas tight with disuse.

She welcomed him, lifting her hips to give him greater access, gripping his arms to make sure he stayed. And then he was in, rocking until they found their mutual rhythm, a connection only this most intimate act could provide. She gazed up at him and got lost in his eyes. Safe. He made her feel safe.

It had been a long time since she'd been anywhere close to safe.

Her body loosened even more, and the wave began to build. She fought to hold it back, to wait until he was close.

"Let go," he said. "It's okay. Just let go." He intensified his rhythm, as if demanding she take her pleasure.

She couldn't stop it. The stress intensified and every muscle clenched.

He grunted and moved faster.

She stared at him, although her vision grew dim.

All she could do was go where her body led her. Her body spasmed—hard.

Seconds later he tensed, his arms flexing hard under her hands.

They moaned together, their rhythm fading at the same time.

When it was over, he sank to his elbows, his weight comforting but not pressing her against the mattress.

"That," he said, "was amazing."

Chapter 21

Megan awoke with a start, uncomfortably realizing she was not alone in bed. Dylan breathed heavily beside her. She reached for the robe that she always kept on a nearby chair, slid out of bed, and pulled the fabric around her.

Her movement must have woken him. His eyelids popped open and a second went by before he registered where he was. Then a slow smile grew across his face. "You are the most beautiful and satisfying woman I've ever met."

What was she supposed to say to that? No one in her life had ever lavished her with praise like that. At least no one who meant what they said. Too many of her kin were adept at pretending to compliment someone while wrapping the words around a thin, excruciatingly exact, stiletto knife.

"Thank you," she murmured.

He flicked off the covers, and she looked away. Silly to be embarrassed after what they'd done an hour earlier, but there it was. She gave him a few seconds, then glanced at him from underneath her pale eyelashes. His jeans were back on and he was sliding into his shirt.

She moved toward the open door, but he caught her.

After kissing her gently, he said, "We will need to talk about this, but let's let it settle for a bit."

"Okay," she said.

He sat on the bed and pulled on his boots. "I'm going to go out and check on the alpacas and the repairs I did. There's a few other spots that might need reinforcement."

"You know animals," she said.

"Not as well as Jarod, but yes."

"Can you take a look at Finn? Something seems off to me, but I don't know what's wrong."

"Finn's the male, right?"

"Yep."

"Sure."

Moments later, the screen door slammed.

She pulled her clothes back on, then ran a washcloth over her face. For a few moments she stared at her reflection, checking to see if her experience showed in her face, just like she had when she'd given herself to Macon for the first time. Then she'd been giddy with first love and possibilities. Now her eyes reflected tentative hope.

But hope for what, exactly?

Dylan was in the pen, holding Finn by the halter as he ran his hands over the animal. Megan went through the gate to join him while Flora eyed them from a short distance away. Dylan held the lead out to her, and she took it. He continued his examination of the back legs and hips, worked his way around the other side, and then pried open Finn's lips and checked the teeth. Finn made only a minor protest during the whole procedure, which worried her more than if he'd been feisty.

"I can't see anything specifically wrong," Dylan said, unsnapping the lead. "He seems tired. Old."

"Dr. Nielson can't make it until Wednesday."

"He'll last until then." Finn strolled away, weariness evident in every step. "But you're going to have to face the fact he's not going to last very long. You might not be able to get even one fleece off him."

"I didn't really want him, but Flora was too good to pass up and alpacas don't do really well on their own."

"That guy wouldn't have split them up anyway. I had a feeling he wanted Finn off his hands. So, assuming old Finn is going to kick the bucket soon, are you going to replace him?"

"I think I have to, but it's not really in my budget."

"Yeah."

She was afraid he was going to offer to invest again, spoiling their afterglow, but he didn't. Good. It was a discussion they didn't need to keep having.

But the loss of Finn, if it was going to happen, was going to be a blow to her plans.

Dylan found a few more areas that he needed to fix. "I'll bring my tools back during the week." He glanced toward the sun, which was drifting lazily toward the western horizon. It wasn't the land of the midnight sun, but light would last well past nine at night during June and July.

"I really need to get back to spinning," she said. "I'm determined to get some samples together for Helen by the end of the week. And I want to finish at least one pattern so she can see my work."

"That was a stroke of good luck that she came into the bistro."

"Yeah. It opened up a door I didn't even know was there."

They left the paddock, and he leaned against the fence. A breeze carrying the sweet smell of ripening wheat ruffled his hair. A dusty rabbit peered out from some nearby grass, ventured out a few hops, then thought better of it and went back into the weeds.

Overhead, the cerulean sky arced hopefully.

If only some moments could be frozen in time.

"That wasn't a one-time thing for me," Dylan said.

"It has to be," she replied.

"It wasn't a mistake."

"No. But I'm not ready for anything more. I have a business to build."

"You don't have to do it alone."

"Yes, I do."

"Don't people help each other where you come from?" he asked.

"Sometimes. But with my family, there was always a price to be paid somewhere down the line."

"I think you'll find it a bit different here. We've got Mother Nature to contend with, and everyone needs a helping hand one time or another. If someone's spun off the highway into a ditch, you don't ask his politics first, you help tow him out. If you need an extra hand to bring stock back from the hills in the fall, it's there. If we didn't live that way, we wouldn't survive."

"But that's a casual thing—now and again. You're talking about a longer term situation."

"That's what being a friend is all about. And you don't know it, but you already have helped me. Come here, I want you to see this." He led her to the pickup truck and pulled out a notebook. Flipping through the pages he showed her a sketch of a bird, almost popping off the page with life.

"Wow," she said.

"I haven't been able to pick up a paintbrush for months. Everything I've done looks like garbage to me. Losing the gallery was the last straw. But you've inspired me. I needed to look at things from a different perspective. I've always done large landscape paintings, but what was missing were the details that made something truly striking."

"Looks like you're figuring it out," she said.

"Maybe. Or maybe this is a one-off. I need someone in my corner, supporting my dreams, like you need someone in yours. If that's a trade, then it's a good one in my estimation." He pushed a tendril of her hair away from her eyes. "The rest is icing on the cake." Cupping her chin in his hand, he kissed her.

# # #

Megan spent the next three days on her feet at the bistro or squinting at her grandmother's tiny script in her diaries. Through it all, her mind replayed scenes with Dylan in such intensity that she could smell their sweat as they'd made love and feel the heat of the sun as they'd talked.

She was wrung out. Reading Granny's words was bittersweet. She'd written of her love for Megan and teaching her to spin. There were even reminiscences of her own grandmother and mother, women Megan had never met but who'd somehow influenced who she'd become. Her ancestors had been skilled in the home arts common during the mid-twentieth century, but they'd also been feisty activists, fighting for the right to own their own home and make their own careers.

But there was nothing saying that Megan should have the spinning wheel if anything ever happened to her grandmother.

Why were her relatives going after it? Like she'd told Cassandra, it wasn't worth huge amounts of money. Some, but enough to cover the expenses of a lawyer?

Of course, the cousin was probably doing it for nothing, just to spite Megan. In fact, that was probably the genesis of the whole matter. But what could anyone do to combat petty hatred?

Well, she damn well wasn't going to let them have it without a fight.

When Wednesday morning gleamed bright and warm, she decided she'd had enough of being cooped up with the past. The vet was due in the morning, so she arose bright and early to feed the animals and do some weeding around the native flowers she'd planted near the front porch. The blue flax and the lavender promised soothing colors as the sun parched the prairies toward the end of summer. In the sun, she'd started a rock garden of bitterroot and cacti.

Her shoulders and knees ached by the time she finished the weeding, but it was the satisfying pain of accomplishment. By the time she'd put away her tools and cleaned up, the doc was pulling into the drive.

Dr. Nielson was smaller than she'd expected, around five and a half feet tall and slimly built, contrasting to Megan's own set of curves. The doctor's sleek brown hair was pulled back in a clip. She greeted Megan with a broad smile.

"Sheila Nielson," she said, holding out a hand. "I hear you're new in town, too."

"Somewhat," Megan said and shook Sheila's hand. "I've been here since January, but didn't really start meeting people until the bistro opened in early spring."

"Yes, that place is a nice addition. I mean, a burger is fine for lunch, but every day?" She shook her head.

Megan smiled, liking the vet already.

"I can't say I've worked with many alpacas," Sheila said, "but the basic principles are the same. Let's see what's up with your guys."

Megan led the way back to the smaller enclosure where she'd penned Finn and Flora so she didn't have to go chasing them across the pasture when the vet came. She snapped a lead on Flora and led her back to the shed Dylan had repaired. In the confined space, Sheila examined the female, probing and listening with her stethoscope. Flora was okay with the first few minutes, but then began to stop her feet and try to move away.

"Easy, girl," Sheila said. "Almost done. I'm just going to take a blood sample and then it'll be all over." She looked at Megan. "You're really going to have to hold her. They hate this."

"I'm not a big fan either," Megan said, using her body weight to press the alpaca against one wall.

The doctor was quick, and soon she was able to release the bleating animal to the pasture.

Finn was another matter.

Sheila pursed her lips as she ran her hands over the animal. A few shakes of the head didn't inspire confidence. After the doc had taken blood and Megan had let Finn follow Flora, they went into the kitchen to talk.

"Tea? Coffee?" Megan asked.

"Tea would be great," Sheila said, thumping the dust from her feet before entering the house.

After Megan put the kettle on, she took down the white teapot with the green shamrocks, something that had been her mother's. She'd hidden it away after her mother died, and her relatives had never realized she had it. The earl gray would provide the perfect kick start to the second half of the day.

After preparing the tea to steep, she put the pot on the table, along with two mugs. "Sugar's on the table. Do you need milk?"

"Nope. Straight up works for me."

"Me too."

Sheila smiled at her. It was an expression that went all the way to her eyes. Someone to get to know better. But first ...

"How is Finn?" Megan asked.

"I'm going to have to confirm it with lab tests, but you're right, he's definitely off."

"What do you think it is?" Megan poured the tea.

"Other than old age?"

"Is it something specific? Something treatable?"

"It could be, but it could be an advanced form of cancer or something like that. Any idea how old he is?"

"Not really." She really needed to get better at asking questions before she invested in an animal.

"There comes a point," Sheila said, "when it just doesn't make sense to do invasive treatments. You're not extending the animal's life a whole lot, and it probably doesn't improve their quality of life, either."

"So you're saying I should just let him die."

"I'm afraid so. I'll know more when I get the tests, but it's not looking good."

Megan swallowed her tears with her tea. She'd care for Finn well right up until the end, but it wasn't going to be easy. At eight she'd cried for days when her pet cat died, and her mother had been there to comfort her. How was she going to do it on her own?

# # #

"Well, that was a bust," Dylan said as he and CJ waited to board the plane in Fort Wayne the Friday before Nick was due home from his trip.

"Not entirely," CJ said, taking a sip of the water she'd purchased as soon as they made it through the security checkpoint. "We've got new cousins to add to our Christmas list." She grinned.

"Distant cousins."

"You don't have to grump about everything," she said.

"Harrumph," he muttered and opened up the art magazine he'd purchased.

"At least we know where the deed isn't," he admitted after the plane took off, bound for Minneapolis. Flying anywhere out of

Montana was costly and time-consuming. No wonder he'd never gone anywhere before. "It's probably with the kids that Moonbeam or Rainbow or whatever the heck the girl was who Tom remembered Greg hooking up with. People had weird names in the 70s."

"Peace, love, and all that," CJ said.

"Sex, drugs, and rock 'n' roll was more like it."

"Finding her and the deed is a long shot."

"It's probably in a landfill somewhere," Dylan said, remembering the scene of the sled Rosebud burning at the end of the cult classic, *Citizen Kane*, which he'd seen long ago in college. In his mind, the sled changed to a large document full of fancy script.

"But according to the letter we received from Choteau Mineral Development, they've got the deed."

"So they say."

"So the records agree. The only thing we don't know is how they obtained it."

"Can our lawyers make them?" Dylan asked.

"Hope so. The idea is to get them to come to the table so we can work together instead of spending all our time in court."

"They're going to drill?"

"Their attorneys said they have the rights, and unless we can find an environmental reason to stop them, they can go ahead with their exploration. Our law firm has hired some experts to go with them and document any concerns they may have regarding damage to the land or other environmental factors."

"More money going out."

"Yeah." A frown crossed her forehead.

"Is that a problem?" CJ had been footing the bill for a lot of the investigation into the other branch of the family and searching for the deed from an inheritance she'd received from her late husband.

"There's still enough," she said. "I just hate spending it this way." She grimaced. "It's kind of like buying a new furnace—got to be done, but no real satisfaction in the purchase."

He chuckled, the first time he'd lightened in hours.

She gestured to the magazine. "Are you painting again?"

"Sketching a bit. I don't seem to be able to go through life without creating something, but I'm not sure it's sustainable."

"And you're still thinking about running for office next year."

He sighed. "Most days. Then there are those when I think

packing everything up and running away to Arizona or New Mexico to try to paint again is a better idea."

"You'd leave the ranch?"

"If I have to." Through the window thunderclouds hunkered off in the distance. The plane gave a shuddering jolt, and he gripped the armrest. Almost immediately, the pilot came on the speaker over his head.

"Sorry about that, folks. We've got some turbulence ahead. I'm going to light up the fasten seat belt sign. Please return to your seats and buckle up."

Great. Bouncing around in a tin can thousands of feet above flat land didn't make his day. Was his life going to be over before he even had a chance to live it?

"Cancel the funeral," CJ said. "It's not that bad. Hell, there aren't even any anti-aircraft guns firing at us. Where's the fun in that?"

"You're sick, you know that?" he said as his fingers fumbled with the seat belt.

"Taking pictures in a war zone will do that to you." Her tone was serious.

Another jolt.

"Crap!" he hissed.

"So if you head for parts south," she said, returning to their previous conversation, "how will Megan feel?"

"I don't know," he lied. "We're just friends." Although they were now friends with benefits. They'd talked every day since they'd been together, but he hadn't been able to get to see her before the trip.

"Yeah, right." She stared at him.

He looked back out the window.

"You skunk," she said. "You slept with her."

"None of your damn business."

"What were you thinking?" CJ asked.

"She wanted it, too," he said, looking back at his sister. "And it is still none of your business." He punctuated the last four words with his finger jabbing her shoulder.

"I think it will matter a whole lot to Megan Winkle if you leave town. Not to mention to the rest of the family. It's been nice to have most of us close again. And you, little brother, you'd be desolate without these mountains."

She had him there. The pictures he'd seen of the desert had spoken to him, but his soul would forever belong to Montana. He

Casey Dawes

shook his head to indicate he was done with the subject and opened up his magazine.

Much to his amazement, they made it safely to Minneapolis where they had a two-hour layover. He quickly downed two whiskeys while CJ sipped her beer. She looked askance when he ordered the second shot but didn't say anything.

He needed something to get him the rest of the way home.

Chapter 22

Early Saturday, Dylan pulled into Megan's driveway, parked, then picked the bouquet he'd purchased in town. He'd chewed on what CJ had said all the way from Minneapolis to Great Falls, then drifted to sleep as CJ drove them back to the ranch.

But the sleep wasn't restful. In his dream he was searching, tearing the house apart looking for something. Every drawer he opened, every room he clawed his way through, every book he opened contained the deed to the mineral rights. That should have been it, but terror still stalked him.

Then he reached the attic. Only one object stood there: a simple pine coffin.

Something compelled him to lift the lid, only to stare at his own reflection. Even the corpse's eyes were open. He was dressed in clothes Dylan recognized, but there was something draped from his neck to below his waist. It took him a moment to realize what it was: a lacy woolen shawl done in yarn the same color as one of the alpacas Megan had bought.

A step on the wooden floor alerted him to someone else in the attic. He turned.

Megan stood before him, tears running down her cheeks. She shook her head, pivoted, took a step, and disappeared.

He'd woken with a jerk.

Now, as he stepped from his pickup, a cool wind raised the small hairs on his neck. Like a ghost had walked over his grave. He shook his head. His ancestors were pragmatic Scandinavians not given to spooky tales. Where had this come from?

He hesitated for a moment, instinctively knowing Megan wasn't in the house.

A low, keening wail came from the shed.

Dropping the flowers in the dust, he ran, cursing as his fingers slipped on the latch to the enclosure. In the pasture beyond the shed, Flora stood, shifting from one leg to the other.

"Megan!" he called.

No answer.

He pushed open the door to the shed. The light streamed in,

spotlighting Megan cradling Finn's head in her lap. She looked up, tears streaming down her face, an eerie imitation of the dream he'd had.

"He's dead," Megan sobbed. "She said he'd last for a while, but he didn't. Poor, poor Finn."

"Are you sure?" he asked, dropping to his knees next to her.

"Of course I'm sure. I damn well know when an animal's dead."

He raised his palms. "Sorry."

"Me too. I guess ..." The sobs started again. "It's all too much." The wail broke from her again, and she swallowed heavily. Still the tears ran down her face.

He squirmed his way next to her and put his arm around her. There was nothing to do but let her grieve. Instead, he simply held her and put his hand on Finn.

They must have sat like that for a half hour before she got her sobs under control. Feeling her stir, he got his legs under him, silently cursing the pins and needles that painfully cramped the left one. Megan stared at the hand he held out, then put hers in it. He leveraged her up and guided her around the animal lying heavy on the ground.

"What do I do now?" she asked.

"How about we brew some tea and talk about that?"

She held out her dirt-covered hands.

"How about you get cleaned up," he amended, "and I'll make some tea."

She nodded and bit her bottom lip.

Putting his arm around her shoulder, he guided her to her own back door and ushered her in the general direction of the bathroom. Remembering the cupboards she'd opened, he quickly had water boiling and the tea ready in the pot. Eat. She should eat something. Ah. A leftover box from the bistro with a few pastries ... somewhat hardened.

They'd have to do.

She came back into the kitchen, her face wan and her eyes expressionless. A fresh set of clothes brightened her appearance, but her limbs were lifeless as she sank into the kitchen chair.

"Tea is steeping," he said. "You'll probably need it to eat these." He placed the plate with the freshest pastries on the table.

"I'm not hungry," she said.

"I can't force you, but it would be a good idea. There are things to be done."

She stared at the food but made no effort to pick it up.

Maybe if he put one on the plate in front of her. He poured the tea and moved one of the goodies. After serving himself, he sat down.

"Eat," he commanded again.

"No," she said, a touch of defiance back in her voice.

Good. A step back to life.

He picked up his tea and sipped.

"Damn! That's hot!" The tea sprayed from the mug as he slammed it back down.

She gave a half-hearted laugh. "It's boiling water. What do you think it would be?"

He exaggerated blowing in and out of his mouth, just to hear her chuckle.

Shaking her head, she finally reached for one of the pastries, dipped it into her tea, and gave him a self-satisfied smile. He mimicked her, and her smile broadened, bringing the light back into her eyes.

"How was your trip to Indiana?" she asked.

"Disappointing in a lot of ways. People are nice enough, but the area's too congested for me. The guy we found—I guess he's a cousin of some sort—doesn't have the deed, and he didn't know if his older brother Greg did. Unfortunately, Greg liked to live fast and loose and ODed sometime in the 1970s. According to Tom, Greg had hooked up with several women but never married, and he didn't know if there had been any offspring."

"So you're stuck again."

"Yep."

"Sorry." She sipped her tea.

He waited for her to bring up the subject of Finn in her own time. Meanwhile, he chatted about the restaurants he and CJ had gone to in Fort Wayne, the ball game they'd attended, and the botanical garden they'd visited.

"I think she was trying to convince me that it was okay to leave Montana once in a while."

"You should see North Carolina. It's very beautiful."

"Maybe you can take me there someday."

She stopped her mug halfway to her mouth and stared at him. "Are you planning on sticking around?" Her voice was soft.

"Are you?" he asked. "This is where I live." He tried to make his voice casual, as if his words hadn't meant anything significant, knowing he was lying to himself.

She cleared her throat and put down her mug. "I guess we need to talk about Finn. What do I do next? I've never owned a big animal before, much less had one die on me."

"Since the vet's seen him recently, we don't have to worry about any contagious diseases. There's an association in town that will pick him up and dispose of him safely."

"Can't I bury him here?"

Dylan shook his head. "First, you don't own the land, and second, you don't have enough acreage they require." But the ranch did. "Listen, I have to check with Jarod, but we do have a spot where we bury the animals we've lost. It's been there a long time."

"I'd feel funny burying the animal in your family plot. Thank you. That's a sweet offer, but I think just calling someone will have to do."

"Up to you, but I really think it would be okay."

She pursed her lips. "No. Like I said, thanks. I've got to learn to handle these things on my own." She stood.

His chair scraped on the wooden floor as he rose as well. "Megan. Did I say something wrong?"

"No, not really. Nothing to worry about."

He crossed to her. "What did I do?"

She looked up at him, a haunted expression in her eyes. "It's too ... too ... much for me, Dylan. The other day ..." She glanced in the direction of the bedroom. "It was lovely, but it can't happen again. If we .... well, one thing simply leads to another ... and then it will turn into something I don't want." She straightened her spine. "I have to learn to manage on my own. I think it's best you leave now."

He forced his hands to flex and his feet to become unglued from the floor. "If that's what you want."

"It is."

He started to lean forward to kiss her cheek but thought better of it, turned, and left. On his way to the truck he saw the flowers lying in the dirt. After tossing them in a nearby garbage can, he hauled ass out of Megan's driveway. Out of her life.

# # #

Once she heard Dylan's truck roaring away, Megan relaxed the tight grip she had on herself and collapsed to the floor in a heap.

Stupid, stupid pride! Why had she pushed him away? Finn was dead. She could have used the support. But did she take it? No.

Her sorrow over the animal transformed into a raging anger at herself. She should have waited. Gone to a certified breeder. Gotten a second opinion.

There was no way she should be in business. *Give it up. Go to school and become a kindergarten teacher or something.* She was only twenty-five. There was still time to have another career. Until then, she could waitress.

Or maybe that's what she should just stick to. The work was hard, but if she found the right place, a restaurant that served liquor, maybe a businessman's hangout, all she'd have to do was put up with a few stray hands and she could rake it in. Politically incorrect, but it's the way some places worked.

She'd have to leave Choteau, walk away from another place. It would be harder. This time she knew people; there was a chance at becoming friends with someone. She'd even had a potential boyfriend, at least until she'd flushed the chance down the drain a few moments ago.

The hurt look in Dylan's eyes would haunt her for a long time, but better to cut it off quickly than to get even closer and break both their hearts when the inevitable happened.

Yes, she'd done the right thing. Pushing herself off the floor, she washed her face and hands one last time and retrieved her phone to make arrangements about Finn. The people were wonderfully sympathetic and efficient. They promised they'd be there by the end of the day to pick up the alpaca.

Okay. That was handled. Flora was okay, although she was probably confused about the lack of her companion. Megan started running numbers to decide the best thing to do next. Should she sell Flora so the animal had companionship and she herself could move on? Buy another alpaca? Leave things as they were?

A knock on the door startled her. She hadn't expected the animal crew this fast.

She opened the door, and her heart dropped. A familiar man in a brown uniform, his face dominated by a good-sized moustache, stood on her porch.

Ah, yes, the man whose wife had recently left.

"Megan Winkle?" he asked.

"Yes."

215

"I'm Sheriff Van Sutton."

"Yes." Her right hand was still on the main door, but she hadn't opened the screen door. Did she have to? What rights did she have?

More importantly, why was he here?

"May I come in?" he asked.

She'd watched enough crime shows to know that letting him in gave him access to the place.

"Can you tell me what this is about?" she asked instead.

"We received a notice from the sheriff in Buncombe County, North Carolina. It seems a complaint has been filed against you for theft of an antique spinning wheel."

"I didn't steal it."

"But it's in your possession."

What was the right thing to say next? Damn, she should have set up that meeting with Cassandra.

"Do I have to answer that?" she asked.

"No, but ..." He gestured at the front window where the wheel was plainly visible.

"That's not theirs."

"Well, I suggest you answer this complaint as soon as possible. If not, I'm going to be forced to remove it from your possession."

The world got fuzzy in front of her, and her limbs became almost too heavy to stand. She shook her head to clear it.

"You okay?" he asked.

"It's been a bad day," she said.

"I'm sorry to hear that," he said. "I hope it gets better." He touched his hat. "And answer that complaint." His boots thudded as he left the porch and walked the path to the drive.

After slowly squeezing the door closed, Megan picked up her phone and dialed Cassandra, getting the answering machine. She left a message.

Then she grabbed cleaning supplies and headed for the bathroom. The sucky chore matched the day to a T.

# # #

"Dammit!" Dylan yelled as the head of the bolt broke off in his hand.

"You're too rough with these things," Jarod said, standing up from the tractor he was, once again, working to keep going.

"What's with you anyway? For the last bunch of days you've been grumpier than a hungry bear."

"Nothing's wrong."

"Uh-huh." Jarod handed him the bolt extractor set.

"Maybe if we had money to buy newer equipment, we wouldn't have to spend all our time fixing things." Dylan pulled out the drill and began to remove the damaged bolt from the machine.

"We've got to be cautious. You know that. Paying the lawyers to deal with that drilling company is costing CJ. I wish we could actually talk to someone, but all that happens is that our lawyers talk to their lawyers, and our environmental engineers talk to their geologists."

"What the heck are they looking for, anyway?"

"Energy, I assume. What else would they want?"

Dylan shrugged and concentrated on the bolt, trying not to think about his lack of contribution of anything meaningful ... to anyone.

Maybe he had inherited the genes that had made Seth go wandering off from ranch life. Or perhaps being a younger brother sucked in general. There were no real purposes for second sons. They were supposed to hang around in case the first one got bumped off for some reason.

He was being ridiculous. He and Jarod were a team. Glancing over at his older brother, he knew it was pure jealousy that was driving his mood. From the beginning, Jarod had planned to come back to the ranch. Sure, he'd wanted to rodeo first, but he'd found a way to incorporate that goal with the life he had.

And now he had Samantha and Audie.

"Shit!" He let loose with more cussing as he sat on the nearest bale and yanked off his boot.

"What did you do now? And tone it down. It won't be good if Audie hears her uncle Dylan using all those bad words." Jarod's tone was kidding, but he meant what he said.

And he was right. Now that school was out for the summer, Audie could show up at any time.

"I dropped the drill on my foot," Dylan said.

"You okay?"

"Yeah. It just hurts like a ..." Jarod frowned at him. "A lot. It hurts a lot."

Jarod stretched to standing position. "I can't concentrate with all the noise you're making. Why don't you get out of here for a while til you can calm down and concentrate? You're no good like this. Go see Megan and play with the alpaca. Or saddle up a horse and paint."

Great. His brother wanted him to do two things he couldn't. So far he'd kept the split with Megan quiet, but it was only a matter of time before they found out.

But the sketch he'd made at Freezeout came to mind. Flowers carpeted the hills. Was success in the smaller versions of the beauty around him instead of epic landscapes?

"You're right. I need a break. I'll finish this up and take a ride."

"Leave it. I'll fix it after I finish here." Jarod squatted back down to the tractor.

# # #

A half hour later, Dylan headed up the trail to an area he knew was rich with wildflowers. Unfortunately, his melancholy rode with him.

Nothing was working for him. He'd thought making love with Megan had been a breakthrough, but now she'd banned him from her life just when she needed him most. CJ would tell him he was being too egotistical, that most women were perfectly capable of handling things on their own. And Megan seemed built of that stock. She'd left her lifetime home, come to a strange part of the country, and made herself an integral part of the community while she started a business.

He was still stuck on his family's ranch. He didn't even have a place that was truly his, whether rented or not. At thirty-three, that was pitiful. He really should leave home; the Southwest was supposed to be friendly to artists. At least it was warmer much of the year. Sometimes the dreary months of winter were too much to face, especially alone.

But today wasn't dreary. Instead the mountains lured him west, their peaks aspiring to something greater than the petty efforts of humans. It's what art had always meant to him, a reaching for something that couldn't be put into words, a world greater than himself.

But those grand paintings, like the ones Thomas Moran used to create, eluded him. Or maybe the time was no longer right for big visions. People had narrowed their focus, only seeing what was right in front of them and lacking curiosity for anything beyond.

Lupines began to pop up in small clusters, purple-blue blankets scattered over a bed of grass. He kept urging the horse to higher altitudes, drifting toward the northwest corner of the property, the same area where he and Jarod had found the rebar pounded into the cliff.

They'd never managed to get back up here. One thing had led to another, and real life had taken over. Maybe he should swing a rope over the edge and see if he could see anything. He'd be in real trouble if he fell.

But what the hell did it matter?

He should have thought to bring the drone with him so he could give the cliff a closer examination without risk. But he'd been so eager to get away from everyone that he didn't think about it.

Well, he'd see how he felt when he got up there.

The sun lit a dark purple speck in the grass to his left. He stopped Paint and slid off. Reins still in his hand, he walked to the spot.

Yep, just what he was looking for, a shooting star, a leafless stalk rising to less than a foot topped with a cone-shaped set of purple petals ending in a yellow-orange stamen. This particular specimen was past its prime, but better ones should exist up where the air was cooler, along with the bright yellow glacier lilies that usually accompanied them. Closer to the edge of the pine forests, he might even be lucky enough to see bear grass.

With a little more spring in his step, he swung himself back into the saddle. "Just a bit farther, Paint. Then you can have a rest."

The horse nodded his head as if he understood what Dylan had said.

They had to descend to a valley and climb another hill before he found what he wanted. Here the grassland was a patchwork quilt all the way to where small saplings and young pines had encroached on the prairie. At their edges were the white bulbous shapes of bear grass. He rode to one of the sturdier pines, hitched Paint to it using the lead he'd brought so the horse had plenty of room to forage, and pulled out the lunch Birdie had packed for him.

He really needed to move away from the ranch or he'd never develop any life skills.

Leaning against another one of the pines, he ate his sandwich and contemplated his choices. Something had to change, but looking out across the hills as they descended to the prairie floor, he knew leaving Montana wasn't an option. At least not for any length of time. Once the state had a soul, it had a person forever no matter how far one tried to get away.

But he could move to another town or even a city. He'd enjoyed Bozeman while he lived there, and they had a solid art scene. Next to Billings, the city had the best airplane schedule in the state. And it was only three hours by car from Choteau, which meant he could get home for things like weddings and holidays.

But what would he do for money? That would take some exploring. He had a trust fund of sorts—they all did—but he wanted to use that money as an investment, not living expenses.

A bigger city would mean more opportunities and a better chance to fill the hole in his heart that losing Megan had meant. Although his score with women wasn't impressive. He'd gotten serious with two women, and they'd both left him.

He washed down the water and the bitterness with the water he'd brought with him.

Which blossom would give him the best opportunity to achieve what he was looking to do? He wandered the area close by until he found what he didn't know he wanted: a supremely lit glacier lily. Carefully, he pushed down the grass around it so he could get a clear view, crossed his legs, and began to sketch. With the sun on his back, the sound of his horse munching nearby, and the familiar tool in his hand, peace settled over him.

Maybe he could get through this after all.

Chapter 23

"Gather all the diaries you have that talk about you and that wheel and come into the office," Cassandra had told her when she called Megan back Monday morning. "I've got an opening on Wednesday."

"Wednesday? Won't that be too late?"

"It's plenty of time. Besides, that will give you a few more days to dig up anything else you may have. The sheriff's visit was just a warning shot. I'll contact Jim and see what else he's heard so we're prepared."

In between shifts at the bistro, Megan had scoured every bit of paper she'd retrieved from her granny's house before she'd left. She jotted down all her memories. And she tried not to think about Finn. Or Dylan.

The animal people had been kind, gracious, and efficient. Once they were gone on Saturday, she'd sat done at her wheel and spun for hours without bothering to turn on any music or shows. Just the steady rhythm of the wheel, the twist of the fiber as it slipped through her fingers, and the gathering yarn on the spool. The ghosts of women in her family grieved around her; their presence clear in her mind as they remembered their own griefs, large and small.

It did seem the lot of women to put up with a great deal of pain in their lives, no matter how modern or prosperous the circumstances.

# # #

On Wednesday, she had to plead for the time off to see Cassandra.

"I'm sympathetic, I really am," Courtney said. "But it's our busiest time of year. Fourth of July is Saturday, but all the festivities begin the day before. People are already showing up from out of town. I hear the inns and hotel are totally booked. Even the Airbnbs are full! With Going to the Sun road open in

Glacier, the traffic through town is steady, and they're ready for a stop when they get here.

"I'm sorry about your alpaca," she continued, "but I have a business to run. I've hired another waitress, and Trish's daughter, Beth, is coming in to bus and work in the kitchen."

"It will only be an hour. I promise. I'll make up for it."

"Okay." Courtney shook her head. "I don't mean to be hard-nosed about it, but you want to be a businesswoman. You're going to have to learn that your business always comes first."

"I'll be here for you this summer." Megan hoped she could keep the promise.

"I hope so. Otherwise, I'm afraid ..." Courtney's voice softened. "I'm afraid I'd have to let you go and find someone I can rely on. I don't want to, but—"

"I know, it's business." Megan tried to keep the bitterness from her voice. Courtney was right about one thing though: as much as Megan needed the safety net of this job, she was going to have to let go at some point.

She decided to walk to Cassandra's office along the main street. It was still early enough in the season that the heat couldn't fry the proverbial egg on the sidewalk. Scraggly saplings would provide shade ... in about ten years. Two boarded up stores and a run-down thrift shop indicated the struggles the town was still having to prosper, but the potted plants on corners were bright with freshly watered flowers and the windows of the hardware store gleamed.

After walking up the stairs to Cassandra's office, she let herself into the waiting room as instructed. The soft, eggshell-blue walls set off the red, Western-style leather armchairs and glass tables. Expensive-looking Western artwork completed the look of prosperity and competence.

Cassandra emerged from the inner office looking, as she always did, like a model stepping from the pages of a New York fashion magazine. Megan felt incredibly homespun beside her. How could she ever be friendly with this woman?

Everybody needs a friend. Granny's voice echoed in her head, emphasis on the word body as being separate from every.

"Come in," Cassandra said in her cultured voice. "Coffee? Tea?"

"Water will do," Megan said. "I get enough of the other stuff at work."

"Yes, you probably do. Have a seat, and let's see what you've got."

Megan placed the relevant diaries she'd marked up with Post-it notes on Cassandra's desk. "She never actually says she'll give me the wheel, but she does talk about me spinning yarn for garments for my children."

"Good. That's very good. Do you know how old your grandmother was when she wrote these diaries?"

"Early sixties, I think."

"And you were how old?"

"Ten or eleven." A memory came back, clear as day. They were on Granny's screened in porch on a summer's day not unlike today. Kids voices could be heard from the playground a few blocks over, and an occasional car broke the silence of the street. Every once in a while, someone strolled by on their way to market, sometimes stopping to gossip a bit. But the constant sound, other than the persistent chirp of a nearby robin, was the whir of the wheel.

"I keep trying to imagine you on your own porch, spinning with this wheel," Granny had said, "but the image just won't stick in my mind. I suspect you aren't going to stay in this place. You're going to go make your own fortune." She'd nodded firmly. "Now that I can see."

The warmth from that day still seemed to wrap her in spite of the coolness of the attorney's office.

"She told me a lot," Megan said, "that she could see me as an adult spinning the wheel. Even from the time of those diaries"—she gestured to the pile on Cassandra's desk—"she told me one way or another it would be mine."

Cassandra nodded, but her attention was focused on the pages she scanned, thumbing from one marker to another.

Megan stared at the huge Western painting hung on the wall behind Cassandra's desk. It looked like it had been painted sometime in the 1800s, quick brush strokes of sage-covered prairies, cattle, cowboys on horseback and a gray wolf slunk down between distant rocks. Masterful, reminding her of the painting Dylan had shown her in the capitol building in Helena.

"It's a Charles Russell," Cassandra said without looking up. "My first big art purchase."

"Have you always lived in Montana?" Megan asked.

"No, but I've always felt like I belonged here. Some distant relation was from here a long time ago, about the time of that painting actually. I was born in Ohio, practiced law in Chicago for a while, then came out here." Cassandra gestured to the painting. "Go ahead and look. This will take me a few more moments."

The artwork was amazing close up. Even though the colors were lighter than she'd imagined, the strength of the action compelled her. It was as if every animal was in motion or thinking about it—almost like a frame in a movie, waiting for the next explosion to occur.

When she'd drunk her fill of light and color, she sat down again, sipping the water that Cassandra had ended up handing her.

"Okay," the attorney said, "here's what we're going to do. I have a copy of the complaint, and I'm going to answer it point by point with what you have laid out here. You did an excellent job, by the way."

"Thank you."

"I'll also be asking them to provide the proof backing their claim, which will slow them down or maybe eliminate the problem altogether. It depends on how tenacious they are."

"I'm not sure about that. They are selfish for sure, but I'm not sure how long they can hang on to an idea."

Cassandra chuckled. "There are more people like that than you'd believe. I prefer simply selfish, though, to tenacious and vindictive. That's when it gets expensive."

"Oh. Yes, how much do I owe you?"

"Don't worry about it."

"I couldn't accept it. It'd be like charity." Something she'd always hated, but not as badly as she'd been disgusted with herself for taking Macon's check. That had made her feel dirty, like she'd sold her body for money.

"You know," Cassandra said, "there is a concept of paying it forward. I do something nice for you and you pass it along down the road."

Megan gazed at her, trying to cipher out the trick. The attorney had never seemed warm and fuzzy to her before. Why was she acting like it now?

"Really—" she began.

"Make me a scarf or something if you insist," Cassandra said. "While I've got you here, let's talk about your business and filing an LLC. I can draw up that paperwork for a hundred dollars. Can you swing that?"

Megan nodded, her throat working at the unexpected generosity. After days of things going wrong, friendliness was about to do her in.

"What's wrong?" Cassandra asked.

"It's just you're being so nice, and Finn died, and the wheel, and ..." The tears that she still hadn't shed for all that was wrong with her life began to slide down her cheeks.

"Who's Finn?"

"My ... my ... alpaca." Megan sniffed and looked around frantically for tissues. Cassandra handed her a box from a nearby table.

"Occupational hazard," the attorney said. "People always cry in my office—divorce, child custody, and wills tend to do that."

Megan gave her a wan smile, then blew her nose.

"So any other unexploded mines I need to worry about or can we get back to business?" Cassandra's words were abrupt, but it was if she were unskilled in offering comfort, not that she was being mean about it.

"I broke up with Dylan," Megan replied, although she wasn't sure why. "Well, we weren't really going together ... well, kinda ... I don't know." Another sob hiccupped out.

"The Becks can be a troublesome lot." Cassandra nodded. "You know that Dave Brockman is very interested in taking you out. When you're ready, you might consider it. I'm sure he'd be glad to help you with your business, too."

"Thanks, I'll consider that." Megan pulled herself together. No matter where she went, she was going to need an LLC. The same could not be true about dating.

"What do you need to know for the LLC?" she asked.

# # #

Megan had just finished cleaning up after supper Thursday night when someone knocked on the door. Her heart sank as she went to answer it. What could it be now? She opened it to find two smiling women on the porch, the older one holding a good-sized plastic food container.

Darcie and her daughter, Roxanne.

"Hello," Megan said, pushing open the screen door. "Do you want to come in?"

"Sure," Darcie said. "These are for you."

"Oh, thank you." The ladies followed her into the living room.

"My goodness, that's a beautiful wheel," Roxanne said walking over to it and touching it lightly with her fingers.

"It was my granny's."

"We heard you lost one of your alpacas," Darcie said. "We're so sorry."

"Thank you," Megan repeated. "I didn't realize people knew."

"Small town," Darcie said.

"Too small," Roxanne added.

"Would you like to meet Flora, the one that's left? Then maybe we can have tea and some of these treats you've brought." Megan felt awkward, unused to guests in her home. Other than the vet and Dylan, the mother and daughter were the first.

After appropriate oohs and aahs over the alpaca, they returned to the house where Megan put the pot on to boil.

"We also wanted to apologize for Faith," Darcie said. "We know she was badmouthing the class. I went to see her and told her in no uncertain terms to cut it out."

"We also went to the school and asked that they get you to teach more classes." Roxanne pulled the hand spinner she'd gotten in the first class out of her purse. It was covered with brightly colored yarn. She handed it to Megan for inspection.

The yarn was evenly spun with a good tension and no slubs in it.

"Beautiful," Megan said, giving it back to her.

"I'm trying to convince my husband to get me a wheel for Christmas," she said. "I told him I needed something to keep the twins from driving me crazy. When he gets it, will you teach me to use it?"

"Now, Roxanne, you don't know he'll be able to get one," Darcie admonished.

"Oh, he'll do it, Mom. I promise you he will."

"I'll be happy to teach you," Megan said with a chuckle. She had no doubt the woman would get what she wanted. A little bubble of happiness rose inside her. Friends. She hadn't had any since school. And these ladies had gone out of their way for her.

She made the tea and plated the lemon bars they'd brought, setting out smaller plates and forks for their use. "These look lovely," she said.

"Trish Small taught a class on baking a few years back. This was the only thing that stuck," Darcie said.

"Rumor is you're going out with Dylan Beck," Roxanne said after they'd had a few bites of their snack.

"We went out a few times and he helped me with the alpacas, but it's nothing, really," Megan said.

Darcie and Roxanne exchanged a glance. "That's too bad," Roxanne said. "He's one of the good ones. I went to high school with him."

And probably dated him, too.

"All the girls wanted to get his attention, but he never really seemed interested in anyone. He dated when he wanted, but he was more interested in being friends. Like he was waiting for the perfect match. But anyone could talk to him. He was one of those safe guys who was good at breaking up fights and giving you exactly the answer you needed."

She had to ask. "Did you go out with him?"

"No. My husband and I started going out in junior high, and it stuck." Roxanne had a broad smile. "Although now that he's inflicted twins on me, I may have to rethink that decision. Worse, he wants another one. He says it will be easier to break up fights if there's an uneven number."

"The role of the middle child," Darcie said.

"Except in my case, the middle child will be the one who was born five minutes after the oldest." She shook her head. "Never going to work."

"Dylan's the middle child, isn't he?" Darcie asked.

"Yep," Roxanne said, "CJ, Jarod, Dylan, Cameron, and Kaiden."

"Well, like I said, we were just friends," Megan said.

"I'd double-check that assumption," Darcie said. "I heard from someone at church, who heard it from the housekeeper, who said Jarod told her Dylan was in a bad mood about someone or another. I'm guessing that someone is you." She pointed a finger at Megan.

"You're right," Megan said to Roxanne. "This town is too damn small."

The three laughed and went back to the lemon bars.

It was good to have people in her corner. Maybe she needed to trust a little more and worry a little less.

# # #

"When is Cameron coming back?" CJ asked when she walked into the ranch kitchen. Dylan and Jarod were both there stocking up on coffee before heading down to the barn.

Jarod looked at Dylan.

"I thought he was only staying a few weeks, but it's already been a month. He hasn't said much, just that there are still things to do for his friend's wife."

"That boy is making an art form out of not revealing anything," CJ said. "Speaking of art, how are your sketches coming?"

"You're drawing again?" Jarod asked. "Why am I always the last to know anything?"

"It's not supposed to be public knowledge." Dylan glared at his sister.

She stuck her tongue out at him. "I guess I better get to the office and make sure all the paperwork is up to date. It's sure nice having Samantha handle the books. God, I hated that job." She wiggled her fingers and went toward the ranch office.

In a minute she was back, his sketchbook in her hand. Damn. He'd forgotten it was in there.

"These are really good," she said, flipping through them. "The detail is amazing. You've got a talent there."

"Thanks." So what?

"Did you know there's a good market for drawings like these?" she asked, her gray eyes focusing on him as intently as a wolf's.

"I've never seen anything like them in a gallery," he said.

"Galleries are not the be-all and end-all of art."

"I'm not selling myself out," he said. He'd rather do anything else than become a mass-produced artist.

"You know," Jarod said, "people who can't afford gallery prices deserve art, too."

Dylan glared at his older brother.

"And schools need drawings like these. So do textbooks. And children's books. I was reading the other day that there's a lack of botanical artists. That's something you could do. And by the looks of these, you could do it well."

"Not only art but helping people learn. Win-win, as they say," Jarod added.

"Don't you have cattle to tend?" Dylan asked him.

"I do, but it's your turn today."

"Damn it all!" He slammed his coffee cup in the sink.

"Hey." CJ put her hand on his arm. "Think about it. Do some research." She held up the pad. "These are that good."

"Yeah, okay." He grabbed his hat from the rack in the mudroom as he headed out to the barn to saddle up a horse. The pickup or ATV would be faster, but he needed the soothing gait and relative quiet of riding.

His family was trying to do the best for him, get him out of his slump. It was an intriguing idea and he'd have to give it a serious look instead of dismissing it out of hand. He'd enjoyed creating the pictures of the glacier lily and shooting star. The bear grass had been a challenge, with all those tiny flowers making up the composite, but he'd gotten close to the right idea.

Make a living with his art? It was a pipe dream, but one that blossomed with new possibilities.

He smiled and swung a leg over Paint.

Chapter 24

Friday had been a whirlwind. Megan had worked at the bistro from opening til closing without a moment to get off her feet. Saturday's only saving grace would be that Courtney had decided to close early in order to attend the rodeo.

Megan had been determined to take the afternoon off and work on another pattern. Helen had loved the one she'd previously sent, said it was flying off the shelves, along with Megan's yarn and wanted to know when she was going to produce more of both.

Thinking about the inevitable collision course between her job at the bistro and building her business was giving Megan a headache. The job was her safety net. She needed it.

Didn't she?

Piling the last of the dishes into the bistro's dishwasher, she set it to run.

"That it, Courtney?" she called over to where her boss was running the day's receipts.

"Sure is. I'll see you at the rodeo."

Megan didn't bother to disagree.

But once she slid into the car, she felt differently. Why was she being such a curmudgeon? She'd never been to a rodeo; there were bound to be people she knew, which would be all right if one of those people wasn't Dylan.

She'd treated him badly, but she didn't know how else to be. He would interfere too much with her dream, her life, and he'd want something in return. Heat fluttered inside her as an image arose of his slightly bearded face the morning they'd made love.

Not a bad price to pay.

But no. No entanglements.

Fine. She'd go to the rodeo, grab something to eat that she hadn't served, and learn what all the fuss was about.

Parking was more difficult than she thought it would be. The entire town and miles of the surrounding area must have decided to participate. As she walked toward the wooden structure, the pulse of excitement rose in the air, along with the dust kicked up by hooves and feet.

She paid her entry fee and perused the food vendors before choosing a sinful hot dog loaded with chili. Once she had the thing in her hand, though, she was baffled at how to get it into her mouth.

"Just go for it!" the vendor shouted. "No one'll care if you get it all over yourself. It happens."

But her granny's training kicked in, and she maneuvered her way around the chili dog without getting splattered. She couldn't say the same for the ground, but a small tan dog immediately cleaned up her droppings.

She clambered up to a seat, program in hand, and tried to figure out what was going on. What was a sheep doing in the ring? An assistant tried to get the sheep to move along, but it placed its legs square on the ground and refused to move. The assistant whistled, and a black-and-white dog streaked toward the animal. The sheep bleated and moved toward a chute in the wall.

As soon as it was well away, the announcer's gravelly voice said, "And now for our second entrant in the mutton-busting event, let's give a round of applause for Tim Nielson!"

Was he related to the vet?

There wasn't time to think about it too much because another sheep leapt out of the chute. Who knew the animals could move so fast? When she saw the little boy clinging to the wool, she laughed along with many of the people around her, but soon there were shouts of encouragement.

"Stay on her, Tim!"

"You can do it!"

The ride only lasted a few seconds, but the boy jumped up from the dirt in which he'd landed and waved his arm, a big grin splitting his brown face.

"Enjoying yourself?" a familiar voice asked.

"Oh!" She turned to her right where a small woman perched nearby.

"Oh, hi, Birdie. Good to see you again." Megan smiled. "And yes, I am. Although I don't think I've ever seen a sheep-riding event before."

"It's been a small-town rodeo tradition for a long time. The little ones want to participate, and falling off a sheep is a short drop. They get to experience the thrill and learn the consequences."

Megan chuckled. "Does Jarod have riders or horses in this?"

"Yes, he's right over there."

Birdie pointed, and Megan quickly spotted Jarod ... right next to Dylan. She looked away.

"I didn't know Dylan was helping out," she said.

"Dylan was born helping out," Birdie said. "He was always sorting out problems between his brothers and sister and lending a hand when it was needed. It's coded into his DNA somehow."

"Oh."

"I thought he was helping you out with your alpaca business and all."

Cheers went up as another sheep dashed out of the chute.

Megan searched for the right way to say what she needed to. "I need to do things on my own," she began, "prove myself, you know."

"Hmm."

Another tiny rider hit the dust. This one didn't have the showmanship of the first. Instead she dragged herself from the dirt and slumped off to her father, streaks of tears running down her cheeks.

"This business needs to be something I've built from start to finish," Megan continued, repeating the lines she'd said over and over to herself. "I don't want to owe anyone anything. If it takes longer, that's okay. It'll be mine when I'm done."

"I see," Birdie said.

Megan let her gaze stray to Dylan and Jarod. The two were grinning as they helped a twelve-year-old into the saddle.

"Barrel racing's about to start," Birdie said over the gravelly tones of the announcer naming the winners of the mutton busting. "Jarod's trainees should have a good shot."

"I'm glad."

"You know," Birdie said, "No one ever does anything totally on their own. The American myth of individualism is just that, a myth. We depend on each other in one way or another."

"Yes, that's true, but you mean in the greater scheme of things, like roads, and schools."

Birdie nodded. "That, and, for most of us, more." She gestured to Jarod and Dylan. "They help each other, give and take. It's not discussed. They just do it."

"But I have nothing to give him." Megan's heart ached with the truth of the statement. She was poor in so many ways.

"Not true. We never really know what we do for other people. You opened Dylan up, gave him a way to see his art differently, just by allowing him into your life and making him give up one of his silly notions."

"What was that?"

"That he couldn't fall for someone who wasn't born and bred in Montana."

Megan laughed. There were a lot of North Carolinians who felt the same way, especially when it came to Yankees.

"When I came to Choteau a long time ago," Birdie said. "I was lost. My Daniel had just died, and my son and I were estranged." She shook her head. "I didn't like the woman he'd married and felt my opinion was more important than the girl he loved." She shook her head. "Stupid woman."

"And you've never heard from him again?"

"No. I send Christmas cards and hope he'll respond someday. They never get returned, so I know he gets them."

"I'm sorry." Megan's heart ached for the old woman. She probably had grandchildren she'd never seen.

And if Megan kept pushing people away, she'd probably end up in the same situation.

"Can anyone join this party?" CJ plunked down next to Birdie.

"It's a free country," Megan said, offering a smile.

"I'm so nervous," Samantha said, taking up Megan's other side. "This is Audie's first competition. Jarod says she's ready, but if she doesn't get a medal, I know she's going to be devastated."

"She'll survive," CJ said. "I think this whole everyone-gets-a-medal thing has gotten out of hand. Adversity can make us better people."

"Or we stop seeking something we'll never get," Megan said.

"Profound," CJ ribbed her.

"Yeah." Megan chuckled. Sometimes she did get a little full of herself.

The announcer started talking, and they all leaned forward to watch the action.

The first up were the littlest ropers, trying to throw a rope around a pair of long horns attached to a sawhorse. Amazingly, three out of the five made it, leading to cheers from different sections of the stands. The next group tackled a real calf, a wide-eyed, howling animal that lunged from one end of the ring to another. Only two of those kids made the cut, with one of them being Jarod's trainee.

"Way to go, baby brother!" CJ shouted from the stands.

"Leave your brother alone," Nick said, climbing into the stands beside her. "He's got enough to handle with those kids without you busting his balls."

"Where's Trevor?" Birdie asked.

"Down there somewhere." Nick gestured to a group of teens hanging together on the lower levels of the stands. "They all seem to go in clumps these days."

"But he's still doing okay?" Birdie asked.

"Yeah. He heads back to Seattle to stay with his mom for six weeks on Tuesday, and he's not crazy about that. He's looking forward to taking pictures with the new camera we got him, but it seems there's some girl he's sweet on here."

"It's only going to get worse," CJ said.

"That's for sure," Birdie agreed.

"Oh, goodness," Samantha said. "I can't even imagine Audie being a teenager." She gave a fake shudder.

They all got along so easily. Would she ever be able to feel that comfortable with a group? Just to let all her thoughts and worries hang out there without being concerned that others were judging her?

"Hey," CJ said as the rodeo assistants were setting up for the barrel racing. "I could use a beer. Anyone else?"

"Sounds good to me," Nick said. "And fries?" His smile tried to beguile his girlfriend.

"That'd be nice," Samantha said. "It's hot out here."

"Megan, can you give me a hand?"

"Sure," she said. This could only mean one thing: CJ had been assigned the task of grilling her about what was going on between her and Dylan.

They tromped down the stairs to the beer truck and food booths.

CJ didn't waste any time.

"So what's up with you and Dylan?" she asked as they waited in line.

"Nothing. He helped me out, and I appreciated it. I let him know that, but I was pretty clear up front that I was planning on running this business on my own. It's important to me. Surely, you can see that. You're a woman who runs her own business."

CJ leaned against a railing and studied her. "I do run my own business," she said, "But Nick has been essential to me. In fact, I wouldn't have the career I do without his support."

The line moved forward.

"It's a two-way street," she continued. "The best relationships always are. I help him with his business, both physical labor and supporting his marketing efforts. They're more my skills. We both parent Trevor, even though he's Nick's son. We talk, we communicate. Whenever there's a problem, we stick with it until we figure out how to resolve it."

"You don't push each other away," Megan said, getting the point.

"Exactly."

They stepped up to the window.

"I'll take five beers," CJ said and put a twenty on the counter.

"I can cover mine." Megan pushed her hand into her jean's pocket to grab the crumpled cash she kept there.

CJ picked up two of the beers and handed them to her. "Don't worry. You won't be indebted for a two-dollar beer." She gathered the other three, and they walked back to the stands.

Audie came in third in the barrel racing event for her age group, and she was ecstatic, showing off her ribbon to anyone who gave her the slightest opening. Megan laughed at the antics of some of the professional athletes as they clowned through a halftime show of sorts. Her heart was lodged in her throat, watching young men hang on to wildly bucking horses, grimaces on their faces and arms waving in the air.

At the end, she felt as exhausted as the participants must be.

"The family is going back to the ranch to grill up some steaks. Got some corn, potato salad, and three-bean casserole. There's plenty. Come along." Birdie was issuing a command, not a request.

"I really shouldn't. I don't have anything to bring."

"You really should"—Samantha put a strong emphasis on the word *should*—"give up trying to fight them. The Beck family is a force far mightier than us mere mortals."

"Amen to that, sister," CJ said. "Well, almost sister."

"I can't believe the wedding is only seventy-five days away," Samantha said. "There's so much to do."

"You had to start her up, didn't you?" Birdie glared at CJ. "Now let's get going. It'll take us a while to round everyone up. And you have to go pry your young fella away from his friends."

Nick shook his head. "I've already given him permission to hang out with Sam and Beth Small as long as he's home after the fireworks are done."

"Okay then. Let's tell the boys we're rolling home." Birdie

leveraged herself off the bench seat. "Ugh. These seats aren't getting any more comfortable."

"I'll meet you there," Megan said. "I can't stay late; I have lots to do tomorrow."

"Okay," Birdie said and gave her a stern look. "But you better be there."

"Yes, ma'am."

Megan made her way down the stands, conversations chattering around her, cheers lifting from small groups as they congratulated the riders, odors of spilled beer, popcorn, and animal dung all overlain by a thin layer of dirt. She could almost see herself as a cinematographer would, camera lens following one small lit figure through a background of noise and confusion.

She didn't belong here. How could she ever fit into this world of testosterone, leather, and danger? She'd been raised as a Southern buttercup, not a rugged cowgirl.

The sheriff must have spotted her because all of a sudden he was standing in front of her. "I hear you've got Cassandra Sanders working on your behalf," he said.

"Yes ... sir."

He studied her without a smile. "Good choice. She's my wife's attorney. Soon to be ex-wife, as I'm sure you've heard in this town."

"Um ... I may have."

"So you can imagine I'm not too fond of her," the sheriff continued as if he hadn't heard her.

"No."

"Still, she's a good attorney. She should get you free."

"I hope so."

He nodded and put his finger to his hat. Just as suddenly as he'd appeared, he was gone.

Hopefully, he was right.

Her gaze followed him and in the distance, she saw Dave Brockman. He waved at her.

More unfinished business.

"Hey, you," Dylan said. "Did you enjoy it?"

"I did." She smiled and looked toward Dave. He stopped walking, and his friendly expression turned into a stony glare. Then he turned on his heel and strode away.

Dylan followed her gaze.

"Something between you two?" he asked.

"No," she said. "I told you, I'm not interested in a

relationship. I don't think I can even stay. It's too different. I don't belong here."

"Of course you belong here," he said. "Montanans come from all states. It takes grit to stay, and you've got that in spades."

"I'm not sure about that. I feel so exhausted and alone."

"Well," he said, his voice softening, "maybe if you stopped pushing people away so hard, you wouldn't feel that way."

Her breath shortened. What would happen if she took a risk, if she let Dylan into her life? Would he try to rob her blind like her relatives who treated her like a modern day Cinderella? He had no father to buy her off, so she'd be spared that humiliation.

Everyone said Dylan was one of the good ones.

What if everyone was wrong? She'd be alone again, only this time she'd have to flee with an alpaca in tow. If the alpaca didn't die like Finn had. And her job? How could she possibly give up her job? She'd have no money. She'd lose it all.

Somewhere along the way, her thoughts must have turned into words because she was speaking. Dylan stood patiently before her, waiting for her to spin to a stop.

But she kept talking.

"And now Birdie wants me to come to your place for supper, but I can't because I'm so tired, so very, very tired. And I need to work, to spin ... they want more yarn ... and I want to make more patterns ... I really enjoy making patterns ..."

She must be crying because her face was wet, and Dylan was looking concerned.

"I ... I ..." And she couldn't speak anymore. All she could do was cry.

At some level she was aware that Dylan put his arm around her and led her away to a secluded spot behind a barn where he sat them both on a hay bale. When he pulled her close, she let everything else go and sobbed on his chest, his strong arm around her keeping her safe.

# # #

Once Megan had cried herself out and calmed down, Dylan got her into her car and followed her home to make sure she got there safely. Although she drove slowly, she didn't weave, to his relief. What would happen when they made it back to her place? Would she allow him to be close, to continue to comfort her?

It mattered. Over the last week he'd realized how important

it was for him to have someone to support besides the family. And if she wasn't from Montana, that was turning out to be okay too. Odd how life continued to hand you what you thought you didn't want until you took a second look.

The gravel crunched under his wheels as he turned into her driveway. Cautiously, he approached her car and opened the driver's side door. She looked up from the seat, her face wan and her eyes red, clearly visible in lingering summer twilight.

"I must look a fright," she said, her Southern accent stronger than usual.

"You look like a very tired person, which is what you are," he said, extending a hand.

She leveraged herself out of the seat, and he shut the door behind her.

"Let's get you to sleep," he said, choosing the word carefully.

"Flora ..." she began.

"I'll take care of her."

"Not your job."

"Be quiet," he said and turned her toward the back porch. At the door, she fumbled with her keys until he took them and opened the door and stumbled inside. Using the bench next to the door, he pulled off his boots, not wanting to track rodeo dust and whatever else his soles had picked up inside.

By the time he'd followed her in, she'd made it to the bedroom, where she sat.

"Here, let me help," he said, kneeling to remove her shoes, debating how comfortable he should get her for bed.

When he helped her stand, she clung to his arms.

"Thank you," she whispered. "I'm sorry I'm such a stubborn old ass."

"It's okay. You're just afraid," he said. "It's understandable."

"It's stupid." She bit her lower lip. "I'm tired of being scared of everything. Am I going to fail at business? Is Courtney going to fire me because I can't balance what I need to do to her satisfaction? Will there ever be someone in my life who's there just for me?" A tear trickled down her cheek again.

He brushed it away. "You know the answer to the last one. You just have to let me in."

She stared up at him, her wet eyes sparkling in the setting sunlight shining in through the window. Then she pulled his head down and kissed him, a long, lingering meeting of their lips. There was a hint of sexual passion, but it was more than that. She was letting down a barrier that had kept her sealed off.

"Stay with me tonight," she whispered. "Please, don't leave me alone."

"Are you sure?"

"Yes."

He checked her gaze, searching for the truth, then nodded. "I'll be back in as soon as I take care of the alpaca." And let Birdie know they weren't going to make it. "You get ready."

She nodded.

He released her, hoping she would stay awake long enough to disrobe and climb under the sheet.

When he returned, he found she'd managed to take care of that but was sound asleep. He went back to the living room, slipped a book from the bookcase, and read until his own eyelids drooped. Then he slipped off his clothes and joined her, swiftly falling into a peaceful sleep.

Chapter 25

"We didn't make love," Megan said when she turned to him the next morning.

"Not to be offensive," Dylan said with a smile, "but it would have been a bit like making love to a corpse. I have to draw the line somewhere."

"Did I snore?" She covered her mouth, and her eyes widened.

"Not at all." He propped his head up on his hand. "But you did take up most of the room."

"Well, it *is* my bed," she teased back. Then her gaze tracked beyond him.

"Oh, my god! Is that the time!"

He cranked his head around to look. Seven thirty. Late for him.

"I have to be at work in an hour! I've got to shower and have breakfast!"

His last glimpse was of her naked ass as she leapt out of bed and ran to the bathroom.

It was a very nice sight.

He pushed himself out of bed, slung on his clothes, and went into the kitchen to start coffee. Fifteen minutes later she was out of the bathroom, flushed and pretty, even in her regulation black slacks and white blouse.

"You look nice," he said, pouring her a cup of coffee. "I did like the other outfit better, though."

"My jeans and T-shirt?" she asked.

"The other other one," he said with a grin.

Her cheeks flamed red.

"What do you have for breakfast?" he asked.

"I'll grab something at work." She put down her coffee. "Flora. I've got to feed her and let her out." She looked down at her work clothes.

"I'll take care of it."

"You can't keep rescuing me."

He held up his hand. "Stop. You need to get to work. I'm heading home. There's some things I need to take care of this afternoon, but we need to talk. Preferably when you're awake." He dropped a kiss on her forehead. "Although you're awfully cute when you sleep, too."

The color on her cheeks deepened.

"I really have to go," she said. "Lock up when you leave?"

"When are you done?"

"Six."

"How about I pick up a pizza and meet you here."

She looked like she was about to argue again but shut her mouth and nodded. "Okay. See you then."

He watched her from the window as she got into her car, spun it around, and took off out of the driveway. Someone definitely needed to remove the pressure on that girl.

After feeding Flora and letting her out into the larger pen, he headed home to shower and get his own breakfast.

An hour later, he was back in his cabin, staring at an email he'd received the week before. Following CJ's advice, he'd contacted a few magazines that had drawings of plants and flowers. This one, based in Seattle, had gotten back to him with a request for samples.

While his sketch of the glacier lily was good, he knew it probably wasn't up to their standards, so he had planned to spend the afternoon redrawing it to match what he saw in their magazine, as well as adding watercolor in the appropriate hues. He got out his supplies, lined up a new paper, and began to work.

Finally satisfied, he stretched his back and his paint-smeared fingers. It was amazing that in this age of computerized everything, the art of botanical drawing was still required. Like writing by hand instead of on a word processer, the brush in his hand gave him a sense of immediacy that typing on a keyboard never had.

But still, the things were useful.

He grabbed a cup of coffee and perused the local paper online, smiling at the coverage the paper had given the rodeo. He'd heard that a new couple had purchased the paper from a conglomerate and were dedicated to providing hometown news and flavor. Montana being the place it was, people from Choteau and the surrounding area were steering some of their advertising dollars the paper's way.

One of those ads caught his eye. He knew that house. He'd seen it recently. It sat on the property just south of their ranch, an odd little corner some ancestor had sold off for some reason lost

in time. There was a good-sized barn and about twenty acres that went with it. Not worth anything as a cattle ranch ... but perfect for alpacas and a fiber business.

Was he willing to even think that far ahead with Megan? Falling into bed together and helping her with her business were one thing, cohabiting on any level was another. Still, he really needed a place of his own; living cheek to jowl with his brother and Birdie, and soon to be more, was getting claustrophobic. This place would be perfect—far enough away from the family to call it his own, close enough to help Jarod out without it being a long commute.

He must know someone in that real estate office.

# # #

Dylan met Marsha Allen at the gate to the property. She produced a key, and they headed toward the house.

"No one's living here?" he asked when they stepped out of their cars at the end of the drive. He had vague memories of a retired couple who'd bought the place from the people who'd owned it while he was growing up.

"Nope. An older couple was here for the last ten years, but he died and she went into assisted living in Great Falls." Marsha frowned. "It's tough when the kids don't have the room or don't want to take you in."

"Yeah," he said, wanting to get beyond the subject. The changes a person had to deal with at the end of life were ones he didn't want to think about too much.

"They raised a few sheep, let a local man shear them. I think they wanted them as lawn ornaments as much as anything."

Dylan chuckled. Raising a few animals to make a place feel lived in was a common practice of people who hadn't grown up doing the dirty chores that owning a large animal naturally involved.

"Shall we go inside?" Marsha asked.

"Yep."

The space was nicely laid out. Living, dining, kitchen, and a full bath on the bottom floor with an extra space that could be used as a den or office. Three more bedrooms upstairs and an attic with skylights. The floors were polished hardwood, the walls a recently painted matte off-white.

"It would be perfect for a studio," Marsha said. "That's what you do, isn't it? Paint? I saw one of your paintings at the bistro."

"Yes. When I'm not working with my brother."

"That's another reason I was happy you called. This is such an odd little section of land, surrounded on three sides by your ranch. It makes it a bit of a tougher sell."

Dylan nodded. Too many salespeople didn't know when to stop talking, and Marsha appeared to be one of them.

Once they finished inspecting the house, they moved onto the grounds. In addition to the barn, he could see a covered shelter, its back to the prevailing wind. Perfect for an animal to get away from the elements. The fence nearby was strong and well-maintained.

"Nicely kept up," he said.

"Yes. The people who owned it had enough money to hire people to maintain it after they could no longer care for it themselves. It's really perfect for a young person like you, and perhaps a family." She cocked her head as if looking for some gossip to pass along.

Which she probably was. Information, not land, was the currency of a lot of businesses. In real estate, knowing people's circumstances allowed a Realtor to get a listing or sale faster than the competition.

She told him the asking price. A down payment was well within the capability of his trust fund. And this was the type of investment he'd been looking to make.

"I'll need to get back to you," he said as she locked the door behind them, although he already knew he wanted the place. Badly. Even if he couldn't entice Megan to make their relationship more than it was, he wanted his own space.

And what would it be like to have kids? He'd always thought he never wanted a family, was afraid to screw it up. But a bunch of little redheaded kids?

He smiled and swung himself into the truck. It was just about time to head into town.

# # #

Megan got home and freshened up, only slightly less weary than she'd been the night before. All day she'd thought about the upcoming discussion with Dylan. It was a crossroads, a decision that would push her life in one direction or another, just as her choice to leave her home in North Carolina behind had been.

Sometimes she missed the country homespun life her granny had represented. The neighborliness was similar in Choteau, but it had a different edge to it, more open, if she was honest with herself. But the summers in the South, even in the mountains, were languid in a way the West would never be. The short growing season put too much pressure on everybody to allow them to be subtle.

The saying was that a person could never go home again. It may not be true for everyone, but it was true for her. The nest Granny had created was gone, her parents and brother dead, and the only relatives left were determined to make her life miserable.

Returning to North Carolina was off the table.

The knock on the door startled her from her reverie. "Come in," she called, picking herself up from the couch where she'd settled.

"I hope you like pepperoni and mushrooms," Dylan said as he came into the kitchen.

"I do, thank you," she said. Why was she being all formal? He'd already seen her without her clothes. Not once but twice.

When her hand shook pulling the plates from the cupboard, she knew: nerves.

He must have spotted it, because after putting the pizza box on the counter, he took the plates. "It's okay," he said, looking directly into her eyes. "No one is going to force you to do anything."

She smiled but didn't say anything.

"Hungry?" he asked when they sat down.

"Starving," she confessed, not realizing how much until that moment. There was something about a rich, greasy, cheesy pizza that brought out her appetite like nothing else. She picked up her knife and fork, having learned the Western way of attacking the pie, so different from the fold and eat method she'd grown up with.

Funny how one country could hold so many different cultures.

She savored each bite as she ate it, her mind racing with possibilities the whole time. What was he going to propose? What should she accept?

"So how was work today?" he asked.

"Busy. I was surprised. I guess a lot of people were headed home."

"Or they just didn't want to cook after doing barbeques and

picnics on the Fourth."

She nodded. "What did you do today?"

"Worked on my drawings. CJ had the bright idea I should look into some botanical jobs."

"What does that mean?"

"I'm a little fuzzy on that myself. But it involves doing detailed drawings of plants and coloring them accurately."

"Oh! That's brilliant," she said. "That sketch you showed me of the bird was so detailed. Will you do birds and animals as well?"

"Perhaps. But at least plants stay still." He grinned.

"That's true."

"I'm coming around to her way of thinking. It's a bit more tricky than slapping paint on a canvas, though. The details have to be right, and the lines and color exact."

"A challenge."

"But I like a challenge." His smile indicated he was talking about more than painting.

Her heart gave a lurch.

"Did your family enjoy the festivities?"

"Audie was over the moon," he said. "She couldn't stop talking about her ribbon and praising her horse, Misty. She's a good little kid."

Did he want kids? She didn't even know if she wanted them.

"Samantha and Jarod were apparently all lovey-dovey after they tucked her into CJ's old room. They need to get married. I don't think the rest of us can stand it much longer."

"Did she stay the night?"

"Oh, no. They're waiting until the wedding. They're pretty strict that way. Neither of them swears, either. It's totally annoying."

She laughed. "I'll have to watch my language."

"Oh, please don't," he said. "It's far more fun to watch them squirm."

She shook her head, although she kept smiling. It had been a long time since she'd been this relaxed.

After they'd cleaned up, he said, "Let's take a drive. There's something I want to show you."

"I thought you wanted to talk," she said, nerves re-asserting themselves.

"I do. But I want to do it somewhere else."

"Okay."

They climbed into his pickup and headed south.

She tried to start the conversation several times, but his replies were noncommittal and impersonal. Finally giving up, she leaned back into the seat and watched the play of light over the mountains.

It would never get old. She'd never be able to leave.

Megan sighed, accepting that truth. But if so, now what?

"You okay?" Dylan asked.

"Yeah," she said. "Just content."

"Good way to be."

They passed the turnoff to the family ranch. Where was he taking her?

Shortly after that Dylan pulled into another drive, almost too faded to see. Along both sides of the road ran wire fences. To the right, off in the distance, cattle huddled together. In the distance stood a house and barn, along with several other outbuildings. Twilight softened the edges of everything around her, making it seem like a dream or a movie set.

Beside her, Dylan seemed to tense more with each rotation of the truck's tires. His eyes focused straight ahead, as if he were afraid to look at her and give away whatever he was thinking.

When they got to the house, he pulled beside the locked gate. "Come with me," he said, then got out of the truck and walked around to open her door.

"But how? What? Why?"

"Shhh," he said, putting his fingers to his lips.

He helped her slide through the rails of the surrounding fence, then led her to the front porch of the house. "Imagine," he said, "sitting here in a rocker or in front of a spinning wheel and watching the sun fade over the mountains." He gestured to the plate glass window next to him. "Even in winter, the view would be available."

Taking her hand, he pulled her toward the barn. "Plenty of room for alpacas, horses, or anything else you might need." He pointed to the pasture to the west. "There's good grazing there, I know. Our family's land is on the other side."

"This is all beautiful," she said, "but I could never afford it."

"I can," he said.

She stared at him for a few seconds, then shook her head. "I can't ..."

"Wait," he said. "Hear me out." He took both her hands. "We have something, something I want to explore further. I know it's premature for us to do anything as drastic as move in together, but maybe, when your lease is up, you might think about becoming a roommate." His lips twisted into a gentle smile, but caution lingered in his eyes.

"You mean, move in here, with you, but not in the same bedroom."

"That's generally what roommate means."

"I don't think that would be possible."

"Why not?"

Was he that unobservant? She couldn't be around him without wanting to feel his touch. Even now, currents of desire flowed from her hands to his and back again. And that alone meant she was already in more deeply than she'd ever intended.

"You're thinking too much," he said.

"It's too much. I guess I wasn't ready for this."

"I was afraid you'd say that." He released her hands, then looked around. "I'm probably going to buy it anyway. The attic is a great place to paint, and I need some space from my family." He looked back down at her. "Then, when time comes and things work out the way I hope they will, there will be space for you here." He put his hand over his heart. "And here."

She didn't have words for the feelings that washed over her. Love? Too soon. Relief? From what? Room to breathe. To become who she was becoming?

Acceptance. That was the long and short of it. He accepting her just the way she was, wounds, dreams, and all.

When he bent down to kiss her, she let down another set of guards and accepted his lips. The kiss was sweet and lasted only a few seconds. Then he put his arm around her and showed her the rest of the place.

# # #

"Hear you're buying a house," Jarod said to Dylan as they rode the fence line up to the northwest corner of the property. The drone had indicated some leaning posts and sagging wires. They'd decided to take horses rather than ATVs so they could continue on up to the cliff where they'd found the pipe sticking out.

"Yeah. I need a space of my own. You're going to fill up the house with rug rats. I can just see it now."

"And here I was thinking you were looking for a place that was big enough for a woman, her spinning wheel, and her livestock."

247

"Jury's still out on that one." Dylan stopped Paint, swung off, and walked to a piece of fence. "Let's shore this up. Looks like the wet spring we had loosened the ground some."

"Sounds good." They worked efficiently, repounding the fence post and tightening the wires.

"She can't see what a good catch you are?" Jarod tweaked him as they remounted and continued up the hill. "You've got to do a better sales job."

"Stuff it. I'll do this my own way, thank you. Besides, you're supposed to be concentrating on a wedding."

"Don't remind me. Who knew there was so much to do? And I feel like Samantha wants to invite the whole town. Whoever she doesn't remember, Audie does. And, of course, Birdie has her own opinions about who should be there. We should just take out an advertisement in the paper and be done with it."

"You'll make it."

"I hope so. I've finally understood why people elope."

They moved to a single file as they came to a narrow spot on the trail beside the fence. Dylan allowed his mind to drift to the steady clop of the horse's hooves and the sun on his back.

After they'd walked the house, he'd taken Megan back to her home. She'd invited him in, and he'd wound up staying the night. Something had shifted. They weren't anywhere close to moving in together, but the possibility flowed between them.

When he and Jarod got to the top of the ridge, they tied the horses and tried to work out a way down to the ledge they could just make out below. It was obvious there had once been an iron ladder heading to something, but why had the damn thing been built?

"Here," Jarod called as he hacked away at some bushes with a hatchet he'd brought along. "The brush has overgrown what looks like a path."

Dylan yanked the branches as his brother broke them off. Sure enough, there was a trace of a path heading downhill. It went away from the ladder, but there was always the hope that it would switch back to the ledge they were interested in exploring.

Cautiously, they made their way down the path, which steepened almost immediately.

"It would have been tough to get any animals or equipment down here," Jarod said.

"You assume that someone was after some type of mineral."

"Has to be. It wasn't gas or oil, although someone could be

looking for a seam of coal, depending on how long ago this path was made."

"Silver or copper could also be possibilities," Dylan said.

"Yeah."

The path switched back toward where they'd started, then back the other way. Each time it reversed itself, it became narrower, and soon they were hugging the wall.

"We may not be able to get much farther," Jarod said.

"Nope." Dylan looked down at the almost vertical wall below them. At its bottom, the summer remains of a creek slalomed around good-sized rocks. Surviving a fall to the bottom would be almost impossible.

The path widened for about twenty-five feet, then came to an abrupt end. A ponderosa pine struggled from the hillside, right where the path would have continued if it were still there. About ten yards ahead, Dylan could see where the ledge continued and opened even wider, before it was covered with sagebrush. Based on the darkness beyond the brush, it looked like there may be a cave or inlet of some kind.

"What do you think?" he asked Jarod.

"I don't think we're going any farther," his brother said. "But it sure would be interesting to find out what's over there."

"Looks like a cave of some sort." Dylan looked above the opening. "And see, there's another few spikes."

"Maybe the ledge broke away after a heavy winter storm and they put in the ladder."

"Could be. The trick will be getting down there ourselves."

"Think it's important?" Jarod asked.

"I'm curious, aren't you?"

"What about the drone?'

"I'll bring it up here and see what I can find out, but I'm not sure what I'm looking for. I can't tell one rock from the other."

"Kaiden can," Jarod said. "He should be here for the wedding, if not before, so you can get him to come with you."

"Can we wait that long?"

"I don't see any other choice, do you?"

Dylan shook his head. "We've seen all we can see. Let's head back."

They climbed back up the steep slope, mounted their horses and started down another section of fence. Climbing out of a draw, Jarod drew his horse up short in front of Dylan.

Four men who looked like they were from the exploratory

team the lawyers had told them was coming were headed toward them on a pair of ATVs. Jarod and Dylan rode down to a wider spot and waited.

"Howdy," one of the men said.

Jarod nodded. "Surprised to see you up here. Wouldn't think there'd be any gas or oil in this area."

"You can never tell," the man said.

Dylan looked the four over. "Where's our inspector? She's supposed to be with any group that is doing research."

"She couldn't make it today. Some female issue." The sneer was evident in his voice, although his expression was still pleasant.

No matter how long women had been working in traditional male fields, some guys were simply Neanderthals.

"Well, then you four will just have to turn around, then," Jarod said. "You can't be on our land without our inspector. It's what the courts ruled."

"We're not harming anything," a thin man with glasses said. "Just going for an outing. Beautiful day, you know."

Dylan moved closer to the ATVs and looked pointedly at the equipment tied to the backs. "Don't see a picnic basket." He rode back in front of the lead vehicle. "My brother said to turn around. If you back down a little bit, it looks like there's room to do it."

The Neanderthal looked like he was going to protest, but the thin man said, "Have it your way, but we'll be back. All our surveys indicate this will be the spot where we find what we're looking for."

The second ATV backed up, turned and headed back down the hill with the first following suit.

Dylan looked around at the pristine land and view that ranged from the rugged mountains to the west to the massive butte rising in the distant east. "They'll drill here over my dead body."

"Let's hope it doesn't come to that," Jarod said. "But I wonder what exactly they're looking for."

Chapter 26

"What do you think, Flora?" Megan asked the alpaca. "Should I consider being a roommate?"

Flora simply stared at her, the thick-lashed, brown eyes kind, as if she understood exactly how much trouble the male species could be at times.

"Problem is ..." Megan leaned against the fence, examining the alpaca for any sign of flaws. Before he'd sold them to her, the farmer had shorn the animals. Flora's fleece was coming back in nicely. "I think he's gotten to me. No matter what happens, he's steady and works things out. He treats his sister and Birdie well, too. Oh, I am so not ready for this."

Every day she spent time thinking about his proposal. The property was perfect for what she had in mind. There was even enough room on the property for her to build a store and studio for classes. CJ had offered to help with the website.

All Megan needed to do was commit.

She walked back to the house, ready for another hour of spinning. The summer was moving on. Next week was already August. Business at the bistro was still brisk, but Courtney had said schools in Montana started before Labor Day, and most out-of-state tourists were headed home to prepare for their own children's schools.

All that remained were the senior RVers, and they'd be heading south soon to escape the cold. Especially if they got frost in August, which sometimes happened.

Like he had most nights over the last month, Dylan was coming by in the late afternoon to help out with Flora. He said he was educating himself. More often than not, he stayed the night and they made sweet love before falling asleep in each other's arms.

But was he learning about the alpaca or studying how to make Megan believe in a combined future?

She sat at the wheel—*her* wheel. Cassandra had successfully convinced the Asheville district attorney that her relatives had no case to repossess the wheel. The lawyer's fee had been steep but worth every penny for the victory. After the attorney had called to tell her the good news, she'd crumpled to the floor of her rental and cried. But this time they were tears of happiness.

The gears hummed as she drafted the combination of alpaca and silk she'd ordered online. There was contentment in this life she was crafting for herself. Her latest knitting class was full, in spite of Faith's negative gossip. The shop in Great Falls continually sold out of her yarn, even though she'd raised her prices, as Helen had encouraged her to do. Helen had also passed her work on to the other yarn store owners she knew in the state. People from as far away as Billings had contacted her.

If this kept up, she'd be at a point where she had to take the step of reducing her hours at the bistro, maybe even giving it up altogether. She crunched numbers every other night to make sure she was heading in the right direction. Giving up her safety net frightened her, but taking the leap was the only thing that was going to propel her business forward satisfactorily. In her heart of hearts, she knew that, much as it frightened her to take that step.

A doe drifted from the high grass onto what passed as Megan's lawn before cranking her head around to look behind her. A small nose poked out from the stalks, then the fawn came out on spindly legs. The doe walked over to Megan's carefully tended flower bed and snipped a bud off neatly with her teeth.

"Why, you little ..."

The deer must have heard her because she raised her head and looked at the window wide-eyed while she chewed. Then she reached down and plucked another blossom. The fawn tore at a clump of browning grass.

Megan shook her head. Oh well. If she couldn't share her home with wildlife, she needed to live somewhere else. She watched the pair for a while, then went back to spinning.

Sometime around five, Dylan's truck pulled into the drive, but she didn't get up. They'd settled into a pattern. He'd take care of Flora and then come in. At first, she'd resisted his help, then realized this was his way of dating. Some men wanted to take a woman to a fancy dinner, and some wanted to relieve their burdens.

"Hello?" he called in as he opened the door about forty-five minutes later.

"Hi," she said, setting her drafted wool down and rising.

"I brought you this," he said, handing her a pot of daisies. "I thought you might put them out back."

"Oh, good," she said with a smile. "One more thing for the deer to enjoy."

"Are they eating your flowers?" he asked.

"With a vengeance."

"Irish Spring soap," he said. "Sometimes that will keep them away. At least that's what I've heard. The other idea is to plant stuff they don't like."

"And would daisies happen to be one of those plants?"

"Not a chance," he said, shaking his head. "Birdie had us erect eight-foot fences around anything she's planted. She says she's not working to feed the deer."

"Can't blame her."

"If you move into the house, I'll build you a fence," he said, a wheedle in his voice.

She probably should move in; they were practically living together as it was. But there were things to discuss, things she wasn't even sure she knew the answers to.

"Want to sit on the back porch?" she asked. "I'll grab some beers."

"Sounds good."

"We need a dog," he said as they settled into the worn Adirondack chairs that had come with the rental.

"*You* need a dog," she said. "I already have a pet."

"But think how useful he could be, especially a herding dog."

"Aren't they hyper?"

"A bit."

"I knew someone who had a border collie," she said. "The darn thing could never sit still."

"No worse than kids," he said.

"Do you want kids?" she asked.

He took a sip of his beer, then tilted his hat back. "I never thought I did. Always figured Jarod and CJ would have enough to keep the family going. I didn't want to get tied down. Besides, what kind of living can an artist give kids?"

"How is the artwork going?" she asked.

"The magazine liked the work I sent. They want more. And some scientific organization contacted me. The pay is a lot better than I expected."

"And you've bought a house."

"And I've bought a house." He nodded. "One with enough room for a family." His lips quirked at the edges. "Especially a couple of kids with bright red hair and a smile as big as the sun."

253

Casey Dawes

"Now who's kissed the Blarney Stone?" she asked, matching his grin.

"And what about you? Are you interested in any kids?"

"I think so. With the right person, of course. I don't know about the red hair, though. It's a recessive gene."

"I'm sure somewhere in our crazy past there's a redhead," he said and took her hand.

They were quiet for a while, as the setting sun painted the bottoms of the clouds a rosy pink. From somewhere in the grass nearby a meadowlark's song played like the solo flute in an orchestra. Flora leaned over the fence and inspected the ground beneath her.

Peace settled over Megan. She could almost hear Granny whisper, "When you find someone you can be silent with and still be happy, that's the one for you."

And it was as simple as that. Whether or not she was ready for a relationship, if her business thrived or failed, she was going to need to take a leap of faith and trust that things would turn out okay.

"When my lease is up in January," she said, "we can talk about where I'm going to live."

He squeezed her hand gently. "That sounds good."

She leaned back and closed her eyes. Leaving home had been difficult, but Choteau had definitely been the right place to stop.

The End

Did you enjoy this story? Please leave a review on your favorite online review site.

Why are reviews important to this writer?
- I really want to know what you think. What did you like? Where did I miss the mark?
- Other readers are more willing to take a chance on a new author when there are reviews.
- A good number of reviews help a book get better rankings on booksites, as well as opportunities to promote the book. More people discover authors you already like.

The next book in this series is *Coming Home*, Cameron's story, which will be available Winter 2020-21.

254

Muskoka Hat and Mittens

Brenda Castiel

In the 1990s, I was involved in something called the International DB2 Users Group (IDUG), DB2 being an IBM software product. During that time, I was fortunate enough to meet Brenda Castiel. After we left the tech world, we both got involved in the arts, I by writing and her by designing knitting patterns. She was gracious enough to give me a pattern to put in the book.

The pattern is below. Alternatively, you can access a downloadable copy, along with the chart, by going to: https://www.stories-about-love.com/knitting-pattern-muskoka-hat-and-mittens/.

Please support Brenda by visiting her Ravelry site: http://www.ravelry.com/designers/brenda-castiel.

Finished Measurements

Hat Circumference: 17 (19)"
Mittens: 9 (11)"
Pattern is written for Small/Medium to fit a youth, and a Medium/Large to fit an average sized adult.

Yarn

Knitpicks Wool of the Andes (100% Wool; 110 yards /50 g),
Colors MC Clarity 25632, 2 skeins,
CC1 Marina 25074, CC2 Conch 25973, CC3 Turmeric 25651, CC4 Hollyberry 23419, 1 skein each.

Needles

US 6 (4.0 mm) one 16" circular needle, or DPNs, or two 24"

circular needles for two circulars technique, or one 32" or longer circular needle for Magic Loop technique, or size to obtain gauge.

Notions

Yarn Needle
Stitch Markers
Scrap yarn or stitch holder

Gauge

22 sts and 26 rows = 4" in Stockinette stitch, blocked.

Notes

In Canada a longish knit winter hat, or stocking cap, is called a toque, or sometimes tuque (pronounced "tuke").

This version is covered with non-traditional fair-isle designs, such as checkerboards, diamonds and chevrons, and is topped with a jaunty pompom. It comes with matching mittens.

The changing patterns and colors will give the knitter enough of a challenge to keep moving along.

Hint: be sure to keep your "floats" loose, or the hat will be too tight. Where the float is 5 sts long, twist the 2 yarns together after the 2nd or 3rd st to keep the floats neat.

Special Stitches and Abbreviations

N/A

Directions for Hat

Note: Change to DPNs when sts no longer fit on 16" circular ndl.

With MC, CO 92 (104) stitches. Join to work in the round. PM to indicate beg of round.

Rnd 1: *K1, p1, rep from * around.

Rnd 2: *Kbl 1, p1, rep from * around.

Rnds 3-20: Rep Rnds 1-2 9 times.

Rnd 21: *K21, kfb, rep from * 4 times, k4 (16) – 96 (108) sts.

Rnd 22: With CC4, knit.

Rnd 23: Purl.

Rnd 24: Knit.

Rnds 25-50: Work Rnds 1-26 of Chart A.

Rnd 51: Work Rnd 27 of Chart A as follows: *k6 (7), k2tog, rep from * around – 84 (96) sts.

Rnds 52-57: Work Rnds 28-33 of Chart A.

Rnd 58: Work Rnd 34 of Chart A as follows: *k5 (6), k2tog, rep from * around – 72 (84) sts.

Rnds 59-60: Work Rnds 35-36 of Chart A.

Rnd 61: Work Rnd 37 of Chart A as follows: *k16 (8), k2tog, rep from *, k0 (4) – 68 (76) sts.

Rnds 62-67: Work Rnds 38-43 of color chart A.

Rnd 68: Work Rnd 44 of Chart A as follows: *p5, p2tog, rep from *, p12 (6) – 60 (66) sts.

Rnds 69-73: Work Rnds 45-49 of Chart A.

Rnd 74: Work Rnd 50 of Chart A as follows: *k4, k2tog, rep from *, k0 (6) – 50 (56) sts.

Rnds 75-76: Work Rnds 51-52 of Chart A.

Rnd 77: Work Rnd 53 of Chart A as follows: *k4(5), k2tog, rep from *, k2 (0) – 42 (48) sts.

Rnds 78-80: Work Rnds 54-56 of Chart A.

Shape Top

Rnd 81: With MC, knit.

Rnd 82: With CC2, *k4, k2tog, rep from *, k1 (0) – 35 (40) sts.

Rnd 83: Purl.

Rnd 84: Knit.

Rnd 85: With CC1, *k3, k2tog, rep from * ¬– 30 (32) sts.

Rnds 86-87: Knit.

Rnd 88: *k4, k2tog, rep from *, k0 (2) ¬– 25 (27) sts.

Rnd 89: *k3, k2tog, rep from *, k0 (2) ¬– 20 (22) sts.

Rnd 90: *k2, k2tog, rep from *, k0 (2) ¬– 15 (17) sts.

Cut yarn, leaving 6 to 8 inches. Using yarn needle, draw yarn through rem sts. Pull tight and stitch down on WS.

Finishing

Weave in all loose yarn ends. Tack down any loose floats. Block hat.

Pompom

To make pompom, take a 3 inch wide piece of cardboard. Lay a length of yarn (in MC) along the length of the cardboard (this yarn will be used hold the pompom together and attach it to the hat). Wind yarn around the cardboard about 100—120 times, using one color or mixed colors. Pull the original length of yarn towards the lower edge of the cardboard, pull firmly around the wound yarn, and tie up tightly. With scissors, cut along the upper edge of the cardboard to free up the yarn. Trim ends to create a nice round shape. Use the tied ends to sew the pompom to the top of the hat

Directions for Mittens

Note: This pattern makes long mittens that continue past the wrist. For shorter mittens, omit one color section, e.g. rows 1 through 7 of the chart.

With MC, CO 36 (42) stitches. Join to work in the round. PM to indicate beg of round.

Rnd 1: *K1, p1, rep from * around.

Rnd 2: *Kbl 1, p1, rep from * around.

Rnds 3- 12: Rep Rnds 1-2 5 times.

Rnd 13: Knit.

Rnd 14: With CC4, knit.

Rnd 15: Purl.

Rnd 16: Knit.

Rnds 17-33: Work Rnds 1-17 of Chart A.

Rnd 34: K2, kfb 0 (1) time, k32 (36), kfb 0 (1) time, k to end of rnd – 36 (44) sts.

Rnd 35 (begin thumb gusset): Work Rnd 19 of Chart A to last st, kfb (Rnd 1 of Gusset Chart) – 37 (45) sts.

Note: Use colors on Chart A to stripe gusset. Yarn not in use will form long floats—these floats should be caught with yarn being used every few sts. Any loose floats can be sewn down at the end.

Rnds 36-46(48): Cont in patt, working Rnds 20-30 (32) of Chart A at beg of rnd and Rnds 2-12 (14) of Gusset Chart at end of rnd – 47 (57) sts.

Rnd 47 (49): Work Rnd 31 (33) of Chart A to beg of gusset, place 11 (13) gusset sts on holder or scrap yarn – 36 (44) sts.

Size S/M:

Rnd 48-49: Work Rnds 32-33 of Chart A.

Rnd 50: With MC, knit.

Rnd 51: Purl.

Rnd 52-60: Work Rnds 45-53 of Chart A.

Size M/L:

Rnd 50: With CC2, k2, k2tog, k36, k2tog, k to end of rnd – 42 sts.

Rnd 51-69: Work Rnds 35-53 of Chart A.

Both Sizes:

Dec Rnd: With MC, *k1, pm, k2tog, work in pat for 12 (15) sts, pm, ssk, k1, rep from * – 32 (38) sts.
Next Rnd: Knit.
Rep last 2 Rnds—28 (34) sts.
Change to CC2.
Rep last 4 Rnds—20 (26) sts.

Change to CC1.
Rep last 2 (4) Rnds—16 (18) sts.
Graft together using Kitchener st.

Thumb

Place sts from holder onto DPNs or 2 circulars. Pick up and knit 3 sts in opening between hand and gusset – 14 (16) sts.
Work in stripe pattern alternating MC and CC1 (one row of each) until thumb measures ¾" less than desired length.
Rnd 1: Knit.
Rnd 2: *K2, k2tog, rep from * to last 2 (4) sts, k2, k2tog 0 (1) time – 11 (12) sts.
Rnd 3: Knit.
Rnd 4: *K1, k2tog, rep from * to last 2 (3) sts, k2(1), k2tog 0 (1) time – 8 (8) sts.
Rnd 5: Knit.
Rnd 6: *K2tog, rep from * to end – 4 sts.
Cut yarn, draw through rem sts, pull tight and sew in end.

Make second mitten to match the first.

Finishing

Weave in all loose yarn ends. Tack down any loose floats. Block mittens.

Chart A

Gusset Chart

14 end M/L
13
12 end S/M

M - Make 1 with kfb

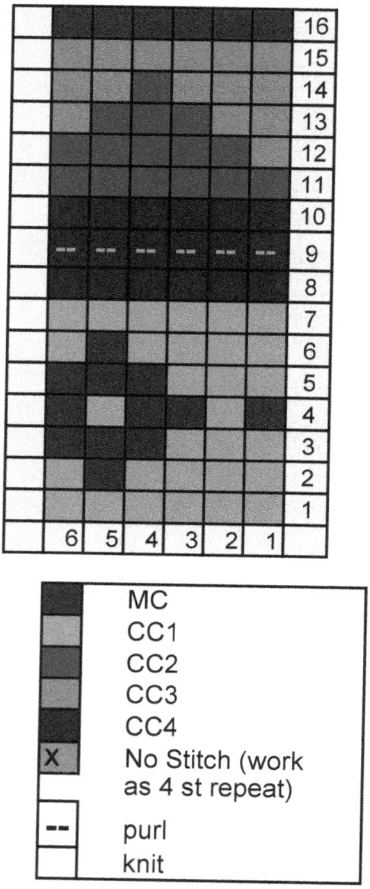
16
15
14
13
12
11
10
9
8
7
6
5
4
3
2
1
6 5 4 3 2 1
MC
CC1
CC2
CC3
CC4
X
No Stitch (work as 4 st repeat)
--
purl
knit

Designer Biography

I've been knitting on and off since my teens, but became somewhat obsessed with it in 2007. I love squishy wools for the short, mild Los Angeles winters, and like light-weight wools, cottons and blends for the rest of the year. I really believe that even beginner knitters can create something beautiful and useful, so I strive to keep patterns simple yet original. I blog about knitting and life here.

I have sold designs to Interweave *Knits, Vogue Knitting, Knit Picks, Knit Now Magazine, Classic Elite Yarns*, and *I Like Knitting*, and have been published in several books.

I produce a monthly newsletter with knitting tips, freebies, reviews, and giveaways -- please sign up on my blog: (http://www.knitandtravelandsuch.blogspot.com/). Get a free pattern when you sign up. Don't worry, it's easy to unsubscribe if you change your mind.

I now have my own Ravelry Group, Brenda Castiel Designs: http://www.ravelry.com/groups/brenda-castiel-designs.
Hurray! Please join us for chat, KALs, pattern support, tips, and contests.

My Etsy Shop is GoodStuffCrafts (https://www.etsy.com/shop/goodstuffcrafts) where I sell project bags and other knitting necessities.

The Story Behind the Story

My husband and I honeymooned in Mendocino, California, and frequently went back to visit when we lived in California. On one trip, they were having a spinning demonstration. I learned the basics of spinning by hand and bought my first spindle. For a while I practiced, then got myself turned around. Since I didn't know anyone else who spun, I put it down. Then life got crazy.

Almost a decade later, my interest in the art of spinning re-awoke, but I couldn't recover the knack for spinning. So we took a trip to the next fiber arts festival we could find, which was on the western Idaho border near Moscow.

My husband has always enjoyed back roads, and I've come along to his way of thinking. It's a slower pace and you can find all kinds of interesting things along the way. One of these places was in Deary, Idaho—the Pie Safe Bakery and Kitchen. That become the model for the bistro where Megan works.

I took a spinning class at the festival and everything clicked again. When I get a chance, I pick up the spindle and practice. Like many fiber arts, it can be very peaceful and calming.

But I am intrigued by the complexities of fiber: where it comes from, the people who spin, and how it gets from animal to my hands without smelling like a barnyard. When Megan came along, I knew she had to share my passion.

And that's the story.

Other Ways to Connect

Join my newsletter list on Stories About Love and get connected with Casey Dawes (Psst: You'll also get a free book.)

Like my Facebook page where I frequently post photos of Montana nature and animals.
(www.facebook.com/Casey.Stories.About.Love/)

Follow me on BookBub to be notified of new releases.
(www.bookbub.com/profile/casey-dawes)